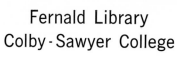

MADELEINE
YOUNG WIFE

Books by Mrs Robert Henrey

THE LITTLE MADELEINE (*her girlhood*)

AN EXILE IN SOHO (*her adolescence*)

MADELEINE GROWN UP (*her love story and marriage*)

MADELEINE—YOUNG WIFE (*a saga of war and peace*)

MATILDA AND THE CHICKENS (*a winter on her farm*)

LONDON (*with water-colours by Phyllis Ginger*)

A JOURNEY TO VIENNA (*the making of a film*)

PALOMA (*the story of a friend*)

MADELEINE'S JOURNAL (*London during Coronation Year*)

A MONTH IN PARIS (*she revisits the city of her birth*)

MILOU'S DAUGHTER (*a winter in the Midi*)

BLOOMSBURY FAIR (*three London families*)

THIS FEMININE WORLD (*Paris dressmakers*)

A DAUGHTER FOR A FORTNIGHT

THE VIRGIN OF ALDERMANBURY (*rebirth of the City of London*)

MISTRESS OF MYSELF

A Farm in Normandy is now incorporated in *Madeleine—Young Wife*.

MADELEINE
YOUNG WIFE

by

MRS ROBERT HENREY

LONDON
J. M. DENT & SONS LTD

CONTENTS

PART I

A FARM IN NORMANDY

From the Authoress to the Reader

The action of this book begins in 1937 and ends in 1953. It is a true saga through peace, war, treachery and violent crime, to the quiet days of peace again. Every character bears his or her own name, and the location of the village is clearly designated.

MADELEINE HENREY

May 1960

1

I HAD often wished to buy a house in France. It nearly happened at Christmas during a week's vacation at Monte Carlo. One morning I had climbed up to La Turbie perched high above the principality and followed the road that is built in the flank of the mountain and leads to Mentone. Suddenly I came upon a house with a red roof and blue shutters clinging like a toy to the rock. But it was not the house that I noticed first. Tangerine-trees dipped their golden fruit over the side of the low white wall. I wanted that place the moment I saw it. I wanted it for the bird's-eye view over Monte Carlo and away over the deep blue Mediterranean that I would have at breakfast while drinking my coffee on the terrace under the multi-colored sunshade.

I was greeted by the barking of a dog and the smile of a woman in her early fifties, whose lips were scarlet and whose hair was dyed the color of golden corn. She must have been pretty in her youth, and from her conversation, studded with quotations from Racine, I guessed that she was an actress. She explained: "I'm obliged to sell this house, as well as my flat in Paris—family troubles, don't you know!" I visited the rooms and inspected the garden, built in twenty or more tiers against the flank of the mountain, each bordered with olive- and eucalyptus-trees and trellised vines, and at the end of each tier was a tap with a hose in order to water morning and night. I then owned $5000, and I was ready to spend all this money, the total savings of a young married woman, on this Paradise.

"How much?" I asked breathlessly.

"Didn't the estate agent tell you?" she queried. "I'm asking 100,000 francs."

I made a rapid calculation, and it seemed to me that at the rate of exchange I would even have a trifle to spare. I was yet to learn that French law called for a state purchase tax of nearly thirty per cent. For the next three days I interviewed lawyers and bank managers in an attempt to deal, but in the end I discovered that I had not quite enough, and this flaxen-haired woman proved hard when it came to splitting francs. I went back to the house each day for the remainder of the week, and each time gazed across the bay toward Italy, dreaming that the place was mine. We left Monte Carlo without buying the house, and for the first few weeks I often thought of the terraced garden and the exotic flowers that grew so easily in the torrid sunshine and, closing my eyes, I could see again the tangerines that were there for the picking, and the little white garage on the other side of the road, set like a jewel in a lemon grove. But as time went on I forgot the house, only to realize how unwise I would have been to sink all my savings in a place over twenty hours by train from London.

The winter passed and spring came, and before summer my mind had unconsciously worked out another plan. It was not only distance that had blunted my regret for the house at Roquebrune. I dreamed of being a young woman with a farm of her own. I needed an orchard, a kitchen garden, cows, and chickens. The house, I planned, would be secondary to the utility of the farm which ought, if properly run, to be self-supporting. There was only one part of the world, I felt, that could give me all this and be near enough to make it practical. That province was Normandy, more akin to England than any other in France.

Though I wanted this farm, when I found it, to be very much a place of my own, an assertion morally and financially, of a young wife's independence, I asked my husband to accompany me on my search. We took the boat to Le Havre on a Friday night just before Whitsun, 1938. We carried hardly any luggage, and we had no idea of where we would go, but as soon as we stepped out of the boat shortly after six o'clock on a cool, clear morning, we hailed a taxi and told the driver to take us along the Seine, past the Schneider works, to the ferry, and across to Honfleur. From here we would follow the coastline past Trouville and Deauville.

Half a dozen times between Honfleur and Trouville I was for

telling the chauffeur to stop. All about this estuary is irresistible.
The mud that is not quite mud but a mixture of mud and sand;
the oil tankers that steam slowly toward Rouen, their propellers
churning the yellow water; the rich green meadows that run
straight down to the water and which are only prevented from
merging with the slime by rickety palisades; the mysterious
lights that, morning and evening, play on the thatched roofs of
the cottages—those thatched roofs bound at the top by caked
earth in which grow yellow and blue irises; the blue and pink
hydrangeas that grow like weeds against the low walls; the
apple-trees and pear-trees in the orchards; the distant glimpses
of Le Havre, with its docks and refineries always covered by a
violet haze; the high-wheeled covered carts drawn by spirited
mares and driven by farmers' wives bringing their milk and eggs
to market, and the smell of the countryside, which is half of
brine and half of hay—all this is irresistible.

Here it was that William the Conqueror amassed his fleet to
sail to Pevensey, here they remained for days quarreling, while
the winds were alternately lulled or contrary. The farmers who
lead their thick-set cattle from one field to another, though
small of stature, have some of the nobility and all the cunning
of their Viking ancestors, founders of the race, who, taller and
more robust than they, pillaged and ransacked by land and plundered by sea. Halfway between Honfleur and Trouville the
brine chases the closeness of the river air and fills your lungs
with refreshing breezes. Rich villas and houses in the Norman
style, with gables, stud the main road.

We reached Trouville and crossed the bridge that leads to
Deauville, where the chauffeur put his head through the window and asked: "Where exactly are you going?"

"I'm not sure," I answered. "Drive on a few more miles."

He obeyed sullenly, suspicious of a woman who did not know
her own mind. I also was angry for not stopping at Honfleur,
instead of speeding along the coast as if the next town must be
better than the last. By comparison, the road we now followed
appeared less wealthy in detail—a long, steep hill to Blonville,
and then down to a flat stretch, with the beach on one side and
low-lying swamps on the other, where the grass was not even
rich enough for cattle to graze on. The beach we came to a
quarter of an hour later was faced by a row of houses, two or

three small hotels, and a low, white casino facing a vast expanse
of golden sand. There was nothing in particular to commend
the place, except that a bright sun played on the vivid colors of
the main hotel, and laughter came from the veranda. I am not
sure that our main consideration for stopping here was not
financial. We would spend a cheap night in one of these rooms
that must capture as much sea air as if they were actually
perched on top of the ocean. We paid off the car, bargained for
the best room, and, five minutes later, were splashing in the sea.
It was as warm as at Cannes, and the sands swept majestically
on either side, with hardly a ripple on their surface. We lunched
on the terrace, where the woman who owned the hotel had
fixed a telescope against the balustrade for her clients to watch
the ships entering and leaving the distant harbor of Le Havre.
The *Normandie* came into sight as we were served with prawns
and cider, and French pride in this giant liner occupied much of
the conversation at adjoining tables during the remainder of the
meal.

Momentarily the sands occupied all our attention, and when
we were not actually in the water we walked at low tide, either
in the direction of Deauville or that of Cabourg—resort of
actresses and *demi-mondaines* in the 'nineties.

It was during our return from here by road one morning that
we ran into all the beauty of the rich pasture country inland.
The hedges garlanded with honeysuckle and wild roses, a donkey in a field, a farm where we were offered a glass of milk—
these were enough to awaken my sleeping lust for possession.

Our hotel was the last building along the front before the
main road turns inland to escape the cliffs which, standing erect
like five black watch-dogs, break the coastline. The sudden
turn of the road is a surprise to motorists arriving from Deauville. They brake savagely to negotiate the right-angled turn
through the village, for the highway across the main square and
climbs away over the hill in the direction of Cabourg.

Halfway between our hotel and the main square was an estate
agent named Duprez, on whose railings was fixed a blue board
where the bargains of the week were put up. Gaston Duprez
could be seen most evenings pacing up and down the pavement
opposite the flight of steps leading to his house. He was the perfect picture of a biblical patriarch, with large caressing eyes of

sapphire blue, an aquiline nose, and a full, though short, jet-black beard that made more ashen yet his parchment skin.

I knew Gaston Duprez as a queer character, but not well enough for me to greet him as I climbed the steps to his house. In the office I found a young woman seated on a high-backed tapestried chair, dictating her mail to a secretary. She was his daughter-in-law, Simone, more striking by the intelligence of her features than by her small mouth and dark, expressive eyes. Her father owned a rival agency near Deauville which, since her marriage, did much to consolidate the already considerable Duprez tentacles. She was gifted with a fine strong voice and a pleasant smile.

"Madam," I asked. "Can you tell me of a small and inexpensive farm for sale in the neighborhood?"

"My husband, Victor Duprez, has one," she answered. "It may be in the market during the next few days. You will find it on the plateau just above the village—a tiny sixteen-century farmhouse standing in the middle of a six-acre field. There are a few more acres you could buy near it. I'm afraid it is too late for me to take you up this evening and my husband is away, but if you care to come back tomorrow, we will drive you there before lunch."

I left her, determined in my own mind to visit the place the same evening. I am not patient when my mind is set on a thing, and I was anxious to find my husband and tell him about it.

We set off at six o'clock.

The road that leads up to the plateau is a white ribbon bordered by rich villas. It seems almost perpendicular so steep is the climb, but the variety of architecture and the beauty of the gardens provide relief. Most of the houses date from the early part of the century when wealthy city folk believed in spacious comfort. A few villas are thirty-roomed affairs built in the Norman style with gabled roofs on which are placed terra-cotta cats and pigeons in lifelike attitudes; others are of red brick, while a few represent the individual whims of their wealthy owners.

This part of the village was beginning to wake from a long winter slumber, for these houses are closed at the beginning of the autumn and only come to life again late in the spring. Gardeners were tending the flowers, watering the beds, and rolling the grass. In another fortnight the curtains would go up and limousines would be parked outside the freshly painted garages. The tennis courts would come to life, and children would run down to the beach with spades and pails. Just now the village was still owned almost exclusively by those who lived there all the year round.

The road is less than half a mile in length. It ends abruptly at something like a roundabout where four country lanes converge—one of them leading down the hill again but in the direction of the station about a mile and a half away across the fields, another to the right where it eventually joins the main highway to Cabourg, and the two others cutting through a curtain of trees into the rich grazing land which is the wealth and beauty of the district.

When we arrived this far, hesitating which lane to follow, we turned round a moment to take stock of the ground we had covered. The village now lay at our feet, the white roofs gleaming in the rays of the setting sun. The sea was a sapphire blue, and to our right the coastline swept gracefully round past Deauville to the long finger which is Le Havre nine miles across the bay. The glittering panorama was as colorful as any picture of the Riviera—far more invigorating in the strong, clear air.

We chose the lane directly in front of us through the wood. It was narrow and entirely roofed in by the thickly leaved branches of the trees on estates on either side. There was no sound but the occasional chirrup of a bird or the snapping of a dry twig, but now our nostrils were filled with a new perfume— that of the undergrowth.

After ten minutes' walk we came suddenly upon our first farm—a cobbled courtyard with a red brick house surrounded by a rose garden. There were stables and cowsheds built in the Norman style. Looking over the low stone wall we could see the milk cans hanging upside-down on wooden prongs beside the hand pump, and in the distance a few cows grazed in the field planted every ten yards with apple trees.

A dog barked loudly at our approach, straining at the leash, and the noise brought a woman from the kitchen garden which in all Norman farms is not far from the house.

"Which is Victor Duprez's farm?"

For a moment she made no answer, looking us up and down. Then, as if to prolong her inspection, echoed:

"Victor Duprez's farm?"

"Yes," I said, "the one farmer Goguet works."

She walked across to where we stood and pointed up the lane.

"He lives in the field next to this one. All you have to do is to walk through the next gate."

The already narrow lane split into two some fifty yards farther along. We chose the one that bordered the field and found ourselves in what was virtually a cart rut, flanked on either side by six-foot hedges in which stood a number of majestic trees that once again made a cathedral dome over our heads with their age-old branches.

Under the honeysuckle and the wild roses that lay in garlands over the prickly hawthorn, the moss-covered ground was white with daisies, golden with buttercups, and blue with gentians. When the hedge had a break in it, or when it was less thick, we could catch glimpses of the pasture fields and the gnarled apple trees with their hooked branches now turning green after shedding their blossom.

As soon as we reached the gate we could see the roof of a house down in the valley. We entered a little nervously, because of the cows that ambled in our direction. There was no path to the house, only a trail, which we followed until gradually we began to obtain a comprehensive picture of the little domain.

The field was long and narrow and led from the gate we had come in by down to a stream at the bottom, whence another orchard rose as high again. The same sort of hedges that flanked the path we had followed divided the field from those of its neighbors, but up against the kitchen garden on our left, from which a moment or two earlier we had seen the woman emerge, grew two magnificent Italian poplars lifting their arms eloquently skyward. These wonderful trees were not in the hedge, but a few feet within the field, and cast their shadow against a pool of stagnant weed-covered water which provided a trough for the cows. Such poplars I have never seen. They were silhouetted clearly against the distant sea, and beyond them, far beyond them, the lighthouse of Le Havre would soon be flashing its beam every eleven seconds. After the pond came the kitchen garden flanked by that of the neighbors, and rich, like theirs, with vegetables that thrive in the black soil. A hundred yards farther on stood a low building, partly of brick and partly of clay, the whole covered by a slate roof, which in the evening light donned the shot colors of a pigeon's breast.

Originally it was a bakery, as was clear from the thickness of the middle wall, the disused oven, and the high chimney. Its three compartments were now used as pens—one for the sow at night, and the others for heifers too young to be put on grass.

Set without rhyme or reason in the exact center of the field was the house.

It was the house of a fairy tale rather than the habitation of a farmer. This jeweled beauty, visible one moment through the trees, out of sight the next because of the uneven ground that was all hill and dale, faced south.

From a distance it seemed no larger than a doll's house. Actually it had the length of three long rooms, and the roof, which surmounted its two stories, was so cunningly designed and the slates so perfectly and so minutely dovetailed, that they shimmered like the chains in a coat of mail.

Most of the façade was of half-timbering, Elizabethan style, each jet-black oak beam, whether vertical or leaning to one side, divided from its fellow by an equal width of the whitest plaster.

The rest of the façade was of stone, so mightily thick that a window set in it and framed by an oak beam had a ledge over four feet deep.

There were two front doors.

They led from the house into the garden that was railed off to prevent the cattle from breaking the rose trees and uprooting the strawberry beds. Even so the hens flopped over the wire netting and made sallies into the house, where they pecked voraciously at the crumbs on the black and white flagstones of the living-room.

I had feared some watch-dog would attack us as we pushed open the garden gate. Barking there was, but from a little white terrier bitch at the end of a long wire cable attached to her kennel under a huge hollow-trunked pear tree. More efficient guards were a goose and gander that arrived from a great distance at our approach, making a great din and stretching their long necks in anger. At all this noise the farmer came out of the house.

"Is your name Goguet?" I asked. "We are friends of Victor Duprez. He has given us permission to visit the farm."

Goguet was in the early forties, with gay, malicious eyes under a heavy crop of black hair, which grew low on his forehead. Advantageous mustaches of a burnt caramel color were well steeped in cider and bleached with apple-jack. His skin was baked a hard brown, and he wore an open shirt. He welcomed us affably and invited us into the house.

In spite of the fact that chickens ran over the floor, and the curtains on the lattice windows were worn and yellow, it was clear that the room into which Goguet led us was magnificent. The great open hearth, on which a black cauldron hung over half the smouldering trunk of an apple tree, had a chimney up which a couple of men could have climbed abreast. Two carved pillars of enormous weight on either side of the hearth appeared at first sight to be of marble, but on closer examination proved to be of Caen stone polished to a shine, and bearing the date of their construction—1555.

These pillars were to be found in replica, not only in the adjoining room, but also in the two rooms directly above, so that one had the impression that the whole house was built round them.

The ceiling was supported by oak beams, so thick that one could see how the axe had felled entire trees in steps. Against the central piece hung the farmer's shot-gun.

Though Goguet had fought in the First World War, he was so essentially a part of his native Norman soil that his talk was that of a man who had never left it. He had three children, he told us; Roger, the oldest, was thirteen, Renée, the little girl, was nine, and Robert, the youngest, was seven.

The two young ones came running in front of their mother, who was bringing home the milk.

The Goguette, as Mme. Goguet was known, had the most magnificent eyes under a mop of jet-black hair. She owned four cows—Rosalie, Paquerette, Paulette, and Marquise—which she called from afar in a strong voice that could be heard from the house to the stream. "Teu—teu" was her call.

"These are friends of M. Duprez," said Goguet to his wife, as she arrived.

The Goguette removed the yoke from her shoulders, and as

she unhooked the chains the handles of the milk pails dropped against the sides with a metallic click. She straightened herself slowly, for the pails were heavy, and, having listened to her husband, wiped the palms of her wide hands against her linen apron before clasping ours.

The two young children fussed over me, while the Goguette went into the buttery.

Goguet moved mysteriously toward the fire-place. From a nail on a high beam he took down a monumental key that looked as if it ought to belong to a cathedral door. This he handed with a wink to his daughter, who made off, post-haste, to the cider press at the bottom of the field. A few moments later she returned with a champagne bottle, which her father received with ceremony. After untwisting the wire round the neck, he uncorked it, saying: "It's last year's cider. This is the right time to drink it."

We were just tasting this excellent cider when a great snorting could be heard behind us. It was Mono, the sow, who was trying to break down the fence to claim her evening ration of dry bread. This brought us all into the garden again, and we took advantage of the incident to visit the Shetland ponies in an adjacent orchard. Victor Duprez had bought this farm to rear horses. It had cost him a great deal more money than his father approved of, and these two ponies, together with a young mare, were all that remained of his live-stock.

Making our way slowly toward the bakery, where Goguet was anxious to show us a young heifer, we say a shadow moving cautiously behind a pear tree. Now it came into the open—the figure of a youth darting to a point of vantage beside the chicken coop; two dark eyes, burning with curiosity, watching our arrival.

It was I who saw him first. I put a hand on my husband's arm. The Goguette, who had probably spied the figure before any of us, looked inquiringly at Goguet. There was no need for me to ask enlightenment. A torrent of explanations suddenly broke loose. Goguet, the Goguette, Renée, and even young Robert, each gesticulating, shouting, pulling at our sleeves, told us the story.

Early that afternoon, so we pieced the tale together, the children, left to their own resources, had gone on an expedition to the pond under the poplar trees. A retired officer called M. Aton had promised them a few cents for each frog they caught in the pool. M. Aton lived in a small house that Gaston Duprez, his brother-in-law, had built for him, and he was a renowned gourmet. None better knew where to find young dandelions for early spring salads, and, having guests for dinner, he planned a dish of frogs.

The pool was full of them. The children had only to throw a stone into the center to see them appear as if by magic from their hiding-places in the slime.

Young Robert was lithe but the frogs jumped away from his grasp with rapid thrusts of their elastic limbs. He seemed to miss each by a hairbreadth.

"Now they've all taken fright," said Roger. "Let's lie down on the grass until they think we've gone."

Soon Robert's eyes gleamed with excitement, for a frog was moving cautiously by the reeds. Without saying anything he crept forward, and for an instant held the clammy beast in his fingers. Once again, however, the frog cheated its opponent. With a flop it was back in the water.

Robert was annoyed. He had been so sure of success. With childish ill humor, he dived after the animal, landing in the shallow end of the pond. The spring rains had moistened the ground. The slime was deep and treacherous, so that the boy's feet rapidly sank into the slush.

"Look!" cried Renée. "Robert's losing ground. In a moment he'll be under water."

She turned to Roger, annoyed that he stood there with his cap on, sucking his thumb.

But Roger came of a farming race that fears the water more than anything else. Now, as he looked at his little brother, listened to him shouting for help, his nervous system seemed to fail.

"Roger!" cried Renée, with all the contempt she could put in her voice. "You coward, Roger!"

She darted up the little mound above the pond and called for help in that shrill tone she inherited from her mother, the cowherd. A boy, working in the neighbor's vegetable garden, heard her and jumped over the fence. He arrived in time to see Renée herself pulling her little brother out of danger. The risk had been slight. There were not more than two feet of water.

Now that all danger was passed, the blood began to flow again in Roger's veins. He was beginning to realize what an abject figure he had cut. Pulling his cap low over his forehead, he slunk away, sullen, bitter, angry with himself.

We walked back to the house without inspecting the heifer. It would give us an excuse to come again. Goguet offered us the customary drop of apple-jack. We exchanged many compliments and left the farm as darkness fell and the lighthouse at La Havre flashed its distant beam behind the poplar trees.

2

I woke next morning thinking of the farm. The subject was already on my lips at breakfast and if, by any chance, my husband broached another topic, the memory of an orchard, an apple tree, or even a bundle of faggots was sufficient to bring me back to my train of thoughts.

The Duprez seemed eager to sell. When I called at the agency to tell Mme. Victor that I had been there on my own account the previous evening, she said her husband would certainly accept $3,500 for the farm, together with an orchard of about two acres opposite. As soon as I heard the price I knew that the place could be mine if I wanted it. I hurried down to the beach, where my husband was sun-bathing, to tell him the news. He received it with polite indifference. "It's up to you," he said, "that money is what you have earned. I suggest we go for a long walk in another direction today and make a point not to mention the farm again until tomorrow. Like that you will come back to it with a cool head."

Remembering Roquebrune, I agreed. We decided to climb to the plateau again, but to take the road to the left through the trees. This path leads to the village of St. Vaast. It has a surface of sand, and as soon as spring arrives it is a mass of hazels and wild cherries. The cherries grow in great clusters, but so high that they remain uneaten except by the birds. Occasionally children on the way to school climb up a smooth trunk and break down a branch, which they drag behind them, picking the fruit as they go along, but the farmers disdain them, and few even bottle them in alcohol.

The road climbs gently all the time, and through the hedges one sees a repetition of fields planted every ten yards with gnarled apple trees, cows resting in the shade of an oak tree, and small farmhouses with roofs of slate or thatch that seem to have grown up with the rest of the countryside. All the ground is virgin. The plough has never passed this way, nor for miles around. There are neither potatoes nor root crops. Wheat and oats are unknown this side of the plains at Caen. Here the roads and lanes are ever twisting and turning, climbing steeply or rolling down, and because of this the country is known as Norman Switzerland. In spite of the foliage, the heat was tremendous on this May morning. We noticed that quite a number of small paths crossed our road transversely. They resembled tunnels, because the branches of the hazel trees joined completely over the center, making a perfect dome. For this reason the ground underfoot is moss-covered and almost damp, even at midday when the sun is strongest.

We took a turning to our right and found that it led steeply down to a clear rivulet, which crossed our path over a bed of pebbles. From here the ground rose steeply once more. The young leaves in the hedges were a tender green and the torrid humidity was almost West Indian. The path led to another narrow road at right angles to it, and which was only wide enough for a cart to pass along. An Alsatian, tied to its kennel in front of a one-storied house of caked loam and half-timbering, barked furiously at the sound of our footsteps. On the opposite side of the road a five-barred gate led into a field.

"Look!" I exclaimed. "There's a cow all by herself."

I took a lump of sugar from my bag and, holding it in the palm of my hand, offered it to the animal, who ambled cautiously but heavily toward me, accepting the gift with pathetic surprise.

"She seems friendly," I said. "I wonder if I could get her interested in a bunch of marguerites,"

"Personally," answered my husband, "I'm for leaving these animals strictly to themselves."

We kept to our bargain, and however much we thought of the farm neither of us spoke of it.

The next morning I suggested we should have a look at the field which Victor Duprez offered to throw in with the property. We arrived early and found Goguet sharpening his scythe under a pear tree.

"Tell me," I asked, "how many acres do you farm altogether?"

"Fourteen," he answered, "The six-acre orchard in which the house stands, and which we call the home orchard, three acres opposite the gate you have just come in by, known as the Point because of its triangular shape, the Little Court and the Little Valley two hundred yards up the lane, and the Burgundy hay field."

"Does Victor Duprez own them all?"

"Yes," answered Goguet, "he owns all of them and another on the opposite bank of the stream called the Picane, which horses have grazed on for the last two years and poor grass they have made of it."

"Are the Little Court and the Little Valley in good condition?"

"I will take you up there now, if you like, but the ground is hard and the cattle ponds are dry. This one under the poplar trees is different. There is a natural spring underneath."

"Let us go to the Valleys."

We went to the gate and passed left for about 500 yards along the lane. The two younger children had followed us, and seeing that we raised no objection their voices soon rose above ours.

"You see this orchard next to the one on which our house stands," cried Robert. "It belongs to the Poulins, who live in the farm just before you come to ours. The field is opposite. That is the Point. On the next one lives M. Groscol. Ah! Here is the gate that leads to the Little Valley. Daddy, shall we jump over it, or have you brought the key?"

Goguet put his hand into his pocket and pulled out a key with which he unlocked the padlock of a five-barred gate. I expected the children to leap forward, but hardly had young Robert passed through the gate than he stood still and pricked up his ears.

"Listen," he whispered. "I am sure the bull is watching us on the other side of the hedge. I can't see him yet because the trees are too thick, but I can sense him."

He took me by the hand and, making me kneel beside him, peered through a break in the hedge.

"There. Can you see him now?"

"Why, yes," I answered. "The funny thing is that he seems vaguely familiar. And what is that dog barking up the lane? I wouldn't be surprised if this is where we landed yesterday when we thought we were miles away."

I walked back into the lane, and twenty yards farther on discovered the little farmhouse where the Alsatian had barked at our approach the previous day.

"You are right!" I exclaimed. "And I fancy the 'cow' I fed with sugar and marguerites must be a bull."

The whole company hurried to my side and stood considering the bull from a safe distance—all but Robert, who looked up at me with admiration in his dark eyes as he muttered:

"You gave him sugar, lady? Aren't you afraid of bulls?"

I expected to find a sarcastic smile on Goguet's lips. Far from that, he seemed impressed. It is true that Robin, as we were later to learn, was no angel. Groscol was partly responsible for the animal's vicious temper.

Groscol (Thick-neck), who lived in the house opposite, was a farm laborer who hired out his services either by the job or by the day. He paid $20 a year rent for the house and the kitchen garden, but the fruit in the orchard and the cider press were retained by the owner. The lovely orchard in which he lived was known as Berlequet. He had a wife, whose hair was the color of dried straw cut straight as barley on a thatched roof, and four children—all young girls. This was almost a dishonor in a Norman, for the race prides itself in producing a preponderance of males. Groscol was a good farmer, being of farming stock. Physically he was a giant with ingenuous blue eyes, and he had a slight stutter, which he lost when he was drunk. His bouts of inebriety were longest at certain seasons and coincided with the completion of such jobs as the cutting of logs in winter, the distillation of apple-jack in April, haymaking in July, apple picking in October, and cider making in December.

As the liquor mounted to his head, Groscol, armed with a hedge-bill, strode in his tall rubber boots across his orchard to a favorite cherry tree at the top of the lane by the Little Valley. There was a fork in this tree providing him with a commanding view over the adjoining lanes and fields. He sat there for hours, his legs dangling over the side, as he smote the air with his hedge-bill, convinced that each blow into space was cutting a neighbor's head off. Before beheading a victim, Groscol passed judgment in a voice so loud that on a still night it was known to carry over half a mile.

His vociferations provided the most appalling scandal and made him bitter enemies, not the least of whom was the Goguette, who did not dare pass the gate of the Little Valley to milk her cows when Groscol was seated drunk in his cherry tree.

"Keep away from here!" he cried. "Only honest women are allowed on this path. It's no good trying to impress me with your four cows. Four cows in four years! I'd like to know where they came from. Don't you think I remember the day when you first came here dragging your three brats behind you like a gipsy? It's not I who would drink the milk from your cows."

Behind the turn in the lane, the Goguette, petrified, would halt before this verbal onslaught, her hands tightening their grip on the handles of her empty pails. Her dark eyes would flash angrily as she meditated revenge. Now she would make a detour of half a mile, but to do this she was obliged to cross over land that was not hers, and seeing this Groscol would raise his voice louder still. Everybody knows that when a Norman is drunk he cannot stand a neighbor crossing his fields. He will even padlock his gates or stand barring the way with a scythe. As soon as he is sober he opens everything wide, even to the door of his own house, inviting strangers in.

Thus the Goguette would slink across another's orchards on her way to milk her cows, and Groscol would continue his diatribe until his throat was parched.

Then the giant would slide down from the branch of his tree and, refreshing himself with a long pull of cider, turn angrily on Robin, the Poulins' bull. He had an idea that Robin leered at him. Groscol's stride was less certain now. He would lurch across to the gate and, falling heavily on his knees, put his thick neck through the wooden bars, imitating the loud roar of a savage beast.

This infuriated Robin. The bull doubtless thought that this conduct was an attack on his personal dignity and, shaking his heavy head, he would advance menacingly toward the enemy.

Nobody knew exactly how long this game lasted. Groscol's wife may have had a rough idea, but she was wise enough to hide in a corner of the house with her four little girls, who clung crying to her skirts.

Yet, ignorant of these facts, I continued to envelop the now placid Robin with a look that was almost affectionate.

"Why, yes," I muttered. "I gave him a lump of sugar, but it's true I didn't realize he was a bull."

We walked back to the gate of the Little Valley and filed into the field. A narrow strip some three hundred yards in length led into the main orchard, planted with apple trees the majority of which were already some fifteen years old.

It was now apparent why there were so few roads in the district, and why the rights of way across orchards led occasionally to bitter quarrels. The stream which watered the bottom of the field in which Goguet lived meandered on its uneven course along the valley from which the ground rose fairly steeply on either side. The country was just a patchwork of orchards of varying sizes, divided by hedges in which there were narrow openings to allow cows to pass from one field to another when the land belonged to the same man.

Few were the owners whose fields were all contiguous. Most farmers were lucky to have three together and the rest dotted about amongst those of their neighbors, and a man might have to wait the best part of a lifetime for some coveted orchard to come on the market, especially if it was watered by a stream.

The Little Valley was divided from the water by a long sloping orchard known as the Big Valley flanked by another hayfield called the Molière, and a thick wood which Victor Duprez had long since given up any hope of purchasing. The land belonged to the widow Paul who had no intention to sell.

This widow Paul was over eighty, and though her husband had been dead for fifteen years, she never abandoned widow's weeds. Both her family and that of her husband were brought up on the land. Paul, all his life, had rented the fields and woods that belonged to the local château, a Louis the Thirteenth gem of which one had a splendid view from the Goguets' bedroom.

The château stood, framed by the trees of its noble park, some three miles distant as the crow flies, high up on the hill that rises beyond the stream. The light played on it capriciously.

Sometimes the sun's rays made it stand out in all its glory, but in stormy weather it would disappear mysteriously amongst the trees—invisible even to those who knew where to look for it.

In the evening I have seen its harmonious lines bathed in delicate changing tints, making of it a thing of indescribable beauty.

The only son of its noble family was killed in action early in the First World War—the first of the village. During the next four years, before mass, the priest prefaced a growing list of dead with the name of this young aristocrat.

Since then the château was kept in a sad state of repair. A sister lived there occasionally. She drove down to the village in a cabriolet, thus joining with the farmers in their defiance of the gasoline age, and her visits were more often to attend mass than to go shopping.

Though this family was so sorely hit by the war and impoverished by a generosity that was beyond its means, the tenants of the farm made a small fortune. Milk and butter rose in value in 1914, the apples were bought at high prices by the State for making alcohol, and wood replaced coal. Paul built himself a house of his own overlooking the road to St. Vaast. Though continuing to work the land belonging to the château, he now lived in the center of some sixty acres which he had managed to buy at various times with his savings. The new house was an ugly construction of red brick, on the chimney of which he affixed the letter "P," so that his descendants, working in the fields, should look up and think of him with pride.

Paul died very soon after moving into his new home. His eldest son carried on with the farm of the château, leaving the widow in the big house.

It was on her land that Groscol lived.

The Big Valley was to the west of the Little Valley, and one passed from one to the other by a narrow opening in the hedge. The larger field made an almost perfect square planted with young apple trees which Victor Duprez had bought the previous winter and which Goguet had put into the ground, protecting each, as is the custom, with metal spikes known as "corsets" to prevent the cows from breaking the young trunks. These trees were planted during a cold spell, and night frosts had killed at least a quarter, which would have to be replaced next February. The grass was almost to hay length because the cows were not feeding there any longer, the cattle pond being dry.

Beyond the western hedge ran a lane, which was the continuation of the one we had taken to reach Groscol's house and which turned sharply to the left some fifty yards beyond his domain, skirting the field in which the bull lived.

One had to get back into this lane to reach the Burgundy, Goguet's hayfield, for the Big Valley and the Burgundy were divided by a tongue of land which belonged to the widow Paul, and which gave access from the lane to her big field watered by the stream.

Victor Duprez had offered large sums to the widow for this tongue of land. He would have been able, by knocking down one of the hedges, to enlarge the Big Valley and bring it right up to the Burgundy, into which he could have cut an entrance. But the widow refused to sell, and she became more obdurate as Duprez offered more money. The Burgundy was much the same size as the Big Valley, but, being for hay, was bereft of trees. In the center was a small square barn which served for storing odds and ends during the hay season. It was typically Norman in construction, and though these old barns are still fairly common, many are falling to pieces for want of attention. They are made of mud and half-timbering. This one had lost its thatched roof at some period of its career and was covered by two sheets of corrugated iron. The beams were almost white with age, and the mud, which took the place of plaster in more substantial buildings of the period, had in places crumbled to dust, leaving gaping holes.

On my way back to the farm I dropped Goguet a hint that I might buy the property, or at least a part of it. He had doubtless already guessed what was going on in my mind, but he was shrewd enough to say nothing. His lease with Duprez ended at Christmas, which left me free to keep him or to look out for another farmer, but the problem was where I could lodge Goguet or his successor when I took over the house he now lived in.

Subconsciously I was working out the possibility of building a farmer's house and some modern stabling for the cows. I dreamed of an almost feudal establishment in which the farmer, ourselves, and our beasts would live round a courtyard so that my husband and I during our visits here would have all the advantages and all the fun of living on a farm. It even struck me that the farmer's rent and the vegetables we could grow in our garden would make us independent if anything went wrong in town.

Lack of water was going to be difficult. The Goguets relied entirely on the stream and on the rain-water tank at the back of their house. This problem was even more serious than the fact that there was neither gas nor electricity.

"What we want," said Goguet, "is a well. M. Duprez has promised me one for the last two years now."

Yes, that is what we needed, but how much does it cost to sink a well, and how could we be sure there was any water?

Knowing how much progress had been made in the electrification of rural districts, I was surprised about the electricity, but it struck me there might be a lot of fun in making our little citadel entirely independent.

I put this idea up to Duprez, senior, later.

What I liked about him was the way he bit into a problem the moment you put it up and explained all the solutions in detail.

"The well?" he said. "I'll ask a water diviner to trace an underground passage, and when we've found it I know a man in Bernay who'll come and sink the shaft. I reckon, judging from the farm next door, that we ought to find a flow at twenty-five or thirty feet." He said that it would cost about $20 a yard to build.

Goguet's new home? He would design a house and stables divided by an archway all under one long thatched roof. He would erect it at right angles to my own house in order to form an interior courtyard. A third wing would be open to the wind on two sides and be used for storing a governess-cart. We could also stack our winter's supply of wood there.

"This is going to cost me a great deal of money?" I ventured.

"Wait till I draw up the plans," Duprez answered. "I think we can do the whole thing for $2,000."

Of course I knew I was wrong in wanting to build. Everybody told me so. Whereas I might make money by buying the fields and buildings as they stood and selling the property when prices had risen, as they must do, with inflation, I would certainly lose all the money I spent on improvements. Besides, what would anybody else want with two houses on one farm?

"Don't do it. Don't do it," said my conscience.

"Nonsense!" said my other self. "You can spend a little less money on furs and dresses. The great thing is to prove that a woman can do things by herself. I want to be a woman who owns something in her own right. I want to create a township in miniature, producing my own food, my own water, my own light, to build a place in which I can have a baby and bring it up with all this round me."

"Let us look at the inside of farmer Goguet's house," suggested Duprez. "We must know if the house is sound."

The house was magnificently sound.

Just as there were three large rooms downstairs, so there were three rooms on the floor above.

Goguet's bedroom was large and airy and bathed in sunshine from early morning until afternoon. A large window with one immense pane of glass faced east, revealing the coastline toward Le Havre and, immediately opposite us, the château surrounded by its trees. The entire window swung open on hinges so that the magnificent landscape beyond looked like a living picture framed in the wall. The effect was superb. The other window was latticed, Elizabethan fashion, and faced south across the garden. By leaning my head out I could see the entire length of the field from the entrance gate to the stream.

The fire-place, framed by immense pillars of carved stone exactly similar to the ones below, made the bed look as if it had been placed in the corner of a cathedral. In fact, the same stone was used for the pillars of London's Westminster Abbey. The ceiling was supported by great oak beams.

The children slept in the center room. It was about half the size of the Goguets' bedroom and had one lattice window and the same stone pillars which here seemed even more impressive. The walls were covered by a faded yellow paper, which we ripped away, revealing half-timbering of unparalleled beauty on every wall. It was a museum piece. I have never, in all my life, seen anything to equal it.

The third room was the largest of the three. It was the oldest part of the house, with the result that the wall into which the window was built was at least five feet deep. One wall was timbered, the others were covered with white plaster, and even later I never dared remove it. If there was half-timbering, it still lies hidden. The fire-place had the same stone pillars as in the other two rooms, but I cannot think why, because there was none in the room below, and the chimney did not lead anywhere.

The floor was rather like a ploughed field. Some farmer had once kept chickens here, and even Goguet used it to store his apples and potatoes.

A concealed door led upstairs to an attic. It was warm under the slates, and the oak beams were fastened securely one into the other with thick wooden pins. This attic ran the whole length and breadth of the house.

Duprez was of the opinion that what the place needed most was a good airing and a coat of paint. Before driving me back to the village, he suggested we should go down to the bottom of the field and look at the cider press.

It was a long building with stone foundations, indiscriminate half-timbering, and a deep thatched roof. Because the grass sloped steeply to the water's edge, the top end of the building had a wall of only six or seven feet, while the bottom end had one twice as high. It was full of the craziest notions. There were barn doors just below the thatch, ladders hanging on wooden pins under the eaves, stacks of sawed apple trees ready for the ambulating distiller when he came along with his alembic to make the apple-jack, outside stairs each step of which was a great chunk of oak worn to the point of rot, and up which one was obliged to climb to reach the hay lofts. There were two creaking doors, one leading to the vats, the other to the presses.

The thatch in the long roof was in some patches almost new, in others so old that it had deteriorated into a moss-covered green, but the ridge of the roof was from end to end a mass of multi-colored irises. The building which, in spite of its several uses, was always known as the cider press, was joint property with the adjoining farmers. Both of us had our hay lofts, and there were different portions of the roof for which we were legally responsible. The actual cider press was a joint affair and the arrangement, which was four hundred years old, gave each of us the right to use it on certain specified days during the cider season.

Victor Duprez had often tried to buy out his neighbor's interest. The adjoining farm belonged, not to the Poulins, but to a wealthy notary at Caen, who was born there. He was adamant in his refusal to sell. It was the same story as the tongue of land dividing the Big Valley from the Burgundy, from which the widow Paul would not part.

The Poulins' farm was, in many ways, a model one for the efficiency in which it was run, for the cleanliness of the buildings, and for the family's unity.

There were three sisters, Madeleine, Nénette, and Louise, and two brothers, Peter and Ernest.

Madeleine, the eldest, was married to a farm hand called Montague. She was recognized as the head of the clan. Her advice was sought, not only by her sisters, but also by her brothers. Every morning she harnessed the mare and drove in a cabriolet to deliver farm produce to the customers and solicit new orders. She surrounded herself with eggs, butter, milk, cream, cider, apple-jack, fowls, ducks, and geese. In summer she added freshly cut flowers and lettuces; in winter faggots and logs. She was entrusted with all the money, which she kept under her bed in the largest room of the red-brick house. Physically she was tall, red-haired, scrupulously clean about her person. She kept her own counsel, seldom speaking to strangers more than was necessary for her commerce. Her dresses were simple and invariably black, for she had not been out of mourning since the death of her eldest brother during the First World War.

Madeleine Montague seemed to have inherited something from both her parents—the patience of her mother, long since dead, and the flair of her father, whom the family had only just buried.

Poulin came from Touques fifteen years ago with only one cow, but a nice fortune in the bank.

Under Poulin's administration the new farm did well. It comprised fifty acres, which was well above the average and the number of cows rose rapidly from one to just over twenty, but the whole family had to work hard to achieve this result. Poulin got drunk regularly five times a day, but he was up at 5 A.M., and for the next fourteen hours his eyes missed nothing on the estate. There was none to equal him as an administrator. Not the least among his qualities was his gift of instilling the team spirit in his family. He knew that the only way of making the estate pay was for his children to toil as no servants would have worked—all day long and without payment. Each had his or her allotted post, and if anybody grumbled he pointed out that each would be entitled to a share in the fortune when he was dead.

Now that he was gone this tradition continued under the direction of Madeleine Montague, his eldest daughter.

Nénette, Madeleine's next sister, was tall, pale, thin as a reed, with straight, sun-and-weather-beaten, flaxen hair. She was as hard-working and capable as her health was poor. At thirty-two she was already a tired woman, for she drove the plough at the age of twelve at their farm at Touques, where there was arable land. Shortly after her arrival in the new farm she was trampled on by a cow. Rescued by Victor Duprez, who happened to be passing, she was rushed in his car to hospital at Deauville (for which Samaritan act she never even thanked him), but she escaped with her life, although she lost a breast and suffered serious injuries to her stomach.

Within a few weeks she was back at work, never dreaming to complain.

Louise, the youngest girl, was her father's favorite child. She had long, nondescript hair, and wore pince-nez of thick glass, because of her short sight. She did not work out of doors, but was the lady of the needle, making her sisters' dresses and her brothers' shirts and overalls, mending stockings and socks, washing the linen in the river, ironing, sewing on the buttons. She married an ironmonger whose shop was in the village square.

The two sons were relatively young. Peter shot hares and rabbits, and now that his father was no longer there to keep him in order, preferred his motorcycle to the farm cart. Ernest was twenty and looked like becoming a good farmer. His sisters had a special affection for him because they had virtually brought him up, Madeleine Montague being fifteen years his senior.

The relations between the Montagues and the Goguets were variable. At times Goguet would cross over the hedge to drink at their cider press and invite the men to come over and drink at his. At other times the two families were not on speaking terms.

I soon discovered that it was to Madeleine Montague I had

spoken when we first came up the hill, uncertain of our way. I recognized her a few days later when she invited me into her cool brick house, where the copper pans shone and the parquet of venerable oak shimmered like a looking-glass, polished by all the girls in turn when they came in from their work on the farm.

With such neighbors I had no fears about their interest in our cider press. I could not then foretell how rapidly the family would be broken up. To Gaston Duprez, who went out of his way to explain clearly the question of joint responsibility, I pointed out that an arrangement which had existed for so long might safely continue for at least the period of my ownership. He agreed, and we walked down to the water's edge.

A ring of ashes, as if Red Indians had camped there, showed where the Goguette boiled her washing. She stood the copper on a trivet supported by three bricks to give depth to the hearth, and it took her less than a minute to build her fire of dead leaves and twigs and set it roaring in the wind. If a woman can kindle a fire in any weather, runs a Norman saying, she's an ideal housewife. Goguet had arranged a small dam in the stream, so that the Goguette could rinse her wash in clear water. Here she kept the box on which she knelt when scrubbing, her rubbing board, and the trestles on which rested the dripping clothes.

The ground where we stood was churned and pounded by the cattle that went to drink in the crystalline water which meandered over its pebbled bed.

We crossed the stream, stepping over three or four boulders while holding to the low branches of the trees. The orchard on the other side rose precipitously as far as the road which leads to St. Vaast, and on its higher slopes it is both verdant and sunny, but its chief beauty consists in the wide, sweeping view across the bay to Le Havre.

It was from the top of this orchard, so peaceful now, that one day I should see, in all its appalling horror, the death pangs of a mighty city.

3

Not until the end of June did Victor Duprez definitely agree to sell me his farm. "Come next week and we'll go to the notary," he wrote. "Meanwhile, my father is busy drawing up the plans for your new building."

As soon as I received this news I telephoned from London. I had almost given up hopes of buying the farm. Three of my letters had remained unanswered. In response to another, Victor's wife wrote to say that her husband was trying to enlarge a farm he owned in the plains of Caen, and that unless these negotiations were successful he would have to withdraw his offer. The delay made me all the keener and was, in itself, exasperating because I began to think he was planning to increase the price.

"I will be with you on Saturday," I told him over the telephone, "and I will bring the money."

I crossed the Channel with nearly $5,000 in my hand-bag, because the notary refused to accept a check on London. He said it would take too long to clear, and that he was accustomed to settle these deals with cash.

When I bade farewell to my husband on the Friday evening, the thick wad of French bank-notes almost prevented my bag from closing. I slept uneasily on the boat, although I managed to get a cabin to myself and was able to put the money under my pillow.

I arrived in the village soon after 9 A.M. and booked the same room at the hotel that my husband and I occupied during our spring holidays. Victor Duprez told me he had made an appointment with the notary for midday. This man of law lived in a large house facing the sea front. The sound of the waves beat-

ing against the foreshore at high water rolled through the northern windows of his study and lost themselves in the stillness of
the park into which the southern windows led by a short flight
of steps. The notary was a little man with neat mustaches,
mocking blue eyes, and an impeccably cut suit. There was a
heavy oak desk in the middle of his study, which he used for
the signing of documents. Another, much smaller, at which he
sat when alone, stood under a huge gilt mirror, into which it
was his habit to look up quickly as the clerk opened the big
double doors. This trick allowed him to size up his clients in a
split unsuspected second before he turned to greet them. By
that time he had a shrewd idea of what the peasant mind would
shortly try so hard to conceal.

He was a man from central France who, some thirty years
earlier, had come as a clerk to the notary who then owned the
practice, and whose daughter fell in love with him. He had
fought throughout the First World War and photographs of
Verdun hung on the walls. His smile was delicious and he had a
gift of expressing himself with devastating clarity. His voice attacked an enemy sardonically and stopped dead when it had finished saying what it wanted to say, so that those farmers who
feared him most declared that he stabbed them with a smile.

Victor Duprez sat beside me. The sun played on his high
forehead and on his spectacles, which, hiding his blue eyes, reflected the sallowness of his complexion. Politics were discussed
for a while; the possibility of war and what we in London
thought. The notary was severe in his criticism of English politicians. Self-conscious as a schoolgirl, dressed in a white blouse
and black tailor-made, I listened to him blaming England for
allowing Germany to re-fortify the Rhineland. But he blamed
his own country and accepted the inevitability of another war
with polite irony. He accepted it completely and coldly. No
doubt assailed him. He asked none of those questions which a
man asks in order to bolster up his own morale; recited none
of those platitudes which even the best-informed men carry
about with them. He was resigned, but inconsolable because he
had a son of military age. I tried to tell him that I had so much
faith in our country that I was buying a piece of its soil. "Yes,"
he said, "land isn't a bad thing to buy, especially for somebody
who owns sterling. But you are unwise to build when property

values are falling and the cost of building is rising because of this Socialist regime which you in England have helped to impose on us. As for trying to live beside a Norman farmer, I consider it sheer madness. The peasant and the townswoman are irreconcilable."

"Do you really think so?" I asked. "Goguet seems a pleasant man."

"You will see," he said.

Victor Duprez took not the slightest part in this conversation. He never pressed me to buy. He gave me the impression of doing me a favor, and though I found it hard to believe at the time, I know now that he was perfectly honest. He never did want to part with his farm. It was his father who believed that land was made to be sold. He treated me with the cold politeness that a well-bred Frenchman treats a woman.

"Well," said the notary, "here are the documents in duplicate. Let us read them aloud."

I listened attentively, but how could I expect my entirely feminine mind to understand these matters, and by the time that four hundred years of a farm's history had been unrolled in a preamble of legal jargon, I was already engaged in day-dreaming. Happily the notary was as scrupulous as the vendor.

"There is a small wood," said Duprez, "that I bought for a few dollars some months ago. I have never seen it, but it may come in useful. If you like I will throw it in."

He explained that it was about two acres in size and mostly planted with oak. A stream ran through the bottom.

"That is very generous of you," I said.

It was now time to hand over the money, and I took it out of my bag and placed it on the table. The vendor does not claim it until, some weeks later, it can be proved that there is no mortgage. I never saw the money being counted, yet I am convinced that it was done, but delicately, during a long discussion on trivial matters.

Ushered to the door by the clerk, we walked across the beautifully polished parquet. The sea was running out on sands of gold, on which not more than a dozen people could be seen, for it was yet too early for the holiday crowds. Victor Duprez invited me to lunch at Trouville. In the evening I went to his home for dinner.

But first I paid a visit to the farm.

When I trod the grass of my orchard, when I saw the sun setting behind the house—my house—the clouds sailing gently past my poplars, the apples growing on my trees, I knew that I was going to love the place.

The Goguette made butter for me to take back to London. She filled a canister with cream.

I took a parting glance at the Point, which was mine also, thought I had still to buy the Valleys and the Burgundy. When we were with the notary, Duprez offered to give me an option, not only on these, but also on the Picane. I could not make up my mind which to choose. The Picane was less rich in grass and farther from the house, but it was watered by the stream.

The notary told us that an option was not valid by law.

"In that case," said Victor Duprez, "you have my word that the offer remains open for two months."

I believed him and he kept his word. All the same, if he had refused to sell me that land, my own would have been too small to be of practical use. And to think I was already planning to build on it!

Victor Duprez lived in a tiny villa under the shadow of the church, and each time the bells chimed one had the impression of being in the belfry. The rooms were so small and the passage so narrow that he removed all the inside doors, but the place was cosy and he had made a magnificent library. He lived at a furious speed, rushing round the countryside buying and selling estates, visiting clients in Paris and staying up in night-clubs till dawn, but he was knowledgeable on many subjects, which made him a delightful companion, though he was said in business to be even shrewder than his father.

Mme. Duprez was an excellent cook. She had been to Trouville that afternoon to buy fish for dinner, and to a neighboring farm for the butter and the cream. Receiving no answer at the front door, I walked straight in and found her in the kitchen.

"Do you like herrings cooked in cream?" she asked, looking up with a smile, as if I made a habit of dining here. "My husband won't be a moment. He's coming with Peter Gravé, the builder, who is bringing you an estimate."

We laid the table together. The linen was of rare beauty. There was no getting away from it. The Duprez all had finely

developed taste. While we were doing this Duprez and Gravé
arrived. Victor, neat in a striped suit which he favored because
he thought it gave him height, begloved, immaculate. Gravé,
rotund, rubicund, an ample jacket hanging without form or
shape, a cap pulled well over his eyes, which he took off as soon
as he saw us, and which he screwed into a pocket.

We went up into the library, where Mme Duprez served us
with drinks and where, after a few moments' conversation, inspired by the leather bindings and gilt edgings, I discovered that
my future builder was also an avid reader. He told me his
father had sent him to the university, but refused to hand him
over control of the firm or give him more than an inadequate
allowance, though he was now virtually its chief. He was a big-
hearted, sentimental fellow, who had spent some time in a German prison camp in the First World War. The village gave him
a lot of drinks when he returned—too many, for soon he began
arriving drunk at the comfortable home his wife had made for
him.

At first she was patient, knowing that he had suffered a good
deal and now only had one lung. Then she scolded and threatened to leave him, but the bottle proved too strong. In his moments of soberness he was a good husband, and told us rather
naïvely that he had suggested a holiday in the Pyrenees to win
back his wife's affection. She accepted, but at the last moment
insisted on bringing a young cousin, with whom she had been
flirting. All three went off together in a motor-car, which Gravé
bought specially for the occasion, but a month later he returned
to the village alone. His wife had eloped with her cousin. Gravé
was more sincerely grieved than most people thought, but he
said to his friends with a laugh: "I have not lost everything. I
have seen the Pyrenees!"

His coat pockets always bulged. In one there was a novel or
a collection of plays, in the other were various things useful to
his profession, such as a tape-measure. He brought out, for my
benefit, a large sheet of foolscap, on which he had noted the cost
of the buildings he was going to erect on my farm. The estimate
was only a few dollars more than Gaston Duprez forecast. I gave
him about half the total, and asked him to start immediately, because I hoped to come and supervise the work.

This was the last Saturday in June. Gravé promised that the house would be finished in six weeks.

Victor told us at supper that he had spent the afternoon at Caen, where he went to see a nun who had been left a rich property in the neighborhood. She belonged to a strictly cloistered Order, and it took a long time to persuade the Mother Superior that it was imperative that the legatee should make a personal visit to the estate. After permission was obtained, Victor drove the nun and a chaperone in his car through the streets of Caen. His client, a St. Ursuline, had not left the convent for thirty years, and her surprise provided Victor with stories that delighted us. We parted as the church bells chimed midnight, and after spending the night at the hotel I returned early the next morning to London.

Three weeks later my husband and I had to go to Paris for the state visit of the king and queen. We decided to leave two days earlier and see what was happening at the farm. This time I brought enough money to buy the Little Court, the Little Valley and the Burgundy, sacrificing the Picane in spite of the fact that Victor offered to sell it me for only $175 an acre. I was to buy it fifteen years later at fifteen times the price. I signed the contract on the morning of our arrival and, accompanied by Gaston, immediately went off to inspect Gravé's work on the building.

The foundations were already built and the bricks laid to the height of half a dozen rows over which the hens flopped to gobble up the worms and insects in the newly dug earth. I made a great fuss in my keenness to hasten everything on, and I got results, being the only person in the village to build a house that summer.

Because I was a woman, everybody was eager to help, in spite of the troubles put in our way by the so-called Popular Front, which was doing its best to slow up work of every kind throughout the country. Gaston Duprez, his blue eyes sparkling above his black beard, looked like the lord high executioner as he walked up and down, lifting carefully gaitered feet over stacks of timber and sacks of cement. Gravé followed at a respectful distance, his hands clasped behind his back and his cap pulled over his face. The two men met only by accident, or, rather, it was accidental on the part of Gravé, who disappeared quickly when he saw his architect appearing over the brow of the hill. Nevertheless, the combination was good. Gaston had the ideas, and Gravé, when he was sober, knew how to execute them. Goguet was intrigued and polite. He wanted a job with the workmen because, as he told me with a disarming smile, it would be pleasant to contribute to the building of his own house.

"That sounds fair," I said.

"If you feel like living in the house," he answered, "we would be happy to give up our bedroom. There is plenty of space downstairs."

I accepted his offer gratefully, and told him that as soon as we were back from Paris my husband and I would stay for a month or more. By then the new house would be nearly ready for the Goguets.

"But you are not leaving till to-morrow," Goguet insisted. "I will have everything ready for this evening."

He had no trouble to persuade us. We dined with Victor Duprez and his wife, and they drove us back to the farm at midnight, more out of compassion than anything else. They could not understand why we were so anxious to sleep at the farm when there was a comfortable hotel in the village.

We parted at the white gate at the top of the field. It was a starlit night, but there was no moon, and the journey to the house drenched us to the ankles because of the heavy night dew and cost me a pair of new silk stockings. We lifted the latch of the heavy oak door as Goguet had instructed us. There were still embers in the hearth, and the smell of burning apple trees was delicious. We fanned the flames and threw a few faggots into the center, which filled the room with a warm glow and dancing shadows. The Goguette had left us two candles to light us to bed, which we held in front of us as we climbed the staircase leading to the upper floor.

The room had been arranged in our honor while we had been away. There were clean sheets on the rickety iron bed, covered over with a counterpane of multicolored bits and pieces, a prehistoric toilet basin and jug of cold water on a plain deal table, under which was a chipped pail. On the mantelpiece stood a faded photograph of Goguet in his wedding suit and of the Goguette in her veil, another of our farmer in his soldiering days, while his military bugle was nailed to the wall. We made an inspection, each in turn, holding our candles above our heads, the flickering light playing on the thick rafters. We flung open the windows, which had been carefully closed because peasants hate the cold night air.

The firmament was a mass of stars, and strange noises rose from below—the cows tearing at the grass which bordered the western window, and the two Shetland ponies chasing each other round the apple trees.

The bed was hard and so uneven that we kept on rolling into metallic pockets during the night, but though our backs were sore we slept soundly until the cock started to crow at daybreak.

In a corner of the room was a tall mirror-faced cupboard in which the Goguette stored her linen and her better pieces of china. Swallows had made their nest at the top of this cupboard, and we suddenly saw the male dart out into the garden. From time to time he would come back, feed the babies perched on the handle, and admire himself in the mirror. We wondered at first how the birds managed to live in this room, the windows of which were closed all night, but on reflection we realized that the farmers rose at 6 A.M. and from then until nightfall the windows were wide open.

Six o'clock struck at the very moment and we heard heavy footsteps in the room below.

Goguet was advancing in his jack-boots toward the hearth, into which he spat resoundingly.

A moment's silence and then the Goguette knocked what was left of the logs against the hearth, shaking out the charred wood. We could hear her stacking them against the sides of the chimney while she swept the embers into a shovel. Now the outside door opened on its dry hinges, letting in a stream of sweet early morning air. The cats that had been out all night miaowed with pleasure at the thought of a saucer of milk and a cushion to sleep on. The Goguette, having exchanged her slippers at the door for a pair of clogs, flung her shoveful of cinders into the garden, returning with an armful of faggots to make her new fire. In less than a minute the dry wood was crackling and a tripod fixed in the center of the flame. The Goguette put on this tripod a soot-covered saucepan of black coffee.

I would doubtless have been less bruised had I slept on the floor. One of the ponies must have been immediately beneath the window. His neighing, so close, gave me a start. I looked out. The sun was rising over Le Havre, and already the château was bathed in delicate coloring. Our cows were down by the river, and in the hundreds of meadows on the hills opposite other cows moved among the apple trees, the leaves of which were now a darker green.

The smell of the Goguette's fire came up in whiffs through the window, mingling with all the other smells of a summer morning in the country: the grass still soaked in dew, the cows' dung, and the roses in the garden.

From downstairs came new sounds of activity, the cups and saucers for the morning coffee, which the farmers drank black and in which Goguet put a thimbleful of apple-jack and two pieces of sugar, which, without waiting for it to dissolve, he ground with a spoon against the side of the cup.

It was time for the Goguette to go milking. We heard her wooden clogs resounding against the flagstones as she went to fetch her pails. The children were getting up, and their shrill voices filled the house, their exclamations pitched a half-tone higher and a little louder, because they knew we were upstairs. They wanted to interest us. My husband had got up also and was making an amused inspection of the room. Opposite the cupboard, where the swallows had built their nest, was another wardrobe in which reposed Goguet's wedding suit, obviously the one in which he had been photographed, and a great number of dark bottles full of apple-jack, the smell of which was quite enough to keep the moths out. Somebody was coming up the stairs whose step was light and childish. It was Renée with our breakfast. She had run out to fill a jug of fresh milk from her mother's milking pail.

Her little brown face was all smiles, and she referred to me as "the lady."

"Has the lady slept well? Does the lady take sugar in her coffee?"

From the orchard now came a great and mighty cackling— the goose and her gander stretching forth their long necks as they advanced to the foot of our window, followed by a dozen balls of yellow fluff, the new family. We threw them a piece of bread and the parents fought for it with much beating of wings and excited cries.

I dressed quickly and went through the garden where the dew still hung lightly in the petals of the roses, into the field where Toxie strained on her leash. Fortunately I had brought bootees for the grass was soaking, in spite of the fact that it had not rained all night and the sun was mounting in the sky.

It was now possible, by following the foundations, to get a rough idea of what the new building would be like. As Duprez had already showed me on his blue-print, it stood at right angles to our own house, leaving a passage of five or six yards between the two, through which we would eventually be able to reach the inner courtyard.

Whereas our house and its garden faced due south Goguet's new home and the cowsheds, all in one long building, would face west, in the direction of the main entrance gate of the field. Nobody would therefore be able to come down without being seen from our farmer's front door, which opened straight into their main room where there would be a hearth nearly as big as ours.

His parlor, in the exact center of the façade, jutted out from the main alignment. This was Duprez's idea, to give the carpenters a chance of showing their skill in the hips of the roofing and the thatcher an opportunity of making something more complicated than one long, plain roof. On the other side of it was the arch (formed by the continuation of the thatched roof) that divided Goguet's house from the stables, and through which he could pass a horse and cart into the courtyard.

Under the whole length of the thatch would be a huge loft, which would make a right-angled turn inward at the end of the stables to continue over the cart-shed.

But so far all these were only squares on the ground mapped out by the two-foot-high walls of brick.

At eight o'clock the workmen arrived—the bricklayers and the cement mixers; old Berthelot with his horse and cart, his long trailing mustaches, broad shoulders, and leather whip; Gravé, collarless and tie-less, who had been out fishing all night and who brought a present of half a dozen mackerel and some flounder; Marino and Primo, the Italian plasterers.

Goguet, perceiving from afar all this ado, walked up the hill from the cider press, where he had been eating a second breakfast consisting of a large chunk of bread and a piece of cold bacon, washed down with many glasses of cider drawn straight from the cask. His job was to make repeated journeys to and from the stream with buckets of water to mix the cement. He had no trouble in finding occasional help from his colleagues, who discovered that the cider press being at the water's edge amply compensated their labors. The children in black aprons went off to school with their satchels filled with books and cold sausage. Their cries of "Eh, là!" could be heard along the path as they progressed slowly, thrilled by the activity round them.

The Goguette was in her buttery straining her morning milk, occasionally crying out to a baby heifer in the stables.

These stables were put up by Victor Duprez. They consisted of half a dozen boxes built against the back of our house, with a slanting roof of red tiles. They dampened the lovely stone wall, blocked up two windows, one in the passage on the first floor and the other in a small room beside the buttery downstairs, and brought the animals far too near the house.

We had no need of any stabling till the winter. The heifer's place was in the "bakery." I decided to have Gravé pull the stables down immediately in order to get some light and air in the upstairs passage. I would stack the old wood and tiles for future use. Gaston Duprez, who heard of this decision as soon as he arrived on the scene for his morning inspection, thoroughly disapproved. He knew his son had spent $300 to put up this place, and it shocked him to think the money would be wasted. I said it was my house and I intended to do as I pleased. As we both had quick tempers, a short quarrel took place, but Gravé received his orders. The stables would be torn down.

After lunch we left for Paris, where we spent a week in the splendor of the Republic's welcome to the king and queen. We found time, however, to choose a bed to replace the one in which we slept during our first night at the farm, and we had it sent so that we should find it all ready for us on our return. I also spent a morning chasing sheets and blankets, and we wrote a letter to the Goguette asking her to make up the bed for the following Sunday.

Meanwhile Gravé kept sober for a whole week and drove the work forward, so that on our return we found the walls at window height.

Gaston Duprez had summoned a water diviner, who discovered an underground flow a dozen yards in front of what would soon be Goguet's front door. A well-sinker from Bernay was coming to start work the next day.

This was splendid news, because Gravé warned us that his men would not be able to come on Mondays, so there would be two consecutive days wasted each week. "The workmen are keen enough," he said, "but the Popular Front insists on the forty-hour week, and I don't dare break it too often. I stretched the point last week because the national holiday would have put the men out of work three days out of seven. Now you will understand why nobody wants to build a house this summer."

It broke my heart the next morning to see the place deserted for I knew how important it was to press things forward during the dry weather, but toward eleven o'clock a truck lumbered over the brow of the field, lurching across the bumps. It came to a standstill with screaming brakes, and as we ran forward to meet it we saw a motor-cycle following behind ridden by a tall, fair youth wearing a blue sports shirt and blue trousers to match.

From the truck clambered a big, heavy-set man, with a strong jowl. He was Tavernier, the well-sinker, and the motor-cyclist was his son. Two young workmen jumped out behind Tavernier and stared to unload. They were introduced to us as Robert and Alphonse. Robert, small, dark-haired, who, as he stripped himself of his coat, revealed arms tattooed with serpents and naked women to remind him of his campaigns with Lyautey in North Africa. Alphonse was tall, good looking, with powerful biceps, and a beret placed at a rakish angle on his head. Spades, picks, pails, a large trestle, and a winch with enough rope to hang all the inhabitants of the village, were piled on the grass.

I asked if they had come direct from Bernay.

"No," answered Tavernier, "we arrived yesterday, as you can see from the sunburn these young fellows picked up on the sands. They spent their Sunday bathing."

They led a gipsy life.

As soon as they started on a new job, Tavernier, his wife, and the boys stacked their requirements for a month on the truck and upon reaching their destination rented a small house. Mme. Tavernier brought her own washing machine, her sheets and and blankets, her knives and forks, and the big black pot in which she boiled her stew in the evening. She was an excellent laundress and a good cook, both essential qualities, because her husband, knowing how exacting was their craft, forbade his workmen to stay out late at night.

Led by Tavernier they came to inspect the spot where the well was to be sunk. The water diviner had marked it with a small heap of stones surmounted by a stick, and it was exactly halfway between Goguet's new house and his manure-heap.

"So this is where the water's supposed to be?" said Tavernier, looking round. "What an idea to summon a diviner. We could have found it just as easily ourselves."

He walked beyond the bakery to the hedge which divided our land from that of the Poulins, and taking a knife from his pocket cut himself two young hazel-nut twigs where they join at the fork. He made this in the form of a wishing-bone, removing the leaves.

His elbows clamped to his ribs and the twig grasped firmly in both hands, the ends turned lightly back with his thumbs, he advanced slowly with measured step.

"What are you doing?" I asked.

"Watch the hazel," Tavernier explained. "When it starts moving from the horizontal to the vertical there will be water underneath. Here goes. But mind, I'm exerting no pressure."

He started moving slowly forward again, and after every twenty or thirty yards would relax and start again. At last he moved over the spot on which the diviner had placed the stones, and there his twig started rising.

Not satisfied with this, Tavernier approached the place from a dozen different angles, finally circling round it. The flow appeared to come from the direction of our house and to make off toward our neighbor's farm. "Watch again," he said; "the wand rises when the stream is coming from its source and falls when following the current."

This lesson in magic appealed to us all. We spent the best part of an hour wandering round the field with hazel wands. We must have looked like inmates of a lunatic asylum. Tavernier, who had gone farther afield than any of us, came back with the news that the flow came from the bottom of the field, passed under our house, and must be the same from which the Poulins drew their water.

"They tell me their well is only twenty-five feet deep," he said. "What did your diviner say?"

"He claims there are two sheets," I answered; "the first at thirty feet, which will prove inadequate, and the second at one hundred feet, which will give us more than we need."

"These diviners are mere theorists," answerd Tavernier. "We shall find enough water at twenty-five feet."

Robert and Alphonse had brought out a tape-measure, and having cleared the stones away drew a circle one yard in diameter. Stripping to the waist, Robert began to dig, while his companion took the earth away in a barrow. "I'll put it in the foundations of the new building," he said. "The bricklayers will need some earth there before long."

"Funny you didn't know how to find water," Tavernier said, while he rolled himself a cigarette. "It's scientific, you know. Like determining the sex of a baby before it's born."

"What's that?" I asked.

"Have you got a sou?" Tavernier asked, flattered by my interest. "A sou with a hole in the center. Here's one. Now, what I need is a short piece of common thread."

I went indoors and fetched him what he wanted. He cut a piece about two feet long, and tying one end to the sou, through the hole, held the other between his finger and thumb. As soon as the coin had finished rocking he called me and said:

"Put your hand just underneath the coin, madame."

The sou hesitated for a moment and then, gathering momentum, started to go round in circles. "I'm not moving a muscle," said Tavernier. "You can try it yourself in a moment. Now, madame, remove your hand and ask your husband to put his there instead." I followed his instructions and, after a moment's hesitation, the coin started to swing pendulumwise. It was really impressive.

"I have four children," said Alphonse, who was passing with his barrow. "We always knew what to expect, a boy or a girl. All you have to do is to place the coin above the baby when it's still in its mother's womb."

"But isn't the coin more influenced by the mother than by the child?" I asked.

"Not as long as the coin is right above the child," said Alphonse. "All our farmers near Bernay know when to expect a heifer or a bull-calf."

"The same thing applies to eggs," put in Tavernier. "If you give me half a dozen I will tell you what the chicks will be."

"Your turn, Alphonse," exclaimed Robert, who had already dug a hole about a foot deep. They changed over, Robert wheeling the barrow and Alphonse taking the spade.

When they reached three feet they ceased work.

"That will be enough for today," Tavernier announced. "We will be here at eight tomorrow and start seriously."

He picked up a sod of earth from where his men had been digging, and rolled it in his hand.

"I wonder what we shall find on the way down—loam, green sand, black sandstone, water? Probably something like that."

"Does it ever happen you go on and on without ever striking water?" I asked.

"No," he answered. "I invariably give satisfaction; but my eldest son is in charge of a team working at Le Havre just now, and he is a little anxious—one hundred ninety feet without finding a damp stone."

He threw the earth down and, putting on his coat, said:

"Your farmer should find another place to stack his manure. If we get some rain the dung water might percolate down the sloping ground into the well."

As soon as he had gone I went in search of Goguet to tell him what Tavernier had said.

"We could move some of the manure today," I suggested. "The workmen can all give a hand in the morning. We can take it near the hedge."

Goguet's face fell. "But what about my pumpkins?" he cried. "If I uproot them now I'll have no soup all the winter."

He cast a tender eye on the dark leaves and yellow flowers sprawling over the top of the manure.

"Which would you rather do?" I asked. "Poison your water supply or go without soup?"

He made no answer, but I know how much he felt the loss of his pumpkins. The Norman farmers pick them before the first frosts and fix them on the stable rafters so that they get the last rays of the autumn sun.

Goguet came back in a moment with a pitchfork and a barrow.

"We would do better to wait till Berthelot arrives with his horse and cart," he said

Climbing to the top of the heap I slaughtered his pumpkins. I knew he would never do it himself. He looked at me angrily, and, as he did not move, I attempted to start the work but the caked manure weighed down my fork, and I blushed under his silent sarcasm.

He then told me he must go and visit a cow that was about to calve. I sat down on the heap and tried to plan something more scientific with a pipe at the bottom to drain off the dung water into an underground tank. I would talk to Gravé about it in the morning.

Goguet came back a few minutes later wiping his mustaches. I knew that he had only gone as far as the cider press.

"The cow?" echoed Goguet. "She's all right. There'll be nothing fresh before the new moon."

"I am not very good with the spade," I answered. "Do you mind if I take a turn at the barrow?"

The ground sloped down from the manure-heap to the new house, but climbed steeply from there to the hedge. My accomplishments had hitherto been exclusively feminine and I was quite unable to push the barrow. Or was it that Goguet, angry that a woman should try to give him orders, had piled the barrow too high?

"Personally," reiterated Goguet, resting on his fork, "I still think we would do better to wait for Berthelot."

The next morning I was up early, and long before the arrival of the workmen began planning the great clean-up in my house.

For the time being I could do little about the ground floor, given that my farmers were living there, but I was determined to have the upper floor thoroughly overhauled during the coming fortnight. The first thing to do was to persuade the Goguette to remove the cupboards from the center room, where her children used to sleep. I caught her as soon as she came in from milking and put it as diplomatically as possible. After all, her husband was earning good money by working on his new house, and, besides, they would soon have the water at their own place, which would save the Goguette no end of work.

She said she would fetch her husband to help her clear the room right away, and I then walked up the field in the hope of meeting Gravé coming from the village. If necessary I would go and see him at his office. My anxiety was unnecessary. I saw him ambling down the hill in a pair of khaki linen trousers, engrossed in a book which he held in both hands just above his paunch, like a priest with his missal. He looked up at my approach and touched his cap.

"Good morning, Gravé. I was just coming down to see you. What are you reading so early in the morning?"

He showed me the cover before stuffing the volume in his pocket.

"Oh!" I exclaimed. "The plays of Porto-Riche. So you favor the triangle love dramas of 1900."

I stopped short, realizing how tactless I was. He was quick to see my embarrassment.

"It does me good," he said with a smile, "to know there are other poor devils in the same state as myself."

"The well-sinker came here yesterday," I said, changing the subject abruptly. "He told me we ought to move the manure-heap. I thought you might put a couple of men on the job with Berthelot's horse and cart. What do you think about building a cement pit?"

"You might as well," said Gravé. "Although I think you'll be about the only farmer's wife for twenty miles around to do such a thing."

We walked as far as the bakery, where he took out his foot-rule to measure the ground.

"How would it be," he asked, "if we built a cement trench at the back of your bakery? Look, the ground falls away from there, so that if we make your pit opposite the cart-shed it can be fed not only by the three sties in the bakery, but also by the new cowsheds."

"How big will you build the pit?" I asked.

Gravé took out his rule and measured a square on the grass.

"About the size of a small swimming-pool," he answered, "and about as deep, but we will have a little brick wall above ground to keep the manure in. The dung water can be drained off to a cistern."

On our way to the house we found Berthelot limping along

beside his mare. He was as short-sighted as a bat, but his tall
stature and walrus mustaches gave him an air of undeserved
ferocity. He had been with the firm all his life, having looked
after the horses of Gravé, senior. Peter's father was in the habit
of buying a new motor-car every year, but never once rode in
it, preferring his horse-drawn cabriolet.

"What are you doing this morning?" asked Peter Gravé.

Berthelot pointed with his whip at a rusty old drinking-trough
fixed up in his cart.

"Very well," said Gravé, "when you've brought up enough
water from the stream for the workmen, give Goguet a hand in
moving his manure-heap over to the hedge."

The place was already getting busy. The bricklayers were
adding another row to the walls of the house, the well-sinkers
were hard at work, and Marin, the carpenter, an elderly man
with white hair and a carefully brushed suit, was standing over
his frame beside our garden.

"Come up stairs," I said to Gravé. "We can have a look
round."

Pencil and note-book in hand, Gravé visited every room with
me. Most of the doors would have to be replaced and the half-
timbering needed careful handling. He would treat the oak and
put new plaster where it was falling out. An entirely new floor
must be laid in the largest of the three rooms, the one used in
days gone by as a hen coop! Stout nails were hammered into the
beams, from which successive generations of farmers hung har-
icot beans to dry, and there was no window pane at all, doubtless to make a draught and air the hay which Goguet stored there
until my arrival.

Gravé put his head out and called to his carpenter.

Marin arrived a few moments later, accompanied by "Deaf
Joseph," his mate, who was Gravé's uncle. The two carpenters
made an excellent team, Marin specializing in beams for roofing,
which is a Norman gift handed down for centuries, Deaf Joseph
making the smaller things like parquet floors, window frames,
and doors. Both men were of village descent. Marin's wife was,
for some thirty years, the local midwife. Each time a birth was
expected Marin used to hurry home to prepare the donkey cart
in which he drove his wife to her work, arming himself when it
was at night with a medieval lantern.

Deaf Joseph owned a little farm on the road to St. Vaast, composed of a small house and seven acres of land. He leased this farm to his only daughter, and though, by French law, she was sole heir to the property, woe betide her were she ever late in paying the rent!

She had married a man called Giles.

Giles was an electrician in a munitions factory along the coast, and was credited with Socialist views, but as soon as he returned home he busied himself on the farm. In autumn, because he was unable to get home before dark, he picked his apples by the light of an acetylene lamp. In summer he cut all his own hay with a scythe, tied it up in bundles, and removed it to his barn in a wheelbarrow.

The farming community distrusted him for trying to prove that an amateur, knowing nothing about the land, can surmount most difficulties by a little intelligence and a lot of work; but he had the townsman's fear of a cow.

Happily his wife was braver. She looked after the one cow they had bought the previous year. She was also rearing a heifer, and supplemented the milk by keeping a goat, which browsed under the hedges at the end of a rope.

Just now Deaf Joseph lived in a log cabin half a dozen fields farther up the road. He owned a villa in the village, but rented it to holiday makers each summer. Sometimes a neighboring farmer would bellow in his ear:

"Aren't you frightened, Deaf Joseph, of living all by yourself in this lonely field?"

"Why should I be frightened if I can't hear anything?"

He was an excellent workman, and I was lucky to have him at my farm. Some of the men like Marin and Joseph were craftsmen no less cunning than those who built great cathedrals in medieval times. Modern Paris sent for the Norman slater when there was repair work to be done at the Louvre. It was known that he carried on with pride the traditions of his ancestors. Marin promised to put the carpentry work of the upper floor in hand while waiting for the builders to finish the walls of the new building. He advised spruce for the parquet in the end room, because oak was almost impossible to obtain. A couple of men would start planning the ribs to support the new floor while Deaf Josph would take all the doors off the hinges and cut fresh ones in the shop. In spite of the fact that we had been obliged to waste the first two days of the week, I felt that things were now beginning to hum, and I implored Gravé to make up for lost time. From what he said I gathered that, momentarily at any rate, he had every intention of doing so.

It was the middle of August, and Goguet asked for a week off to bind his hay. He had cut the long grass, white with ox-eye daisies and yellow with buttercups, at the end of July during his lunch time and in the evening. Both the Goguette and Roger took their turn with the scythe, and I was surprised to see how rhythmically and untiringly worked the boy who had behaved so childishly the first day we made his acquaintance. The Goguette took no rest these days, washing her linen down by the river, tending her house, feeding her family, milking her cows, making the butter and the cream, and finding time to spend long hours haymaking. Dressed in her blue apron, with a wide-rimmed straw hat hiding her olive features, she used to bend over her rake in the evening or scatter the hay before stacking it in the dome-shaped ricks studded about the field.

Renée was not strong enough yet to do much more than gather the stray ends and jump with her young brother on the ricks to beat down and compress the sweet-smelling hay, but she was lively, and her movements were so rapid that she ended by doing a good deal more than most children of her age. Robert knew where his father kept the keg of cider, from which they all drank in turn straight from the tap-hole. It was hidden among the pimpernel which grew under the leafy hedges, and it was as cool there as in a cellar. The Goguette claimed to lose more weight during haymaking than during all the rest of the year, but her fatigue was not all physical, for her husband was nervous and irritable, though generally sober, until all his bundles were made and safe in the lofts of the cider press.

The year's hay was food for the beasts and often their litter too. If there was not enough, if rain came at the wrong moment, hay would have to be bought and the money taken from savings put aside toward the purchase of the next cow.

It was three weeks now since the hay had been stacked on the Burgundy, and the weather was fine and sunny. Goguet took his bicycle and hied to Dannestal, where he fetched his brother-in-law Adrien, the binder. It was a Monday morning when he started work, for binders like to begin a new field early in the week in order to be sure of spending Sunday at home. Sinewy, fair-haired, and booted, Adrien went to the Burgundy armed with a pitchfork, which he used for tossing a quantity of hay from the rick to the ground. This he divided into two parts: the first he kneaded into a sort of square cake, rolling the ends inwards. When it was tight and compact, he knelt down, placing his right knee in the center to keep the bundle in position while he made another cake of exactly the same diameter with the rest of the hay. His shoulders were strong and square, but the veins of his forehead, beaded with sweat, stood out as he thumped and crushed the bundle with both arms from the elbows to the wrists.

The hay was dry and kissed by the sun. The Goguette drew out from the rick a handful of hay which she pulled evenly toward her, twisting it the while into a strong cord which she ended by making two yards in length. Quickly she handed it to the binder, who now clamped his two cakes one against the other, their even surfaces outward. He passed the cord round, tying it with a slip-knot which he drew so tightly that his neck bulged with the strain. Then he threw his shoulders back and, getting up, tossed his bundle into the cart.

Goguet paid by the hundred for these bundles, and a good binder would make two hundred between dawn and sunset. When winter came, Goguet gave two a day to each of his cows, one in the morning and one in the evening, and not even the cord would be wasted, for in a trice it unwinds itself and mingles with the rest.

In the evening, because these bundles must not stay out in the dew, the cart, which Goguet borrowed from the Poulins in return for services past or in the future, rumbled down the narrow lane past Groscol's house, the barking Alsatian, and the gate that leads to the Valleys. It was not just a cart full of hay that Goguet and the Goguette followed, but a known quantity of bundles to feed a known number of cows through the winter months.

The day Adrien made his last bundle, when not a wisp was left on the Burgundy and when the great beams of the cider press creaked under the weight of the hay, the Goguette killed her plumpest chicken and Renée went down to fill a jar of cider and a keg of apple-jack for the farewell dinner to Adrien.

Tonight Goguet could get drunk. His beasts would not starve this winter.

It was the last Monday in August. Alphonse, the well-sinker, and young Tavernier arrived just before midday on their motor-cycles from Bernay, where they had spent the week-end.

Robert and his chief were at the well at Le Havre, which was now presenting grave difficulties. Ours was already forty feet deep, but on Saturday progress had been slow because of a treacherous layer of black sand, and over the week-end I noticed that the cement ridge at the mouth was damp in spite of the dry weather.

My husband and I followed the sinking of our well with pas-sionate interest. The first twenty feet took little more than a week. The third day, old Tavernier fixed a wooden trestle sup-porting a windlass across the orifice. There was a handle on either side to wind the cable, and when it was somebody's turn to go digging he would be let down astride a narrow cradle with his pick and a bottle of cider. As soon as the digger was safely at the bottom his companion at the winch brought the cable up again and sent down the heavy pail, which was continually be-ing emptied by Goguet, who was now definitely assigned to the well-sinkers.

At twenty feet it was time to cement the walls of the well. Tavernier believed in the most primitive methods, and had in-vented four curved wooden casings which clamped into a hol-low circle, leaving about a foot between the outside of the cylin-der and the walls of the well. Into this cement was poured and left to dry overnight.

This operation was repeated every three feet down, the joins beings filled in by hand. Since Robert's departure for Le Havre, Alphonse was nearly always at the bottom of the well, and as I passed that way I could hear the sound of his ribald songs rising from the bowels of the earth.

On this Monday morning young Tavernier gave us a sly look as soon as his companion disappeared below ground.

"Alphonse had a thick night at Bernay," he said, laughing. "He looks washed out."

After filling a couple of pails we got the signal to haul him up. "The air is foul below," he spluttered. "Give me something to drink."

Goguet handed him the communal cider bottle and he took a long draught, but his features were ashen and his eyes so haggard that we were not surprised when he disappared behind a cherry tree in a fit of vomiting. It was past midday. There was nothing to be done till after lunch.

The team came back at two o'clock. Alphonse had recovered his equanimity and young Tavernier was in fine fettle, having been well fed by his mother in their villa by the sea.

"Come on!" he cried, lighting a cigarette as he swung on the cradle. "I'll have a look down there myself."

Alphonse went over to the winch, letting his companion down slowly while talking to Goguet, who was standing beside him.

My husband left me to hold a watching brief while he went over to inspect the manure-heap, which was now finished, and of which I was inordinately proud. I was getting anxious about the well, because the work was proceeding much less rapidly since Robert's departure. The team spirit had gone, and it was no good expecting Goguet to take his turn below. He would not have gone down the well for a fortune.

At about twenty-five feet a hoarse cry was heard.

"Bring me up quick."

Alphonse bent over the winch, but the weight had suddenly increased, and he called to Goguet for help. They realized now that something was seriously wrong, and both men put all their strength into the task of winding the cable. I peered over the orifice, expecting soon to catch a glimpse of Tavernier's cap.

Straining my eyes I suddenly perceived a body coming up through the blackness of the hole. Tavernier, in crying out, had inhaled so much gas that he had fainted, his body collapsing across the cradle, his head and legs hanging limply downward.

The men, bending over the winch, could see nothing. I realized how acute was the danger because Tavernier's head would, in another moment, be shattered against the base of the trestle which cut across the orifice.

It was too late to cry out. I threw myself against the free winch and the weight of my body acted as a brake.

Alphonse now saw in what posture his companion was returning to the surface. He called a couple of plasterers working near by to help Goguet hold fast to the winch, and with my help he swung Tavernier round.

The operation was delicate, for the inanimate body might always slip off the cradle and be hurled to the bottom, but what saved him was his height. His long knees acted as a wedge. As soon as Tavernier was safely on the grass he opened his eyes and exclaimed: "What am I doing here?" He remembered nothing at all—not even that he had shouted for help.

We closed the well that afternoon by putting a couple of planks across the orifice, covering the grass round the edge with implements and stones to prevent the animals from approaching. The gas cleared within a few days, and by the middle of the week a candle sent down to the bottom on the cradle came up still alight.

The thatcher was called Caesar Bianchi, but he was so thoroughly Norman that if his ancestors were Italian they must have cooked spaghetti for the Conqueror.

He came one fine day on his bicycle and looked at the timbered frame of the new building and sampled our cider in the press room, because it was in the barn above that he would keep his rye straw. He had ordered it from the Limousin and a truckful was on the railroad somewhere between Limoges and Deauville. The only thing about Bianchi which did not belie his name was his fair hair, turning slightly gray over the temples. He took life philosophically, too much so, because he always had more work than he could handle, although he was the only thatcher in the village, whereas when he was an apprentice there had been a dozen. Most of his work was the repairing of old barns and cider presses, nearly all of which were thatched, but the little house he lived in on the cliffs had a tiled roof and was fitted with electricity. He did not smoke, but drank his pint of applejack a day, which commands respect even among farmers, some of whom claimed to drink up to forty pints of cider between dawn and bedtime. On the other hand Bianchi had the excuse that after a couple of hours perched on a roof-top he came down with his teeth chattering and his bones frozen.

I went down to see him in the cider press and told him I

hoped he had ordered enough straw, because if we were obliged to wait three weeks for the railroad to send a truck across the entire length of the country again, we would be faced with a long delay. The trouble with a thatcher is that you make a contract with him for the whole job. He supplies the straw, which means that he always hopes to do with less than he really needs. At the last moment he has to send a wire to Limoges for more, and that is an invitation to the rain to soak your house.

My homily was a complete waste of time. He would not have listened to me, anyway, but as it happened I had broken in on a piece of news.

"They say it's her daughter who is forcing the sale," Goguet was saying, as he filled a bowl of cider from the cask in my honor.

"What sale?" I asked.

"I thought you would have been the first to know," said Goguet. "The Paul sale."

"Oh!" I said. "The widow Paul? What exactly is she selling?"

"Her daughter at Caen," put in Caesar, "is forcing the sale of all the land on both sides of the stream because she claims she was not given a fair share at her father's death."

"Yes," said Goguet, "that is how it is. In Normandy every child has the right to an equal share of the father's estate. If one of them is dissatisfied, he can force a sale of all the land and be paid in cash."

"Could they not come to an agreement?" I asked.

"From what people say," explained Goguet, "she was not listening to reason. You know what it is. She probably believed she was being cheated. That is how all the big properties are broken up."

"So Berlequet the lovely orchard in which Groscol lives is up for sale," I cried, "and the Big Valley, going down to the stream, and the wood, and the Molière hayfield. . . ."

"And a lot more beside," Goguet answered. "Le Cour du Cerf, for instance. But if you ask my opinion the land is already sold."

"To whom?" I asked.

Goguet shook his forefinger knowingly.

"Who buys all the land round here? Victor Duprez, of course."

Without appearing too interested, I brushed the hay from my skirt and walked back to the house. I could not understand why Victor Duprez had told me nothing. He had sold me his own farm only a few weeks ago, so he surely did not want the Paul estate for himself. Unless, of course, he was acting for somebody else who was bidding for the entire property. I was worried. I knew that part of this land which adjoined mine would one day be necessary to me if I wanted to make my farm a going concern. If I let it go now I might have to wait ten or fifteen years. Perhaps I would never get it.

I found the workmen busy when I arrived at the top of the field. Barbe, the painter, was there in his long white coat. He used to spend long afternoons seated at the big table in the farm, working out minute estimates on foolscap paper with a pencil stub poised between two fingers of his right hand, because the rest had been shot away. By a judicious first marriage and wise investments, Barbe was a rich farmer as well as a successful painter. His workmen were ambidextrous in the sense that they milked his cows and cut his hay with one hand, while painting his customers' villas with the other. This method brought profit to both parties because it kept the men busy throughout the year, whereas normally they would have been thrown out of work in the winter.

Barbe was jealous of my well, or rather what we all hoped would result from it. He spent a great deal of time questioning young Tavernier, and I guessed that before long he would place an order for one on his own forty-acre farm.

Gaston Duprez was here today and so was Duclos, the gardener, whom I had summoned to build a garden all round my house. The existing one was too small. It lay like a strip of carpet in front of the house so that the cows, and even Mono, the sow, used to stand for long hours below our bedroom window. At night the noise was appalling, and what was worse the animals tore down the tiles by rubbing their backs against the wall.

Duclos was a little man with huge black mustaches, who wore the traditional blue overalls of his craft and spoke to his clients with old-world courtesy in the third person. He would advance, cap in hand, toward me and say: "If madam will allow me to make a suggestion, she will plant King William pears like those I am in the habit of planting for Monsieur le Baron."

He was gently tyrannical, and having rolled off a dozen incomprehensible names would add: "Of course, madam must understand that we gardeners always speak of such things in the Latin tongue."

The garden must be gay with flowers. I enlarged it by as much again in front and carried it right round the house, taking in two excellent cherry trees and a sturdy greengage. The earth had to be dug and manured, and the fence changed and enlarged. Barbe would paint the railings in white when they were put in place. I was very anxious to mix vegetables and fruit with the flowers. Apart from roses and lilac-trees in front and a wall of hydrangeas behind, because these flourished in the shade, the ground would be prepared to receive lettuces, carrots, turnips, and bushes of red and black currants. Duclos was an expert in fruit trees. I told him to plant one hundred and twenty cider apple trees in the Big Valley and two dozen Cox's in the little orchard opposite our bedroom window.

He was thus waiting for me at the door, his cap in one hand and a hothouse plant in the other, which he offered me with a bow so low that his head almost touched the ground.

Gaston Duprez, having finished his inspection, came over to greet me. He said that during the next few days the window frames would be fitted in Goguet's house and in the stables, and the outside walls covered with rough plaster to hide the bricks. Whenever possible I used to accompany him, as an act of courtesy, to the gate at the top of the field, where his car would be waiting for him. On the way I told him what I had just heard about the Paul estate and asked if he intended to offer me any of the land.

"It has been bought by my son Victor," he said, "but we buy to sell, and you can have what you like on the condition it does not hamper our chances of getting rid of what remains."

"In that case," I answered, "if you can spare a moment we might go and look the land over now."

Gaston was infinitely easier to deal with than his son. He treated property in terms of cash, whereas it always hurt his son to sell orchards which, deep in his heart, he would have liked to own. Victor made a hard deal, almost hoping that his clients would refuse.

I took Gaston across the Little Court (facing Berlequet) to

the Big Valley, that sloping orchard with its fine wood running down to the stream. The Molière hayfield spread its beauty with only a hedge of tall trees dividing it from my own Burgundy. I could not afford to buy Berlequet, a farm nearly as big as my own, or the Cour du Cerf (the field of the Stag), another magnificent orchard facing Victor's Picane across the stream. That would have to wait until I was a much richer woman. But the Big Valley, the wood and the Molière would link up naturally with the land I already owned. They would make my property compact, every orchard communicating with the other, give me an extra hayfield which I would need as soon as we had more cows, a quarter of a mile of beautifully clear, running water in which my animals could drink, and all the timber and logs I needed. It was in the wood that the men who built my house four hundred years ago had quarried the stone for the pillars of the chimneys. There were rabbits, a host of cherry trees, some oak and silver birch.

"My son bought the estate from the Pauls at an average price of $185 an acre," said Gaston. "You can have as much as you like at $225."

"How large is the wood?" I asked.

"About two acres," said Gaston.

"But everybody knows," I went on, "that woodland in Normandy is of no value. You can not put cows to graze there. Would you, therefore, deduct the acreage of the wood?"

Gaston was in a good temper.

"Yes," he answered. "If your offer is firm."

"It is," I answered.

That is how I suddenly doubled the size of my estate. I was now a woman owner in a big way. In the winter I would pull down the hedge that divided the Little Valley from the strip that Victor had tried for so long to buy. Duclos would plant more apple trees down by the river, and instead of leasing the wood to Goguet with the rest I would reserve it for myself so that I could do what I liked with it.

We were now in the first week of September, and my husband decided to go back to town, leaving me alone for another fortnight. He drove to Rouen, where toward midday there was a train that connected at Dieppe with the one o'clock steamer. A pastry-cook stood in the narrow street that faces the cathedral parvis, where the cakes had not their equal in France. It was under the famous-clock that gives the street its name, and having bought there one of those strawberry tarts nearly two feet in length, my husband gave it to the chauffeur to bring back to me.

I was sitting under a pear tree when it arrived, having sought the shade to escape the scorching heat, and I had brought down in a basket the four kittens that Finette, our white cat, had presented us with a fortnight ago. I put the tart beside me, when suddenly Mono, the sow, came lumbering that way. Big pigs will sometimes eat little cats. I bundled the kittens in the basket and seized the tart in my other hand, but the tart slipped out of its carton and Mono made short shrift of it.

The trouble was that henceforth Mono went wherever I went. She apparently expected more strawberry tarts.

4

WHEN the September crisis became acute, my husband telephoned suggesting it might be wise for me to come back. The
reservists had already been called up in France, and our veterinary surgeon was among the first to go. At Le Havre the
dockers, who were nearly all Communists, were enthusiastic in
their desire to fight Nazi Germany, and there was such a spontaneous speed-up in the loading and unloading of vessels that
work which usually took a week was rushed through by them
in twenty-four hours. Germany later wrecked this spirit by her
open pact with Russia. There would have been no sabotage of
war effort in France if war had been declared in 1938.

I returned to find Londoners frantically digging trenches in
the parks, trying on gas-masks, and mounting over-age anti-aircraft guns on the Thames bridges. We lived through a week of
anguish while Neville Chamberlain made his flights to Germany.
Work on the farm came to an abrupt end and Gaston Duprez
sent me a registered letter asking for his architect's fees by return of post in case war broke out.

My position was an unhappy one. The thatcher had not yet
done a quarter of the roof, the well-sinkers had gone without
finding water, and it was clear that everything would be left unfinished. My savings were virtually lost.

Munich gave me back my farm, but the piece of paper that
the British prime minister waved in his hand as he stepped out
of his airplane was not inspiring. I decided to go back to France
and hasten the completion of the buildings so that when war
broke out, as it must do sooner or later, I might live there.

I was determined to make the place independent of the outside world in time of war. The problem was an enthralling one,

and I tried to make none of the mistakes that people made in 1914.

Though I arrived nearly ten days after the Munich accord, life was not yet quite normal in the village. The trucks had all been requisitioned and taken up to the Maginot Line, so that the grocers were without coffee and the bakers short of flour. The reservists were being demobilized, but their relief to be home was tempered by a sort of shame at having let down Czechoslovakia. Many of our workmen had been called up on the eve of having their first holidays with pay, legacy of the Popular Front. It was now too late to claim the promised vacation. They were given an extra week's wages instead.

The first people to make a reappearance at the farm were the well-sinkers, who almost immediately struck water. This was at sixty feet, and the flow was nearly 200 gallons an hour. It was the best news for a long time, and an analysis showed that the water was crystal clear.

The weather was glorious: rainy nights, but warm, autumnal days, during which Goguet started picking his apples, of which there was a bumper crop. Although he was not entitled to make use of the new fields which I had bought from the Pauls until he signed a fresh lease at Christmas, I gave him, in a fit of generosity, not only the immediate enjoyment of them, but also the apples, and as he now had far more land than was justified by his cattle, I made him a present of a young cow on the condition he bought another out of his savings.

We went to fetch them from a neighboring farmer because Goguet claimed one should never buy a cow at market, first because cattle dealers are thieves, and secondly because cows born nearest your land give the best milk. One we called Blanchette, because of its white spots, the other Queer Eye, because of the strange markings above its right eye.

The apple harvest is the high spot of the year, set in all the splendor of autumn long after the holiday makers have returned to the city. One morning Goguet set out with a long pole of smooth cherry-wood, twice his own height. It was as thick as his fist at the base and it tapered away at the top. He severed each apple at the stalk, and his arm worked so quickly that the fruit fell in cascades from the tree without ever a branch being hurt. As soon as the first tree was bare Goguet's family came along with baskets of wire netting, which they filled at great speed emptying the apples into hemp sacks which the buyers from Trouville supplied. Four baskets go to a sack and twenty sacks to a ton. The Devonshire cider firms took five tons from us that autumn because the home supply was poor owing to spring frosts. The Goguette's mother, Granny Hommet, arrived with her husband from Annebault to lend a hand. She was a little woman of sixty-two with white hair made up into a neat bun above her head, and a face as wrinkled as her native apples after two months in the loft. Energetic, and clean as a new pin, she had brought ten children into the world of whom the Goguette was the seventh. Two older ones, who were deaf and dumb, made lingerie in a convent at Lisieux, a son had gone to Canada, whence he sent her letters written in a mixture of French and English which, if I was not there to translate, she put into the pocket of her apron, saying philosophically: "If he writes, he's well."

Granny Hommet was a dressmaker, or, more accurately, she hired her services in neighboring farms for a day or two of mending. She put new seats to trousers, made wedding dresses, or sewed black crape on the men's coats after a death in the family. She was doubly welcome because she was an excellent milkmaid, so that a farmer's wife could leave her in sole charge knowing that the cows would not go unmilked. On cold days she arrived with a black shawl and a foot-warmer filled with red embers, which she tucked away under her voluminous skirts while sewing at the threshold of the front door. She was an expert apple picker, gathering up eight at a time, her fingers combing the grass with an inward movement.

The baskets of open-work are shaped like a baby's cot with a short wooden handle above. In the poorer farms mothers used to line them with a blanket to put their new-born in.

Old Hommet occasionally came up from the cider press, where he spent most of his time, to join his wife. He had started life as a carpenter and more especially as a cooper, exchanging this profession, when his eyesight began to fail, for that of the village grave-digger. Fourteen years older than his wife, he spoke of her as the "old lady," and was still hearty enough to cut a hayfield all by himself. Being a good Catholic, he never missed mass. Nor, indeed, did his wife. They would arrive at our farm early in the week, but always left by Saturday night, returning home by bicycle which he learned to ride at the age of sixty-five, in order to be sure of getting back to Annebault on Sunday morning.

The apple harvest at our farm lasted the best part of two months, and as the days shortened the nights seemed to become more splendid with periods of clear moonlight, by which Goguet drove back Bichette, the mare, from the two Valleys, with the cart stacked with sacks of apples, filling the night air with an almost intoxicating smell. At times we used to join the strange procession along the undulating lane, hear Goguet's deep voice urging on Bichette with cries of "Heu—heu!" and see from afar the lights of the farm, where the Goguette was cooking her evening soup before going off to milk her cows.

Giles was waiting for me one evening. He wanted to know whether I was going to install electricity at the farm. He had a grievance against the mayor, who he imagined was preventing the power cables from pushing out in his direction because of his political views. Being a factory hand and used to city life, he missed electric light in his shack. I do not know whether the mayor really had a grudge against Giles. The fact remains that we were singularly unlucky. Only one estate had electricity, that of Mme. Michelin, whose house and farm were opposite the Poulins'. This wealthy industrialist had asked her neighbors if they would share the expenses of bringing the cables up to the plateau, but not even the Poulins accepted. They thought there must be a catch in it.

"What is your suggestion?" I asked Giles.

"That we should sign a petition and send it to the mayor," he said.

"What will that do?" I asked.

My neighbor looked doubtful. "We might get it next year," he sighed.

The lack of electricity made my farm extremely self-contained. The immediate problem was how to work the well which was far too deep for a hand-pump. Gaston Duprez put me on to Dauvilaire, the slater, who overhauled the roof of our house. It was he who re-domed the Paris Invalides with gold leaf. He was also a plumber and kept a shop in the village. Dauvilaire suggested a two-stroke engine, which would be housed in a little structure above the well, the whole surmounted by an umbrella-shaped thatched roof. The water would be driven up into two big reservoirs, one in the loft above Goguet's house, the other above our own, so that we would have running water everywhere. He would also make himself responsible for turning the buttery in our house into a bathroom.

I needed a tripod and a roasting-spit for the fire in the big room, and learning that the easiest way of obtaining these rather medieval implements was by going to Dozulé on market-day, I asked farmer Déliquaire to drive me there in his buggy.

Déliquaire had the farm on the other side of the road to St. Vaast just across our stream. He came from the same village as Goguet and had done his military service in the same regiment. After that he became groom to an American financier, who had a villa near Deauville and a stud for racehorses. You would have said that Déliquaire had become American by contact, even to his rather angular features, blue eyes, and fair hair. He never went around collarless like his neighbors, but took pride in his smartly cut shirts and shining leather top-boots, and would do almost anything for a packet of American cigarettes. He had often gone shooting with his master, and so when he married the parlormaid and set up as a farmer he would go off with his gun under his arm, followed by the cocker spaniel that his erstwhile employer gave him as a wedding present. He farmed thirty-five acres which he rented from a very old farming family, and he did very well.

Almost everything at his place was on the instalment system. His house was like mine, a sixteenth century period piece with the most beautiful fruit trees in front and at the back a perfect view across the bay to Le Havre.

It was a Monday morning, the day before Hallowmass, that I went over to join him for the trip to Dozulé. Déliquaire, wearing a pair of corduroy trousers and a canary-colored waistcoat, was harnessing Rosette, the gray mare. When everything was ready, Roger, the eldest son, held the mare while his father fetched his gun to have it repaired in the market-place. Madeleine, his sweet wife, ran into the buttery to fetch the twenty-pound slab of butter which since four o'clock in the morning was ready to be wrapped in her cleanest napkin and placed in a wicker basket of exactly the right size. The basket had no cover, but a handle on either side. Mme. Déliquaire tied the ends of the napkin over the top, and a lovely picture it made as she brought it out into the courtyard for her husband to lift into the back of the buggy. She was back a moment later wearing a huge black straw hat decorated with a wisp of imitation Paradise. Instead of the blue apron that suited her so well and in which she was plump and pretty, she had donned a pleated silk skirt and a yellow jumper that descended limply below her waist. I would have preferred to see her dressed in more bucolic fashion, but was I not myself in a white blouse and short black skirt?

On our return to the farm we found that Goguet had spent several hours storing his apples in the hayloft above the cider press. For the last fortnight they had lain in an immense heap on the grass in our field, halfway between the entrance gate and the house. They might really have stayed there until Goguet was ready to make his cider, but the cows eat the apples greedily and can fall ill. Goguet had sold most of the pears for alcohol to the distillers, but because the crop was large they only took a percentage from each farmer. He was left with a few tons he would deal with in the spring.

Bianchi was finishing the roof of the cart-shed. He claimed to do a yard a day but was becoming more and more erratic. Nevertheless, Goguet's house was nearly ready. I was longing for the day when we could get him in. I was very bitter that I had bought a house that was not yet my own, but I was determined not to grumble for fear of the notary getting to hear of it, which would allow him to say with that exasperating smile: "Madame, I told you so."

Marino and Primo, the Italian plasterers, had spent the morning filling up small cracks at the back of our house, for the wall was of stone slabs—there was not a brick anywhere. I found them carrying on a long-distance conversation with Bianchi, who was astride his roof with a sheaf of rye straw of about his own height. It transpired from this conversation that there had been another case of suicide by hanging in the neighborhood, the second in three months. A farmer of nine or ten acres of land on the road to St. Vaast, after a quarrel with his wife, returned home to find her hanging by a cord from the rafters of the hay barn. The subject of the quarrel was unknown, but nobody thought for a moment that a domestic dispute was in itself a reason for this woman of mature age to end her life by hanging, rather it was suggested that it might be due to a sudden attack of madness caused by over-indulgence in apple-jack.

Goguet gave his own views on the subject after supper. The Goguette had gone to the village to help with the washing-up at the house of the veterinary surgeon who was entertaining his future son-in-law. She had disappeared into the night, swinging her lantern, her clogs oozing water. She used to take them off at the gate at the top of the field, hiding them in the ditch ready for her return, for the orchard was so boggy after dark that one struggled ankle deep in mud.

There being nobody to shepherd the family early to bed, we gathered round the fire which Mme. Hommet stoked up in the big room. Goguet was turning over in his mind the appalling happenings at the farm up the road. He was sitting in a corner of the fire-place, his angular knees well apart and his hobnailed boots, covered in dry mud, planted fairly and squarely on the red tiles. He had taken a pinch of tobacco from a square brown-paper packet and was making himself a cigarette, while his son Roger, celebrating the first occasion on which he had not been packed off to bed immediately after dinner, was whittling small slices off the edge of the white deal table where we had eaten our supper. He was determined to test the jackknife his father had given him for his thirteenth birthday.

"You know the woman who hanged herself?" Roger began, laying down his knife a moment to scratch the back of his head on which still reposed his old cloth cap.

"What do you know about it?" snapped Goguet, who never missed an opportunity of coming down on his eldest son, partly, as he explained to me so often, because the child's ill health had cost him since he was born the sum of 423 francs and 65 sous in medicaments.

Without flinching at the harshness of the paternal voice, Roger answered:

"Perhaps you haven't seen the village magazine?"

This time we looked up eagerly. What had the parish magazine got to say about it?

"It says," Roger continued, "that the priest warns intending suicides that in future they will not receive a proper funeral service."

"Did you know?" asked Goguet, looking intently at me as he held his half-made cigarette in a horizontal position so that the tobacco wouldn't fall out. "Did you know, Mme. Henrey, that one of the richest farmers round these parts hanged himself in your cider press—the one at the bottom of the field?"

"Heavens!" I exclaimed, rather perturbed by this revelation, as indeed Goguet had hoped I would be. "When did that take place?"

"Before the Poulins took the farm next door the estate was farmed by a man called Anger," said Goguet. "His wife inherited quite a lot of land, nearly a hundred acres, about a mile beyond your Burgundy. One day he was found hanging from a beam above the cider press which, as you know, belongs half to you and half to Bonpain, the notary at Caen. Anger must have got in from the adjoining field without being seen by the farmers who lived here. His widow moved after that to her own property, which she still runs, taking her produce to town every day in her buggy."

"What is the reason for all these suicides?"

"Wait till you cross our orchards, tripping over the pitfalls after dusk while Groscol sits howling on the fork of his cherry tree," said Mme. Hommet.

Roger's knife hung poised above the table he had been chipping like a mischievous child. His eyes bulged, and I expected to see his soiled cloth cap rise above his bristling hair.

"Talking of suicides," continued Goguet, "I reckon some people are right to attribute them to madness. There is the asylum at Caen, for instance. It is the biggest in the province. One family in every three in this village has some relation locked up there."

He took a long breath, giving us to suppose that he was about to reveal some important secret. Then, looking over his shoulder at the curtained windows, he said:

"It was a night like this, and we had spent the whole day picking apples. I was fresh from the army and working on a farm near Annebault. We were all sitting round the fire—the farmer, his wife, a couple of young women, and myself, when suddenly there was a knock at the window."

He paused so that we should fully appreciate the significance of such a happening, because one night has fallen the peasant barricades his door and fears instinctively all that arrives from without. The night, with its eerie stillness or its boisterous winds, is the unknown enemy.

"There was a second knock," he went on, "louder than the first, and the farmer, rising silently and taking down his shotgun from the rafter where it hung, went to peer through the window. Then we heard him laugh. 'It's the milkmaid!' he cried. 'Who is the fool who locked her out?' He threw his gun on the table and, looking at me, said: 'Go and let her in, Goguet.'"

"The milkmaid! We had all forgotten about her. She was a queer soul, who kept to herself and frightened us all with her rather daft look, but the cattle liked her. They understood her better than we did. I was sitting right over the fire, just as I am now, and smoking a cigarette. I wondered why the farmer refused to let her in himself, so, grumbling a bit, I rose and opened the door. It was a horrible night, with the wind blowing half a gale, but the girl instead of hurrying in stood and stared at me, while the draught caught the fire and filled the room behind me with smoke. I went up to her, and it struck me that she must be ill, so I held my hand out. At that moment she bent down and bit me in the wrist like a savage."

Goguet pointed to the wound, showing us the deep scars where the girl's teeth had entered the flesh as far as the bone.

"When her jaws closed in on me like a young horse," he went on, "I yelled for the farmer. After all, she was his responsibility. Meanwhile, though I was crazy with pain, I tried to get my arm round her, but she slipped out of my grasp with a snarl, making off between the trees.

"The farmer and I chased her for half an hour while the wind howled. You should have seen us slipping over the cow dung, tripping up over the pot-holes, crashing our heads against the tree trunks. She was raving mad when we caught her. It must have come on all of a sudden.

"'Go and get the hay cart,' said the farmer. 'We must take her to the madhouse at Caen.'

" 'Not in the hay cart,' I answered. 'One man couldn't hold her all by himself at the back; besides, look at the distance. We'd take four hours on a night like this.'

"We tied her arms behind her back, but she bucked and bit and screamed and drove her head against the wall till there was blood everywhere.

" 'You will have to order a car from the village!' I shouted to the farmer.

" 'A car!' he choked. 'You don't realize how much that would cost me.'

" 'I have a fair idea,' I answered, 'but I know exactly what sort of mess we'll all be in by tomorrow morning if you don't get rid of her.'

"As I was speaking she swung herself round and drove her teeth into his arm, clinging to him with locked jaws like a bulldog.

"He let out a yell of agony and called to his wife to bring a bucket of water to throw in the mad girl's face."

Goguet wiped his brow with a big red handkerchief. There were actually beads of perspiration on his forehead so deeply was the incident embedded in his mind. His voice became low and confidential.

"One of the women went down to fetch the car, and we succeeded in getting the poor girl inside it. Imagine how, after the long night drive, during which we never had a moment's respite, fighting and struggling against the demented creature, we finally reached the great portals of the asylum.

"The doors opened on creaking hinges as the clock struck midnight. Blinking in the sudden light, I looked from our lunatic, now slightly quieter, to the farmer, whose mane of thick black hair was disheveled, whose cheeks were furrowed with cruel red lines where the girl's fingernails had scratched the flesh, whose collar was torn open, whose eyes were dim and bloodshot, and whose forehead was bruised by the low branches of the apple tree during our chase in the darkened orchard.

"Meanwhile the girl stared in front of her with large blue eyes that gave her a strange beauty. Fascinated by the contrast, it was a moment before the horrid implication hit me. If looks counted for anything, the warders would assuredly think that it was the farmer, and not the girl, who was mad. It was up to me to save him, if I could, from this predicament.

"At that very moment the sound of a heavy lock snapping behind us made me jump. I guessed, without daring to look, that the outer door was now securely fastened. We were all three prisoners in a lunatic asylum.

"The farmer must have been thinking the same thing. Up to now he had seemed too overcome to speak. I felt, rather than saw, his eyes turn in my direction, and I admit that I was so sorry for him and so anxious about his future, that I never dared return his gaze.

"Then he spoke, and his voice was almost angry.

" 'Pull yourself together, Goguet,' he said between his teeth. 'You look like a tramp. A tramp, did I say? No, worse than a tramp. Your trousers are split up the side and your shirt is full of blood. Haven't you got any self-respect? I wouldn't be surprised if they marched you off to a padded cell.'

"I felt as if somebody had struck a knife into the small of my back. A nasty cold shiver ran like forked lightning all over me. I feared, so young, to be deprived of the immensity of nature, of the orchards and fields of our province, and of the rivers and streams that water them.

"We had been moving aimlessly across the flagstones.

"Another door closed with a metallic click.

" 'What is your name?' asked a warder, advancing upon me as he rattled a huge bunch of keys.

" 'It is not my name you want,' I answered. 'Ask the farmer here, who employs me. I am only a farm-hand whom he brought along to help him overcome the girl. She is crazy.'

" 'That is all right,' said the warder. 'When I want your life story I will ask for it. What is your name?'

" 'He is quite right,' put in the farmer, regaining confidence. 'Let me introduce myself. I am a landowner at Annebault. My milkmaid here attacked us both savagely at the farm this evening. We hired a taxi and brought her straight here.'

" 'Did I nothing!' suddenly cried the girl, waking from her torpor and plunging forward like an angry beast. 'Mad! mad! Who said I was mad?'

"The warder gave a short blast on his whistle and reinforcements rushed out to overpower our dairymaid, who was now lashing out in all directions."

Goguet paused in his story.

"Yes," he muttered, after a moment. "They locked her up, and what is more important they let us out, but if you ask my opinion it was a narrow shave."

Roger must have heard the tale a dozen times, but he appeared thrilled. He was impressionable by nature, though this sensibility was increased by the influence of his employer. She was the widow Dufour, a woman of sixty-three, who was for ever fearing assassination since her house had been broken into one winter's night.

She lived in the center of a two-acre orchard and, although she had only one cow, the cheese which she made was appreciated by gourmets as far away as Honfleur, where she drove to market in a ramshackle truck which had seen service in the First World War. Roger claimed that she could never succeed with a cheese without humming the *Song of the Lark*, and there were times when he fled the buttery to escape the monotony of her incantations, but there was something uncanny about the way the old lady farmed her plot of land, and Roger, who was not capable of doing anything worth while on his father's farm, was learning to become an excellent market gardener under her direction. The widow Dufour's fruit trees were as famous as her cheese. Some people said that her big White Heart cherries were the most luscious in Normandy. And, in addition to all this, there were her chickens and her pigeons and her rabbits, which she reared and plucked and skinned and sold at market with the aid of her young apprentice.

"Mme. Dufour is going to leave her place at Christmas to live with her son-in-law at Pont L'Éveque," said Roger. "I suppose I can go with her?"

Goguet was about to answer when there was a sudden tapping on the window. We all looked up, to see the door open and the Goguette march in.

"Hé, la!" she cried, kicking off her clogs and banging her lamp on the table. "Ten o'clock and not in bed yet, Roger?"

We all rose rather meekly, and, lighting our candles, trooped off to our rooms.

Barbe came to see me the next morning to ask if I knew that Duprez had done him out of the contract for painting Goguet's house. I said I knew nothing about it. Would it not be better to go and see Gravé? Clearly Barbe had already done this without success, so that he considered me his last hope. But I refused to intervene, saying that I could not do more than give him all the work in my own house.

Later in the day, along the tree-domed path that led to our farm, I saw coming toward me a little Humpty Dumpty, followed by a tall girl with an olive complexion. He waved his short arms at me and, with a grin that stretched right across his round face, announced that he was Ramon Andreux, the painter, and that the girl was his daughter.

Andreux was quite a character in the village. He had turned up one fine day at the end of the First World War, accompanied by his wife, the prettiest little Spanish girl you can imagine who, in spite of the fact that she was a mere child of fifteen, already bore an infant in arms. There was no man, when Andreux first arrived, who was not bewitched by the loveliness of his young wife and by her warm voice that could be heard singing the melodies of her sun-kissed land. She presented her husband with a baby almost every year, and by now time had changed her from the ravishing girl whom Andreux brought to town, into a corpulent matron with jet, glossy hair.

Her husband was in competition with Barbe. His eldest daughter was eighteen years old and inherited from her mother such splendid eyes that, looking into them, one had the impression of peering into the mysterious waters of the Amazon.

Only a few weeks earlier Andreux had discovered a young cousin among the Spanish Republican refugees brought to the village by sympathizers who had rescued them after Franco's victory. These families were accommodated in a fine estate bordering the domed path that led to our farm. It was called the Pelouses (Green Lawns), and was a little château of modern construction with white verandas and big airy rooms. It was now owned by Arcueil, a Communist borough of Paris and used by it as a holiday camp for city children, who were sent there throughout the summer for periods of twenty-one days. The Goguette supplied the milk during July and August, which gave us the excuse to look in from time to time. The largest and sunniest rooms were turned into dormitories, with the children's kit folded neatly on each little camp bed. The long tables in the dining-room were always laid for the next meal, a bowl and spoon for each child. It was infinitely touching until one looked skyward at the red flag floating from the mast planted in the center of the lawn and heard the ribald comments of these Parisian children, who raised their clenched fists as one passed by.

At eight o'clock each Saturday evening a cinema performance was held in the infirmary for the children in the camp, and to this were invited the neighboring farmers and their families. The Goguets never failed to attend, although young Robert fell fast asleep after the first half-hour. At ten o'clock a bespectacled pianist struck up the "International," and as the guests streamed out of the door a member of the party, wearing a badge portraying the hammer and the sickle, handed a sugar apple to every guest.

The Spaniards who had taken the place of the Parisan youngsters were haughty in demeanor and proud in their penury. They even hauled down the red flag for fear of hurting the feelings of the village folk, and all one saw through the hedge were long lines of washing hanging out in the autumn sun. The local Communist party collected masses of knitted clothes for their guests, who, finding they did not fit, handed them to the womenfolk, who undid them stitch by stitch, washing the wool and re-knitting it according to their own ideas.

Andreux, in spite of his political sympathies, was not often there. He was mostly to be found carousing with Pierre Gravé or accompanying him on his fishing expeditions. But when he attended to business he did good work and was rapid. Soon the interior walls of my new farmhouse shone a bright yellow to give an effect of sunlight, and within a fortnight all was ready for the Goguets to take possession. The Goguette's sewing-machine and her kitchen range led the way, while her husband battled with the family wardrobes. There was the one above which the larks had built their nest, and the other which was of heavy Norman style, given by Mme. Hommet to her daughter for a wedding present. The back was so dilapidated that it fell to bits as soon as it was moved from the propped-up position in which it had stood for the last five years. The pots and pans, the tripod and the roasting-spit, were carried ceremoniously from one house to the other, also the gramophone, pre-1914 model, with its metal horn, that Roger played on Sunday afternoons, and the brass hanging-lamp from the living-room, with its chandelier effects and jade bowl swathed in greased muslin, of that peculiar pink which one associates with seaside rock, to prevent the flies from tarnishing its bright surface. This and the gramophone had been presents at one time or another from M. Aton, who had such a partiality, nearly fatal once to Robert, for frogs.

My house seemed very large after the farmers had gone, but at last it was mine, and the workmen could get down to their task of redecorating it. Dauvilaire had his plumbers waiting to install the bathroom and the central heating. Deaf Joseph and his carpenters would make new doors for the front of the house. Barbe had his men waiting to paint the whole of the interior as soon as the builders were ready. I ordered a Swedish Aga cooking-range and a gasoline-driven refrigerator for the kitchen, while oil lamps would be sent from London for all the rooms. My presence would only hinder the proceedings. I handed over the keys to Gaston Duprez and left for England during the last week of November.

5

ONE of the most rigorous winters within living memory was over, and my house was now ready to be lived in. I had gone over two or three times a month, mostly at week-ends, to supervise the work which took much longer than I expected. No sooner had Dauvilaire installed all the water system than the fierce, cold snap that covered all Europe froze the pipes, many of which burst. As the workmen were still there, we went over the whole lay-out in the light of this experience and either re-laid the pipes much deeper in the earth or encased them with straw.

I took my husband over on April first, eager to show him the transformation scene. The house was now a little jewel, sparkling in new paint. I had telephoned Dauvilaire to put on the central heating and light the Aga stove in the kitchen. This stove was to create a sensation in the village, where only Guérin, the cattle dealer, had a similar once. It remained at an even temperature night and day, and consumed little more than two tons of coke a year, which would simplify the problem of storage if war broke out.

The policy of appeasement had failed, and every week brought us new crises. Could we pass the summer without being involved in war? Something of immense importance was about to happen in my life. I was going to have a child in a couple of months. I never had the slightest doubt but that it would prove to be a boy. The sou swung pendulum-wise each time I carried out the well-sinker's test. He was to be called Jean-Robert.

For this reason the channel crossing presented a certain danger. On a previous journey I had consulted the village doctor to warn him he would soon have a new patient, and because I was suffering all the inconveniences of my condition, he insisted that I should choose a day when the sea was calm. Happily, it proved so, but the journey from Le Havre took some two hours longer than it should have done. We were held up at the river ferry over the Seine, and it was past eleven o'clock when we arrived at the farm.

The path leading up to my front gate was banked with violets, and the fields and woods were full of primroses, but because of the severe winter frosts the countryside was not yet fully green, and freshly cut logs lay in thick, slimy mud.

We found a huge bowl of spring flowers on the oak table in the living-room and the trunk of an apple tree smouldering in the four-hundred-year-old fire-place. After an excellent lunch made on the Aga, a procession of tradesmen began to call at the farm. Many of them, like Dauvilaire, had taken a personal pride in their work and wanted to thank me for employing so many people during the dead winter months.

Another of these was Roginsky, of whom we were to hear more before long. Nearly all the furniture and the decorations of the house came from him. He had found us the old Norman grandfather's clock that chimed the hours twice, the massive oak buffet with its carved doors, and he had supplied the beds and made the mattresses with wool from the sheep near Caen. Nothing was too much trouble for him, and the materials he used were so good that it was a joy to handle them.

He wore a beret and had small, closely cropped mustaches, deporting himself as a man of substance, which in fact he was. At the end of the 1914–18 war Roginsky had married the daughter of a wealthy Belgian refugee, and with her money had opened a shop, where he specialized in Norman furniture, supplying the villas along the coast. His taste for decoration was sound and he was quickly able to expand his business, selling curtains, blankets, and household linen—everything, indeed, that a woman needs to make a country house gay and comfortable for the summer months.

Roginsky put his profits into real estate and soon owned quite a block of houses between the sea and the main street, but his wife died after only a few years of marriage, leaving him two children, a boy called Riquet and a girl, Andrée.

Our return to the farm coincided with two important pieces

of village news. The first I learned in London by cable on the eve of our departure. Gaston Duprez was dead. The disappearance of this patriarch from our midst robbed us of a picturesque and powerful figure. The other news was that Riquet Roginsky, the furniture dealer's son, had just married Nénette Poulin, the tall, pale girl from the farm next door to ours. They had met when Poulin's eldest daughter, Madeleine, married Montague, her father's farm-hand. Montague had asked Riquet to be his best man and Nénette had been her sister's bridesmaid, holding up the white satin train. The romance must have started during the wedding breakast, when they sat next to each other.

So Nénette was leaving the Poulin farm.

On the surface the marriage appeared a wonderful thing for Nénette. Riquet was rich, and although he was pale and gawky, Nénette was pale and thin also, and her eyes were dim and tired under her flaxen hair. Moreover, she was six years older than he.

Nénette would leave the Poulin farm with her share of the stock—a couple of cows, her hen coops and her chickens, and her milk-cans. Riquet was going to give her a farm of her own— or, rather, Roginsky was buying it for the newly-weds.

I had not yet seen Riquet's farm, but I noticed that his father was continually noting some little thing he liked about my installation, so that he could adopt it for his son's house.

As soon as he had gone, we went to see what new arrivals there were in the farm. Pierrette and Pierrot, the goose and gander, were making a terrific row at the door of their coop, where eleven tiny balls of yellow fluff had just come into the world. For the last month Pierrot had paced up and down the threshold like a sentinel, driving off all intruders except Toxie, the old white terrier, but although they knew her as the farm's watchdog, and to a minor extent as their ally, she took no liberties.

When it was feeding time for the goslings, the Goguets braced themselves up for the comedy that never failed to take place. The first job was to catch Pierrot and hold him fast by tucking his wings under one arm and his neck under the other. In doing this Goguet looked rather like a snake charmer. Now that Pierrette was no longer under marital control, she could be booed away while the Goguette slipped the food into the coop. It consisted of a plate of bread and milk, and a small square of tender turf to teach the babies to graze, for a grown goose grazes, ten birds eating as much grass as one cow.

Pierrot and Pierrette had a marked affection for me based on greed, which made them run cackling to our garden gate each time I appeared, in the hope I would bring them a crust of bread. Although they had not seen me for several months, they welcomed me as warmly as did Finette, the white cat, who could not be persuaded henceforth to return to the farmer's house, where she belonged. She knew that her cushion and her bowl of milk were always ready for her beside our stove, and she paid us the compliment of having all her kittens under our roof.

In the old bakery there were two heifers, the oldest of which was only four weeks. They were still uncertain on their legs and were the offspring of the two young cows Goguet bought in the autumn, one of which I had given him.

The youngest of the baby heifers was called Shrove Tuesday, because it had arrived into the world on that day, and the other one was called Matinale, because of her early morning arrival.

We found Goguet in his big, low room, entertaining the butcher with a glass of apple-jack. He had built a balustrade round his front door and installed geraniums in tubs on either side, but the ground was a quagmire into which one sank ankle deep. It seemed difficult to believe that all this would be grass in a few weeks.

The butcher had come to kill a pig. He was a man of good breeding, who had the reputation of having squandered a fortune, retaining nothing but his violin, which he played admirably. Employed by Guérin, the cattle dealer, his business was to go round the farms slaughtering pigs which the farmers wanted for their own food. Apart from the hams that would be hung in the chimney, and those parts of the animal that would be salted, the skin of the intestines would be washed in the stream and used to envelop the black pudding which the Goguette cooked in her cauldron over an apple-wood fire. The next day she distributed pieces of the pudding to her neighbors, who would return the courtesy when they killed their pigs.

Roger was working at Pont L'Évêque, where the widow Dufour now lived, and he only came home at week-ends. He had fixed up a cage in the cart-shed in which he kept pigeons, but they were not allowed out because of the thatch.

Dr. Lehérissey called in the evening.

He was slim, gray-haired, with long, tapering fingers, and was of an old Norman family in the Manche, the piece of coast that juts out with Cherbourg at the tip. He owned land there.

A devout Catholic, a Royalist, president of the ex-service men's association, he liked to talk politics, though he judged his compatriots severely.

I felt tolerably safe in his care, for he was one of those general practitioners whose most precious knowledge is based on long experience. He gave me a rapid examination, seemed satisfied, and delivered himself of a short homily to the effect that his old professor used to say that women were made to have children and that this was their natural state. The falling birthrate was, according to him, one of the scourges of the age, and he prophesied it would lead to his country's downfall. He was eager to know what people in England thought about politics, and said that, in his opinion, war was imminent. His bitterness toward the Popular Front, which he claimed was destroying the Frenchman's love of hard work, added a note of sadness to his charm. His visit was a rapid one, but I knew that we should have plenty of time to know each other better.

After ten days of alternate sunshine and torrential rain, the garden began to give signs of beauty. The lilac came out and lettuces and carrots filled the long beds near the rain-water tank at the side of the house. One morning, just as we were getting up, there was the most appalling din from the track that led down to the cider press. The geese cackled furiously and Toxie led a chorus of barking that was echoed by all the dogs in the neighboring farms. Above all this came the shrill cries of the children, who ran out of the farmhouse in their black overalls with their satchels over their backs, shouting: "It's the applejack man!" All thoughts of school were swept out of their minds by the sight of the cavalcade which came jolting down the hill, bumping and clattering over the pot-holes. Finette, our white cat by adoption, leapt off the bed, sending a milk jug crashing to the floor. It seemed that the entire farm was under the influence of the commotion, and even the new pig, that a few days ago had barged into the base of the well cover, smearing its snout in red lead which made it look like an allegorical beast in a Venetian carnival, ran to and fro as if the devil had got hold of its tail.

Through the window my husband and I could see the procession coming nearer. It was led by Goguet, looking tremendously important as, every now and then, he gave instructions and warnings in a martial voice. The machine was drawn by a rather tired-looking mare and accompanied by its owner, who time and again glanced up to its summit to see that no essential piece was missing, shaken down by the rough passage across the field. The hot morning sun smote the cucurbit, making the brightly polished copper shine intensely. The machine was an ambulating still, in which we were going to make our apple-jack, and it was carried on large steel-rimmed wheels; the tall narrow chimney made the whole contrivance look rather like an antiquated locomotive. We hurried down into the garden just in time to find the Goguette arriving with the milk. She told us that the distiller had come over from Bellay's farm, which was a dependence of the Green Lawns, and that the mare was Bellay's, because by custom the farmer for whom the distiller has last worked is obliged to provide him with a horse to take his still to the next job on the condition the journey does not exceed ten miles. An ambulating distiller lives in the farm where he works, but goes home every Saturday night to put on a clean shirt and take his earnings back to his wife. During the next ten days Goguet was never in his house. Callers were referred to the edge of the stream opposite the cider press, where he held court, accompanied by the distiller and by old Hommet, who lectured the company on the subject of casks and barrels. He had stacked several cords of wood against the outer wall of the barn and he had chosen very dry cherry and poplar to produce a quick, bright flame under the boiler.

The distiller looks after the alembic and watches the fire, but the farmer pumps in the cider and controls the apple-jack as it comes out, for these things are of more interest to him than anything else under the sun. Goguet dug a ditch along which the residue could run off. This river of hot cider waste could be smelt from our garden when the wind was right, and looking down into the valley from my window I could see the white smoke from the still curling away in wisps across the stream. The children used to take their bread and butter down to the still at midday and munch away with their bright eyes full of wonder as they dangled their legs over the side of a wheelbarrow. Goguet asked me how much apple-jack I wanted for myself, and I ordered twenty-two quarts, for which he bought a well-soaked rum keg. I planned to put it away for my son who was shortly coming into the world, and if we looked after it well, adding a little more every year to make up for that which was imbibed by the wood, I supposed it might reach perfection by his twenty-first birthday. Old apple-jack was a rarity that even money could not buy. Our apples were the best in the neighborhood, and even those of Déliquaire, for some curious reason, could not compare with them.

By the time the lilac was in full bloom we saw the post office engineers arrive with half a dozen telephone poles, which they ran up with incredible speed across the field. I had asked for a line some weeks earlier, expecting to find the same difficulties as I had encountered for electric light, but this time I had a pleasant surprise. The installation cost me less than $5. The chief engineer was twenty-eight, the father of two young children. He had been called up during the Munich crisis and rushed to the Maginot Line from which he had only just been released.

"I was bound to be called up because of my job," he explained. "The experts are called up first and demobilized last."

He said he had a cousin who had not been given a day's leave from the damp frontier fortress in nine months in spite of the fact that he was the sole breadwinner of his aged parents. Our engineer fixed up the telephone within a couple of days, convinced that war was only a matter of months.

Renée was preparing her first communion. She used to trot off to mass on Sunday mornings, which was followed by an hour of catechism at the local Sunday school. Her memory was prodigious, and she could rattle off her questions and answers after reading them over three or four times, though she never had the slightest idea of their meaning.

We used to watch her returning across the field a full half-hour late for Sunday lunch, red as a turkey and laden with all the things that her parents had asked her to bring from the village—the day's bread, a newspaper, a packet of tobacco for her father, and the empty milk-cans which she collected from her mother's clients.

"Good gracious, Renée, you are breathless!" I used to call out to her as she passed by. "What have you been up to?"

"It's the priest, madame," she would answer. "He's been explaining a lot of explanations."

Her chief idea was to get home before the family had finished the choicest morsels of the midday meal, for they never thought of setting anything aside.

The first communion was to take place on Whit Sunday, and for a fortnight beforehand Renée thought of nothing else but the white organdie dress with its long sleeves and high neck, and the white bonnet and long veil which she would wear on the great day. Though some families in the village owned communion dresses that went back four and five generations, others borrowed them from neighbors, and this is what the Goguets did for Renée. The dress and bonnet were loaned by Andreux's daughter. The painter brought them round in a carefully packed parcel, and after the usual exchange of compliments and the clinking of cider glasses, Mme. Hommet, the dressmaker, spent an afternoon making the necessary alterations, for a first communion dress is made purposely with a number of wide pleats in the skirt to allow successive adjustments. The rehearsals were numerous. First to satisfy the family that all was well, and then for me. It was during lunch one day that the little figure, all in white and shimmering in the sun, suddenly appeared in my doorway. I broke into a paean of praise as, in duty bound, she made her pirouette so that I could inspect the dress from every angle. She was already a little woman, growing more like her mother each day, and her black hair and olive complexion contrasted with the snow-white muslin. The presents arrived a few days before the ceremony. M. Aton gave Renée a pair of white shoes, and father Hommet a wrist-watch from Lisieux, which came from the jewelers in the main square. This watch produced much excited comment from the family. Never had anybody seen such a beautiful time-piece, but when it came to putting it on Renée's wrist not a soul was able to fathom the working of the clasp and everybody became red in the face making vain attempts to perform this delicate operation. An emissary, in the form of young Robert, was sent to recruit my help on the grounds that being a townswoman I must certainly know the secret. I arrived on the scene to find Goguet, the Goguette, and the Hommets bending over the unfortunate child, whose arm was being pulled in all directions. When the watch was finally fixed, the wristband was found to be much too large.

"You must take it to the watchmaker in the village," I said, "and ask him to shorten it."

Goguet's face fell, for the peasant in him was suspicious.

"It comes from Lisieux," he argued. "The jeweler here might well tamper with the works out of spite."

This was an argument that all the family could understand.

"Do as you please," I said, "but don't you think that the jeweler in the village would be only too glad to earn a few francs for making the alteration? He must make a living, like everybody else."

"We might risk it," declared Hommet, "on the condition that one of us watched over him while he worked."

"Meanwhile," said Mme. Hommet, "I am going to give Renée my present."

She gave her granddaughter a rose-colored china cup portraying Sainte Thérèse, the local saint, upheld by two angels. From my husband and myself the young communicant received a warm Shetland shawl, for we had noticed that she shivered all the winter.

The similarity of gifts received from the wife of the veterinary surgeon and from Victor Duprez, to whom the family owed so much of its good fortune, produced a minor drama. Both these people had gone into the same shop and bought identical prayer books, which fact was deplored by the Goguets, for a present is a present, and while the number of friends who gives them is limited, the appetite of the Norman farmer is insatiable. From her mother Renée received a rosary, and from her father nothing.

On Saturday afternoon, after leaving school, Renée paid a few visits in the village. She was supposed to call on her acquaintances and ask them to forgive her for any wrongs she might have done to them so that her conscience would be clear on the morrow, but humility was not one of Renée's strong points, and after touching lightly on her painful duty, she cunningly changed the conversation to more congenial topics. She hurried back to the farm for another glimpse of her dress and to bathe her feet and to wash her hair which she put in curling-papers for the night.

She was sent to bed at the ordinary time because early next morning she would have to deliver her mother's milk as usual. At eight o'clock, however, Mme. Hommet was ready to take her to the village, not in her finery for fear it should be spoilt on the way, but with her white dress and veil pinned up in a table-cloth so that she could carry them under her arm without any danger of crushing the newly ironed muslin. The Goguette had got up at dawn to iron her daughter's clothes. Renée would change into them at the veterinary surgeon's house in the village.

At eleven o'clock the church bells pealed, and by this time the May sun had come out in all its glory, melting the morning hoarfrost. The procession returned to the farm half an hour later, where the Goguette was preparing the meal. She had worked hard cleaning the house, burnishing the brass, cooking the vegetables, and milking the cows. Now Renée came, leading the way in her white dress and veil. She was erect, self-conscious, but proud. The heifers, who were over by the Italian poplars, looked intently at their young mistress and then galloped across the grass, halting suddenly within a few feet of her. Roger, awkward, wearing a blue suit that the Goguette had gone specially to buy at the market at Trouville, shambled along in a pair of shoes far too tight for his feet accustomed to slippers and clogs, but he had a new cap with a visor that made him look like a motorist of the 'nineties. Young Robert hopped from side to side in spite of his patent leather shoes. He was proud of the gray ribbon tie that his mother had made him and was wondering just how much he would be able to eat at lunch. Mme. Hommet trotted dutifully beside her husband, who wore an alpaca suit which, next to Goguet's black coat and black hat, made him look like a tripper in Cairo who had linked arms with an undertaker.

The Goguette stood on her threshold to welcome them. Her hair, washed and curled for the occasion, had nevertheless become disheveled from bending over the log fire, where the vegetables cooked in black pots. A quarter of an hour later the veterinary surgeon and his wife arrived in their car bearing newly made cakes which they had baked at home. We were invited to the feast, but refused, in order not to give the Goguette more work than she could manage. As it was, young Robert came knocking at our door a few minutes later, whispering in his adorable way: "It's mother who sends me because we haven't any knives."

"No knives?"

"You see, normally we eat with our jackknives, but mother says that as there are guests to lunch we ought to have the real thing."

Whenever the Goguette wanted something she sent us Robert, knowing we could not refuse him. We gave him the knives, together with the roast that I had made in the Aga.

Goguet had bought a bottle of red wine for his guests. This was to show that he had expended money on their entertainment. In point of fact neither the Goguets nor their guests did any more than criticize the wine and ask each other how anybody could drink anything else but cider. They tasted it, made polite grimaces, and all but spat it out on the floor. Then Hommet winked at the company and, leaving the table, went to the great collection of champagne cider that stood ranged along the window in thick, wire-corked bottles.

The rejoicings ended but late in the day. After lunch the men trooped down to the cider press, leaving the women to themselves. We saw them marching down the field, like Red Indians, in single file, each in his shirt-sleeves because of the heat, but all wearing hats to keep a measure of decorum.

Next morning I heard a rumor that Victor Duprez, who had retained the Picane as well as the two important pieces of land left over from the widow Paul estate—the Cour du Cerf on the near bank of the stream, and the pretty Berlequet farm where Groscol still lived—was to buy a small country house with a kitchen garden and a farm of its own, on the far side of the Point, the triangular hilly meadow near my entrance gate.

The house, built in the solid, though uninspiring, style of the 'eighties, belonged to a M. Allard, who was in residence most of the year. Any sale of land is a matter of immense importance in a farming community, but this one was of particular interest. M. Allard was one of those men who none of us thought would ever leave his estate. He was elderly and rich, but it seemed he was going to leave at Christmas. Victor Duprez now found himself the owner of more than forty acres which, by a miracle, formed one solid block watered by two streams, the one which flowed past the bottom of our fields and another which ran through the wood and the orchards belonging to M. Allard.

At first we wondered whether Victor, according to custom, had bought to sell. We soon learned that it was a private deal. He was head of the firm now, and it was with relief that he was able to satisfy his ambition to own a farm in this rich valley. The new purchase more than made up for what had happened a year ago when his father had made him sell his farm to me. We soon heard that Victor was going to live in M. Allard's house and that his wife hoped to have a baby in the New Year. But what was going to happen to Quettel, M. Allard's farmer? It appeared that he also was leaving. Victor was anxious to farm the land himself and make Camembert cheese. Goguet could not get over this. He pointed out that Camembert is made in districts inland where there is a less ready market for the milk, but it was his opinion that Victor was indulging in a childish fancy. He wanted to be able to put his own cheese on his dinner table and say to his guests: "This is my cheese. I made it."

Quettel had been M. Allard's tenant for twenty-two years. He was attached to the farm which he looked upon as his own, but now there was no room for a tenant. Quettel would be obliged to leave at the end of his lease, which was at Christmas. It must have been a bitter blow to him. The place suited him because of its small size, which allowed his work as a farmer not to conflict too seriously with his functions as the village beadle. He wore the traditional waxed mustaches to go with his bi-cornered Swiss hat, and when you saw him walking early in the morning beneath his apple trees in his silver-striped trousers, you knew that later in the day there was going to be a wedding, a funeral, or a baptism, and that soon he would put on his braided coat and sash and exchange his pruning-knife for a halberd.

He was dignified, whether at church or in the fields, and though, on occasion, he got as drunk as any Norman, he did so discreetly in his own cider press, without offending his neighbors. His wife went in her donkey-cart to market twice a week to sell the produce of the farm. There remained some speculation about Groscol's future. His shack was now in the middle of the new property and no longer had much reason for being there, but the social laws of the Popular Front made it almost impossible to get rid of a tenant with young children, even if his lease had come to an end. The only way out of it was to find him another house somewhere else, but Groscol had an unenviable reputation, and nobody would have been rash enough to saddle himself with such a tenant for life. It seemed hard to buy a piece of land, pay one third of its value in an initial tax to the State, and then be unable to turn out a tenant at the end of his lease. This law was the creeping hand of socialism, for it meant that a man was no longer master of his own property. It was, of course, the pendulum swing from a state of affairs which existed at the beginning of the century, when owners would not let their land to peasants who had big families for fear they could not save enough to pay the rent.

So Groscol went on living in his shack. But just now Victor needed a bailiff, and Groscol would suit him admirably. I was not told how much Victor paid for the Allard estate, but land was becoming increasingly difficult to obtain, and whenever a small farm was put up for auction the value showed an increase.

The notary claimed that wealthy industrialists in the north and northeast, fearing that war was imminent, wished to invest in farm land in the west. Though this artificial rise made no difference to those of us who had no intention to sell, it gave us a certain moral satisfaction, enhanced by the peaceful atmosphere of our green orchards and quiet lanes.

But though we were far from city life, the fear of war was continually manifesting itself in the price of pigs or the shortage of chicken feed. Goguet had a cow called Rosalie, which he had bought when he first came to the farm. She must have been twelve years old, as far as he could judge, for he had brought her back from market. He was now anxious to sell her, for she had developed milk fever on the last two occasions she had calved, and he feared that the third occasion might prove fatal. The matter was practically settled when the cattle dealer telephoned to say he was making no more commitments until the end of the month, because war seemed so certain. Goguet was vexed about this delay. Rosalie was almost due to calve and the whole idea was to get rid of her first. Three days later he came to tell me that the dealer had changed his mind. Because he was making up a whole train of Norman cattle to be sent direct to

Spain, where they would be used to re-stock the farms following
the civil war, he would take the cow after all. I was sad to see
our poor Rosalie led off. She was made to walk all the way to
Trouville station under a hot sun. Fortunately she calved before she could be put in the truck and was therefore saved the
journey to Spain. Put up for auction locally, she was bought by
a young couple who had a tiny house and two acres of land a
mile away from her old home. Goguet saw her later. She had
calved perfectly.

By the first days of June our garden was beginning to repay
Duclos for his labors. There were roses of every kind, from the
sweet-smelling English varieties to the fat, prickly, French moss
roses, quantities of nasturtiums and sweet pears, two young fig
trees which he had doubts about in spite of their sunny position
in front of the house, a bed of strawberries, and bushes of red
and black currants and gooseberries. I pestered Duclos for a vine
which would take to our Normandy soil. He brought me the
only one that flourishes so far north. It was called the Madeleine,
and I put up in its honor a light steel trellis against which it
could climb. The cherry and greengage trees which had done
but indifferently in former years became suddenly laden with
fruit owing to the rich earth and manure that Duclos had heaped
on our garden. The strip at the back of the house was a mass of
hydrangeas, of colors that ranged from every hue of pink to
every shade of blue. My mother, who had come over to join
us in view of the coming addition to our family, was given sole
control of all the vegetables in the garden, and because of her
unlimited patience she obtained results which even Goguet eyed
with jealousy.

My walks were now limited to the neighboring orchards. This
hilly country was not ideal for me, and I was weakened by a
diet of Evian mineral water and plain vegetables. I decided to
take a daily charwoman, and arranged to share the services of a
person who worked for the wife of the local garage proprietor.
My help arrived one afternoon, a fine, tall woman, rather corpulent, with rich dark hair done up in a bun, clean and delightfully garrulous. She had a profound affection for her husband,
who had been employed by Barbe to paint my house, and her
gratitude to me for being instrumental in giving him work
throughout the winter made her doubly anxious to please. Her

name was Mme. Bayard, and she always referred to her husband by his surname, though often qualifying it with a choice of adjectives such as "my poor, good Bayard." They were the most happily married couple in the village.

The hours she put in at my house provided me with a picturesque commentary of village affairs, for she knew the pedigree, love tales, and idiosyncrasies of every single inhabitant. Her mother delivered the mail in the First World War, and had brought up her three daughters, of which my charwoman was the youngest, in an atmosphere of such courage and honesty that it was reminiscent of another age. The old lady now had a market garden down in the marsh land by the sea and reared Angora rabbits for the English market. She also re-made mattresses, and was employed all the more willingly because people knew that she was too honest to do like many other mattress makers and steal large quantities of beautiful white wool. Mme. Bayard followed the news from the outside world by striking a mean between the state radio and the nightly terror talks of the traitor from Stuttgart. Her chief concern was not to lose her husband, who had lived as a child under German occupation during the First World War.

Their home was a little wooden house on a piece of land that Bayard had bought near the main road to Cabourg. The house was a reconditioned British army hut which Bayard had found at Deauville when the army stocks were being liquidated after the war. He took it to pieces at the depot, brought it to his piece of land, and put it up again plank by plank. Then he painted it, decorated it, and built a garden round it. He was a handy-man.

A few days after Mme. Bayard arrived, my husband was obliged to leave for London. He asked Caffet, the garage proprietor, to fetch him at the farm in the evening and drive him to Rouen, where he could catch a train for Dieppe, crossing the channel by the night steamer. Frightened by a new watch-dog outside the farmhouse I slipped on the hard, dry ground while saying good-by to him, and almost had a miscarriage. The doctor came to see me in the evening, but in spite of an anxious night all ended well.

6

It was a hot, sultry day in late June and the sun was hidden by low black clouds. The hard earth, cracked like baked clay by a spell of warm, dry weather, seemed waiting to quench its thirst as soon as the storm broke. I rose from a chair and walked over to the wide-open door to contemplate for a moment the wilting flowers in the garden. I was depressed and felt a sudden desire to escape from this oppressive atmosphere by crossing my orchards as far as the big hayfield, where the grass was not yet cut.

"Let us go for a walk," I called out to my mother, who was bending over the lettuces. "Bring Toxie. The exercise will do her good."

We climbed slowly up the field to the path that led to the Valleys, while the terrier ran in wide circles, yapping delightedly like all dogs which, having spent most of their existence tied to a kennel, suddenly find themselves free to go where they please.

The hedges were filled with wild strawberries, and the approaching storm brought out their perfume threefold. The fruit rotted under the leaves of the honeysuckle and the dock. Nobody bothered to pick these succulent berries except young Robert Goguet on his way to school, and even his healthy appetite was not sufficient to make the slightest difference.

The Molière hayfield, the one bordered by the wood, was now at its most lovely stage. The marguerites had attained all their majestic splendor, and soon the tall grass would be ready for the scythe. Tired by the long climb, I sat down on a big heap of logs and fell asleep, while my mother picked armfuls of daisies, and Toxie ran after the baby rabbits hiding amongst the faggots on the border of the wood. A fine drizzle woke me half an hour later. It was as if a mist from the sea was holding up the big drops that should have announced the beginning of the storm. I rose and climbed over the gate leading from the Molière to the orchard that sloped down to the water. Standing on the patch of bracken, one had a magnificent view of Victor's Picane rolling up on the other side. The topmost trees appeared to merge into the black clouds. I felt as if my ankles were dragging chain and ball. If anything happened to me, I thought, this was the place I wanted to be laid to rest. I remained for many minutes gazing straight ahead while the fine rain fell like dew on my hair. Did I really like this property? Was I right to have spent so much money on it? I knew, at heart, that the answer to these questions depended on an event that could not be very distant now. I dragged my steps back to the house, listening to, but not understanding, what my mother was saying.

By the time I reached the garden the rain had stopped without so much as softening the outer crust of black earth. This was the longest day of the year. I smiled at the thought, and sitting at the big table wrote a few letters. When I finished the last one the words seemed to dance on the paper.

"The long day has no end and I cannot settle down to anything," I wrote to my husband. "I have sent a few words to the people I love best, for I may be prevented from doing so before long. It is hard to be separated from you just now. Forgive me if this letter seems inadequate, but I do not know how to express my fear and emotion."

The clock struck eight and it was almost dark enough to light a lamp. A few big raindrops hit the window-panes loudly. This time the storm was breaking. I tried to make myself a little more comfortable in another chair, but it struck me that the wisest thing would be to go to bed, for it was pointless to drag my melancholy from the door to the fire-place.

My mother, who came up to help me slip into the cool sheets, stayed in the room for half an hour, and then hurried down to call the doctor.

By the time he arrived at the gate in his car the rain was falling in torrents. Turning up the collar of his mackintosh, and pulling down his hat well over his eyes, he ran down the field, which was now a lake because the rain was falling so fast that it had no time to sink into the hard ground. The wooden planks across a rivulet beside Goguet's house were submerged. The doctor never could understand why people who had improved an estate so considerably appeared to have no road sense. It was unthinkable not to have built a car approach to the house. The cattle troughs were overflowing and the cows were huddled together under a pear tree near the hedge. There was no sign of the farmers, and even the dog remained silent, preferring the relative comfort of her kennel.

Welcomed at the door by my mother, the doctor shook himself and threw his raincoat against the back of a chair near the fire. After a few brief words he came up to the bedroom, where he looked at me with that kindly, knowing smile born of understanding and long experience, which was much of his charm. He decided it was time to telephone to his nurse, but discovered that, for some reason, the dialing system appeared no longer to act. An attempt to call the chemist met with no better result and the exchange was as silent as the night was boisterous. Cursing at this ill luck, the doctor made a last experiment. He dialed the number of Roginsky, the furniture dealer, next door to whose house lived Mlle. Lefranc, his nurse. This time it worked. Roginsky promised to go round himself and deliver the message. A quarter of an hour later the young midwife arrived in a short, narrow, gray skirt and a woollen jumper with puff sleeves. She was gay, cool, and efficient, and took possession of the room with a happy assurance.

The next thing was to summon Vanneufville, the chemist, who arrived, thanks once more to Roginsky, with the baby scales in his arms and water dripping from his hat. A moment later the telephone rang and the doctor was called to an accident on the Deauville-Cabourg road. Seeing that I was in no immediate danger, he snatched up his hat and his bag and fled up the field, forgetting to take his coat, so that by the time he returned he was drenched to the skin. The accident had happened halfway up the steep climb from the village and was caused by a motorist skidding on the waterlogged asphalt.

The doctor now held a brief consultation with Mlle. Lefranc. There was nothing fresh. I was quick to see that he was turning over in his mind the possibility of going home and coming back later. My idea was to keep him at all costs. Quickly I gave orders for a bed to be made up in the big end room, and luckily the doctor, who had been up all the previous night on another maternity case, was just beginning to feel the effects of his long vigil. He went to bed on the understanding that the midwife would wake him as soon as anything happened. Mlle. Lefranc arranged a lamp by the window and another by the stone chimney that, with the rain and wind beating outside, took on an even more sepulchral appearance than normally, but for the time being she lighted only one, shading it to allow me to snatch any sleep I could. Roginsky had made this room one of the pleasantest in the house. Its bright chintz curtains and gay furniture, its complete modernization, from central heating to running water, did not clash with the beams of solid sixteenth-century oak which supported the ceiling. Mlle. Lefranc chattered gaily while she bent over the lacquered cot. It had arrived only two days earlier, painted in light champagne color and decorated with Pompadour roses. The trim midwife was making it up expertly with the sheets and blankets that had just come from Paris.

But still nothing happened.

My mother came up from the kitchen, where the faithful Aga stove kept up its constant nocturnal heat. She brought a bowl of freshly made coffee with enough rum in it to have put the unfortunate midwife out of action if she had not noticed it in time. The travail did not start till after midnight. Becoming acute every quarter of an hour, the intense pain kept on waking me. I bit my pillow savagely not to utter a cry, but during half-consciousness it annoyed me to hear my mother and Mlle. Lefranc talking in low tones about trivialities by the fire-place.

I concentrated on the oak rafters until I knew every bulge, every crack, in the wood. The birds announced daybreak by the scratching of their beaks against the window-panes. The storm was over and the sun, rising from behind the château, dispelled the last billows of the turbulent night in a warm, tender glow. Soon after five the Goguette walked across the field in her clogs to open the pen where she kept her geese. The thirsty earth had drunk in the torrential rains and the grass had revived green and fresh, but so soaked that the Goguette's clogs could be heard oozing water. She opened the door of the coop and the goose and the gander spread their wings, preening themselves

after the long night's immobility, before hurrying over for a
bath in the cow pond. A few minutes later the Goguette was
back with her pails, for the cows had spent the night in the field
and were now gathered together near the cider press.

When she brought the milk to the door she learned from my
mother what was taking place upstairs. She gave a loud cry of
"Hé, la!" Neither she nor her husband had heard anything. The
doctor, the midwife, and Vanneufville, the chemist, had crossed
and re-crossed their threshold without disturbing their heavy
sleep, the watch-dog had remained silent in her kennel, the geese
in their coop. She set down the milk-can and fled in the direction of the farm to spread the news.

Meanwhile I was still suffering without result. Mlle. Lefranc
kept up her vigil while my mother made the coffee and heated
the milk. The doctor got up at seven, ate his breakfast downstairs,
and smoked his first cigarette of the day. Then he came to me.
I could see that he was far from satisfied. He left the room and
returned a few minutes later wearing his white coat, and for
three hours worked hard with Mlle. Lefranc to obtain some result, but their efforts were in vain. The doctor and the nurse exchanged glances and went down to the big room where my
mother had lit the fire. Should they call an ambulance and drive
me to the nursing home at Deauville? It was an experiment
fraught with danger. The midwife strongly opposed the suggestion on the grounds that, quite apart from the risk of transporting me across bad roads at this critical stage, the moral effect might prove fatal. She asked for half an hour's grace to see
what could be done. Her opinion prevailed, but at the end of
this period there was still no result.

There was now no choice but to use the forceps, but help
was imperative for this operation, and Mlle. Lefranc decided
to run across to the Poulins' farm.

As she was hurrying down the stairs she was met by my
mother.

"Where are you going?" she asked anxiously.

"To fetch the Poulins."

"But won't I do?"

The midwife paused.

"Very well," she answered. "I would not have asked you, but
if you have enough courage it would save time. All the same, we

shall need another person. Run and fetch the farmer's wife and bring her up with you."

The doctor dipped his arms as high as his elbows in a solution of iodine before putting on his rubber gloves. The operation had hardly begun before the Goguette, who, in the fields was as strong as a man, gave a cry of warning and fell across the bed in a dead faint.

She came to a moment later swearing she had been put under by a whiff of chloroform, but the situation was critical by now, and it was too late to find somebody else.

Having sent the Goguette back to her cows, the doctor, the midwife, and my mother, whose nerves were of steel, started afresh. This time there came into the world a boy, who turned the scales at seven pounds. The clock of the village church was striking midday and a smile of triumph spread over the doctor's features. It was the sunshine after the storm.

Half an hour later my husband, returning to his flat in London, was met by a telegraph boy, who handed him one of the familiar yellow envelopes. He ripped it open and read: "It's a boy. All's well."

He read the laconic message half a dozen times, and in his exuberance concluded that I must have had my baby without the slightest difficulty. It was only when he spoke to the doctor by telephone that he learned about the forceps, but even so he decided not to leave London until he had cleared up his work.

Three days later my husband, coming down the field, found my mother and Mlle. Lefranc just leaving to put the faithful Toxie to sleep. The terrior was old and suffering, and the change to a life of plenty after long years tied by a chain to her kennel appeared to have increased her ailments. Her affection for us was touching. During the night that preceded the birth of my son she had never moved from the sofa in the big room downstairs, her pathetic eyes wide open. She sensed that something was happening, and a couple of days later, when she was brought up to see me, she inspected the baby in the nurse's arms and then leapt into the cot, where she laid her jowl on the pillow for the fraction of a second as if to make contact with her little master.

Mlle. Lefranc told my husband how much more serious the accouchement had been than he seemed to realize. She asked him to stay in the garden a moment while she came upstairs to announce his arrival. He found me propped up in bed, and our son sleeping peacefully in his tiny Pompadour bed by the window. We made an arrangement for the midwife to come twice a day, at eight o'clock in the morning and at six in the evening. Though not exactly pretty, she had an agreeable profile, dark hair, laughing eyes, and an extraordinary liveliness. It was a joy to watch her handling her charge, administering his shampoo and swathing him, French fashion, in a blanket passed under the arms and pinned behind the back in folds that looked like a nun's head-dress.

My son was all head and sleeping-bag, with a bib round his neck, but he had a whole lot of silken hair, which his nurse parted at the side, and his cheeks were pink like our Normandy apples. Mlle. Lefranc's tongue never stopped wagging. After taking her hospital degrees she had come straight to the village, and had brought every child for three miles around into the world during the last eight years. She entertained us with intimate close-ups of all our neighbors.

The fact that I had produced a son first time enhanced our reputation. Congratulations were showered upon us and the mayor seemed to think we had honored his village, for he came in person to tender us the felicitations of his council. Duclos, the gardener, filled the house with exotic plants, which he grew under glass for wealthy clients at Deauville.

For the next three weeks my husband and I enjoyed the quiet of our new home. True enough, the political picture was becoming increasingly acute, but apart from consolidating our reserves in case war broke out, I was utterly engrossed in the joy of watching our infant become bigger and healthier. The doctor paid us frequent visits, but they became more social than professional, and he went back each time with the best rose from the garden in his buttonhole, and the pick of farm produce.

One morning Goguet came to tell us that his cow, Paulette, was about to calve. I was especially interested because, until my son's arrival, we had never been quite sure who was going to be a mother first—Paulette or I. A kind of sympathetic understanding bound me to the cow which was positively touching.

Since dawn Paulette was all by herself in the orchard adjacent to our garden. She remained motionless in a corner under the walnut-tree, looking pathetic. From time to time Goguet would go and make an inspection, coming back almost on tiptoe.

Towards midday he arrived in a terrible state, asking my husband to telephone to the veterinary surgeon because the calf was wrongly placed. Paulette was clearly in for a bad time, and Goguet, faced with the danger of losing both his cow and the calf, was prepared to pay the fee of a veterinary surgeon, although this would cut seriously into his profits. My husband was fortunate to find the man at home, and he promised to come immediately. I was not yet up, so my husband came to break the news to me in bed. Meanwhile Goguet coaxed his cow out of the orchard and into the cowshed, while the Goguette went across to the Poulins' farm for help.

By the time she came back with Montague and a farmhand the veterinary surgeon had arrised and was preparing for the operation. A man stood by with the rope, and a few minutes later Paulette brought a beautiful heifer into the world. The relief was general though it affected the onlookers in different ways. The veterinary surgeon sponged his forehead with a red handkerchief, the Goguette looked with damp eyes at the heifer as it tried to stand on its long delicate legs and then broke out into a loud stupid laugh.

Hearing all this commotion and angered by the laughter, I left my bed and, crossing the narrow corridor, put my head out of the courtyard window to harangue the crowd. Paulette's suffering, I shouted to my husband, was not a thing to laugh at. I, having so lately brought a baby into the world, could appreciate what the unfortunate animal must have gone through. I felt absurdly resentful, and my legs were shaking. Presently Montague went up to my husband and said:

"Congratulations. I hear you have a fine boy."

"Thank you," my husband answered, "but it appears you forestalled me by a few weeks. What is your son's name?"

"Michael," answered Montague proudly. "You must both come and see him. My wife would be very pleased."

My husband drove to Trouville after lunch and bought a perambulator, which he brought back on the roof of the car. Returning through the village he stopped at Roginsky's, and chose one of those colored parasols that French people use on the beach. This was exactly what I needed to protect our infant from the sun when he was out in the garden. There was quite a crowd in the road watching a drunken man disguised as Neville Chamberlain with a battered top-hat and an old umbrella.

"Oyez," he cried. "Je suis M. Chamberlain."

It proved to be our old friend Gravé, who was at the start of one of his long spells of inebriety which could easily last a week or so. Nobody in the village was surprised when he performed in public. He was regarded with amused indulgence.

During our absence in London his father had sold his business and retired. I imagine that Peter was heir to quite a fortune, but he was never sober enough to say anything.

When my husband was back at the farm he stood the perambulator amongst the rose bushes, and having put the infant inside covered it over with a mosquito net because the wasps were after the greengages. Goguet used to go on expeditions at nightfall to burn them out of their nests and to seek out the abodes of the hornets in hollow apple-tree trunks.

As soon as I was strong enough to go out we decided to pay the promised visit to our neighbors. We found Michael Montague in his cot in a corner of the big cool kitchen, where splendidly polished brass pans hung from the wall. Madeleine Montague was delivering the milk in her covered cart and we were welcomed by a brunette we had never seen before. She was Yvonne, wife of Ernest, the younger of the two Poulin boys. The marriage had taken place in May. Ernest was still doing his military service, and was not due for release until October, so that his young wife had seen practically nothing of him since the wedding. She came from a neighboring village called Formentin, where her parents, M. and Mme. Castel, owned a small inn and six acres of land on which they kept a few cows and some prize chickens. Yvonne was looking after Michael with the same devotion as if he had been her own son, having allotted herself this task in a house where she was almost a stranger. The farm still seemed flourishing and the house was as well kept as ever, but it appeared strange to think that Nénette had left it. Riquet and she had now moved into their new home, so that Madeleine Montague was obliged to do the rounds in the evening as well as in the morning. It was hard work, and she would never have managed had it not been for Yvonne minding the baby, but even this did not quite compensate for the loss of Nénette and the fact that she had removed as part of her dowry several cows, the covered carts, and Fanny, the mare. The kitchen garden was no longer what it was, for vegetables had always been Nénette's strong point. I asked Yvonne if she had yet visited the Roginsky farm, but she answered curtly, which seemed to suggest that relations were strained. This jealousy was to be expected, for while the Poulins and the Montagues were tenants Riquet owned his land.

Bidding farewell to Yvonne, we walked back to the farm. On the way Barbe overtook us, driving his light truck. He stopped at the fork of the lane where it branched off to M. Allard's house and told us that Tavernier had made him a well and that he was delighted with the result. "Thank you for the idea," he added. "You must come up and see it. The whole installation works by electricity."

"Where are you off to now?" I asked.

"Victor Duprez is redecorating M. Allard's house so that he can move in at Christmas," answered Barbe. "A Trouville firm is to do the structural alterations because, since the Gravés have packed up, there is not a builder left in the village."

Barbe held out his big friendly hand with the fingers missing, and jumped back into the driving-seat. We watched the truck disappear under the arch of trees and heard it chugging painfully up the hill.

"Victor is doing himself well," I said, laughing. "But he is a brave man to start building now."

7

ONE morning toward the end of August Mme. Bayard sent us word that she would not be coming that afternoon. Her husband was a reservist and had just been ordered to join his regiment at Caen. The officers had been called to barracks, and because Bayard was an orderly he was needed at the same time. Late in the evening Mme. Bayard decided to come and see us after all, and we saw her striding down the field with her young son, Jean-Louis, holding her hand. Tears rolled down her cheeks as she greeted us. "They have taken away my Bayard," she sobbed. We gave her what comfort we could, and sent her away a little happier.

The next day she came to work as usual with her face all smiles. Bayard had left his barracks before dusk and spent the night at home. Guérin, the cattle dealer, had taken him back to Caen at dawn in his truck.

"He has promised to come back every night," she announced as she tied on her blue apron. "What do you think, madam, is there going to be a war?"

She planted herself with an air of determination in front of the sink and cocked up one ear for the answer, but finding that it proved non-committal prodded the water impatiently with the dish mop. A moment later she spun round with the mop in one hand and a wet plate in the other, holding them at arms' length so that they dripped on the flagstones. "Bayard has no luck," she declared. "Fancy spending all the years he ought to have been at school hiding from the Germans in occupied territory, and now having to leave his wife and child because the Nazis want to start another war! What do you say, madam, is that fair?"

Mme. Bayard's natural optimism was clouded by what the traitor of Stuttgart announced each night over the radio. His voice was a poison she loathed and was yet unable to dispense with, and she could never persuade herself to go to bed until she had listened to his virulent prophecies. For the next few days, however, she had the joy of seeing Bayard come home each night. His presence reassured her, and she began wondering whether things would not settle themselves as they had at Munich.

Big changes were taking place in the village. Nearly all the owners of villas had returned to Paris as soon as the officers were called up. Their wives came back with the children and seemed prepared, if necessary, to take up winter quarters there. Roginsky was working overtime, and so was Dauvilaire, for these big villas were not built to live in during the cold, damp months ahead, and few of them had central heating. Business was brisk and industrial firms in Paris were buying empty houses for the families of their employees, installing dormitories and cold water showers.

On Saturday evening Goguet had just come back from the Burgundy when the sound of drums rolled across the orchards. At first one might have thought that a regiment was passing along the road to St. Vaast, but the noise was too intermittent for this, and there was no tread of feet. Then a single drum was heard in the courtyard of the Poulins. We ran up to Goguet's kitchen garden and looked over the hedge. A man with long, unkempt mustaches was beating a drum slung across his shoulders, and having roused all the dogs to fury he cleared his throat and yelled out the order of mobilization. The drum of another crier could be heard from across the stream in the direction of Déliquaire's farm. The news was being broadcast from barnyard to barnyard.

"That means I must report to Dozulé within twenty-four hours," grumbled Goguet. "Why could they not wait until the apple crop is gathered?"

Later in the evening the text of the mobilization was posted up at the café at the corner of the main road.

Victor Duprez came to see us. He had been requisitioned to serve conscripts with their calling-up papers and was rushing round the countryside in his car. Goguet, who had taken the news tolerably well, became moody toward dusk. He went to bed early, but was unable to sleep. As a matter of fact, his nights had been disturbed of late because he and his wife were taking it in turns to keep an eye on Monette, the new sow, who was expecting her first babies. Neither of the Goguets was very expert in breeding pigs.

Goguet was beginning to realize just what that drum in the Poulins' courtyard signified. He would be sent to the front, and might well be killed. At the best he would be absent for months, perhaps years, far away from his cider press and his orchards, while his wife made all the money. Each time he woke it was to find beads of feverish perspiration on his forehead.

"Léontine," he wailed, "I don't want to go to the war."

The Goguette slipped out into her kitchen, where she made him infusions of camomile and peppermint, but she could see that his nerves were so shaken that unless she took him to Dozulé herself in the morning he might do something stupid. Toward midnight Goguet became increasingly nervous, and his wife was finally obliged to feign sleep in order not to answer his cries of distress.

He rose at dawn and announced his intention of bidding farewell to his neighbors—the Quettels at M. Allard's farm; the Poulins, of whom only Montague and the women were left because Ernest was still doing his military service at Caen, and Peter, being a reservist, had gone a week ago; the Déliquaires and the Giles.

He came back feeling braver, having drunk copiously at each farm, and it was decided that he and his wife would go to Dozulé on their bicycles and that they would pick up Déliquaire and Adrien, the binder, on the road to St. Vaast, for both these men also had orders to report at Dozulé by nightfall.

Before their departure Goguet arrived at the threshold of our house. He wore a clean shirt and newly pressed trousers, and had slung over his shoulder the haversack he always took with him when going out in the fields to cut his hay or pick his apples. He looked smart and quite composed, and said to us pathetically: "Well, here I am. I'm off now!"

His tone of voice gave one the impression that he was being condemned to a life term on a penal settlement. It was so touching that I kissed him on both cheeks and wished him luck. His three children hovered in the background, each with a bottle of cider, a chunk of bread, and a pear.

"What are you going to do with the youngsters?" I asked the Goguette.

"They are going to spend the day with a neighbor," she answered, "but Robert's making a long face because he does not want to go."

"You can leave him with me if you like," I offered. "What do you say to that, Robert?"

The youngest Goguet beamed with pleasure and his smile was more than his mother could resist.

"Very well," she answered, "but mind you be good, young man."

I told Goguet that as long as it was in my power, I would look after his family during his absence. I added that I was delighted to have him as a tenant, and that I hoped he would come back covered in glory.

We waved to them all the way down to the stream, and all the way up the orchard on the other side until they reached the road to St. Vaast, where Déliquaire was waiting for them, leaning on his bicycle. The weather was perfect, the sky a deep blue, and the sun as warm as in July.

At midday we heard over the radio that Britain had declared war on Germany and that it was only a matter of hours before the French Government made a similar announcement. Young Robert Goguet behaved like a little gentleman at lunch, proud to eat for the first time in his life with a knife and fork, and to drink his cider in a wineglass instead of in the thick opaque tumblers of the farm. He was intrigued and a little flattered to think that my infant son bore the same Christian name as himself, but there was another angle to this question which he had no doubt been figuring out for some time in his little mind, for he suddenly sat back in his chair and asked:

"And you are a Robert also, aren't you, lady?"

"How so?" I queried.

"At the entrance gate," he explained, "the notice board reads, 'Ferme Mme. Robert Henrey.' "

"Why, yes, that is right."

"So you see," he exclaimed triumphantly, "in spite of the

fact that you are a woman, you are 'Robert.' We are all Roberts here!"

Toward evening the sound of drums came across the fields once more. This time the crier was ordering us to black out our windows by nightfall. I ransacked my cupboards and found a length of thick blue linen which Roginsky had sold us with the parasol. It could be hung round the umbrella to form a tent, but as we had no use for this the material proved ideal for cutting up into curtains.

My mother and I were busy on this when the Goguette arrived. She looked tired and told us that the journey to Dozulé had taken over three hours because the company had grown all along the road as more and more neighbors joined it. After picking up Déliquaire and Adrien, the binder, they had gone to fetch Camille, Goguet's brother, who had been supposed to leave with the reservists a week ago, but he was afraid, and barricaded himself in his little house, threatening to shoot any policeman who attempted to break in. When his brother knocked at his door the company in the road looked so merry that he was unable to resist the prospect of the numerous drinks that would enliven the journey to Dozulé. Collecting Camille, the cavalcade made a detour to Annebault to say farewell to the Hommets, and on the outskirts of Dozulé a call was made on Goguet's mother who had a farm there which, upon her death, would be divided amongst her children.

The streets of the little market town were so crowded that it was almost impossible to move. Thousands of men were arriving from miles around to report to the military authorities.

The Goguette was relieved that she had delivered her husband safely to his barracks and all the more so because of what Camille had done. She disliked having anything to do with the police. Now she was not only tired, but a trifle sad, and she had probably cried on the way home. We delivered up her son, praising his behavior, and settled down to a quiet supper.

As darkness was falling we went into the garden to see the effects of our black-out. It was not perfect, but there was nobody to bother us anyway. As we were going back into the house we heard a man lumbering across the field. It was not possible to recognize his features, but from the way he was lurching from tree to tree it was obvious that he was drunk.

Intruders were so rare that we decided to stand our ground, but before the man reached our garden gate we had recognized that he was none other than our Goguet.

"Is the war over already?" I asked.

Goguet explained that the military had sent him back because there was no more room in the barracks, but that he must return in the morning. My mother and I went to the farm where his wife gave a cry of surprise. Her husband's return gave her another sleepless night, for this time Goguet was violently sick. He rose at dawn and, borrowing the Goguette's bicycle, went down to the village for a hair cut, having been severely reprimanded because he had arrived at the barracks the previous day with the locks of a poet. When he reached the barber's shop he found Peter Gravé, our builder, in the middle of the road throwing pebbles at the barber's bedroom window to wake him up, and before long they were joined by a number of unfortunates who had been similarly rebuked. Goguet returned to the farm soon after seven with his hair cut so short that he looked quite a different person. He came to take leave of us again. "This time, ladies, I'm off for good. Destination unknown," he announced. He was very sorry for himself, but a redeeming feature of his exile was the knowledge that Peter Gravé was waiting with Déliquiare just above the stream and that they would pick up Adrien, the binder, at the crossroads. They were supposed to report at Dozulé by 10 A.M., for the task of requisitioning horses in nearby farms. It meant a lot of walking, but also a lot of hospitality if they came up against friendly farmers, and it invested them with pleasing authority.

On my way to the village, after Goguet's departure, I met Groscol driving his hay-cart. His four children were valuable assets now because they entirely exempted him from military service. He could look forward to being one of the few young men left on the land, and if there was going to be as much money made out of farming in this war as there was in the last he could be reasonably sure of getting his share.

The village was crowded with evacuees, and the casino was being turned into offices for the clerical staff of a Paris rail terminus. Every hotel was full, and anybody who had a villa for sale was sure of getting a fantastic price. The shopkeepers were selling out their depleted stocks, and the grocers were already short of sugar and coffee, because normally the season would now be over. With business so prosperous everybody was optimistic. "It's not like the last war. This time we're armed," they said.

I returned home just before lunch, and meeting Mlle. Lefranc asked her to discontinue her visits. Although this was primarily an economy move it suited the midwife who had become frantically busy, as many women who had just arrived in the village were expecting babies.

Late that evening Goguet returned home once more, dragging his feet as if they were lumps of lead. He had received permission to sleep at the farm because there was still no room in the barracks, but he would be obliged to leave at dawn the next day to take a string of horses from Dozulé to Caen where they were urgently needed by a regiment that was getting ready to move off shortly to the Belgian frontier. The only horses that were now left in the farms were the grays and piebalds, because they were supposed to be too easily visible to the enemy, and any farmer who was lucky enough to have one of these animals was at once offered more than twice its normal value.

Knowing that he was being transferred to Caen, Goguet took it that his good fortune had now come to an end, and when he bade his third farewell next morning it was with tears in his eyes.

"Well," he said sadly, "I don't suppose I shall be seeing this place for quite a time now."

At ten o'clock that night he came back once more.

His arrival was a pitiful sight, for his feet were so raw with walking that he had slung his boots round his neck by the laces, and was carrying his socks in his hand. He was more tired than drunk, and was no longer capable of uttering a single word.

The next day when my mother and I called at the farm we found him with his feet in a tub before a wood fire in the big red-tiled room. As soon as he had reached the barracks at Dozulé, he had been sent with Gravé and Adrien to Caen with the horses. The three men stopped at every inn on the road, and having put down numerous absinthes cried out: "Hitler will settle the bill." Some of the publicans shook their heads and laughed it off, others chased our brave soldiers into the street and called them thieves; but with the help of these generous libations Goguet, Adrien, and Gravé arrived safely, but weary, at Caen, where, having handed over their horses, the colonel told them to go back home and wait until he sent for them. This news was tantamount to demobilization, and they faced the twenty miles' walk home with new vigor. It was a long trail, however, and they had probably never tramped so far in a single day.

For the next few days Goguet hobbled about in a pair of slippers that the Goguette made for him out of an old carpet, and they were much too large for him. Morning and evening he waited anxiously for the postman, fearing that the dreaded recall to Caen would arrive, but nothing came, and gradually he settled down to normal work on the farm, where, because of rising prices, there was plenty of money to be made. The wood of oak trees that Victor gave me when I first bought the property proved invaluable. It was also very picturesque. One reached it by following the path that led past Groscol's house, and cutting across a meadow belonging to Mme. Anger, widow of the farmer who had hanged himself in our cider press. The wood ran all along the bottom of this meadow and was full of big trees, some of them attaining noble height. There was also a stream running in the valley at the bottom of the wood, and this was the one that watered M. Allard's orchards. The water was clear and cool and ideal for trout. The trees leaned over and spanned it in places, making giant bridges. My mother and I loved this wood because it was all our own and our tenant had no right there. We decided to clear the undergrowth in parts where in springtime the mossy ground was carpeted with primroses and violets, and we planned to cut down sufficient undergrowth to provide us with fuel for all the winter.

One Sunday evening in October, as we were returning from our work, we saw Mlle. Lefranc's beautiful car drawn up in the lane outside Berlequet. It was just after seven, and night was falling. There could only be one explanation of the presence here of the midwife's car—Mme. Groscol was having another baby. This time our tall, powerful neighbor need have no fear about the future. Five children would keep him out of the army for the entire war.

We pushed on to the gate leading to the Little Valley, where Mlle. Lefranc caught us up. She told us that everything was well, and that it was a girl. "But would you believe it," she asked, "Bichette, the Shetland mare, is in the kitchen with Groscol?"

This was Victor Duprez's pony, which we had found on our farm when we first visited it. She was a beautiful beast, but very wild, and Goguet could do nothing with her. After we had bought the farm Victor gave Bichette to Groscol, and they became inseparable friends. The mare followed her new master like a dog and rested her head on his shoulder, and in the evening when the door of the shack was open Bichette thought nothing of walking straight into the kitchen, and it never entered Groscol's head to shoo her away.

When her baby was to be born, Mme. Groscol cleaned out her house from floor to ceiling. The cracked tiles were scrubbed until they shone like mirrors. From time to time during the travail, Groscol opened the door of the bedroom where Mlle. Lefranc was looking after the patient and asked in a gruff voice that he tried hard to soften: "Well, how goes it?"

Mme. Groscol, looking up from her pillow, would then catch a glimpse of Bichette's shaggy mane just behind her husband's shoulder, and thinking of her clean floor, she would cry out between her pains: "Will you get out of here and mind your own business!"

As soon as the child was born the midwife opened the kitchen door to break the news.

An oil lamp, suspended from the ceiling, threw a warm glow over the table, at which two people were sitting with tears rolling down their cheeks in front of an empty bottle of apple-jack. One of these was Groscol, the other a neighbor called Mme. Kettel, who had looked in on the excuse of helping with the accouchement, but who had been quickly bundled out by Mlle. Lefranc. Between these two people Bichette was quietly munching the sugar that remained in the bowl on the table.

"Come, now!" said the midwife, who eyed this scene with indulgence, "it's all over, M. Groscol. Go and see your wife, but do not scold her."

Groscol rose wearily, and comprehending the midwife's meaning, brought his fist down on the table.

"I thought so!" he exclaimed. "I'll bet it's another girl!"

Then a gleam of compassion spread over his rugged features.

"Never mind," he said. "Depend on me, miss, I'll be good."

A few days later I made up a parcel of baby clothes and some biscuits for the older children, which I took to Groscol's house, but I left the packet hanging from the door handle so that Groscol would find it when he came in from the fields. Although there was nothing to show who had sent it, Mme. Groscol guessed that it was I, and she told her husband to go across and thank "the lady who lived opposite." The genial farmer was keen to show his gratitude, but before going he fortified himself with long pulls of apple-jack, for he would be obliged to cross Goguet's field and pass in front of his enemy's house. The two men had never been on speaking terms, and Groscol and the Goguette had a vendetta. Only a few nights earlier Groscol had publicly announced from the top of his cherry tree that he would shortly be obliged to cut off the Goguette's head with his scythe, and the Goguette had accused her gigantic neighbor of stealing the honey from the beehive in the hedge dividing the Little Court from the field where Mme. Anger kept her bull. But Groscol was touched by the present I had made his wife, and he had overheard the midwife say that I had knitted the garments myself.

He walked resolutely down the hill with that long, rhythmical stride that was his, and opened the gate that led into our field. He was carrying a stout whip and he had drunk just sufficient to give him confidence. He followed the rut in the grass that led to the bridge over the rivulet and, passing the farm, opened the gate that led into our garden, where I was pulling up weeds.

Groscol doffed his cap and leaned back against the railings as if to stress the point that he was on my soil and not on that of our tenant. Groscol stuttered before a drink, spoke fluently afterward. He made a little speech of thanks, but something told him that Goguet was listening from behind the gable of the buttery. Groscol slapped his whip against his leggings in an effort to contain his feelings.

"Well, it's nice of you to have come," I said. "I suppose there's no scarcity of work just now?"

"Nothing to grumble about," said Groscol, loud enough for his voice to carry as far as the farm. "Especially when a man knows his job."

The last words were a cut at his enemy, but on second thoughts Groscol decided to make his attack more direct.

"That fellow who's spying on me from behind his buttery thinks I can't see him, but, bless me, I can smell the tobacco in his pipe. There's no danger of him coming out, the coward. He knows I'd tickle his cheeks with my whip!"

Goguet did not move from his hiding-place. He parried Groscol's abuse with cunning, and he knew the law almost as well as the notary. He was aware, for instance, that if Groscol lost his temper and attacked him in his house, he would have a case at court, whereas at present Groscol was a guest on my land. So he slunk back into his living-room, burning with resentment at the thought that I had sent a present to his enemy.

Groscol, having delivered himself of his feelings, felt better. He invited me to come and see his wife any time I was passing and, turning round, walked majestically up the field, looking neither to the right nor to the left.

A few minutes later Mme. Bayard arrived. Her husband had been drafted to the Belgian frontier, returning to that part of the world where he was born, and where as a child he had lived under German domination. He wrote a letter to his wife every day full of minute details of his soldiering life.

The cadets from the military college of St. Cyr were quartered in one of the largest villas and they spent several hours a week throwing grenades into the sea. They were the only young men one saw about the place. All the rest had gone to the front. Victor Duprez was laying pipe lines with the Standard Oil, Peter Poulin was in the Maginot Line, and Ernest, his younger brother, who had been doing his military service, was sent to join a motorized unit. Neither Dauvilaire nor Barbe was left with any workmen and, from what Mme. Bayard told us, Barbe was particularly unfortunate.

At the end of August he had collected his men, of which Bayard was one, and had them pull down the cowsheds on his farm. As soon as the buildings were flat, war broke out and his men were called up. He was left with the prospect of having no accommodation whatsoever for his cattle all the winter. Happily, Primo and Marino were there. Our two Italian plasterers offered to build new cowsheds. The Italians were making use of their neutrality.

Mme. Bayard used to arrive crestfallen at my farm. She was vexed that while her husband was on the Belgian frontier, Goguet and Montague were both enjoying the advantages of family life. Goguet was exempt from military service because he was the father of three small children; Montague because two fingers of his right hand were missing.

One evening at the Poulins' house Yvonne, after minding Madeleine Montague's baby all day, announced naïvely to her sister-in-law that she herself was expecting a baby in April.

"Won't it be sweet to see them together?" she exclaimed, holding the infant Montague at the end of her arms.

The news produced a reaction that Yvonne could never have guessed. The Montagues foresaw that in this war they were going to work for two soldiers at the front and for the wife of one of them, who was about to have a child. They decided to look for a farm of their own. They could then insist on a general share-out and leave Yvonne, three months before her delivery, to fend for herself on a huge farm from which most of the cows had gone.

The Montagues found a farm at the bottom of the road to St. Vaast. It was here that the woman had hanged herself the previous summer, and now the farmer had died, leaving the place vacant, but it was a very humble affair compared to the present vast estate of forty acres. They would have to live in a tumbledown house of one story instead of the big red-brick dwelling where their airy bedroom overlooked prosperous orchards and a considerable area of spacious stables and commodious cowsheds, but they would be working for themselves, with a low rent and the certainty of rising prices, and if the new farm was small it would at least be richly stocked.

The Montagues made their plans adroitly. Madeleine knew many of the customers personally, and some would doubtless follow her. Meanwhile her husband worked as he had never worked before to remove his share of the wood and hay. For this reason he hired Goguet to help him cut several cords of dry lumber to make logs ready for sale in the winter when there might be a serious shortage of coal.

Yvonne had been without news of Ernest for thirty-two days, and as a result she had a breakdown for which the doctor ordered her complete rest. Yvonne's room was the smallest in the house, and being obliged to remain in bed, she was at the mercy of her sister-in-law who sent up her meals by the maid as if she had been a child in disgrace.

One morning Mme. Castel drove up in her covered cart, and having seen her daughter's pale face demanded an explanation from the Montagues. When she learned that they were determined to go, she went back to Yvonne and told her that she would have to decide whether to return and live at Formentin or ask for a new lease of the big farm. Yvonne insisted on staying on, for Ernest had told her that nothing would make him leave the place of his birth. He wanted to carry on the traditions of his father, but the problem that faced his young wife was considerable. It meant that she and her parents would be responsible for an immense farm with insufficient cattle to stock it, and not enough people to work it, for there was no chance of hiring anything but casual labor.

M. Castel, however, was willing to do a lot to please his daughter, for she was his only child, born after nineteen years of marriage. He decided to put his little café up for sale, but though people were eagerly buying farm land it was difficult to find buyers for real estate. While waiting for a purchaser he would spend one week in two with his daughter.

Once a week we used to go down to the village to get our provisions, but although prices were rising there was an abundance of everything. The only shortage was in coffee, which the grocers turned to good account, for they dealt it out in packets of a quarter of a pound only to those who bought a minimum of goods at their store. One was thus tempted to buy a great many things which were quite superfluous, and husband and wife would split up the shopping list to obtain two packets instead of one.

My mother and I had stocked the farm just before war broke out with all the things most likely to become scarce. We had enormous reserves of sugar, flour, and canned milk. Our house was a citadel that could have resisted a six-month siege, but as the months passed wearily by, these things appeared more and more plentiful. The country gave one the impression of limitless wealth.

Just before Christmas there was a scheme for rationing gasoline, but, as farmers, we were allowed more than we needed for the pump in our well, and the restrictions were as elastic as the black-out, which nobody heeded seriously as soon as it became clear that the enemy was not yet intending to bombard us from the air.

The farmers soon became very prosperous. The price of butter rose almost every week, and a cow was worth twice as much as before the war. These values were brought home to us one December afternoon when the notary put up for auction the stock of a tiny farm on the road to Cabourg. It had been owned by a woman called Mme. Fillon, who, in the absence of her second husband who had gone to the Maginot Line, was not only running her farm but taking the produce to market in his covered cart. She was not a very expert driver, and one day the pony shied and threw her out with such violence that she was killed outright. The property could not be sold because it belonged to her small children, but her six cows and all the stock fetched prices that produced a revolution in the farming community.

Her cows were the first to fetch $150 each, which was double what they were worth three months before, and the scraggy little pony that killed her, in itself not a very good reference for the animal, was sold for $450 or three times what she paid for it.

Goguet was now quite reassured about his future, and he no longer even troubled to look up when the post-woman passed that way, but it irked him to feel that he was under the constant supervision of a woman owner. The fact that I was his best customer and constantly gave him small jobs for which I paid him handsomely had ceased to matter.

The peasant is not very grateful for easy money. What really delights him is to get the better of his neighbor by some act of cunning which he fondly believes will never be noticed. It is a state of mind almost incomprehensible to townspeople. If he can cut down a tree to which he has no right, or spirit away a pile of bricks which does not belong to him, he is happy all the day long. Goguet never bargained to have me living on the farm all the winter. The fact that I had not espoused his quarrel with Groscol vexed him bitterly, and he sought some method of revenge. He found it during the cold spell that preceded

Christmas when his chimney, being new, started to smoke as do nearly all chimneys in big farmhouses where immense black cauldrons are suspended over green logs.

I used to see him pass by our house in the morning simulating the most acute attacks of the shivers.

"What is the matter, Goguet?" I asked.

"Our house is worse than an ice-bank," he answered, his teeth chattering. "It is not habitable."

"I will have Dauvilaire look at it, but he has got no more workmen and it will not be easy. On the other hand, your contract ends at Christmas, and if you find the house cold there is nothing to stop you leaving."

"You can't throw us out," he snapped back. "Even if I don't renew the lease, my wife and children have a right to stay for nothing."

Goguet, for once, had shown himself ignorant of the law, but as I would have hated to lose this rascally Norman I answered:

"If the house is not habitable, Goguet, would you want your family to remain?"

"I'll tell you what," said Goguet, "I'll forget the chimney if you give me a six-year lease."

"Very well, but the rent will be based on the average yearly price of butter, so that I am insured against inflation. That is fair enough, is it not?"

"No," said Goguet. "I am not taking any risks."

"Nor I," I answered. "No landlord gives six-year contracts in the middle of a war. You can have one year and then we can reconsider the matter."

He went away mumbling, but I was far too tenderhearted not to worry about his chimney. I telephoned Dauvilaire and asked him to come up and inspect it.

"I know you are frantically busy," I said, "but I would be very grateful if you could spare the time."

He arrived that same afternoon.

"All these farm chimneys smoke in this ice-cold weather when the doors and windows are closed," he said. "The hearth is much too big. Why doesn't he install a small wood stove?"

"And who is going to pay for it?" asked the Goguette, who was standing beside us.

"In that case," said Dauvilaire, "I will heighten the chimney in the hope that it will improve the draught."

For the next few days Goguet said nothing more, but when Mme. Bayard arrived her face was purple.

"And to think," she proclaimed at the top of her voice, "that while that pig is filling his pockets Bayard's feet are frozen at the front! Why does not Goguet offer to change places with him?"

In due course Dauvilaire arrived to heighten the chimney, so that it surmounted ours, and he fixed a vane at the top, after which we all sat in Goguet's kitchen with the doors and windows closed to see what would happen.

It was a beautiful room, with a high ceiling and a tiled floor. The fire-place was nearly as large as ours, and Duprez, in designing the house, had recalled our hearth, with its big marble pillars. Gravé, with all his faults, knew how to build. No farmer for twenty miles round was lodged in so princely a manner as Victor's ex-cowherd.

"It's not smoking any more," announced Renée, who was sitting in the fire-place with her feet right against the glowing logs.

"Wait until the wind turns," objected Goguet. "You are just wasting money putting that vane on. For a few thousand francs more you could have rebuilt the chimney altogether."

I looked at Dauvilaire and led him quietly out of the farm, resolved in future to be like Mme. Paul and Mme. Anger, and refuse to replace a single tile for a tenant.

8

On christmas eve Goguet brought us the traditional log. It was of elm and as big as he could carry.

"There's a piece of wood that will last you all day and all night," he announced proudly.

It was bitterly cold and our field looked like a Christmas card, for snow had fallen over the frozen grass and lay on the branches of our apple trees and on the hedges.

The nights were magnificent, so clear that the stars shone like diamonds, so light that they were reminiscent of the Scandinavian banks. But it was not a happy Christmas. People were querulous and few had their menfolk back on leave.

I went down to the village to buy toys for the children in the farmsteads, taking with me an Airedale I had brought from England because we had difficulty in finding locally an efficient watch-dog. All Goguet's dogs slept profoundly throughout the night and nothing woke them. Our Airedale, that we had christened "Chinka," was about eight months old—a wonderfully bred beast but so highly strung that she shied violently at the slightest noise. Duclos, in particular, was terrified of her and used to stand pitifully, cap in hand, outside the garden gate until I came out, but Chinka was just as frightened of Duclos. She used to slink back into the house at his approach, with her tail between her legs. Her chief quality was an unbounded affection for my baby. The Airedale slept at the foot of the cot and, although we never had an opportunity to test it, she would doubtless have guarded the child against an intruder.

I took the dog past the church, where there was a Christmas tree with the candles burning, to the paper shop kept by a man called Leleu, a big fellow with a deep voice, who gave strangers the impression, when he opened his mouth, of wanting to swallow them. He had gone through the last war without a scratch, and that included the Chemin des Dames. His son, a blond Viking, was one of the few men from the village to get Christmas leave, and he served in uniform behind the counter.

The Norman regiments gave more soldiers to the nation than those of any other province, and for this reason they excited the hatred of the Nazi radio commentators, who promised to send them into Silesia when France was conquered. Stuttgart radio did a lot to poison the Christmas spirit in our village, for more and more people listened to it, and for five nights out of seven Albrecht, one of the Nazis who spoke in French, addressed himself especially to the Normans. He described their green orchards, their fat cattle, their beloved apple trees, and added: "Your life is easy and pleasant now. It will be cruel and lonely in the arid desert where we are going to deport you."

It was as if our people were mesmerized by this sinister voice. Albrecht was the son of a German who had owned a villa on a high cliff above our village in 1914. The father had left at the last moment, setting fire to his house and escaping with his little boy who, twenty-five years after this ignominious flight, was instilling venom into the countryside.

Leleu's shop was always crowded, for he sold tobacco as well as books and papers, and one heard the latest news there. He was well placed, being opposite the mayor's parlor and the market-place, where vegetables were just now rare and expensive, because of the frost which made it wellnigh impossible to dig them out of the frozen ground. Coffee was still a rarity, although we were invariably told that supplies would become normal again before long, and chickens were not within the reach of any but the rich.

I bought a few toys for the Goguet children, knowing that they would get none at home, and some chocolate for the soldier Bayard, who, having been on leave three weeks ago, was not likely to have another spell at home for at least two months. His wife would send him the chocolate in her next parcel. Our butcher had saved a bone for Chinka, so that she would not be without her Christmas present, and so, loaded with all these things, I started the long climb back to the farm.

I followed the main road, walking behind a band of children

who, headed by their young mistress, sang *The Lark, the Gentle Lark,* which song the Normans took to Canada when they colonized the province of Quebec in the seventeenth century. We had seen these children before, because they held paperchases across our fields, and in preparing these games their little blond heads clustered round their mistress made a pleasing picture. They turned right just before reaching the café which is in front of M. Allard's estate, for they lived in a large house, almost a château, on the cliff where Albrecht, the spy, had owned his villa.

I watched them go, and as their voices died down I noticed that an elderly woman, with tears streaming down her cheeks, was also looking intently in their direction.

"You are doubtless wondering why I should cry like this," said the stranger, wiping her eyes, "but I am Polish. Ever since I have been evacuated here I am without news of my own young children, just about their age. When I see those youngsters and hear their laughter, I think how wonderful it would be if my kiddies could be with them. Do you know who they are? They are little Jewish children evacuated from Paris by one of the Rothschilds who bought the finest villa on the coast for them."

As I listened, Chinka caught sight of the dogs from the café and raced across the road to them. She was not yet trained to stay at heel, and was gone in a flash. A heavy truck thundered round the corner, and before I could move or even utter a warning shout, my dog was dead. Those deep, kind eyes were wide open, and still so full of fun that she could not have suffered. Chinka was buried that afternoon in a corner of our orchard under the shadow of the big walnut tree, and the house seemed strangely still without this affectionate animal that had taken so large a place in our lives. The bone that the butcher had given us for her Christmas dinner lay like a mute reproach on the kitchen table, and we missed her presence everywhere—in the bedroom, where her place at the foot of the cot was empty, on the stairs, which she mounted four at a time, and most of all in the big room by the fire, where she sprawled at full length, with her long paws on the tiles.

While I was crying for the loss of my dog, Mme. Gilbert, a corpulent soul with fair curly hair that made her look much younger than she really was, knocked at the door. An itinerant haberdasher, this woman kept her stock in a large black box between the handlebars of her bicycle. It was incredible how varied was her store. She sold soap and bottles of cheap, strong perfume which the young men on the farms gave to the serving-girls; ribbons and elastic, shoe-laces and buttons, knitting-needles and skeins of wool. Mme. Gilbert was quick to notice my red eyes.

"You have been crying, my little lady!" she exclaimed sympathetically. Her false teeth deformed her words, giving an impression of imbecility which was quite erroneous. I told her about Chinka, and she answered:

"But, my good lady, what would you say if you were I, with four sons in the Maginot Line and not one able to come on leave? It is a sad Christmas, indeed."

I suggested she should warm herself for a moment by the fire in the big room. The sun was hidden in a gray sky and more snow was on the way. Mme. Gilbert propped her bicycle against the half-timbering and accepted the invitation.

"Where did the accident take place?" she asked.

"On the road to Cabourg, by Berthelot's café."

"Accursed spot!" lisped Mme. Gilbert. "I was run over there by a truck and spent nine months in plaster. But there, I mustn't grumble. I'm on my legs again."

She told us that her four sons were born during the last war, when her husband was at the front. She was working in a munitions factory in Paris. When the war was over and Gilbert came home, his wife said to him: "It's nice to have you back, but the factory is closed and we've got to earn a livelihood." She reckoned there would be work to do in the devastated regions, because her husband was a plumber by trade, and she proved right, because they came back to Paris a couple of years later with a few savings. Gilbert now began looking for a steady job.

"You know Dauvilaire?" asked Mme. Gilbert. "He was doing a lot of work in Paris at the time, and my husband joined his staff. That is how we came here."

She was too good a saleswoman to allow sentiment to interfere for long with her trade, and before leaving the house she sold me a pair of gloves for my infant—the first he ever wore.

"The poor body!" she exclaimed, when she caught sight of

him. "He'll catch cold with his little hands uncovered in this biting cold."

As she was wheeling her bicycle up the field, Victor Duprez came along to wish us a happy Christmas and to see our son. He was demobilized temporarily and explained that things were so uncertain that business was at a standstill. The value of land was still increasing, but there were practically no sellers. "All the same," he said, "I shall go ahead with my alterations if I can get any workmen from Trouville."

He was on his way to see Goguet, who was to help him plant a number of apple trees as soon as the ground unfroze. He added that his wife was expecting a baby in March, which explained his sudden interest in my child.

It was three o'clock when he left, and the cows were already ambling up to their stables waiting to be let in and mooing with impatience while the heifers stood huddled together under a pear tree. Our pipes froze and left us without water, so that we were obliged to go down to the stream and fill a wheelbarrow with blocks of ice.

Once more the serenity of the night proved almost supernatural. Many of our farmers went to midnight mass at the medieval church in Annebault, hamlet of only a few hundred souls, where the priest decorated his own Christmas tree, distributing small presents after the service to the faithful.

The moon was full and strong, and the stars shone like lamps in a night-blue sky in which there was not the suspicion of a cloud. The farmers who were coming back our way grouped themselves for company along the hilly roads, through orchards where the naked arms of the apple trees threw uncanny shadows on the snow. It invoked the painting in the Tate Gallery of the dead rising up from their graves. Nobody had ever seen the stars so fixedly bright, and most fathers spoke of their sons on the eastern frontier where frozen limbs caused more casualties than Nazi bullets. A long succession of nights like this had spread the tale that these scintillating stars portended nothing good. Parisians, who may have been influenced by the dimming of the city lights, said a great calamity would fall upon the land.

The great freeze lasted until the sixth of January, when our pipes started to burst in the loft, the water trickling through the ceiling of our bedroom soon after dawn. Dauvilaire sent us his only available workman during the morning. He proved to be Gilbert, the husband of the itinerant haberdasher, a good-hearted fellow who was almost completely deaf and who talked to himself during the whole time he was mending the pipes, occasionally breaking into a peal of laughter at his own thoughts.

Goguet waded across the field in his top-boots to start lopping the hedges. Taking advantage of the fact that I was breast-feeding my baby and could seldom leave the house, he cut down a long line of trees bordering my wood. It was an exceptionally picturesque corner, and I was rather angry. Farmers are not allowed to cut down trees, even in hedges, without permission and in this case I had reserved for myself the entire wood and its borders, but the price of logs was by now so high that Goguet hired a man to help him. Since the war he was making it quite clear that he resented a woman owner and that I would do much better to remain quietly with my baby and my knitting, and in a way I felt terribly helpless and incompetent.

I took the matter up immediately but he parried my attack with a counter-offensive. Did I know that his chimney now smoked so badly that one of his children had narrowly escaped a serious illness? If that happened, he said, I would be in a most unenviable position.

"I will take care of that, Goguet, but you must cut down no more trees. I shall send you a registered letter to that effect this evening."

"Very well," he conceded, "but it is time I had my contract. Unless you give me six years I will not stay."

"That's up to you," I answered. "I will telephone the notary tomorrow, and we can sign the agreement, but it will be for one year, not six."

"Then I'll leave at Christmas," he threatened.

I was vexed about my trees and not very interested in his threats. If once it became known that the farm was vacant, I would have a dozen people clamoring for it. I could not believe that Goguet would be so obstinate.

At the house we were running short of wood, and it was impossible for me to order a cord from Goguet, knowing that he would sell back to me at an enormous price those same logs he had stolen from my wood. His theft already represented nearly six months of his rent. At this point, my husband suddenly flew over from London and I suggested that he and I should cut down what we needed from my big wood near the Allard estate.

We set out one morning with the garden wheelbarrow and two totally inadequate instruments—a short, blunt axe that we were in the habit of using to split the brushwood, and a small handsaw.

There were no cows in Mme. Anger's field, only a friendly donkey browsing by the entrance to our wood. It was my dream to buy one as soon as my son was old enough to be driven to the village in a donkey-cart. We planned to build a small stable in a corner of the orchard adjoining our house, which we were going to reserve for our own use by the terms of the new contract. As it was cut off from the main field by a palisade, it would provide my son with a place of his own when the garden became too small for him, and if vegetables became scarce we could use the edges for planting potatoes.

Nobody within memory had ever used our wood and there was no real entrance. We had cut away just enough undergrowth to wriggle through, and we always left the wheelbarrow on the grass in Mme. Anger's field. The doctor had warned us against these rough, prickly shrubs, because the goldfinches use the thorns as larders, spiking weevils on them ready for some future meal. When one pricks a finger on a thorn storing a not very fresh weevil, the result is a sore which is almost impossible to cure. We managed to clear a path from one side of the wood to the other, and discovered that the ground under the brambles was moss-covered, and if one looked carefully one found primroses and violets already in bud, though not yet in bloom, and a quantity of wild orchids. More or less in the middle of one slope we found a poplar rather more than thirty feet high, which we decided on the spot to level down. Nothing prompted our decision beyond the fact that the trunk was just the right girth for the logs we had in mind.

We made a V-shaped cut in the side of the trunk where we hoped it would fall, but the axe was so blunt and small that this work took half the morning, and by lunch-time we had decided that other weapons were needed to cut down a tree. I decided to go down to the village and, without appearing too ignorant, ask the local police superintendent, whose wife owned the ironmongery store, for his advice. I was lucky enough to find three foresters in the shop who had passed most of their lives cutting down trees but who still liked to argue about the best way of doing so. The argument suited me admirably, for I had only to listen carefully to discover the rough principles of the business. The superintendent sold me a two-handled saw, an iron wedge, and a wood cleaver.

"And now, my little lady," said the superintendent, "whenever the saw sticks tell your husband to widen the gap with the wedge. But take care the tree doesn't fall on your pretty head."

I called at the blacksmith's to have the axe mounted, and returned to the farm too late to go back to the tree. The next morning we returned to the scene of our labors and cut through more than two-thirds of the tree with no effort at all. It was a warm, springlike day, and we decided to go down to the stream for five minutes' rest while planning just how we were to make our tree fall where we wanted it to. We stood beside the limpid water where it ran in cascades over small boulders of granite. Here and there some large tree, its trunk rotted with age, had fallen across the stream to form a bridge for the squirrels. There were enough faggots from broken boughs to last us through several winters. On the other side of the water the wood extended in the direction of the field which bordered M. Allard's house. A slight wind brushed through the naked boughs and suddenly a creaking, cracking, rending sound reached us. We looked at each other, knowing but too well what had happened. We raced up the bank to find that a gust had caught our tree from behind and, severing the piece that was uncut, shot it beyond its stump, driving the base into the soft ground. The topmost branches were caught up in the boughs of a nearby tree. All we had to do now was to saw off another slice and allow the trunk to slide down progressively. We were not very proud of ourselves but things worked out just as we thought, and during the next few days we cut nine or ten fine logs, each about a yard in length, which we split up into four with the wedge. We carried these, two by two, as far as the entrance of the wood where we made a pile of them ready to be carried back in the wheelbarrow. These long trips back to the farm proved the hardest work, for Mme. Anger's field rose steeply and the lane past Groscol's house was high in mud and half-thawed snow.

But spring was not far off. One sensed it everywhere: by the sun that became warmer each day, by the grass that was coming up a tender green, and by the appearance here and there of the first daisies that escaped the eye until one looked for them.

We stored the logs against the stone wall at the back of the house, and arranged the brushwood and faggots alongside. Now that I had taken over the orchard next to the garden I planned to cut down one or two of the dead apple trees to add to my store. Duclos and I had marked these trees the previous summer, and he was going to replace them with a dozen young fruit trees of varied kinds such as cherries, plums, and peach-trees.

I had even less idea of how to cut down an apple tree than a poplar, but as I was keeping this orchard for a nursery it hardly seemed to matter if I left the stump, a dangerous practice where cattle graze. It might even have its use because I could axe wood on it. One morning, therefore, when Goguet was out hiring his services elsewhere, I decided to make a start, and, putting up a ladder, lopped off the branches. It was tough going because of the pith inside—which, incidentally, burns admirably—but in rather more than an hour my tree was felled to within eighteen inches of the ground. The Goguette came along as I was struggling to splice up the trunk and, discarding the wedge, swung the axe over her shoulder with the strength of a man and brought it down at the end of the log, splitting the trunk from end to end.

Meanwhile the coal for the stove was running short, and there was no more to be had. The Aga burned anthracite or coke, but the anthracite, which came from England, was requisitioned, and the coke was being used for the blast furnaces. Some of our wealthy farmers like Barbe took their trucks to Le Havre in the hope of buying a few sacks but most of them returned empty-handed.

I went down to the village after lunch and discovered a merchant willing to sell me five sacks of coke at an exorbitant price, but the most difficult was to find a vehicle to transport them to the farm. There were no cars or trucks, but Victor Duprez whom I met in the village square, offered to send Groscol with Bichette and the hay-cart. However, I was not anxious to take advantage of his offer, foreseeing serious trouble with the Goguets if their rival were suddenly to swing into their field.

There was a taxi driver who was occasionally to be found in the square, though I never quite discovered where he came from. He must have been a bird of passage from Cabourg or from Trouville. I suddenly saw him coming into the café for a drink and, knowing that the best approach was to offer fifty per cent above the fare, I closed the deal before he had time to make objections. The five sacks were parked on the pavement outside the coal-yard, and we did our best not to fill the cab with coal dust. We drove off and, ten minutes later, landed safely with our cargo at the top of the field.

It was a problem to know where to put it. Norman houses are built without cellars, so that when we first moved in Gravé built us a brick shed with a zinc roof near the stables, but it contained only a ton, and this was our reserve in case of emergency. I decided to turn the small room beside the kitchen into a storehouse. Having cleared it of furniture, we brought the sacks down the field by wheelbarrow, and deposited the coke on the tiled floor. The walls were of stone, and at least three feet thick, so there was our cellar ready made.

The next day the notary telephoned to say that my contract with Goguet was ready for our signatures, and he asked me to come along after lunch. I went in search of Goguet whom I found in the Poulins' cider press just across the hedge. The Montagues had now left for their new home, and the big farm next door was being run, in the absence of Ernest, by the Castels and a hired boy. Yvonne could do very little. She was expecting her baby in less than two months. Goguet, who before Christmas had helped the Montagues to empty the place of as much stock as possible before their departure, had now succeeded in making himself indispensable to their successors. Castel and he had long drinking bouts together in the cider press, and from the way Castel looked I suspected that Goguet had told him that I was a difficult woman.

The old man unfroze, however, when I admired his prize fowls which were in truth splendid, but, unfortunately, this hobby occupied so much of his time and was so unremunerative that the rest of the farm looked more and more neglected. Goguet told me he wanted his wife to be present at the signing of the lease, but that she would follow on her bicycle, so, collecting my husband, we all three walked down to the village.

Although I guessed that the proceedings would be stormy we carefully avoided the subject. Indeed, Goguet was unusually talkative and he yarned continually, but in spite of all his cunning he was unable to hide something that lay heavily on his heart, and this something was the fact that we had cut down so large a tree without asking his help. He angled craftily to discover if it was for lack of funds that we had taken to cutting our own logs, and when his subtle questions proved abortive, he recounted in detail the accidents that he had seen overtake the most expert lumbermen.

"As for apple trees," he said, "you have the idea all wrong. You must dig out the master root and pull down the tree, otherwise the cattle might trip over the stump."

The Goguette was already there when we reached the notary's house and, after a short wait, we were ushered into his presence. The man of law had carefully arranged two chairs to the right of his desk on which he asked the Goguets to sit, while two others, opposite his own desk, were for us.

He plunged straight into the contract he had drawn up, in which it was made clear that, during the tenancy, Goguet could not hold me responsible for his chimney. When he finished reading the document he looked at Goguet who for the last ten minutes had sat on the edge of his chair, his elbows resting on his knees, his cap twisted in his hands.

"I must have a new chimney," he said stubbornly, as if reciting a set piece.

"But I understand that it has been seen to?" said the notary.

"It has been seen to," said Goguet. "But does that mean that it's any better?"

"Yes, for sure," put in the Goguette who, in conversation, was of everybody's opinion, knowing full well that she always went her own way. "It doesn't mean anything."

"I have yet to hear of a farm chimney that does not smoke when the wind is the wrong way," said the notary, "and I fancy that yours is no worse than the rest. Have you any suggestion?"

"If it were my house, I'd pull the chimney down and build another," said Goguet.

"You mean personally?" asked the notary.

"Why, no," answered Goguet, puzzled. "I mean that if I

were the owner of the house I'd have enough money to employ a man to do it."

"I am afraid these are not normal times," said the notary.

"Just to give you an example," said Goguet, "during the cold snap in January, the cider on our table in the big room was frozen when we woke up in the morning. I bet you would not live in a house where the cider froze!"

"I think you are wasting my time," said the notary. "I do not think you want to sign."

"I want a nine-year lease," said Goguet.

"For sure," said the Goguette. "Nine years."

"Nine years?" echoed the notary. "It was six some time ago, now it is nine. There is something about this draughty house that makes you ask for a singularly long lease. I am sorry, it cannot be done. I could not advise any owner to accept."

"Then," proclaimed Goguet, agitating his cap, "I will leave at Christmas."

"Precisely," said the notary dryly. "That is when your lease ends."

"Ah, but I won't go if the war is still on," said Goguet, "and what is more, you will not be able to make me pay a rent. It is illegal to throw a family out during war-time."

"You must revise your ideas about the law," said the notary. "Land must be farmed and you will have to make place for somebody else who is willing to farm it."

"If the contract is only for a year, I refuse to pay the fees," said Goguet. "I would much prefer a simple agreement made at Dozulé market."

The notary brought his fist down on the desk.

"But you certainly will pay the fees," he declared. "I will see to that."

For once the notary seemed on the verge of losing his temper. He remembered where he had been in the last war. Faced with the stubbornness of this peasant, he felt like commiting an unprofessional act. He did, indeed, allow himself to ask:

"Why are you not called up?"

For the first time Goguet lifted his eyes from the ground and looked the notary squarely in the face.

"I have three children."

"Have you registered them at the town hall?"

"I should say so," answered Goguet with alacrity. "You won't catch me in the army again if I can help it."

Silence fell over the room. The drama was deeper than this superficial quarrel which, in ordinary times, could have been settled over a glass of apple-jack. The notary was wounded in his love of country, and it was as if in a flash he had seen the possibility of defeat. He passed his hand over his forehead like a man chasing an ugly thought and, bringing back his famous smile, queried:

"Are you both agreed on the lease? Then you must initial over the pencil marks and sign your names at the bottom of the page."

Two days later I suggested we should call on Nénette Roginsky at her new farm. It was a fine sunny afternoon, but the recent rains had turned the fields into swamps, immersing the spring grass and young clover. Fording the swollen stream by our cider press, we climbed up the orchard opposite as far as the road to St. Vaast, where we turned right past Déliquaire's farm and that of our friend, Giles. In many of the orchards the farmers had already laid low the apple trees which had been killed by the winter frosts. They had been felled in the way that Goguet had explained to us, by digging round the base for the master root until the whole tree could be brought down by a rope. Mme. Paul's red-brick house, the one with the initial fixed to the chimney, was now occupied by an ex-service man who had lost an arm in the First World War. He was farming the fields east of our stream which the Pauls had sold at the time of the split-up.

It was a good half-hour's walk to the Roginsky farm. It faced the main road, with a garden and a short drive in front, a low Norman house all bathed in sunshine on this February afternoon. Though we had never seen it before, we knew at once that it was theirs. With two stories, like ours, it had the same green shutters and cute white doors with windowed tops that I had designed for my own house.

We rang the bell, but there was no answr. The windows had bright chintz curtains with red squares and they were gathered with a bow in the center. This might have been the home of Tom Thumb in a fairy book. We peeped through into the kitchen, shimmering in white paint, with a brand-new white en-

amel stove and exactly the same sideboard, table, and chairs
which Roginsky, the furniture dealer, had made for our house.
There was electricity laid on everywhere.

We looked into the adjoining room and saw a big double
bed, and beside it a pale pink cot with a tiny baby sleeping inside. Everything was so fresh, so neat, so perfectly clean, that it
was a joy to see. We walked round the house and found a half-
timbered barn divided into three compartments. In the first was
the covered cart that we recognized as the one which Nénette
used to drive to the village when she delivered the milk from the
Poulin farm, in the center of the barn was the cowshed, and the
end compartment was a stable for the pony. Voices reached us
from the bottom of the orchard, and a few moments later we
came upon Riquet and his wife. They welcomed us with cries of
delight, and led us into their home. Riquet went first. He wore a
beret and a blue pullover, and his long, thin legs and gawky arms,
his high cheekbones and big pointed nose, made him look like a
bird of prey about to take flight. Strangely enough, Nénette
resembled him, or, at least, she had certain points in common
with her husband, such as her straw-colored hair, that crowned
her angular features, and her wide-lobed ears that peeped from
beneath her hair.

Riquet delved into a pocket and brought out the front door
key with a flourish of his arm and a high-pitched laugh. He was
so proud to have a front door and a family of his own. On the
threshold Nénette and he took off their top-boots and exchanged
them for slippers not to dirty the shining parquet floors. It
seemed criminal that we should enter this doll's house without
doing the same, but they waved our objections aside and ushered
us into the kitchen.

"Look!" exclaimed Riquet, dancing round the room and waving his arms excitedly. "Isn't it cosy here? Isn't the stove a
beauty? We had a blue one at first, but Nénette sent it back
because she wanted everything in the kitchen to be white—
white!"

Riquet's laugh was unreal and made one flinch, but his enthusiasm was that of an overgrown child, and he looked radiantly
happy.

"Come and see the baby," said Nénette. "It doesn't matter
if we wake him because it's time for his bottle."

She led us into the bedroom and, bending over the cot, took the infant up in her arms and gave him to me, watching expectantly for the reaction that one mother seeks from another in such circumstances. He was a poor, weak little creature whose wan face seemed already tired of life, but Nénette looked after him with the same scrupulous attention which she bestowed upon her house, and when I had taken him and had sat down in the arm-chair, rocking him in my arms, Riquet, beaming with pleasure, went off to the kitchen to pour the milk into the saucepan and make the bottle himself.

"Your house is a real jewel," I said to Nénette. "How happy you must be in it."

"I thought we'd be happy," she sighed, "but we're so far away from everything. Why, if we run short of flour or need a box of matches, I am obliged to harness the pony and drive all the way down to the village, and there is no market for the milk here. Isn't that right, Riquet?" she asked, raising her voice for it carry as far as her husband through the open door.

"Nénette hankers after the old farm," he said dully, returning into the bedroom with the bottle in one hand and the saucepan in the other. "She has the place in her blood. All the Poulins are like that. They can't keep away from it for any length of time. Of course, it was a fine place. I'll admit that, but then so is this, if it wasn't that I have to go away and leave her all alone."

"But where are you going, Riquet?"

"Into the army, of course."

"Into the army?" we cried, my husband and I together. "They're going to call you up?"

"Yes," he answered. "I shall be gone in a week's time."

His voice quavered, but it was from a feeling of helplessness, not from any lack of courage. He feared to leave his wife and her tiny baby and all the work to do in this lonely outpost— Nénette, whose energy was almost consumed, whose poor tired brain was unable to key itself up to the task of organizing a new manner of life.

But Riquet? It seemed unbelievable that the military should seize on him when there were so many healthy men still on the land. It would be murder to put him into the Maginot Line.

"But are you sure?" we asked again.

"I am being sent to Blois," he answered. "It won't be too bad, because I can buy a little house there and Nénette can come and join me."

"Yes," said Nénette. "He is going to be in the Algerian Sharp-shooters, and perhaps he will stay at Blois for quite a time, because their headquarters are there. Now this is where you can help us. We want to sell this house, and I am sure you must know a lot of rich English people who would like to own a farm in Normandy."

It was a grim joke, indeed, to picture Riquet wearing a *chéchia*, but one thing was certain, and that was that Nénette could no longer stand her new house. Her voice when she mentioned it was harsh and determined, and she even spoke of living with her sister, Madeleine Montague, while Riquet was settling things up at Blois.

When the baby was back in his cot a young serving-maid came with a bowl full of eggs, for with the approach of Easter the hens were laying well.

"You must come and see my hen house," said Nénette. "You remember that it was I who looked after the hens at the Poulin farm."

A flush of pride spread over her face as she said these words.

We rose and followed her to the barn, where she had built the poultry house amidst the solid oak beams which, like ours, must have been centuries old. The pony's harness hung from a nail in the wall and adjoining it was the stout bull halter.

We left them as the sun was setting, for Nénette had her cows to milk.

9

THE pear trees that climbed up the front of our house were in flower on Palm Sunday. They were the precursors of blossom time, for in less than three weeks our Normandy orchards would be all pink and white.

Renée left home early to find a sprig of box, which the priest would bless at mass, and which she would hang on the wall above her bed until next year. She followed the path that leads to Berthelot's café, because she knew that there was a hedge of it in the grounds of a disused laundry.

On her return we heard that Mme. Duprez had given birth to a still-born child. Judge how great was her sorrow, for the Allard estate had been purchased for the new arrival, and Mme. Duprez *mère* had covered the cot in which all her own sons were born with flounces of priceless Brussels lace in readiness for the great day.

Mme. Bayard arrived after lunch. She told us that one of our neighbors had fallen from a ladder while cutting down the branches of a tree and broken a rib. He was known as "Old Porquet," and for twenty years had looked after the farm of a Paris industrial magnate who had his house beside it. Porquet had left two months ago to become gardener at the villa where the students of the military college of St. Cyr were quartered. He had an amazing war record which he never spoke about, and three sons, of whom the eldest worked in a munitions factory near Cabourg, the second was preparing to enter the Church, and the third was to be a teacher.

"It serves him right," declared Mme. Bayard, as she told us of his accident. "A man with a son taking Holy Orders has no business to cut down trees on Palm Sunday."

That was all the sympathy Old Porquet got.

Goguet did not broach the subject, but he doubtless felt some satisfaction that his warning to me was so rapidly confirmed, for Porquet had been cutting down trees for nearly thirty years. Our relations with the Goguets were guarded. My farmer was cunning and shrewd, but he was the quintessence of the Norman, and if he bore me any malice he was too crafty to show it. For my part I was eager to live on friendly terms. If I could not have an honest tenant I would accommodate myself with a picturesque one. But the Goguette was harder to deal with and her actions more difficult to interpret. Her vendetta with the Groscols grew more vicious, and when Mme. Groscol came one morning to sell me some leeks from her garden, the Goguette, having covered her with insults, turned to me and shouted:

"And next time you want any milk or butter don't come to me for it."

I immediately took her advice, and that evening Helen, the Castels' serving-girl, brought us our milk.

Helen was a buxom child of fourteen, with big healthy cheeks that might have been scrubbed pink with a hard brush, and clear eyes the color of ripe hazel-nuts flashing with mischief and the joy of being alive. She smelt of carbolic soap and clover hay, and was so appetizing that the young men of the farms said of her:

"She's edible."

Her visits gave us immense joy, for she brought us all the news which she expounded with a delightful lisp, holding the tips of her fingers against her comely breast. Each day she arrived in a clean overall of a different bright color, perfectly laundered, and she wore her long hair done up in a snood.

Yvonne, to whom she was attached, had brought her from Formentin, where she had served in the Castels' café and where she had learned the quick repartee which was the salt of her conversation. The farm amused her, but she missed the customers of the café and the tips she used to earn on Sundays.

"You know," she confided one day, "I don't make much—one hundred fifty francs a month, that's five franc a day." She rattled this off in one breath, and her happy smile and childish lisp dispelled any suggestion that she was not satisfied at a wage of about twelve cents a day.

She told us that the Castels were finding it impossible to sell their café, and that Yvonne was expecting her baby for early April. It was Helen who milked the cows, but there were only six, so that more than half the land was idle.

The Goguette made no comment on my new arrangement, and her prudence was increased by the fact that her husband continued to be employed from time to time by the Castels, but the loss of my custom began to show itself at the end of the week when she added up her earnings, and she was vexed to think that our good money, thanks to her angry word, was going across the hedge into a neighbor's pocket. After a few weeks she had worked herself up into a great state of suppressed anger, and began to meditate revenge. But she was determined not to put herself within reach of the law.

One day, while I was bathing the baby, I heard strange noises in the corridor above. Thinking that the cats were chasing each other on the staircase, I took no notice, but having finished bathing the child, I went up to call the animals to order, but neither Finette nor the kittens were to be seen, only a pile of stones on the carpet. "They must have come from the eaves," I thought, "but how?"

As I went over to the open window a pebble hurled from the courtyard caught me on the temple. It had been thrown by young Renée who, standing by the cart-shed, was pelting the house.

"What do you think you're doing, young lady?" I asked, puzzled.

The little girl, whose arm was raised in the act of throwing another stone, let it fall to her side. For a moment it looked as if she was going to apologize, but she changed her mind and, as if taking a great decision, her dark eyes narrowing, shouted across to her young brother squatting on the steps of the buttery:

"Say, Robert, have you seen Groscol lately?"

"No," answered Robert, disinterested.

"That's funny," said his sister. "I suppose he hasn't been round to see his new friend today."

The insult had scarcely left her mouth than she heard her father's heavy step behind her. He had swung round a pile of freshly cut logs, and when he was right up against her, so that she could see his shadow on the wall, he thundered:

"What's that you were saying?"

Her slight, lithe frame trembled, for the voice was charged with anger.

"It's mother's fault," she whimpered.

"Very well," he answered, clutching his daughter by the back of her apron and boxing her ears with unbridled ferocity. "Just take that on account."

He threw her to the ground as if she had been an animal, and without looking up at our house went his way.

Early in April, Duclos arrived with five men to plant our fruit trees in the orchard adjoining the house, and the work was finished in the course of one day. He also pruned the rose trees, and declared that my vine had outlived the frost and should produce grapes in the autumn. It was a fine piece of news, for the poor thing had looked so miserable during the winter that I had given it up for lost.

"You know," said Helen, when she came with the milk that evening, "it has been so hot that I was up at four today to make my butter, and now I must hurry back to look after my rabbits and calves."

"In that case," I answered, amused by her use of the possessive pronoun, "I won't keep you. By the way, is there any news about Yvonne?"

Helen beamed with importance.

"Why, yes," she said. "There is. It may be any day now."

"In that case," I said, "tell her that she has no need to send you all the way to the village when she is ready for the midwife. You are welcome to use our telephone at any time of the day or night."

At midday on Sunday Helen paid us a surprise visit. She wore a Sabbath overall of pale blue with a brooch containing large bright stones, and had fixed a ribbon in her hair. Black shoes replaced her week-day clogs, for she had been to mass at six.

We guessed that she was bringing news, for she was on her way to milk the cows, and the cans hanging from her yoke glistened like silver. Our farmers were beginning to milk three times a day now and the Castels had two cows that had just calved.

Helen's eyes sparkled as she beckoned me and said: "Mme.

Castel sends me to ask you if you could telephone the midwife. I think something is happening."

"Very well, Helen. I'll see to it."

As soon as the serving-maid had disappeared, we telephoned to Mlle. Lefranc, but she was in bed with a high temperature.

"I'll warn the doctor," she announced. "Meanwhile, perhaps you could go over to the Castels and keep me in touch."

It was warm, but a fine drizzle was falling. Taking a raincoat and top-boots, I went over to the Poulins' farm. Our orchards were now in all the glory of the pear and apple blossoms, and the hot rain made the hedges smell delicious.

The low room of the farm was empty. It was here that the Poulins had their meals at a long deal table scrubbed twice a day until it had become white and scarred. On the wall above hung the shining copper pans. A bell under the roof of the house used to call the large staff to their midday meal, but we had not heard it since the departure of the Montagues.

I sat by the door to take off my top-boots so as not to spoil the parquet floors, and as I was doing this a woman came into the room carrying a pile of sheets.

She must have been in the early fifties, with well-tended gray hair made into a bun at the back, and dressed in black, even to her stockings and felt slippers. She moved across the room so silently that she seemed unreal. Having looked at me intently she said:

"I take it you are the owner of the farm next door. I am Mme. Pinson. Perhaps you will be able to tell us if Mlle. Lefranc is on her way up?"

"That is what I intended to tell Mme. Castel," I said. "I am afraid the midwife may not come. She has just finished a difficult case and has overtired herself."

"I'm not surprised," answered Mme. Pinson. "The case you refer to was that of my daughter, Mme. France Marie. I live on the road to St. Vaast, between the Déliquaires and the farm which the Montagues have just taken. I shall be glad if you will call one day."

This invitation from a peasant woman was given with such authority that I could not help but be surprised. Moreover this woman spoke elegantly and with such assurance that, in spite of her surroundings, one might have taken her for the Mother Superior of a convent or the housekeeper of a feudal home.

"Who can she be?" I thought, as Mme. Pinson put away her linen in a vast oak cupboard and led me upstairs.

Yvonne was lying on a massive peasant bed of shining walnut which stood high, not only by reason of its monumental legs, but also because of the number of downy mattresses piled upon it. Her mother stood motionless beside her with Yvonne's head ensconced in the bend of her arm.

Mme. Castel was a short, trim woman, almost bald, but with a bun, no larger than a pigeon's egg, done up with two or three pins. She looked as if she had remained thus by the bedside for hours and was capable of going on for ever.

I halted, waiting for some sign from Mme. Castel, whose keen, clear eyes, usually so alert, were now exclusively centered on her child. Seeing that the old lady appeared to take no notice of my presence, I turned my attention to Yvonne. The young Poulin wore a nightgown embroidered in red wool, the collar of which fitted tightly round her neck, while the sleeves were gathered modestly at the wrists. This garb made her look like a young lady in a boarding school.

She was the first to speak, and her words were addressed to her mother.

"Have they given the medicine to the calf?" she asked. "I do hope Helen will remember to massage it in the way the vetinary surgeon explained."

Then, lifting her head slightly, she added for my benefit:

"Would you believe it, we have lost two calves in a month. What will Ernest say?"

Her head fell back on the pillows, and these remarks were followed by a low groan. A few moments later she exclaimed:

"To think that Ernest doesn't even guess what's happening! You will have to send him a telegram, mother, stamped by the mayor and the police, so that he is given three days' leave for the baptism."

"That's all right," Mme. Castel answered. "You must deliver the baby first."

More groans followed this maternal advice, and then Yvonne cried:

"Oh, mother, don't it hurt?"

"Offer your sufferings to the Virgin," said Mme. Castel.

The door opened and Helen advanced her rosy cheeks.

"Madam," she exclaimed, "twelve little chicks have just come out of their shells, and the new heifer is in the courtyard trying to walk for the first time. You ought to see the way she's sniffing the spring and putting out her tongue to catch the raindrops. Oh, it's lovely out, madam!"

"Thanks, Helen," muttered her mistress, "and give the dogs their supper, because when I'm not about everybody seems to forget them."

"Ought I to tell them about Mlle. Lefranc?" I wondered. It struck me that it might be wiser to say nothing, for Yvonne seemed so worried about the loss of her animals that she might think that a fresh calamity was about to fall on her.

My doubts were settled by the sound of a car in the road, and, looking out of the window, I saw it was the doctor.

"Thank goodness for that," I thought. "Mlle. Lefranc must have told him, after all."

The doctor came straight up to the bedroom and, taking a quick look round, seemed to weigh up the situation. Mme. Castel continued to clasp her daughter as if to save her from some unknown danger, while Yvonne groaned a little louder. Unimpressed by this touching family scene the doctor turned to me and asked:

"Where does one find a wash-basin in this house?"

Without waiting for an answer, he opened a door opposite the one by which he had just come in and found what he was looking for, but taking up what he imagined was a cake of soap, he exclaimed:

"Heavens! What on earth is this?"

"Why, it's a piece of Camembert cheese," I said, laughing. "They must keep it here to eat when they're hungry at night."

After a brief search I found a slab of carbolic soap, and the doctor, having washed his hands and put on his white coat, cried:

"Come on, let's get to work."

We returned to the bedroom to find Mme. Pinson standing beside Yvonne in a dignified pose.

"Courage, little one," she crooned. "It will soon be over."

Her words failed to obtain the impression she hoped for.

Yvonne answered her admonition with an uncomprehending stare. Then, turning to Mme. Castel, Mme. Pinson, nodding her head wisely, proclaimed:

"Ah, dear madam, believe me, I have seen some children brought into the world."

"And I," muttered Mme. Castel proudly. "I can flatter myself that few women have had my experience."

"Well, ladies," broke in the doctor, "for two matrons who know so much about it, I see you are not even capable of making a bed. Look at this mess!"

Brushing them aside, he took hold of Yvonne and plumped her to one side. Then, beckoning to me, he caught up the sheets and with my help re-made the bed in a trice. An hour later he flung me the tiny heir to the Poulin dynasty, saying:

"Hi! Dress that for me, will you?"

I began to clothe the infant, but, looking up, saw Mme. Pinson, whose eyes were fixed upon me so intently and with such strange insistence that I shuddered.

I left the house as soon as I could and hurried home, where I found Mme. Bayard cleaning the kitchen. I told her about my experience, and added:

"By the way, Bayard, I met a curious woman, called Mme. Pinson, at the Castels. Who is she?"

"She is the most respectable and the most respected woman in the village, but as soon as she crosses the threshold of a house, discord and tragedy follow. Nobody suggests that this is her fault. Her conduct is always exemplary, but even her sons-in-law are so scared of her that one of them moved to Rouen before the war not to have to live in the same village. He is in front of the Maginot Line now, and his wife has just had a baby. Did she tell you about that?"

"Is France Marie the name?"

"That's right," answered Mme. Bayard.

"But what does Mme. Pinson do in the Poulins' house?"

"She is supposed to have had a great influence on the old man Poulin. Shortly before his death he had promised to marry her."

"Well," I said, "I had better be telephoning to M. Castel at Formentin. I promised his daughter I would let him know."

I went to the telephone and asked to be put through to the café. Castel answered in person.

"You're the grandfather of a fine baby boy," I announced.

"What?" shouted Castel excitedly. "And, to begin with, who is that speaking?"

"Your neighbor," I answered. "The young Mme. Poulin has just asked me to give you the news."

"Do me a favor," implored Castel, hardly able to contain his joy. "Go right round to the farm, without losing an instant, and have one of the farm-hands harness the mare and fetch me in the covered cart. I want to kiss my grandson this very evening."

An hour later the Castels' covered cart clattered down the path on the long journey to Formentin. Goguet had offered to accompany the lad, for they would be driving by night with shaded lamps.

They returned at two in the morning, and by dawn Castel was already on the return journey, for he wanted to open his café at the right time.

10

A TELEGRAM from Ernest announced that he was being given three days' leave for the baptism of his infant son, and that he would arrive at the end of the week.

Mme. Castel was determined that her young son-in-law should find his farm impeccable. Nothing must make him regret the quarrel that had sent his sister Madeleine Montague to form a home elsewhere. During the next few days Mme. Castel embarked on a gigantic spring cleaning to make the red brick house shine from top to bottom, but with her daughter in bed and the baby to look after, she found herself seriously short of staff.

For example, there was the washing that normally Yvonne, Helen, and she used to rinse in the stream at the bottom of their orchard, all three kneeling in boxes built at the water's edge. Now it happened that the Goguette overheard Mme. Castel discussing her troubles.

"If it's to lend a hand," said the Goguette, "I'll be glad to do your washing with mine. As a matter of fact, I'm going to light my copper this afternoon."

Mme. Castel had known the Goguette all her life, for they came from neighboring villages, but she had never voiced a very flattering opinion of her, and it was not entirely to her liking that Goguet should spend so much time with her husband in the cider press when he was paid for a day's work. But this offer was extremely generous, and Mme. Castel revised her feelings. It saved her from an awkward situation, but in order that the Goguette should not be out of pocket, Mme. Castel supplied the soap.

The Goguette spent all the afternoon by the stream, and in the evening the linen was hanging right across my field, gently floating in the breeze, and in order not to have to bring it in at night, the Goguette moved her cows to the Valleys, for they had a habit of eating the most indigestible things.

The baptism was to take place on the day following Ernest's arrival, and it was timed for six in the evening. The Castels' two covered carts would take the family from the farm to the church, but one could hardly describe it as being a gathering of the Poulins, for there would be some notable absentees, such as Peter, who was in the Maginot Line, and the Montagues, who were not even sent an invitation. One could hardly blame Yvonne for this, because Madeleine Montague, after making her life unbearable, had marched out of the house swearing she would never set her feet in it again, but Ernest, when he came back, was soon regretting his eldest sister's absence, and after spending an hour or two at his wife's bedside, and admiring his infant son, went round in secret to the Montagues' house.

He had only to cut across his orchards, jump over the stream, and walk fifty yards along the road to St. Vaast, where the farmhouse lay behind a clump of trees. It was really nothing more than a small whitewashed cottage, and its only wealth was its cleanliness.

Ernest came away in tacturn mood. Indeed, he was so grumpy that Mme. Castel, who had not been told of his visit, was quick to guess, but being a wise woman she said nothing.

Nénette drove over to her brother's house in her pony-trap. She was presenting her nephew with his baptism dress and being, since her marriage, the wealthiest member of the family, she saw to it that the present was magnificent. Her swollen eyes and strange manner might have alarmed Ernest at any other time. Riquet was at Blois. His wife was in despair, for she felt incapable of overcoming her loneliness. Her baby was not sufficient company. His cries often annoyed her. Her house, with its green shutters and white paint, full of expensive furniture, became loathsome to her, especially in the evening, when she sat alone at her kitchen table to eat a meal she had cooked without enthusiasm and for which she had no appetite.

Louise Rossé, the youngest of the Poulin sisters, was to join the party at the church. Her good-looking young husband, Jules, the ironmonger, was in the same regiment as Ernest, and had congratulated the proud father before he went on leave. She closed the shop early and waited for the cortège to arrive. The two covered carts clattered down the hill, reaching the church a few minutes before the hour. In the first was Mme. Castel, with the baby enveloped in white tulle and fast asleep, and Ernest was the driver. The second was driven by old Castel, with Nénette beside him, and at the back was Castel's sister from Le Havre, who was sitting on a kitchen chair. The church bells pealed as they arrived in sight of the village, and the shopkeepers round the ironmongery store came to their doorsteps to watch.

Mme. Pinson had remained at the farm to cook the immense dinner for which the Castels, because it was a meatless day, had killed at least ten chickens and a number of rabbits. She was helped by Helen in a velvet dress of turquoise blue with puffed sleeves.

The next morning, as the Goguette was going to the village to order her buckwheat, Mme. Castel gave her a pretty box of sugar-almonds tied up in ribbon for washing her linen, but as soon as Ernest was back at the front the Goguette sent Renée round to the Castels' with a bill for eighty francs.

Victor Duprez was now pushing actively ahead with the alterations at the Bruyères. He also planned to rebuild Groscol's house, and turn Berlequet into a model farm.

We were in early May, and one evening Helen told us that Peter Poulin was coming home on leave from the Maginot Line. Yvonne was anxious about his reactions, because at the time of the split-up Peter sided strongly with Madeleine Montague, to whose farm he had removed all that constituted his share, including his cows. Like Madeleine, Peter said he would never again cross the threshold of the old home. When he arrived on leave he went directly to the Montagues', but his longing to see the red brick house was more than he could stand. At heart he would have been more than willing to make peace with Yvonne, for the anger of the moment had now subsided, and only his pride remained.

As soon as he had a moment to spare Peter, while still in uniform, set out on the traditional round, calling on all his neighbors, after which he would change into slacks and potter about the farm for the rest of his leave. The way to the Goguets' was along the road to St. Vaast as far as Déliquaire's farm, and then down by our cider press. But Peter did not take this route. Instead, accompanied by a farm-hand, he went all the way round by the path that led past Yvonne's house, and which would bring him to our front gate.

When he reached the low stone wall in front of the Castels' courtyard he spoke to his companion louder than was necessary to give himself plenty of assurance, for he could see that Mme. Castel was rinsing her milk-churns by the well. The two men walked straight along the path, but as they reached our hedge Mme. Castel called out:

"Well, Peter, are you not going to say good evening?"

Peter did not yield to her kindness.

"Good evening," he called out, continuing his way stubbornly.

Five days after his arrival the sound of drums was once more heard over the countryside, and on this occasion the students of St. Cyr, in their picturesque uniforms, did the drumming.

The announcement they made was of the utmost significance.

All leave was immediately canceled, youths of eighteen were to report to the authorities, and those men who had hitherto been declared unfit for military service were to be re-examined by doctors who had orders to be much more severe.

When Peter Poulin heard that he must return the same night he resolved to call on Yvonne after all. He felt he could not go back to the front without seeing Ernest's wife and the first-born. He, for whom the Poulin caste had always meant so much, was now determined, whatever happened, to hold in his arms the first Poulin to be born in their beloved home. Peter changed rapidly into uniform and hurried round to Yvonne. He went straight up to her and kissed her on both cheeks, without offering the slightest explanation, and he greeted Mme. Castel, who had known him all his life, with the same affection as if no quarrel had ever existed between them.

When Peter said good-by it was clear that he felt more satisfied, but like so many young soldiers in the village, he appeared to have no hope about the future. He was going back to the front convinced that he and his fellows would be swallowed up in some immense disaster, and on the doorstep he held Mme. Castel's hand for some moments before saying: "Think of me when I'm away. I know I'll never see this place again."

Among those declared fit for military service during the next few days was Maurice Porquet, whose father had fallen from his ladder while cutting the branches of a tree on Palm Sunday. Nobody ever understood how it was that Maurice had managed to keep out of the war, for he was twenty-six and of splendid physique. Up to now he had been helping his father to garden during the day and at night he worked in a munitions factory near Cabourg. The exemption he had enjoyed so miraculously was not without minor drawbacks, for he could never pass through the market without all the housewives chattering behind his back.

"Some people have all the luck," one of them would say.

"Yes," answered another, "and yet they seem to have normal sized arms and legs."

"Well, never mind. I hear that with this new order all the raw recruits are going to be sent straight into the firing line, and if you ask me it serves them jolly well right!"

Young Porquet received his calling-up papers the next morning, and set off to work that night with a heavy heart. Having climbed the hill by Berthelot's café, he raced down the next one on his bicycle, but he skidded half-way, crashing against a cement pylon with such violence that his skull was fractured.

He was rushed to hospital at Pont L'Évêque, where his suffering was so intense that the doctors were obliged to put him in a strait jacket. We heard of this accident when a fellow workman went to break the news to the wife, who lived with her little girl in a lodge on the estate where the Porquets worked as gardeners. She was a good-looking Breton woman, who had never quite recovered from milk fever that set in following the birth of her child three years ago. The problem was to tell her what had taken place as tactfully as possible so that she could go and see her husband in hospital before it was too late, but though she was informed with infinite care, the young Mme. Porquet remained dazed on her doorstep, her troubled eyes staring without comprehension in front of her for long after she had been left alone.

The estate was a sort of model Versailles, with lakes and ornamental waters, and while Mme. Porquet was thus trying to get her brain to function, she became dimly aware of her little girl, who was crying for help. The child, taking advantage of her mother's distress, had clambered over the edge of a slimy pool to try and catch the goldfish she saw flashing past in the bright sunlight, but she lost her footing and fell into the water.

Her mother rushed in to pull her out, but the shock further unbalanced her mind, leaving her during the next few days in a torpor.

Three days later the village bell tolled for the death of Maurice Porquet, and on the eve of the funeral the bier was exposed in the church so that all his mates in the factory would have an opportunity of paying their last tribute.

They came silently, respectfully, cap in hand, leaving their bicycles against the wall of the church, as night was falling, and passed into the dim interior, lit only by the flickering candles. In the main street at the close of this warm summer day the shopkeepers were putting up their shutters. From afar came the music of the gently rolling waves breaking against the beach.

Suddenly the muffled roar of a dozen heavy bombers flying wing to wing right over the house-tops rent the stillness of the night, and the street, half empty a moment before, became filled with an excited crowd peering skyward.

Nobody dared say what was in his heart, but each nodded significantly. The answer followed swiftly. From the direction of Le Havre came a deafening thunder of fierce explosions so that the ground rumbled underfoot, while windows shook and doors quivered.

There was a rush for the beach. Any fear of personal danger was swept away by the desire to watch the aweinspiring spectacle from the grandstand of the breakwater. Within a few minutes the short street leading to the sea was black with people running, jostling to get to the sands in time.

Across the bay small tongues of flame appeared, growing in intensity as the first docks began to blaze. The sky was silent by now, the raiders having sped away after dropping their bombs from only a few feet above their objectives.

A quarter of an hour later another wave of bombers thundered through the night and, passing above the village, made out to sea in the direction of Le Havre, where they dropped their bombs all at the same time with a deafening, crashing roar.

It was as if the raiders, now that their attack was robbed of the element of surprise, were anxious to unload and disappear as quickly as possible. But the arrival of this second wave gave people the idea that these attacks might go on all through the night, and now the crowds on the beach were swollen by the arrival of others rushing from the villas higher up, who were determined to take refuge in the chalk caves of the cliffs, although the tide was rising.

Nobody slept because, without warning, the village was plunged right into the war, and the next morning, when the bell tolled for the funeral of Maurice Porquet, the deceased, who the previous evening had been on everybody's lips, was now, in spite of his coffin being in the church, entirely forgotten because of the tremendous happenings of the night.

In the middle of the service when the church was packed and the choristers were echoing the priest's mournful *de profundis*, every siren between Cabourg and Honfleur started to wail and then, above the deep strains of the organ, came the high-pitched zooming of numberless planes, and each person in the church looked furtively back at the closed door, hoping that he would be the first to reach it in an emergency.

At the end of the service the congregation hurried out into the sunshine, breathing more freely, each going his way.

Life seemed worth living after all, and the streets were as gay and crowded as ever on this perfect May morning. But round the corner came a procession of limousines from the rich villas.

Their owners no longer considered our village safe.

11

ONE afternoon I decided to take my son for an outing in the perambulator, and as I wondered where to go it struck me that Nénette might like to see the child, but when I reached the Roginsky farm I found the doors locked and nobody in the fields.

The house was just as enchanting as ever. It was indeed the sort of place that, as a girl, one imagines when reading the end to all good story books: "they lived happily ever after." The cows were grazing peacefully under the apple trees, a lazy dog stretched its legs in front of a sky-blue kennel, merely wagging its tail when I tried the doors and peered through the windows. Nénette had made a magnificent vegetable garden, which must have cost her months of hard work, and Duclos himself could not have planned it better. Not an inch of soil was wasted, not a weed to be seen.

When there was no longer any hope of finding Nénette, I decided to turn back, for it was an extremely hot day, and distant thunder could be heard, and as the road was bordered by high trees, mostly poplars and cherries, I wanted to be home before the storm burst.

I followed the main highway leading from Lisieux to Caen for a couple of hundred yards before turning into the road to St. Vaast. In spite of its broad, tarred surface, the traffic was normally slight at this time of year, but to my surprise I was continually having to run my perambulator against the bank because of big private cars speeding westward and clearing away all obstacles in front of them with long shrieks of their powerful hooters, and as they disappeared in a cloud of dust all that was visible were stacks of expensive luggage and a big "B" at the side of the number plate. Their owners were wealthy Belgians fleeing as far as possible from their unhappy land.

The storm broke half an hour after I arrived home. It was so severe that the first roses in the garden were dashed and the cows were so restless that the Goguette had difficulty in milking them.

When Helen came and heard about the expedition to the Roginsky farm, she said:

"You had no need to go so far. Mme. Nénette was with Mme. Castel all the afternoon, and the poor woman was in a terrible state. She cried all the time."

For the last few days, indeed, Nénette had spent the afternoons calling on her sisters, Madeleine Montague and Mme. Rossé, or looking in at the red brick house next door. On this particular afternoon she arrived at the Castels' immediately after lunch and, placing herself at the corner of the big table where, before her marriage, she always sat during meals, recalled how her father and mother used to sit at each end, with their large family and the servants gathered round them. The memory of these happy days so affected her that she collapsed, and in an effort to calm her Mme. Castel suggested she should stay the night.

"I can't," Nénette sobbed. "I've got Suzanne staying with me."

Suzanne was old Roginsky's daughter by his second marriage. She was twenty-one, and at the beginning of the war was engaged to a young farmer called Peter Levêque, whose family had once occupied our house.

The marriage had been fixed for the end of September, but Peter Levêque was called up at the mobilization and rushed to the Maginot Line. Suzanne was far too impatient to take her father's advice and wait till the end of the war, so when, toward Christmas, she discovered that by a new law she could marry at the front without the permission of her parents, she eloped to a convent at Bar-le-Duc, and the marriage took place there a few days later.

It was not the first time that M. Roginsky had been up against one of his children. Harried on all sides, Suzanne got a job behind the counter at a baker's shop in the village, for her husband's allowance was too small to live on, but her life was so dreary that when Nénette suggested she should come and sleep at her farm, Suzanne accepted.

That evening the two women, having put the baby to bed, talked interminably in the white kitchen after supper, but Nénette was shaken by the storm and Suzanne noticed with alarm that for the first time her companion was showing signs of hysteria, shouting, quarreling, and sulking without reason. This went on till the early hours of the morning.

"I tell you," cried Nénette, "I see them as clearly as anything —your husband, Riquet, and my two brothers. They're dead. All dead."

"Don't be so foolish," said Suzanne. "Riquet isn't even at the front, and Peter and Ernest have both been on leave during the last few weeks. It's two o'clock, and unless you go up to bed right away, I'll fetch my brother-in-law."

She was exhausted, and her head was aching violently, for she had worked all day, weighing and selling bread under the eyes of an irascible employer, and Nénette's behavior in this lonely house was exasperating.

"All right," agreed Nénette suddenly, "I'll go."

Toward five o'clock Suzanne, turning over in her bed, while still half asleep, heard Nénette coming back from the orchard, where she had been milking her cows. Then she heard Nénette kick off her clogs against the rail by the kitchen door and drop her churns on the tiles. A moment later she was off again to feed her chickens, calling them as she threw the corn over her shoulder.

"Thank goodness!" thought Suzanne, reassured by her stepsister's happy voice. "Nénette has become normal again."

She dozed off once more, only to be awakened half an hour later by the serving-maid, who rushed into her room crying:

"Come quickly. Madam has hanged herself in the cartshed!"

"Hanged herself?" echoed Suzanne, stunned by the news, and wondering if she wasn't dreaming. "What on earth are you talking about?"

She threw a dressing-gown over her shoulders and rushed out. Nénette was hanging dead from the rafters, swinging by the bull halter. She had mounted the covered cart, which she had pushed from under her feet.

Dressing hurriedly, hardly knowing what she was doing,

Suzanne sprang on her bicycle and rode to the village, where she went to fetch the doctor and warn the mayor. She then woke up Mlle. Lefranc, who drove her back to the farm, where they found Nénette's four-month-old baby awake in his cot smiling angelically.

"What shall we do with him?" asked Suzanne, distracted.

"We'll give him his bottle first," answered Mlle. Lefranc, "and then I'll drive you both round to your mother."

The news of Nénette's suicide ran through the village during the morning, and was voiced from farm to farm. Though telegrams were dispatched to Ernest and Peter Poulin, neither of the brothers received them, for by now the Belgian retreat was at its height. Riquet, by a miracle, was still at Blois, and he was given permission to return for the funeral, but meanwhile the Poulins made arrangements to relieve each other in the mournful task of sitting up with Nénette until the arrival of her husband.

Montague and Mme. Castel, who were not on speaking terms since Madeleine Montague had quarreled with Yvonne, kept vigil the first night. For a time these arch enemies faced each other in silence, for though they met in a common sorrow, they were not yet willing to call a truce, but shortly after dark the droning of the Nazi night raiders, distant at first, soon right over their heads, made the watchers look up nervously, for they knew too well what would follow. The enemy had arrived on schedule every night since the first terrifying attack a week before.

Thirty seconds later the house began to dance to the rhythm of sickening thuds.

"There they are, over Le Havre," muttered Mme. Castel.

"I suppose so," answered Montague.

"It's louder than ever tonight. Soon there'll be nothing left. They've already destroyed the big department store and the main café and part of the ocean dock. They say the enemy is attacking the city systematically zone by zone."

"Maybe."

"And then what will happen?" asked Mme. Castel, raising her voice in an effort to drown the distant thunder. "The traitor of Stuttgart says that when Le Havre is wiped out they will bombard Deauville, and afterward it will be our turn."

"Have you heard about all the people who left the village

today?" asked Montague. "A lot of our customers have closed their villas and have gone to Brittany. There are rumors this evening that the boys from St. Cyr are leaving."

"What worries me," said Mme. Castel, "is that I can't get any more corn, and you know how Castel feels about his hens, especially now we've got such a lot of chicks."

"One thing's certain, and that is that if this offensive lasts for long we can't count on military aid for bringing in the hay, and my farm-hand is joining up to-morrow."

"You have no right to complain," snapped Mme. Castel. "Yvonne and I are all alone on a forty-acre farm."

"Well, you wanted it, didn't you?"

"We wanted it?" rapped Mme. Castel angrily.

Her words wilted as the second wave of bombers came over their heads.

On the third day Riquet arrived after traveling for eighteen hours, and his father, who was on the platform to meet him, embraced his son with tears in his eyes.

"Is she worse?" asked the young soldier, who had not been told all the truth.

When he saw his father's distress he guessed that Nénette was no longer there, but he supposed, because of what people had been saying in the train, that she must have been machine-gunned while milking her cows. For some days past Nazi airmen had been amusing themselves by flying far from their bases and shooting at women working in the fields.

Riquet was now to learn the truth, but his father, knowing his son's sensibility, recoiled from his painful task. He waited until they were in the car on thir way to the farm and, staring at the road ahead, his hands clutching the driving-wheel, Roginsky broke the news as gently as possible, but he dared not look at Riquet's face, and was thankful that the noise of the engine partly drowned the low sobs of his boy.

"She couldn't live without you," Roginsky was saying. "You understand that, don't you?"

Riquet made no reply, but when he reached the house, with its green shutters and the garden which Nénette had made so beautiful, he ran into the room where his wife lay and, throwing himself beside her, asked:

"Oh, Nénette, why did you do that to me?"

Roginsky was unwilling for his son to remain for more than a few minutes, for Riquet had eaten nothing during the last twenty-four hours and the shock was enough to unbalance his mind.

He drove him home, where Riquet found Suzanne, one of the family again, holding his baby lovingly in her arms, and after lunch Roginsky told his son to go on foot to the various farms where Nénette had her friends and invite them personally to the funeral.

Riquet followed once more the route he had taken when announcing with a glowing heart the birth of his baby four months ago. That was the coldest day of the winter, and now, under this broiling sun, his heart was chilled.

When he reached our farm and saw the house so like his own, he fell back into an easy chair and for quite a moment said nothing, his eyes staring vacantly in front of him. He was dry of tears, and looked pitiable in his uniform, which was far too large for him, but after a time he brought out a number of photographs of Nénette, one of them showing her in her wedding dress, another, of which he said: "I don't like this one. It makes her nose too pointed," just as if he would find her in the orchard milking her cows when he got home.

As he spoke Renée and her young brother raced across the field beyond our garden, one of them shouting:

"I brought down the nest. There were three baby birds in it."

"There!" exclaimed Riquet sadly. "Did you hear what those kids were saying? Another home has been broken up."

He relaxed after a time, and even suggested a stroll in the garden.

"At least," I said softly, "you have the child. Nénette was very fond of him."

Riquet hesitated slightly, and said:

"If she had really loved her baby she wouldn't have left him."

He went down our field, past the cider press, to Déliquaire's, but his back was bent and he had the gait of an old man.

Riquet's grief was appalling, and everybody in the village felt the deepest sympathy for him, but many had now the impression of living in a nightmare.

The next morning the Goguette and I, enemies of yesterday, went together to Nénette's funeral.

"Well," said the Goguette, "life goes on. One Poulin disappears just as another is arriving."

"What do you mean?" I asked. "Who is expecting a baby now?"

"Madeleine Montague," answered the Goguette. "You'll be seeing her at the funeral this morning. They say it's for early July."

"Good gracious!" I exclaimed. "But if she's coming to the service, who will look after the little boy?"

"There's a terrible to-do about that," said the Goguette. "Mme. Castel offered to do so and Montague accepted, but when his wife got to know of it she was furious and sent the child to Mme. Pinson's house."

"Then the Montagues and the Castels are not going to make matters up after all?" I said. "How did Mme. Castel take the insult?"

"Badly," answered the Goguette. "She thought, after the wake, that everything was going to be all right again. Now, it's clear that in spite of Nénette's death, Madeleine Montague is to remain as bitter as ever."

The church was crowded when they arrived, because the funeral brought together the farmers and the villagers, for the Poulin-Roginsky interests were widespread. Nearly all the congregation followed the cortège up the long hill to the cemetery. Again the sun beat down fiercely from a cloudless sky.

Although the road was wide, the procession was continually being stopped by the flow of cars speeding westward, and now they were coming, not only from Belgium, but also from the eastern provinces. The invaders had crossed the bridges of the Meuse and the country was once more overrun. The realization of this tragedy spread consternation.

On my return to the village I did the shopping, for it was no longer possible to get anything delivered to the farm because of the absence of transport.

The main street was in effervescence, and though it was a so-called meatless day, the butchers had received instructions to open their doors in order to serve the refugees, but few of these remained long enough to partake of a meal. They grabbed sandwiches and loaves of bread while waiting for their cars to be filled with oil and gasoline, and if one asked them where they were going, they answered:

"Straight ahead—as far as it's possible to go."

Their eyes were bloodshot and terror had seized them altogether. It was not death alone they were fleeing from, but wholesale massacre.

I came up against Mme. Bayard outside the baker's shop.

"I've had a letter from Bayard," she said. "He's in Alsace."

She could hardly contain her joy as she pulled the letter out of her bag, adding:

"I feel ashamed of my happiness, for it looks as if Bayard, after being so unlucky, is having a break at last, for only a few weeks ago he was on the Belgian frontier, and now he's safe in the Maginot Line."

Old Porquet passed by as she spoke and, looking furtively round, slipped into the café to have a quick drink. A moment later a young woman with fair hair and blue eyes, wearing a gray costume and a claret-colored hat, brushed past on her way into the paper-shop.

"Who is that?" I asked. "I saw her at the funeral."

"Don't you know her?" asked Bayard. "She's Mme. France Marie, Mme. Pinson's daughter."

A crowd of refugees stood outside the garage waiting for their cars to be mended, for there had been many mishaps due to speeding under a weltering sun with loads far in excess of normal. Some had red crosses painted on the windows to show they carried an invalid or a member of the family who had been machine-gunned on the road, and those who had died on the journey were carried along in the flight to save the bodies being trampled by the advancing enemy.

The next morning we heard that the entire stock of Nénette's farm had been bought by a dealer from Dozulé, for it was not practical to hold one of those auctions presided over by the notary which lasted all day and to which people drove from miles around—the doctor's wife to show off a new hat and choose a plump chicken, the owner of some villa to bid for a copper warming-pan which he would take back home to decorate his drawing-room. A month ago our neighbors would have seized the opportunity to buy Nénette's cows, for they all knew what excellent animals they were and how well she kept them, but now the farmers, seeing how many people were leaving the village, were showing great caution. Nénette's relations had other reasons also for not wishing to add to their herds. The Montagues had insufficient land to buy more cows and the Castels, who had too much land, had insufficient money.

Goguet might have bought an animal to replace one that was getting old, but he decided to wait.

Meanwhile he would take his butter to Dozulé himself that morning, leaving his wife to look after the farm, so, taking the carefully prepared basket, he slung it across the handlebars of his bicycle and set off early.

He found to his surprise that, instead of the busy street market, with the farmers' covered carts tied up along the pavements, the town was filled with military trucks and refugees. The prices on the butter market had slumped so much that he could not decide to sell, for it was the first time in his life that he saw this basic commodity slip away from the gold standard. There were buyers at six cents a pound and not very keen ones at that.

The farmers considered themselves insulted and would have preferred to give it away, but Le Havre was burning and the railroad track to Paris cut, and in this torrid heat it was impossible to prevent the butter from melting.

Goguet decided to bring his basket back, but in the marketplace he met his sister-in-law, the wife of Adrien, the binder. She was without news of her husband and had just lost four cows lacerated by a bomb which an enemy airman had dropped in her orchard.

Refugees were pouring into the town, and not all of them had traveled by car. There was a Belgian peasant woman who arrived in a covered wagon, American style, drawn by two farm horses. The outfit had been shelled and machine-gunned during the first 100 miles of the journey, the woman driving like mad with her nine children through burning towns and roads encumbered by war material.

Seven out of her nine youngsters had been killed on the way, and each time she had halted only long enough to lay the little victim on the roadside and make a sign of the cross.

Goguet returned to the farm late in the afternoon, and his sound peasant mind was trying to assess the things he had seen and heard. The previous day he had lost a good gardening job at a nearby villa because the owners had fled, a job that was worth two dollars a day, and now he was faced with the fact that butter was virtually unsalable.

It was his custom to come as far as our garden after supper and to chat with his arms resting against the top of the fence. The sun was so hot during the day that the cool of the evening was a welcome relief, but these neighborly talks were prompted not so much by this as by a desire for companionship during the time that preceded the nine o'clock bombardment of Le Havre.

Nobody could settle down, let alone sleep, before the enemy arrived.

I was watering the garden as Goguet came along.

"I saw some English soldiers at Dozulé," said Goguet, filling his pipe. "Funny uniforms they wore. Like mechanics' overalls, if you understand what I mean, but in khaki. No, I've got it. They're just like those ski suits the young people from the villas wore during the snow this winter."

"That is battle dress," I said.

"It's decidedly practical," said Goguet. "Our boys were envious, for they hated their puttees."

The next morning we learned that Roginsky had let Nénette's farm to some people from Deauville who could no longer stand the bombardment. Riquet had gone back to his regiment, and there was a demand for accommodation inland, for there was a general belief that the raids would follow along the coast after Le Havre was destroyed, and already the picturesque old town of Honfleur had been bombarded from the air. Deauville's huge military hospitals were being rapidly evacuated, and we were next on the list.

Victor Duprez had been called up urgently and had left for Rouen, whence he was to be sent straight into battle, and his wife had fixed up accomodation for a dozen friends from Le Havre in her big house, work on which had come to an abrupt stop. Her guests slept on mattresses in the drawing-room, and their cars were parked in the drive waiting to take them farther away at a moment's notice if the situation became critical.

Meanwhile the news spread that Mme. France Marie had become the first war widow in our village. On her return home after attending Nénette's funeral she found a letter from her husband written in a hospital train while passing through Nancy.

It will be remembered that he was engaged in leading expeditions into no man's land beyond the Maginot Line, and on one of these three of his men were killed, and he himself was left seriously wounded on the outskirts of a wood.

The Germans took all their uniforms in order to equip their parachute troops, and France Marie was found absolutely naked.

"I ought to count myself lucky," he added, "because the war is finished as far as I am concerned, although you'll never see me walking on two legs again, but I expect I shall get a good pension from the police force, and they'll certainly find me a soft job somewhere where we can live in comfort and bring up our child."

A couple of hours after she had received this letter, the telegraph boy called at her house with a notification from the War Department that her husband had died at the military hospital at Rennes. The unfortunate woman was feeding her five-week-old baby, so that, accompanied by Mme. Pinson, she had to take him on the long journey into the heart of Brittany.

The young wives in the village were dismayed because, for the first time, they faced the tragic consequences of war. Yvonne was especially depressed, for she had received no news of Ernest since his return to the front, and when the postwoman came to our farm she made a long detour so as not to pass in front of the red brick house where Yvonne was waiting, and where she would be obliged to say:

"There is still nothing, madam."

The Castels' farm was now terribly forlorn. Louise Rossé came to spend each night with her sister-in-law, but the news she brought from the village added to their pessimism and, though she had received a letter from her husband at the front, it was so strange and incoherent that she was convinced he had lost his reason. Mme. Castel was giving hospitality to an aged relative from Le Havre. He was eighty-five, and had twice been evacuated from his native city since the Franco-Prussian war of 1870, and he now spent the long days dressed in an alpaca coat sitting thoughtfully under an apple tree.

Montague was lucky enough to be discharged a second time by the army medical board, but he was put at the disposal of the Home Guard, and told to form a corps of anti-parachutists. The need was obvious, for parachutists were flopping down at night all over the countryside, and every day one heard of fresh damage which they were supposed to have done. A time bomb was placed on the main railroad track running into Caen, and three Nazis who were caught limping near by were taken to hospital.

Montague came down our field one evening wearing brand-new leather leggings and his gun was slung across his shoulder. He had never looked so smart or so martial. Goguet, who had not been able to find any work on neighboring farms since the bombardment of Le Havre, decided to look after his own, and he was sharpening his scythe under a pear tree in front of our garden before starting to cut his hay in the Burgundy next morning.

"Good evening," Montague called out. "We didn't see you on parade before lunch."

Goguet hung his scythe over a fork in the tree to give him plenty of time to think up an answer, and queried:

"What parade?"

"The anti-parachutist corps," answered Montague.

"How was I to know there was a parade?"

"Didn't they tell you?" asked Montague.

Goguet put both hands to his heart and declared:

"The best proof is that I wasn't there."

After the preliminary fencing, Montague continued:

"We're all in it, you know. Peter Gravé has been guarding the railway station and Deaf Joseph is on the bridge over the main road, and Old Porquet's standing in front of the casino in case any of them try and land on the beach. You must come with your gun."

"I don't mind bringing my gun," said Goguet suspiciously, "but I've got no cartridges."

He was already afraid that it would cost him something.

"The Government's providing the cartridges," said Montague, "and we may even get paid."

"That's different," said Goguet. "Who else is in it?"

The proposition was beginning to appeal to him, especially when he heard the name of Peter Gravé.

"There's Déliquaire," said Montague. "He's come back so ill that they're going to discharge him from the army." Lowering his voice, he added: "We're not asking Groscol. They reckon he's not the sort of man you can rely on."

"All right," said Goguet. "I'm with you. Tomorrow you'll find me at the Burgundy."

12

MY HUSBAND was in London in early June and was not intending to go back to France for several weeks, but when the German army broke through Holland and Belgium, sweeping across northern France, he became alarmed, and applied for an exit permit.

The channel steamer, the last to make the journey, took three days to reach St. Malo. From here he had an adventurous trip by motor bus to Fougères, where he prevailed on a French soldier who had been repatriated after the evacuation of Dunkirk to drive him to Villers.

Five minutes after leaving Caen my husband started to shiver. All the afternoon they had driven under a boiling sun, and now, without warning, they encountered intense cold. The transition was so great that they knew it could not be natural, and the most curious thing about it was that, though there were no clouds, the sun was not visible any longer, and the sky, instead of being a deep blue, was a nondescript gray.

As they went forward and passed from the plains to the orchards and valleys of Norman Switzerland, it was as if all life had stopped in the fields. The cows were lying huddled together under the trees, the hens had gone to bed, the geese to their coops, and the birds, which had ceased to sing, skirted the tops of the hedges.

But now my husband recognized every turn in the road, every field, every property, and felt a tremendous exhilaration. He ran to the gate of our farm at the very moment when my mother and I were coming up the field with the baby between us.

The sky had cleared by now, and the sun came out as if nothing had happened. It bathed the thatched roof over Goguet's house, and I had never seen our farm look so lovely. The grass was a perfect green. The Italian poplars stretched their arms to heaven and the air smelt of newly mown hay. The Goguette was milking her cows by the cider press, and the garden was a mass of roses. Everything looked so prosperous, so utterly peaceful, that I hated the idea of talking war, and I suddenly felt convinced that we should hear on the radio that the enemy had been repulsed. My son had grown bigger, fatter, and more playful during my husband's absence. His two perambulators and his toys stood in the garden path between the big cherry tree and the strawberry beds. He had a new contrivance on wheels in which he could stand up and push himself along without fear of falling over.

I had ordered a rabbit hutch, which now stood at the back of the house between the red currant bushes and the pile of logs we had cut down together in the big wood. As soon as the rabbits heard us coming they put their noses up against the netting asking for lettuce leaves. I had dug a strip all round our orchard which I had planted with potatoes as a war measure. Goguet came along. He was delighted because we had given him permission to keep a heifer in our orchard, but I took him to task because there were no corsets round the new fruit trees and said that if he wanted to have the heifer there, he must at least put down stakes. This detail worried me, and I made him promise to see to it in the morning.

"What are we going to have for supper?" my husband asked me. "I've had nothing to eat all day."

"Neither have we," I answered. "And at lunch time it was dark as night."

"So something was wrong?" he queried. "We ran into a patch of ice-cold weather just after Caen."

"I'm not surprised," I answered. "Come as far as the Point and I think I can show you the reason."

We walked up the field and, crossing the lane, clambered to the top of the promontory, where the marguerites were growing a couple of feet high. The Goguette had obviously not put her cows here lately, or perhaps our farmers were keeping it for hay. The plateau was one of the highest on our estate and, looking right over the tops of our buildings snugly ensconced in the hollow of the field at our feet, we had a wonderful view across the bay, beyond the estuary of the Seine.

From a point due east as far as the eye could see, rose a huge column of smoke belching skyward like a volcano in eruption.

"That smoke is coming from the huge refineries at Port Jérôme," I said. "The biggest gasoline storage tanks in France. Our troops set fire to them at dawn so that they would not fall into enemy hands. We only saw the sun at five o'clock this evening."

As the crow flies, Port Jérôme was some fifteen miles from where we stood. Boats plying upstream to Rouen picked up their river pilots there because the Seine is particularly treacherous at this point, and there was a ferry. We used to take it when the one at Berville, nearer Le Havre, was out of order. Millions of gallons went up in flames on this historic Sunday, and later we learned that the smoke had spread as far as Paris. I turned away from this picture with a feeling of sickness, but I kept on fighting to hide realities, and these hours were a terrifying mixture of joy and consternation.

"Come on," my husband shouted, to dispel the horror we had just witnessed, "take me to the wood. It does me good to make contact with your land again."

We went as far as Groscol's house and, crossing the Little Valley, arrived at the big orchard. Shrove Tuesday and Matinale, heifers of the two cows that Goguet and I had bought two winters ago, were grazing between the ferns and the end of the wood. They were at the angry age, and had become terribly wild, and they started to chase us so that we had to hold them back with a stout stick.

We came home by way of the Burgundy, not to be late for the supper which my mother was making. We had it in front of the Aga in the kitchen.

"How wonderful to receive your telegram!" I exclaimed. "We had almost decided to take the baby and join the stream of refugees trekking west."

"Thank God you did not!" said my husband. "It would have been the end of us all."

As we were finishing our meal we heard airplanes overhead.

They flew in circles over the farm for a full minute and then made off in the direction of Le Havre.

"Friends or foes?" queried my husband.

I laughed.

"We're getting used to them," I said. "They come at all hours now—day and night. Listen!"

The house shook as the first stick of bombs fell over Le Havre.

"Do you want to go up to the Point again?" I asked. "If they are bombing Le Havre we would do better to cross the stream by the cider press and climb up to the top of Sandret's orchard."

We had no need to hurry, for the enemy was taking things in the most leisurely fashion, returning again and again to the target area to watch the effect of the bombs.

The sun was still warm, although the day was drawing to its close. The raiders passed like streaks of silver, low over the green orchards and the blue sea, dipping over the noble city to release their bombs. All the coast we knew so well and loved so much was breaking out into sheets of flame and billowing clouds of smoke—the ocean dock where so often we had watched the giant *Normandie* gliding in from the horizon as we lay on the grass chewing a daisy; the graceful houses built by Louis XV; all the wide streets and colorful market-places where I had gone so often to buy dress materials or knitting wool.

As the flames spread we heard the most sinister noise of all, the crackling of burning timber, followed by the distant crashing of masonry. Soon dozens of little fires spread to merge into one great inferno, which sent up huge clouds rolling along the estuary to meet the black smoke from Port Jérôme.

The work went on relentlessly, methodically, and when the raiders had dropped their bombs they swooped to within a few feet of the ferry at Berville, and it seemed to us that they were machine-gunning the people trying to cross to our side of the Seine.

Five minutes later the sky was clear of planes. They had gone as suddenly as they had come, but the coast from Le Havre to the medieval jewel that is Honfleur, beloved by painters and poets, was writhing in agony.

Too moved to speak, we went along the road to St. Vaast, opposite Déliquaire's farm. A woman was trudging up the hill

with a young child asleep in her arms. She asked us the way to
the Maison Verte. It was just before one came to Mme. Paul's
old house, where the ex-service man now lived.

"You'll know the Maison Verte," I said, "because it's painted
green and there are red and white curtains in the windows. It's
a real doll's house."

She thanked us, and was passing wearily on when I called
after her:

"By the way, where do you come from?"

She turned round and answered:

"Rouen. The Germans are in the town."

The news was devastating. It meant that the enemy had not
only broken through the defences of the Somme and the Bray,
but had crossed the Seine and were within a few miles of us.
They might arrive at any moment, cutting off our retreat.
Bombs are nothing compared to the terror of an advancing
army.

"Did you see them?" I insisted.

"They machine-gunned my shop," she answered. "I owned a
pastry-cook's."

"Tell me more," I asked. "It's announced on the radio this
evening that the advance is checked."

"That's what we thought," she answered. "The Germans
were supposed to be at Amiens, seventy miles east, with our
best regiments barring the way behind two strong lines of de-
fence. Then, at ten o'clock this morning, as we were going to
mass, two tanks came down the cathedral street. We took no
notice of them, except to make some remark like: "Wait till
the Jerries see those fellows.""

"Then the tanks we thought our own opened fire and swept
the pavements, choosing the top of the rue de la Grosse Horloge
where it meets the cathedral parvis, the most crowded spot in
the town."

"You don't think we repulsed them? Isn't there a chance of
that?"

"As the first tank drove across to the south side," she continued, ignoring my anxious questions, "our engineers blew up
all the bridges—the one opposite the big café which sent the
enemy, imprisoned in fifty tons of steel, plunging into the river,
the Corneille Bridge, and the gigantic transporting bridge that

crashed into the water on top of a ferry-boat carrying two hundred people. It was hell let loose. Our guns opened fire from the south side of the river, bombarding our own cathedral, though the enemy had only sent those two tanks."

"We must have repulsed them," I said.

"They're everywhere," said the woman. "They've taken Pont de l'Arche this afternoon. The country is overrun with them. Everything is on fire."

She turned to climb up the hill and, nodding farewell as she clutched her sleeping child, we saw her go off, weary and broken-hearted.

We walked quickly back to the farm. The sun had set, and it was getting dark.

"Do you realize," my husband asked, "that Rouen is only fifty miles away? A motorized column could surprise us during the night."

"Meaning that we should leave this evening?" I queried.

"Yes, but how? What a fool I was to have let my driver go. He could have taken us back to Fougères."

"If you feel that way about it," I said, "let's go down to the village and see if we can get a car."

"It might be a good idea," he answered.

We looked in at the house to tell my mother what we had heard and then set off briskly in search of transport. We both knew only too well what would happen if we left things to the last moment. The baby might get crushed or machine-gunned. The first thing to do was to try and wake the garage proprietor's wife, but though we rang her bell and knocked at her window, she refused to answer.

A car was standing by the curb at the back of Roginsky's house, and when we came level to it we found Mlle. Lefranc piling up suit-cases. Her good humor was so infectious that we were soon laughing in spite of the tragedy that had brought us into the village so late. We told her what we were doing, and she said:

"I'm stacking up just in case."

"Where will you go?"

"I'm not sure," she answered. "Either to Lion-sur-Mer, just above Caen, or to St. Nazaire, where my brother-in-law designs submarines."

She began telling us how her little cottage at Lion had cost her only $100 because when it was put up for auction there were but two bidders.

"What worries me," I said, "is how I am going to get the child away without a car. I suppose you haven't time to drive us as far as Caen tonight?"

"Impossible!" she answered. "I'd be gone already if it wasn't that Madeleine Montague is expecting her baby at any moment. I don't want to leave her in the lurch."

Madeleine Montague! I had forgotten all about our neighbors in the turmoil of the last few hours. At least my family had the good fortune to be reunited, but Yvonne Poulin was still without news of her husband; poor Riquet had been sent off to the front and there was every likelihood that Peter Poulin had perished in Belgium.

"What's happened to Nénette's baby?" I asked. "Is he still with Mme. Roginsky?"

"No," said Mlle. Lefranc, "that's the tragedy of it. Mme. Montague has taken him. Soon she will have three infants to look after in that tiny house."

"Well," I put in, "we must find some way of pushing farther west for a few days. There's a saying in this war that if you don't want to be caught unawares you must put a good sixty miles between yourself and the enemy."

"Try the tailor's next to Mme. Rossé's shop," suggested Mlle. Lefranc. "They're always hard up, and as they own a car they might be willing to help."

It was less than a hundred yards away, at the corner of the street that led to the church. We went there accompanied by the midwife, and threw stones at several of the windows to wake the family, but there was no answer.

The church clock struck ten, and we were obviously wasting our time. The local wardens were patrolling the streets shouting at anybody who was showing the merest suspicion of a light. They made a great deal of noise and appeared very full of their importance.

We bade good night to Mlle. Lefranc and set off home, taking the steep path that led to the roundabout above the villas.

At the top of the hill we were challenged by a couple of sentries, who told us we ought to be in bed at this hour.

"What is the trouble?" my husband asked.

They led us to a field, whence we could see across the bay. Le Havre was in flames from end to end.

"The night raid has started," they said. "You had better be off in case they start dropping their bombs here."

We quickened our steps, thinking of the house, which by now was doubtless rocking, and our baby asleep in the bedroom. We knew that we should have to leave our beloved home in the morning.

The bottom had fallen out of my dream farm.

13

WE WOKE up to another of those mornings during this memorable June when a heat haze covered the countryside. Before breakfast the sun was already drawing off the light moisture from the ground and the dewdrops from the rose petals in our garden. I helped my mother make the bed and tidy my room, for I was determined that our house should be trim when we left it. I even dusted the furniture, straightened the pictures, and carefully arranged all those little treasures with which a woman fills her home. Then I went out into the garden and cut the most beautiful roses to decorate the low room, but I allowed the Aga to burn out.

Soon after eight my husband and I went down to the village again. We called at the bank, where I had opened an account, and were fortunate in being able to draw out quite a considerable sum of money. Then we crossed the road to buy a morning paper, and found Leleu on his doorstep. He looked terribly haggard and said that he had not slept all night trying to calm his wife, who was in despair. Their Viking son had been in the big retreat from Boulogne to the Somme, and then through the nightmare of St. Valéry-en-Caux, fighting his way back from there to Rouen. Leleu brought out a letter from his pocket, which he must have read a hundred times, and showed us this passage:

"Do you remember, father, how you used to tell mother and me about the horrors of Verdun? They sounded so appalling that I never quite believed you. It would have been so easy to exaggerate with the passing of time. But if I wrote now of the things I have seen, it is you who would call me a liar. The

enemy are savages and the road from Boulogne is strewn with
the hands and feet of tiny children."

But Leleu had an argument that instilled hope in his breast.

"Our villagers are unwise to leave," he said. "The Germans
will not be so stupid as to waste their time pushing on to Paris
to drink champagne. They will start an invasion of England
immediately, while they have everything in their favor."

In the market-place we found Mme. Groscol watching the
cars preparing to leave. Her eyes were filled with tears and she
seemed lost. Her plan was not to flee until the enemy was actually in sight and then, with her husband and her five children,
to take to the road on foot blindly.

The notary was standing outside the mayor's parlor. The
fears he had always entertained were now proving true, and in
his case there were no broken illusions, but only the fulfillment
of a tragedy he had seen clearly from the beginning. During the
last ten days his wife spent long hours praying in the church,
for she was a devout Catholic. Their second son was on the
eve of being called up, for he was seventeen. Perhaps the speed
of the retreat would save him at the last moment. I tried to tell
the notary that our army was being reorganized after Dunkirk
and was already returning to France, but he was not impressed.

He had never put much faith in British aid and had frankly
said so.

We went back to the garage with no real hope of finding a
car. That proved to be the case, but Mme. Bayard, who worked
for the proprietor's wife in the morning and for us in the afternoon, was there. She put her head out of the window.

"I thought you would be going," she said. "But what am I to
do? How will Bayard find me again if I disappear, and what's
to happen to my dog? I can't let the poor animal starve."

I think it hurt us more to leave Mme. Bayard than any one
else in the village. We kissed her affectionately on both cheeks,
and neither of us dared turn round to take a last look at her
misery. I insisted that if there was really no car to be found we
should put the baby in the perambulator and do like Mme.
Groscol, escape on foot. Then I thought of Dauvilaire, who had
always had a soft corner in his heart for us. It was not entirely
because we had been good customers, but his partner, Mathieu,
had a son, too young to be in the army, though physically a

giant, who had spent many years in England and loved our country. Father and son were in the shop when we arrived.

"Where do you want to go?" asked Mathieu, when I told him about our troubles.

"I don't know," I answered, "but anywhere west of Caen. That would give us time to make other plans."

"My son Giles is at a loose end until we go away ourselves this evening," he answered. "I'll have him get his car right away. He'll be delighted."

"Of course I would," said Giles Mathieu. "Dauvilaire has gone away with the truck, but we still have the Sedan. It shakes a little, but I don't suppose you will mind that."

One would never have guessed how generous the offer was from the offhand way in which it was made.

On the doorstep we met the doctor, with his dog, Fellow.

"Well," I said, "I suppose I'd better say good-by. I'd like you to know how grateful we are to you, doctor. Our little boy owes his life to you."

His kindly eyes had a look of infinite sadness, and he seemed grayer and older than when I had last seen him. He asked me where I was going, and when I told him that I had no plans, he tore a sheet of paper from his note-book and wrote down for us the name of a property he owned near Granville.

"There's nothing much there," he said, "but my friends will make you welcome."

This place was three-quarters of the way to St. Malo, where, if things really became critical, we hoped to find a ship to take us back to England, so I accepted gratefully. The only point was whether Giles Mathieu would be willing to take us so far. But we looked it up on the map, and he appeared satisfied he could just make the return journey in the day. The doctor said he would remain in the village until the end. He had sent his wife and daughter to relations at St. Brieuc, since when Fellow had been wandering disconsolately in the village looking for them.

My mother had everything ready for our departure and our baby was washed and dressed for the long journey. Mathieu came into the kitchen to have a glass of cider, and we took both perambulators, the big one and the little one, which we fixed securely to the luggage grid with stout ropes. Once we had packed the baby linen and the feeding-bottles, together with a supply of Nestlé's, we took a last look round the house. The bedroom was bathed in sunshine, and I opened my wardrobes, filled with my dresses, my furs and hats, and looked at them with tears in my eyes. My linen cupboard, scented with lavender from my garden, was my pride. The books I had taken a lifetime to collect glittered in their leather bindings, my baby's cot was all ready for him to sleep in.

I kissed the pillow in the cot when nobody was looking, and I steeled my nerves, driving my nails into the flesh of my hands. I knew there must be no choosing of this or that to take away. The sacrifice must be complete or it might cost us our lives. Leaving the bedroom where my son was born, roughly chiding my mother for keeping us waiting, I hurried downstairs and looked at the big fireplace, which seemed to beckon me. It had been here since 1555. Would I ever see it again? I opened a drawer and found a box of chocolates I had bought at the shop at Le Havre which must, by now, be a tangled mass of ruins. In the kitchen the Aga shone splendidly and was still warm.

I put up the shutters and locked the doors. The table was laid for lunch. All our hoards of sugar, all our hard-earned reserves of coal, which I had pushed in the garden wheelbarrow from the gate, would not be for me. The garden was a dream. It was a garden in June, a garden that was ours, that we had made from the time it was grass that the cattle grazed on. There were the logs of the poplar my husband and I had cut down. We had been saving them.

The Goguette was leaning over the little white fence of her garden. I kissed her and took young Robert Goguet up in my arms and kissed him also. But Renée stood at a distance, fearing to say good-by. She had enough pride to remember how she had stoned us. I took Goguet's outstretched hand.

"I'll be back soon, but it's safer to get the baby away."

We neither of us realized the terrible drama that would take place on this farm during the next five years.

"Don't forget to put those corsets round the apple trees," I said.

We walked up to the gate where the car was waiting, and I took a last look at my apple trees and my Italian poplars. It is terrible to be attached so much to a piece of land. It hurts to love. The sea was the blue of a picture postcard. What could be so wrong on a day like this?

We called at the Castels', to say good-by. They were planning to leave in their pony-cart the same evening for Formentin, where they would pick up M. Castel. Yvonne was broken-hearted, for she had an idea that she was not doing the right thing by Ernest in leaving his farm. The women had problems that surpassed those of the men just now, and if they wanted to save their lives it meant sacrificing those of the cows, which would perish unless a neighbor had time to milk them. But there was no news of Ernest. He was somewhere in Belgium, perhaps killed by the enemy or sent into Germany as a prisoner. We waved a farewell and turned down the lane that led to Berthelot's café, where we joined the road to Caen, passing the pylon where Maurice Porquet had killed himself.

We were now refugees, like the rest on this crowded road. The preambulators at the back and the bags of baby linen were all the possessions we had saved from our home. But this drive soon gave us the impression of a holiday. It was the first time that I had left our village for the last fourteen months, and our son appeared to be enjoying himself enormously. He chattered incessantly in a language that none of us could understand, but he pointed with delight at everything that surprised him, refusing to sleep a moment. The morning haze was followed, as we guessed, by a day of burning heat, but with the windows open we kept reasonably cool.

We lunched at Villers-Bocage, fifteen miles beyond Caen, a little village with the houses spread on either side like soldiers, and three hotel-restaurants at a crossing. Two of these were full; the third being more expensive had a corner to spare beside a large open window decorated with geraniums on the sill. It was one of those inns famed for its cooking, with three stars in the guide, a dining-room with dark paneled walls and a kitchen where all the pans were of shining red copper. Our son had never fed outside the house of his birth, and he chuckled with joy. We all had a great appetite, and I was anxious that Giles Mathieu should not be disappointed in our hospitality. While we were having coffee a woman passed in the street holding a baby by the shoulders, trying to make him walk. She came right under our window.

"What's his age?" I asked.

"A year."

"Then he's only a few days older than mine. Where do you come from?"

"Le Havre."

She was the typical factory hand, intelligent, but thoroughly Popular Front. One could picture her accompanying her husband to the local Communist meeting.

"How are you traveling?" I asked.

"In the gasoline truck over there," she said, jerking her thumb in the direction of a Standard Oil tank.

"I hope it's full," I said.

"You bet it is," she said. "We have orders to go anywhere, provided it's a long way from Le Havre. I guess we'll be making for Rennes."

She told us that her husband was driving back from Rouen when he caught sight of motor-cyclist infiltrations in the forest of Bourgtheroulde. He jumped down and ran in among the trees to hide from the enemy, but when he returned his gasoline truck had disappeared. It was already on its way to the German lines.

"He had to walk back to Le Havre," she said. "And at the depot each driver was given a truck full of gas and told to clear off."

"How did you cross the Seine?" I asked.

"On the auto-ferry at Berville," she answered. "And we're lucky to be here. A German plane swooped down and machine-gunned us. You know the ferry, don't you? They put the cars on the top deck and the people down below. It was crowded to suffocation and we stayed in the truck, but a coach full of people next to us was so riddled with bullets that not a single person escaped unwounded. The planes circled round while our skipper fought against the current—it's terrible just there—and each time we tried to land on the other side we got more lead pumped into us. Our truck wasn't holed, otherwise we'd have poured gas all over the place and set the ship on fire."

"When did this happen?" I asked.

"About eight o'clock last night," she said.

"That's what we saw while they were bombing Le Havre!" I exclaimed.

"Oh, you can't guess what it was like," she went on. "You

remember how flat the eastern bank is and how Schneider's used it for gun practice before the war? Thousands of people fled from Le Havre yesterday, and when they saw that there was no room for them on the ferry they dumped their cars on the grass and tried to swim across. It was a risk worth taking, because if they had driven on they would have come to Rouen, which is in German hands."

She went to the truck to join her husband, and a few minutes later we also left.

The route was picturesque, and the farther we drew away from the Germans the more enjoyable it seemed. Once or twice we came across columns of British mechanized troops, probably coming down from Cherbourg. Their short, powerful trucks, decorated with fishing nets in which leafy branches were placed for camouflage, delighted the French, who stared at them with interest. Then we might drive for half an hour without meeting a soul, but by four o'clock we were only a few miles from our destination.

The doctor's map was now to come in useful, and we followed his instructions carefully, continuing along the main road until we reached a bridge, and then turning into a lane until we came to another.

Here we were challenged by two anti-parachutists, so drunk that for a moment I feared they were going to shoot us. We gave them the name of the farm and all that we knew about it, but though it was clearly only a few hundred yards distant, the leader insisted it did not exist. He shouldered his gun, and we were obliged to humor him before he allowed us to pass.

A few moments later we found ourselves in front of a porch leading into the courtyard of a grange. Mathieu parked his car at the bend of the road and I went through to investigate.

A priest was sitting in a wicker chair making notes at a small green table under an oak-tree. I asked him if this was the doctor's property, and I showed him the card he had given us by way of introduction.

"I'm very pleased to meet you," he said, "especially as you come from our village, for we are without news of it for the last five days."

As he was speaking a woman came out of the house, and seeing Mathieu standing in front of the car, went over to welcome him. She also was from our village and was staying here with her daughter Ginette. Her name was Mme. Minary.

We unloaded the car and said good-by to Mathieu who was in a hurry to get back, for the journey had taken him longer than he expected, and his own family was leaving the village that night.

The house was a three-storied stone building with gables, and a mass of ivy growing up one side. The doctor had warned us that we should have to make the best of things, but we had not expected to find a place so completely bare. There were big rambling rooms with no furniture at all, not a table nor a chair, only vast fire-places filled with cobwebs. Mme. Minary showed us over, keeping up a low, plaintive monotone which was as depressing as the empty house.

She told us that the place was used as a vacation center each summer for seminarists, and that in the attic we should find a collection of utensils and bedding from which we could make our choice. Ginette would help us draw some water from the well, and when we had put a camp-bed and a basin in one of the empty rooms on the first floor, we would find her in the kitchen.

The unfortunate woman was in a state of profound despair, and had no longer any power of counter-action. She was a widow of the last war and had two sons, one of whom was already a prisoner in enemy hands, the other unheard of since he was drafted to the Belgian front.

A broken axle imprisoned these three people in this comfortless house where, except for a wireless set, they were without news of the outside world. Their original intention was to spend only a few days away from the bombing of Le Havre, but their car broke down at Villedieu, and the garage where they left it was still waiting for the spare parts to arrive from Paris. It now looked as if they might wait for ever. The news we could give them was far from encouraging. They knew nothing of the rapid German advance or of the capture of Rouen, which was carefully hidden by the radio.

Ginette came along and offered to take us to the attic to make our choice of equipment for the night, and we were not sorry to exchange guides, for Ginette had the quality of youth to compensate for her melancholy.

She was dark, lively, and attractive, but her devotion to her mother had doubtless wrecked any chance of an early marriage, for she was unwilling to leave her. We learned from her that the priest was a hero of the last war, in which he was so gravely wounded that his chest was encased in metal. Ginette's father died in his arms during the battle of Verdun, commending his family into the priest's care, and the promise made at that time had been faithfully observed.

The attic provided an astounding collection of bedding and crockery, all in the last stages of decay. The blankets were damp, the camp-beds sagged, and the crockery was chipped. We fixed up one bed in the largest of the empty rooms for my mother and placed the baby's perambulator beside it. We put another bed for ourselves in the passage.

"Now, I'll show you the kitchen," said Ginette.

She led us right across the house into a large raftered room with a huge fire-place and a long table on trestles under the window.

Mme. Minary stood in front of the fire with a pair of bellows, vainly trying to fan a blaze. The doctor's stack of dry logs had been spirited away by his farmers, and, although the country-side was well wooded, it was impossible to find anything in the courtyard but a few faggots.

There was a stove but no coal.

It was not only the lack of fire that worried the doctor's guests, but it was almost impossible to obtain provisions in this isolated corner of the country. Anxious to pay our share of the evening meal, we suggested we should go in search of something if they would tell us the way to the nearest store. They said they were going themselves, but would be happy if we went with them.

The priest stayed in the garden. Armed with binoculars, he made frantic efforts to determine the nationality of each air-plane that passed overhead, and he was full of theories about the noise of their engines and the toy balloons enemy airmen were said to release above their targets before dropping their bombs—a myth that spread all over France.

The hamlet we were bound for was about a mile away. The countryside was green and marshy, and the hedges were covered in honeysuckle. There were not many apple trees and the pasture land looked far from rich, for whole fields were half under water, and in these grew thousands of multicolored irises of the most flamboyant colors.

There were only two small stores to choose from and neither had anything to sell. The best we could find was a packet of dried Swiss cheese, but on our way back we called at the farm which the doctor owned, and I found a dozen eggs. The farmer and his three stalwart sons had been passed over by the war. The first was too old and the boys too young.

Mme. Minary boiled the eggs over the faggots, and served dinner at the trestle table. It was not a gay meal, and at 7:30 Ginette placed a portable radio on a chair by the window so that we could hear the news. A few farmers wandered in and sat down beside us, but nobody spoke much. We waited in a frozen fear for the reading of the communiqué. Mme. Minary wiped her tears, thinking of her sons, the priest stared at the empty egg-shell on his plate, and the peasants, cap in hand, kept their eyes glued to their boots.

It was Prime Minister Reynaud who told us of the latest catastrophe. Italy, believing the Germans to have won, was to enter the war at midnight. The damp faggots spluttered in the big fire-place and the last comforting flames died down.

The dispirited voice went on without a word of comfort, and though, from time to time, the drone of an airplane could be heard, presumably on its way to Cherbourg, the priest no longer troubled to take up his binoculars.

Ginette was thinking of her car, and announced she would go to Villedieu in the morning to see if there was a way of hastening the repairs, for their situation might become complicated if the enemy continued his advance and they were stranded. The only train to Villedieu left at 5 A.M. from a station three miles distant, but she could borrow a bicycle from the farmer's wife and pick it up when she came home on the midday train.

My husband and I took a short walk before turning in. The holiday spirit had left us. We saw how impossible it was to remain with a baby in this bleak spot, and the gloomy faces of our fellow guests were sapping our morale.

We groped our way to bed with a candle, to find bats in the rafters and rats on the floor. The sheets were so damp that I lay on the bed in my blouse and skirt, and by morning the news had become so alarming that I was determined to find a car, believing that we would be safer at St. Malo. The farmer from whom I had bought the eggs told me that a miller, a hundred yards down the lane, had a telephone, and that he even owned a car. A great big fellow with his arm in a sling, the miller assured me his car was out of order and that, quite apart from this, there was nobody left to drive it.

His place was mill and farm combined. For a little way a narrow stream and the road ran parallel and then the road curved and crossed the stream, disappearing toward the station.

It was in the hollow of this bend that the miller had his domain—a comfortable house facing the big water-wheel, a pond with ducks and geese, a pony in a stable, and a tall granary. The wheat hereabouts grew in small fields between the orchards and the marshes.

I said I supposed it was not easy to run the mill in war-time, and before long we had become the best of friends, but there was no car, and I therefore asked permission to use his telephone.

I rang up every garage at Granville and at Villedieu, only to learn that the drivers had all left, some of them days ago, for unknown destinations. Nobody had a car and nobody had any hope of having one.

I went back rather despondent, for this time I had no suggestions to make, and it looked as if we had fallen into the same trap as the Minarys.

We were sitting in the forecourt just before 11 A.M. when a taxi turned in from the lane. It was Ginette coming back from Villedieu with the shopping, and she told me she hoped her car would be ready at the end of the week.

I asked the driver if he would take us to St. Malo, but he said he was not fit to drive so far, having gone through a serious operation only a few days ago. I offered to pay him twice the normal fare, and he finally agreed to go as far as Pontorson, rather more than halfway.

While my mother packed our belongings, I bade farewell to the priest and to Mme. Minary, explaining as best I could the necessity of our departure. We abandoned the big perambulator and took only the smaller one, and ten minutes later we were on the road again.

We reached our destination just before one o'clock, and, although I did my best to make our driver change his mind, he refused, fearing to fall ill on the road.

In the garage next to which he set us down, I found the owner's wife, who told me that her husband was out on a job, but that when he came back in an hour's time she would have him drive us to St. Malo.

The town was filled with refugees, who arrived in thousands, emptying the restaurants like locusts as they fled farther and farther west. Because of our baby, the garage proprietor's wife offered us the hospitality of her home while we waited for her husband, and she led us to her villa, which was at the side of the railroad track, a few hundred yards from the station.

Her garden was a mass of roses, and as we sat on the lawn we saw a woman leaning over the balcony. She asked us if we had come from far, and when we told her she said:

"My home was on the Belgian frontier, in the Ardennes. I had to leave it in the middle of the night, abandoning absolutely everything. My husband and my son are both at the front, and as they don't know where I am, I can no longer hope for any news."

She had driven across France in her two-seater car, fleeing before the invader.

As she spoke a long train steamed into the station. It was the Paris express to St. Malo, arriving at Pontorson eighteen hours late. It was so crowded that people were clinging to the outside of the carriages with their feet on the running-board and their arms round the window casings; the guard's van was filled to suffocation with women and children, who had eaten nothing since their departure, and jagged glass and bandaged limbs told how the train had been machine-gunned by a German pilot from a height of only fifty feet as it was passing through Le Mans. When the locomotive came to a standstill a man leapt from the train, scrambled over the low fence that divided the track from the garden in which we were sitting and appealed for a piece of bread.

The garage proprietor's wife ran into the kitchen and brought out two whole loaves and the remains of a leg of mutton.

"Thank you," said the man. "We need it."

It did us good to see the woman's spontaneous generosity, but we looked with damp eyes at the train of misery, which a few seconds later steamed away.

Her husband arrived almost immediately, but he was taciturn and surly, probably because he had not slept properly for three nights, and for a moment I feared he would refuse to take us to the end of our journey, but his wife was adamant.

He owned a new American car, and we followed the coastal route from Dol. I was frightened of finding no accommodation at St. Malo, and my first idea was to stop at some small hotel overlooking the sea and a few miles from the city, but although we tried three times to get rooms, everywhere was crowded and we were forced to continue. Had I been successful we might never have escaped.

We reached St. Malo in the early afternoon and drove to the Hotel de l'Univers in the main square facing the old castle, where we were given adjoining rooms on the first floor. The sun was as hot as ever. There had been no break in the heat-wave since the first day of the great German offensive.

14

ST. MALO scintillated. Its colorings were so intense that one was almost blinded by them, and the sea and the sands flashed facets of blue and gold against the background of the stone battlements. The hotels and cafés in the Place Chateaubriand were crowded with allied officers, whose leather leggings were polished to a shine, and the long, narrow, tortuous main street of St. Vincent, up which you climb to the heart of the city, was filled with people gazing at the wealth of luxury goods displayed in the shop windows.

Yet if the famous fish market abounded in crabs and oysters, and if the pastry-cooks displayed cakes with sugar icing and whipped cream, there were other aspects of the city which, though not less picturesque, told of the agony through which it was passing.

The middle of the main square was reserved for military cars, the drivers of which jumped out and stood at attention when red-tabbed officers appeared. Under the shadow of the castle came a continued stream of heteroclite vehicles, bulging and weighed down with bedding and furniture, in which, under which, or beside which, whole families lived and slept, because they had no other place to do so. It was the grand terminus of haunted souls who had driven like mad through wrecked cities and in face of machine-gun fire to escape from their homes. They had reached the place they had picked out on the map because it was the farthest away, and now the sea lay in front of them, but they had no hopes, no plans, only a deep lassitude from driving by night as well as by day.

The foyer of our hotel was the nerve center of the walled peninsular city, for hither came the administrators of many towns, and they brought up-to-date tidings of what the radio continued to hide: The governor of the port of Rouen fled here after giving the order to blow up the bridges over the Seine. He was accompanied by a staff of engineers, and they had driven non-stop from the doomed city when there was no longer any hope of defending it.

The French radio gave out the official communiqués once every two hours, but the 7:30 broadcast was the most important. The loud-speaker was placed in an alcove at the far end of the palm court, and a little crowd of people gathered round it waiting in the silence of despair for those five melancholy notes in slow time from the *Marseillaise* that denoted the stand-by signal.

As St. Malo became more crowded every hour, we wondered what all these people were planning to do. They wanted to live, to bask in an illusion of normality, to look at the shops and not to hear the dread sound of guns.

In Paris you could buy a stalk of bananas for a few cents and a loin of beef for litle more. The people of St. Malo might have done the opposite, raise their prices sky high, and the chief reason they never did so was that in defeat it was possible that money would cease to have any value. What was the good of profiteering?

The arrival of four transports from England sent a breeze of faint hope through the town. They tied up at the quay by the Porte St. Louis, and as our men, fresh and newly equipped, marched under the battlements, the passers-by stopped and cheered. That evening the terrace of our café was enlivened by scores of British officers who had crossed the Channel for the first time. Their presence gave rise to the theory that a stand might be made along the River Loire, and that all was not lost, but later in the day there came arrivals from Cherbourg who told of disastrous night attacks. St. Malo was now the last of the great Channel ports to remain unbombed, and this busy little town, hemmed in by its massive walls, on what was almost an island, would undoubtedly prove an easy target for an aerial massacre.

The next morning three of the transports slipped out to sea. The fourth was to remain until the end to repatriate Britishers. During the next few days the growing fear of air-raids drove many people out of the city proper. Some of these crossed by launch to Dinard, only to find that most of the hotels were closed or turned into military hospitals. The casino on the wide semi-circular bay, which in peace-time is the fashionable center of the beach-front, was being reopened to house the Air Ministry, evacuated from Paris, and the only people on the sandy beach were wounded soldiers, some, appallingly mutilated.

Nature seemed to mock this human suffering. The cliff gardens were ablaze with brilliantly colored flowers that in the hot sun made a picture reminiscent of Portugal's Estoril.

Many refugees crossed to Dinard, but few remained there. They preferred the comparative safety of Paramé, which they could reach more easily from St. Malo, even, if the need arose, along the sands. Near our hotel British soldiers continued until the last moment to fill sandbags which would never be used. Farther along thousands of French *poilus*, surly, unshaven, and with their tunics unbuttoned, lolled on the beach. Reynaud had already made his pathetic appeal for American help. Nobody had any more faith in the future. Officers no longer strove for discipline in the barracks.

It was then that we knew that we should not see our farm again. Our departure was a matter of urgency.

We went to the British Consulate, where the staff was already packing, to obtain our embarkation permits. Here we came up against officialdom in its worst form. A boy sat at a little desk in the consul's anteroom giving out exit permits to British subjects. We received two without difficulty for my husband and myself, but there remained my mother, whose passport was French. I pleaded vainly for a human interpretation of the regulations, pointing out that she had come over from England solely to help us with our child, and that her home was, like ours, in London. But my pleading was in vain.

Should we have stayed in France rather than leave her alone to fend for herself on the eve of an invasion? But would our presence have helped? Both my husband and I would have been interned by the Nazis, and our baby might have died. The problem was the cruellest that can face any person. I felt a criminal in deciding to return. I felt worse when we left my mother at the bottom of the companion-way to climb into the crowded transport, where one could hardly breathe for people.

My husband and I leaned over the side of the ship, unable

to do more than make signs at my mother, who remained motionless below, her eyes filled with tears. A dozen airplanes roaring out of the blue swooped toward our vessel, and for a moment I thought we were caught in a trap, for this was the Nazis' favorite way of mass murder.

But they were our planes—British planes. A great feeling of gratitude and pride filled our hearts. Now I thought of the white cliffs of England we should see before long, unless an enemy torpedo sent us to the bottom. We pulled away from the quayside as our planes kept sentinel above, and I dared not even look back to where a dark-coated woman stood taking a last look at us—at the baby which was almost her baby.

A fierce sun gleamed on St. Malo, on its fortified walls, on Dinard, and on the deep blue waters of the bay. Passengers moved from deck to deck, some of them telling of a journey by train from Paris that had taken fifty hours. They had lost all their luggage. Many had been killed.

But we were free.

We were to be given a second chance.

We had escaped servitude and jail. A steward passed with a cup of tea, and it was already English soil on which we trod.

The ship steamed out to sea and skirted the coast northward toward Cherbourg. Long lines of barges passed quite close to us, all making for St. Malo. Some said they had come from Rouen, others that they were being brought by the Germans for the invasion of England. Nobody knew for sure. How could they know? A crippled submarine was being towed into Cherbourg, and later we caught sight of Jersey and Guernsey, which we were seeing for the last time before the enemy seized them.

Anti-aircraft gunners manned their post on the top deck and were given a hand by their fellows from Le Havre, who had escaped at the last moment, leaving the city the mass of flames we had seen from afar. They joked, but they had come through hell. So had our steamer, that had made the journey to Dunkirk seven times through the epic evacuation. British refugee children now played on the decks scarred by bullets. They had seen the real thing during their train trip from Paris.

"You're the Jerry, I'm the Spitfire!"

The next morning we sailed into Southampton Water.

Our second chance had come, after all.

PART II

LONDON INTERLUDE

15

As MY husband had spent the first months of the war in a single room in Clarges Street, near London's Green Park, we took a cab to the Savoy Hotel where he had courted me during that magical spring and summer when, in my little black dress, I was a manicurist in the barber shop. Thus in poignant circumstances did my dream come true of staying at this mighty hotel as a guest, though not as a film star or as an elegant young married woman, but as a disheveled, tearful refugee with a baby in arms, a bundle of dirty linen, a perambulator and a feeding bottle, my entire possessions. My husband, hatless and distraught, ashamed of having been obliged to leave my mother alone, with only a few francs, in a country where advancing armies would cut her off, perhaps arrest and torture her, grimly booked an apartment.

A great change had come over the Savoy. The hotel which, during boom and depression, war and peace, had been filled with politicians, business executives, film and theater stars, was now almost hushed for the first time in half a century. Hardly any guests had remained after the German breakthrough. The famous grill room was closed so that workmen could remove the enormous plate glass windows facing the courtyard and replace them with a brick wall in case of air raids. The great restaurant overlooking the Thames embankment remained open but its normal atmosphere had gone. City stockbrokers who normally patronized it at lunch time, spending their money lavishly on brandy and cigars, seemed to have faded away. In place of them one met groups of Poles, Dutchmen, Belgians, Norwegians, and a few American newspapermen who had just crossed over from France. General de Gaulle, almost unknown as yet, held court at a large round table. French diplomats from the embassy, and members of the various naval, military, and economic missions who had decided to obey the instructions of the Pétain Government, kept as far from the new leader as possible, and even glared at him with undiplomatic rudeness. They intended to insist on their safe conduct home as soon as possible. This international crowd was somber and depressed.

The next evening at about five o'clock I saw a dozen shabby figures walking in Indian file into the reading room. What struck me first about them was their bent and lifeless backs, and the way they sank limply into the settees. Soon their heads were close together as they talked and argued in low tones.

Suddenly I recognized familiar faces in this little crowd. Yes, indeed, they were France's most famous war and political correspondents, men and women whose names were known throughout the world, and whom I had met personally as a young married hostess.

Now they had covered the greatest story of all; but the story was too big and had burned them up. They had no longer any papers in which to write what they had seen; they had no longer any country to call their own. They were cut off from their families, and treated with scorn by their own government which pillaged their homes, declared them traitors for continuing the fight, and deprived them of their greatest heritage—their nationality. They were exhausted and penniless. Their minds were reeling from incomprehension.

A page boy slipped into the room and turned on a radio from which suddenly came a strident voice announcing the terms of the armistice. The refugees, exhausted by excitement and a five days' sea journey in a ship so crowded that there were neither bunks to sleep in nor food to eat, winced at the words. The world they had known and swayed was crashing about them. In the foyer two young women with neat summer hats and flowered dresses broke into peals of laughter.

We occupied a large suite overlooking the river and the hotel provided a comfortable cot for my baby whose cheeks were as pink as a Normandy apple and who gurgled with pleasure every time the telephone rang. My husband and I were both so tired that we resolved to sleep through any raid that might take place. Though I was no longer breast-feeding my son, I had his bottles to give him at regular hours and was glad to put on a nightdress and slip into a cool bed.

There·was, of course, no raid and the next morning, on taking the child out in the perambulator, I found the Strand crowded with Australians and small tough Maoris who had just arrived.

C. B. Cochran, the impresario, met me, and said he was planning to leave the hotel and move into a flat in a great cement and steel building just off Piccadilly, and he suggested I should go and see if we also could find accommodation there. West End flats were at a discount. People had not yet any idea of what would happen when London was raided from the air, and most Londoners who had money were moving into the country for a few months. Those who could not spend all their time away at least made arrangements to sleep a few miles out. I had no difficulty, therefore, in finding a choice of empty flats. The most suitable was a ground-floor apartment with window boxes filled with geraniums overlooking the entrance court. The flat would surely be filled with sunshine all day long. In the absence of my husband, I offered half the normal rental, and refused to sign a lease that tied me down to more than three months at a time. My offer was accepted within a few hours, and we moved in during the week-end.

I liked to compare our building to a luxury liner tied up at the quay of a small port. There was a Diesel room below for the central heating, and a corridor flanked with stout pipes for water and oil which increased this marine atmosphere.

We towered over Shepherd Market—that village sleepily living its own life just behind Piccadilly. We dominated it, almost overpowered it with brute strength, for it is no larger than a handkerchief. But the contours of the market are sharply defined, and it has a vigorous character. From the top of our roof we could look down on Shepherd Street, the market's main street, which runs into the market-place proper with its butcher's shop, its fishmonger, its greengrocer, the oil and candle store, and two public houses.

I owned practically no furniture with which to make my new apartment snug and homely. The bedroom and living room were at right angles to each other, both overlooking the courtyard. The bedroom had built-in wardrobes with an entire wall of mirrored doors. I placed a large double bed as far as possible

from the window and the baby's cot in a sheltered corner. The
living room had cream colored walls, a round cherry-wood table
on which I served the meals, my plain deal writing table which
I used for cutting blouses, dresses and skirts, and at which I sat
when putting down in note books during the long night hours
the poignant memories of my lost farm, for it was during the
terrifying months to come, the long sleepless nights, the incessant pounding of bombs, the shattering of glass, the collapse of
nearby houses, that I felt confusedly the urge to become an
author.

I had no help at all. My husband was soon to be called away
and I was temporarily poor. I had no maid, no nurse, no daily
help, no cook, and I doubt if I slept more than two hours in
twenty-four. The collapse of France at first made Londoners,
not yet tested by high explosive, frightened and sarcastic, and
rather than listen to their bitter criticisms of my country, I kept
proudly to myself. The great comradeship which was to make
London, emptied of all but the brave, a noble and lovely city to
inhabit, did not come till after the first nocturnal onslaught.

Our building bordered by Piccadilly stood halfway between
two great London parks—Hyde Park and the Green Park. I
took the baby in his perambulator to one or the other of these
parks twice a day, morning and afternoon. Hyde Park was
famous for its Daisy Walk which runs beside a fine undulating
lawn bordered by the Row where people used to ride horseback,
and the Dell where the rabbit warrens are. In the days of peace
it was the rendezvous of smart nurses and their young charges,
and photographers used to take pictures of the babies for the society weeklies. Soon there would be no child left in central
London but my own.

These were the days of fierce aerial battles on the southeast
coast. No bombs had yet fallen on the West End. Indeed, big
wagers had been laid in clubs on the day that war was declared
that no bombs would fall for a year on the C police division of
London, and it seemed just possible that these bets would be
won. There were twenty-four plays and musicals in central
London—four times as many as in New York City; and in spite
of the incessant alerts I remember looking up from my sewing
one afternoon to see a carriage and pair swing into the courtyard. The sight of this shining carriage drawn by two splendid

bays seemed almost unreal in a London that only a few minutes earlier had been sheltering from enemy raiders. Our hall porters had by then been issued with tin hats and hatchets, and three of these men hurried forward to meet the carriage. One of them in this accoutrement looked like Don Quixote. He was slight of build, wore steel-rimmed spectacles, and his tin hat, much too large for him, toppled over his eyes each time he made a sudden movement. He was an incredible picture as he raced toward this fine equipage. Lord and Lady Portsea had come to pay a leisurely call on our neighbor, Mrs. Elinor Glyn. Lord Portsea and the famous red-haired novelist had played together as children on the sandy beaches of the island of Jersey.

On Saturday afternoon, September seventh, I had, as usual, taken my baby to the Daisy Walk.

Fall had come to the park; lawns and paths were covered by curled-up brown leaves, but the heat was still reminiscent of mid-June.

There was a fair crowd, and the brown-coated chair seller claimed to be doing even better than in normal years, for there were still many Australian and Canadian soldiers with spare time on their hands.

My baby was just beginning to walk, and I watched him making his first steps accompanied by a Pekinese puppy that we had bought him for company. It was tea time and Londoners lying lazily under the big trees on the lawn were just unpacking thermos flasks and sandwiches from baskets. The sirens wailed, first in the distance, and then nearer, but although a few people were hurried away by a desire to be on the move as soon as a raid was signaled, most of us took no notice. There had been so many occasions on which nothing had been seen or heard.

Then to the east came the drone of airplanes at an immense height, no larger than pinheads. One needed to adjust one's eyes to the light in order to catch glimpses of the silver dots in the sky flashing at one moment in the sun, then disappearing as they banked and turned. As more airplanes arrived the puffs of anti-aircraft fire appeared like little flakes of cotton wool among the formations. Fascinated, we watched all this for nearly an hour but suddenly, with a deafening screech, big guns quite near us spat their metal into the sky. We seized the child and the dog and discovered that by now we were almost alone on the lawn. Knowing that each morning the Daisy Walk was strewn with shrapnel I feared these guns more than the raiders, and we beat a precipitate retreat into Knightsbridge.

It was not until dusk, when the great fires of dockland reddened the sky, that most people realized that the Battle for London had started in earnest, and that the silver specks we had watched at tea time had been fighting for the mastery of the capital.

While this battle for London was taking place the face of the West End changed. Crowds filed through the streets an hour before dusk carrying their mattresses on their way to the subway stations and public shelters.

We had decided for the sake of the child to continue our lives as normally as possible. We slept with the windows wide open without once going into a shelter. Many people looked at me askance for thus exposing the child's life, but he grew plump and rosy-cheeked, oblivious of the thuds that woke us from time to time. Our section was, according to statistics, the most heavily bombed in Westminster, and each morning I wheeled my baby in his perambulator through streets where men were still sweeping away the broken glass. He gurgled with joy at the sight of a house split in two, the bathroom on the third floor ready for somebody to take a bath, a towel lying across the metal rail. Almost every night some landmark near us would go up in dust, and yet our building continued to stand with every pane of glass regularly cleaned by the company's staff. "The child who would not be evacuated" became a local character, and was adopted by our village, who considered him as a mascot. He was watched over with sympathetic part-ownership, and often when my husband jumped off a bus in Piccadilly on his return from the office he was given news of our movements.

In the early hours of a November morning I was wakened by the sound of an explosion a few streets away, followed by another much nearer. We held our breaths expecting a third, because that is how they so often seemed to fall—nearer and nearer. It came screeching down, finishing up with a crisp, angry, tearing punch, accompanied by a blinding flash as the building rocked and everything in the room crashed about our heads. There was a suffocating stench, a moment's complete silence, and then an imperative voice from somewhere in the night. We made a dive for the cot, found the baby intact, and still asleep, and proceeded cautiously to assess the damage. It was not possible to strike a light because our windows were gaping open with the curtains wrenched off, but by a miracle the glass was not broken, probably because the air had been able to rush right in. In the living room, however, where the windows had been closed, all of them were smashed, and the glass pounded to shreds and driven like nails into the opposite walls. Myriads of sharp pieces were imbedded in the plaster. The Pekinese was wailing, and the chairs had been torn to pieces, with their legs thrown in all directions so that we were continually tripping up over broken objects on our way into the kitchen, where it was safe to light a lamp. We dressed hurriedly, chilled by a cold November wind blowing through the flat, and wheeled the cot over a sea of broken glass into the passage where the porters were running along with lanterns, the electric light light having failed. The entrance hall where we took refuge was soon filled with phantom figures difficult to recognize in the semi-obscurity. Wardens and police tramped past with their thick boots, women clad in the strangest garb fired shrill questions at the porters, who reassured them with respectful annoyance. The bomb had fallen on a garage at the corner of our courtyard, but our building, though buffeted, stood proud and true. Nearly every window of its seven stories had, however, crashed into the courtyard, where the glass lay several feet deep.

Soon explosives began to fall again. Each time a bomb whistled down we both rose hastily to throw ourselves over the baby as if our bodies could save him from the explosion, but our haste was such that we invariably knocked our heads together on the way up, relieving our fears with laughter.

Incendiaries fell harmlessly in the courtyard, but a terrible stench of burning wool filled the flat. It was the jumper that I had thrown over the lamp to shield the light. The hot globe had burned a hole right through it.

It was nearly dawn when firemen, worn out with fatigue, arrived to deal with the fires. Soon our main street was oozing with a mixture of water, plaster, soot, and broken glass—a horrible pall of smoke and burned wood and paper choked me. The old houses and shops were left to burn themselves out.

16

OUR VILLAGE was built on the spot—then all green fields with wild bugloss bushes—where Edward I privileged the hospital of St. James to keep an annual fair on the Eve of St. James, the day and the morrow, and four days following.

These fields, through which the Tybourne stream wound between banks and braes, fringed with rushes and redolent with wild mint, were known as Brook Fields, and as time went on the fair was called May Fair.

The Americans came to our village in the chilly fogs of March. They were young, friendly and beautifully dressed, and after dark moved like shadows along Piccadilly, straining their eyes, unaccustomed to the black-out. They stood in little groups at the top of Whitehorse street, an eighteenth century passage linking our village with Piccadilly and the Green Park, humming tunes we Londoners did not recognize, and they talked in low tones, as if fearful to break the silence of the night, and their accents lingered in our ears.

The market was in the throes of depression and we welcomed this friendly invasion from across the Atlantic as a breath of much-needed hope. Singapore had fallen, Ceylon was being evacuated, India and Australia were threatened. Sisters were without news of brothers, mothers wept silently for their sons last heard of in lands overrun by the Japanese; to those who had no ties and who lacked sensibility, the shortage of tea and rice in the village stores came as a vague, misty foreboding of worse things to come. I now took my baby to the Green Park twice a day. There were deck chairs round an artificial lake built by the fire fighters who on so many occasions had run out of water during the worst raids. A duck and drake had taken possession of this sump and we illegally brought them bread, hoping they might eventually produce a family.

My husband now left England and I was alone with the child. Though my farm in Normandy came back often in dreams, I did not expect very seriously to see it again; indeed the end of the war did not seem a matter likely enough to speculate about. My mother I continually saw waving good-by to us from the quayside at St. Malo and on her account my conscience never gave me any peace. I reproached myself with sacrificing her to save myself and the baby, and I reflected that she would never have left London had it not been at my urgent request when I was pregnant and in need of her help.

My flat, without a picture on the walls, tarred paper replacing the window panes and scarcely any furniture, became a place where French, Belgian and Polish officers dropped in uninvited for lunch and supper for the satisfaction they obtained of sharing a meal with a woman and a child, momentary illusion of family life. Often agents who forty-eight hours earlier had been parachuted on French soil returned with a Paris newspaper or a flower picked in a hedgerow.

As the date of the invasion grew nearer, London became strangely still. The U.S. Military Police who, on the instructions of General Eisenhower, wore white helmets, white belts and white gaiters, became more than ever in evidence.

Londoners, blinking in the sunshine of those last few days of April, 1944, looked up into the blue sky when the drone of airplanes was heard and asked themselves whether "it" was for today or tomorrow, this week or next.

There were some perfectly glorious mornings toward the end of April—mornings when the sky was absolutely blue. On such a morning, a little after nine, I pushed the perambulator into Piccadilly from Whitehorse Street to find two long lines of white-helmeted Americans drawn up in the Green Park. These men, whom I soon recognized as the 787th Battalion, were facing Piccadilly, and the Stars and Stripes floated impressively in the breeze. The band, on a lawn a little to the rear, started to play as I crossed the street, and this was the signal for the battalion to wheel to the right and march in that direction. Soon the whole battalion was parading under the trees, making a martial picture in pastoral surroundings.

The sun glittered on the brass and the grass was fresh and tender. In the distance a clump of cherry trees made a splash of white blossom, recalling the orchards where the invasion forces were now gathering in mighty array. The foliage of the hawthorns was several shades deeper than that of the stately chestnuts; the London plane trees were still garlanded with the previous year's blackened seed balls caught up in the boughs which from a distance appeared leafless, though on looking closer one saw that they were speckled with green.

In the hollow, the mountain ash was putting on its spring garb. The elms and the poplars were only just beginning to wake out of their long winter sleep and had not yet joined this symphony of green, but already a distant line of barbed wire was being hidden by a cloak of sprouting shoots pushing upward through the damp soil and stretching their arms bravely over the unsightly prickles. The scent of lilac was about, brought to us probably from the white and mauve blossoms which were just beginning to unfold in the gardens of those once stately mansions that run from Arlington House to the Mall. Yes, indeed, this military parade was set in the most peaceful surroundings. The white helmets and the white belts and gaiters gave these men a picturesqueness that reminded one of the white breeches of the Napoleonic Guard.

The first week in June was charged with expectancy and women in town were becoming a little jumpy because there was no mail from their men stationed on the south coast. They were no longer able to write direct. On Tuesday, June sixth, I was wakened by a telephone call from the editor of one of London's chief evening newspapers who asked me if I could tell him what the coast was like between Le Havre and Caen. As my farm was exactly halfway between these two cities, his query filled me with apprehension. "Why do you want to know?" I asked. He answered: "The invasion has started."

By early fall, thanks to the kindness of American officers traveling between London and Paris, I was able to establish some sort of contact with my mother who was living alone in the front part of an empty and unheated shop near the château of Versailles. She had recovered from a serious illness but had practically nothing to eat; on cold days she went into the palace grounds to gather faggots which she painfully carried back to burn behind her iron shutter. She was experiencing poverty, cold and hunger for the second time.

In London I continued to take the child and the little dog both morning and afternoon to the Green Park where, with half a dozen other women, I used to sit under the Cornish elms beside the sump. We called this piece of lawn our Drawing Room. The others were older than I was. Most young married women were serving in some capacity with the armed forces, working in a government office or evacuated with their babies to the country. As my companions and I sat knitting in our deck chairs, the dog chasing the boy through the long grass, we looked up every few moments to see flying bombs coming toward us from the south, very low, their machinery ticking inside them as if they had been monster alarm clocks. Timed to cut out at this point of their flight, the ticking would suddenly cease, the torpedo swiftly fall, and then from Soho, from Kingsway, from the neighborhood of Oxford Street, came a growling explosion and a tall column of wreckage, powdered brick and smoke. The low houses where my mother and I had lived in a one-roomed apartment when I worked as a manicurist at the Savoy had gone entirely. Weeds grew in the street.

Christmas Day was white—not with snow, but with hoar-frost that lay like a crisp carpet over the parks. The temperature, below freezing, contracted the muscles of one's face, and froze the puddles on the gravel walks. The sump, facing the Cornish elms in the Green Park Drawing Room, had a coating of ice, and the roofs of the black huts studded round the big searchlight looked as if somebody had decorated them with sugar-icing.

The towers of Westminster Abbey, shrouded in mist, took on their medieval aspect, powerful and mysterious. Big Ben tolled the hour, and a taxicab, its hood quite white, drew up at the abbey door, and I followed the occupants inside, where a tall fir tree, decorated with colored electric globes, stood in front of the tomb of the Unknown Warrior, at the four corners of which burned immense yellow candles whose flames, bent by the draught, caused the wax to drip. The scene of the nativity, against a colored oriental backcloth, was softly lit. The nave was warm and wrapped in meditation, and from afar came the voice of the preacher, himself invisible until one had passed silently along the aisle past the organ bridge.

Then one saw him in his white surplice and black stole with a touch of crimson, venerably dignified and austere against the ebony screen carved in front of the massive, fluted, and half-dim pillar of Normandy stone. All the candles of the high altar were glimmering and flickering, shedding a soft yellow and diffused light on fir trees, tapestry, and gold plate.

Already Europe had suffered intolerably. The abbey, with its Norman stone—the same exactly as the huge fireplaces in my house—was a poignant reminder that the churches of Caen and Rouen were shattered, that these splendid medieval cities were laid waste, and that the entire Norman countryside was still strewn with rubble, corpses and unexploded mines. The scene of battle had shifted to the Ardennes. The bombing of England had made us appreciate what it means to lose a home, to see a child lying dead.

My son was now five and I myself taught him to read and write both in English and French. Though many friends urged me to send him to day school, as if there were something morally reprehensible in keeping him at home when it was so easy to get rid of him, I was of the opinion that war had already done enough to break up families. The wealthier people had sent their children to America from which continent they would eventually return estranged from their parents and the customs of their own country; the poorer had parted with their children to comply with the various evacuation schemes. For many, family life had ceased altogether and it seemed to me that so long as I was in the position to enjoy the companionship of my son during his tender years, it was normal that I should desire to continue this privileged state. Each time he looked at me it was with clear blue eyes full of love and confidence. He was now, of course, even more wistful, even more sweetly polite and enticing than when three years later the entire world acclaimed him. Now I had his charming ways, his slightly French lisp, all to myself. No Carol Reed, no Alexander Korda had discovered him. He was my own. He was a child and yet the mirror of my grown-up self. As each bomb fell I bent my supple body over him so that if he were killed I would die also. Separated from him I had no interest to live. Yet I was, as also later, too strict with myself not to be strict with him. My own climb from a girlhood of poverty, my continual desire to write, to read and to reflect, made me at times impatient with the tender mind I was determined to instruct. I would put him across my lap and administer two or three sharp smacks to bring back his attention. I would try to pass it off lightly at the time but I would then become angry with myself. As the morning wore on, I would feel worse, for whereas he had been inattentive, I had undoubtedly lost my temper, and supposing a bomb were to fall or he were to be injured or killed . . . ?

On such an occasion when, shortly after the lesson, I had to go out, imagine what a state I put myself in, knowing that he was alone in the apartment and that at any moment a flying bomb might fall on our building! I had smacked him. My long pointed nails might have torn his skin. He trusted me, and I hit him. I hurried home expecting to find my child at the last extremity but was relieved to discover that the only thing he complained of was a great hunger. The Charles B. Cochrans still lived in our building. Mrs. Cochran telephoned to say that she had arranged for seats to be placed at our disposal for *Alice in Wonderland*, and as this seemed a just recompense for my inhumanity, I hastened to acquaint the child with his good fortune.

For an hour I watched him at the theater enjoying himself mightily, but after the first curtain fell we all left the theater, and parted in Shaftesbury Avenue. He was to be taken on a shopping expedition in Soho while I hurried off to keep an appointment, but no sooner had I turned to go than I heard tiny steps, and the child, his face bathed in tears, threw himself into my arms, accusing me of going away without kissing him farewell. He was already, like myself, a packet of sensitivity.

Though we had more or less written off our lovely farmhouse, we were for ever thinking of it, and from time to time we wrote to one or other of the local dignitaries in the hope of receiving a reply. Weeks and months passed, however, without news, when one morning the child, who used to collect the letters the postman pushed through the door as he made his round of the flats, brought a postcard which in his eyes appeared so dull that, as he handed it to us, he said with a disappointed air: "That is all the postman brought this morning!"

But though he could not guess it, the little blond god was bearing in his hands the cup of plenty. Dr. Lehérissey, who had brought him into the world, was giving him the first news of the house where he was born. We seized the thin card with its two postage stamps—the one still showing the head of Marshal Pétain and the other, of more recent issue, the Arc de Triomphe —and this is what we read:

"Our village, saved by a miracle from the desolation all round us, is intact except for that part of it nearest the railway station. Your house is still standing, though emptied of all its contents. I hope that as soon as these emotions have calmed down a little, we shall have the pleasure of seeing you again, and I pray you to kiss most affectionately on my behalf your son who must by now have become a big boy."

This news was so unexpected that it was difficult to assimilate. We had never supposed that this house, built four centuries ago, could have withstood the impact of the present war. Did we not remember how its old walls had shaken when the German Stukas dived on Le Havre during those hot summer months of 1940 when it seemed that civilization was about to disappear from the earth?

PART III

THE RETURN TO THE FARM

17

MY MOTHER had watched the ship bringing us to England growing smaller and smaller as it steamed away. She cried bitterly, but her thoughts were mostly with my baby son. When I had stood on the boat deck with him in my arms, she had not ceased watching him. He had kicked and struggled. She imagined he wanted to return to her, for she had nursed him and loved him and spoilt him since the day he was born, and now she felt convinced that the ship would be torpedoed or dive-bombed. She could not rid herself of the picture of the baby struggling in the water.

Never had St. Malo looked more lovely than on that June morning, when the battlements of the historic walled peninsular city scintillated in the sun. The ship making its perilous trip to Southampton was an Ostend packet which only the previous day had brought a British regiment across the Channel. The men had marched along the quay, under the gate, and out along the white dusty road leading to the interior. Nobody had seen them since, and my mother hoped that perhaps something might happen to reverse the future of our arms.

The wife of a proprietor of the hotel in the Place Chateaubriand had an honest affection for the English. She had always desired to send her son to London. My mother went back to the hotel and lunched there, but the small bundle of notes, which my husband had given her at parting, now represented her entire fortune. She realized that the hotel was too expensive.

This sudden return to poverty seemed almost natural to my mother, who never appeared destined to enjoy good fortune for long. The last few years during which, thanks to her son-in-law, she had no need to worry about the future, had always seemed

unreal. She had enjoyed herself timidly. Now she was about to
re-enter her former state and would be obliged to stitch and sew
as she had done earlier for me.

In spite of her rheumatism, her fingers were still reasonably
cunning at their craft.

Her chief concern was to find an inexpensive lodging, and
after a few hours of diligent research she discovered a dressmaker who had a room to spare. Though the woman was not
particularly friendly, she allowed my mother to cook her meals
in the kitchen.

Less than two days after the Channel packet had sailed to
England, the first German vehicles drove into St. Malo. When
my mother stepped into the main street after breakfast she
found the town full of enemy troops. They were buying up
everything in the shops, which soon became empty of goods.
No other ship had left St. Malo since the Ostend packet, and
my mother shuddered to think how narrowly we had escaped.

There was a tiny haberdasher's owned by two elderly Breton
women where my mother had bought some lisle stockings.
These wizened old ladies listened to the B.B.C. and were the
first people whom my mother heard stoutly declare that England was, without a doubt, destined to win the war. This was
an excellent reason for her to take a liking to them, and she
used often to go to the shop for an hour's gossip. As the days
passed and the news became more alarming, the kindly women
increased their optimism. Each fresh catastrophe gave them
hope.

She discovered that her elderly friends were not the only
people in St. Malo to hold these views. The Bretons were
toughly resistant from the first and showed the independence
of spirit which has characterized them throughout the centuries.
But as the Germans began to take over the seaport, my mother's
situation became increasingly difficult. Her identity card showed
that before going to the farm in Normandy her home had been
in London.

Every evening when the sun was going down she used to go
for a walk along the ramparts and look out to sea. There was
no more beautiful view than from these medieval battlements,
below which the waves broke over the golden sand, creeping
each moment nearer to the rocks. There was one place in par-

ticular which fascinated her. Steep and majestic, it stood higher than the rest, and my mother's head reeled as she looked downward at the glittering shore. Here the writer Chateaubriand played when he was a child. You will capture the spirit of the place in his *Mémoires d'outre-tombe*. My mother used to stop for a moment on her walks and lean over the parapet, and it became her custom to tarry there each evening. She found sudden quietude after the long day. She was no longer flustered or nervous. The rocks below beckoned her as if they were friends. How peaceful would be that long sleep lulled by the soft beating of the waves.

Calmly she chose the evening of her suicide. She was convinced that the Ostend packet had met with disaster, and she therefore had no longer any reason to live. She reflected with satisfaction that the Gestapo would be cheated of its humble prize.

A few evenings later she walked quickly to the appointed place with neither fear nor regret. St. Malo had charmed her from the first day when, after dinner at the hotel, we had all taken the child in his perambulator, racing with it, each in turn, over the sands. My husband had been incorrigibly optimistic, and I had seldom been in better health. My baby with his platinum hair and rosy cheeks was an angel, and he gurgled and laughed at this unexpected holiday. My mother had enjoyed every moment of this fantastic twilight of happiness.

As she turned the battlement she suddenly caught sight of two steel-hatted German sentries posted at the exact spot she had chosen for her suicide. They had mounted a gun there, which faced the sea.

Slowly she retraced her steps.

On her way back she called on the woman at the hotel in the Place Chateaubriand who, having examined the identity card, called her husband to give his opinion. One of their friends was employed at the town hall, and they decided to call upon him at his house, where they could doubtless find him at supper. It was important that the interview should not take place in public, and the hour was therefore well chosen. My mother was agreeably surprised at the spontaneous offer of these friends, upon whom she had no call, but it proved to her once again that the Bretons were a kind, loyal race.

The town hall official told her that she must ask the dressmaker with whom she lodged to make her a member of the seamstresses' union, which would establish not only her profession but also the fact that she was domiciled in St. Malo; my mother must then make an application to him at the town hall for a new identity card, upon which he would be careful to make no mention of her London home or her connection with the farm in Normandy. He impressed upon her the importance of this last point because the Germans were insisting that all refugees must immediately return to the places whence they came.

My mother hurried back to ask her landlady to facilitate the scheme. At first the dressmaker demurred, but the next morning she agreed to apply for the necessary papers, which arrived toward the end of the week. Then my mother went to see her friend at the town hall.

The Germans were already in charge of the civil administration of the city, but for the moment they contented themselves with supervising the French employees. When my mother handed in her identity card for renewal, her friend placed his thumb over the word London, and rapidly made out a new card. She was then free to go where she pleased.

My Uncle Louis, Marie-Thérèse's husband (whom readers will have met in *The Little Madeleine*), lived at Viroflay, near Versailles. He worked in Paris, at a furniture store behind the Boulevard des Italiens, and traveled up and down every day. Though his flat was so small that it was scarcely large enough for himself, he offered to share it with my mother on condition she kept house for him.

She arrived at the beginning of the winter, when the newspapers were full of the great raids on London which, according to the French press, were gradually wiping out the capital. My uncle's quarters were more cramped than she expected, and she found that to supplement his wages and keep herself warm during the day she would be obliged to work.

There had just opened at Versailles, under the aegis of Marshal Pétain, a workroom for needy gentlewomen. The room was tolerably heated, and there was thin hot soup for lunch. Since the French Army, under the terms of the armistice, had been disbanded, the government found itself with several million unwanted uniforms, which needy ladies up and down the country were adapting for the civilian population. My mother welcomed this opportunity of keeping herself warm, but was surprised by the great dejection of so many people she encountered. Their attitude was in striking contrast with the uncompromising Breton seafarers who never for a moment believed that the Germans would triumph.

My mother's arrival in the workroom, where these ladies sewed under the portrait of the aged marshal, gave its members new hope. She told them about her heartening experiences in St. Malo, and was full of ideas about their work. She had a gift for sewing under difficulties, and I had often laughed at the way that her most beautiful dresses were made with inadequate lengths of material.

Her first task was to turn the rough military trousers into children's coats. Later there arrived at the workroom a crate of bathing costumes seized from a Jewish store, and she managed with infinite patience to unpick these gaily colored materials and transform them into girls' dresses. Her work was sufficiently remarkable to attract the aged marshal's attention when, some time later, he paid an official visit to the workroom.

She had by now inspired all her colleagues with her own faith in British arms, and every morning when the ladies met round the table, those who had listened to the B.B.C. gave an account of the proceedings for the benefit of those who had no wireless sets. Some of these women had come from a Jewish-owned factory engaged in the fabrication of false teeth, closed by the Germans on their arrival. There was also a Russian princess who, after the beginning of the eastern campaign, firmly believed that the Germans would restore the property in the Ukraine which the Bolsheviks had stolen from her. She had an incessant craving for tobacco. Also she could never pass a stray cat without taking it home, with the result that she had sixteen animals living in her small apartment. At first my mother had supplied her with some of my uncle's smoking tobacco, but gradually she became suspicious of her neighbor's political views, fearing that she might have been introduced into the company as an agent for the Gestapo, but as the war continued it became clear that the princess was entirely devoid of malice, her chief concern being to spend her meager pay on cream buns

and tobacco. The women from the false-teeth factory used to
laugh at her, but the princess would answer:

"Give me a little money, a hot bath, and an hour at the hairdresser, and I shall be as beautiful as I ever was!"

In the end she made cigarettes out of lime-tree flowers. Most
of the other women were Bretons, who welcomed my mother
because she had come from St. Malo. She went with them to
mass on Sundays and they comforted one another.

Two years later, however, my mother fell dangerously ill.

My uncle's apartment was inadequate for two people, and
he was far from well himself. He had been deeply affected by
the death of my gay and pretty aunt. Then while the German
armies were surging across France, at the very moment we were
preparing to leave our farm in Normandy, his daughter Rolande
died. I think he would have liked to marry my mother; they
could have comforted each other, but she felt her strength ebb-
ing away from want of air and from malnutrition, and though
her identity card no longer gave her any anxiety, she was in
continual fear of arrest. Every morning she traveled in the electric train from Viroflay to Versailles, and the services were so
irregular that she often arrived at work two hours earlier than
her colleagues, who mostly lived in the neighborhood. When
Pierre Laval was invited to Versailles to review his legionaries,
my mother, because of the crowd, missed her usual train back
to Viroflay. At the station she heard that the passengers had
been collected as hostages because of the attempt against the
French politician's life, and she had the shock of seeing them
being taken away for execution.

Each of the workrooms which formed part of the organization set up by the marshal was visited from time to time by a
doctor, who gave his services for nothing. My mother retained
an old antipathy to the medical profession; not altogether that
she mistrusted them, but she was too shy to allow herself willingly to be examined. By now, however, her condition had become critical and she had no choice.

The doctor had her X-rayed, and told her that she needed
two months' complete rest in the country.

"There is nowhere I can go," she replied.

"You must have a relation—or at least a friend?"

"I have absolutely nobody."

"That is not possible," answered the doctor. "Everybody has a relation, if only a distant one."

"Not in my case," she answered.

He thought she was lying and pressed his questions. Then she told her story. When she had finished he said:

"This is a very strange coincidence. I know Dr. Lehérissey, of Villers, well, and before the war I used to relieve him when he went on holiday. I am also acquainted with Mme. Bayard, your daughter's charwoman, whose son I attended when he had pneumonia. You are quite right. It would not be wise for you to go back to your daughter's farm. You would be betrayed to the Germans."

His manner had altogether changed, and it was obvious that he was determined to help her. A certain Mlle. de X had turned her country house at Marly into a rest home for women from the city who had no means of their own, and the doctor arranged that my mother should be sent there. The house was in the middle of the forest where Louis XV used to entertain the members of his court. The bedrooms were divided into cubicles and it was an ideal place for convalescents. Shortly after my mother's arrival, she became so ill that she was unable to leave her sick-bed, whereupon the matron said to her: "You are more seriously ill than we were led to believe. Your illness is possibly contagious, and I must therefore ask you to go." She was on the point of being dismissed when the doctor arrived and insisted that she should stay.

For almost a fortnight she lay in semi-consciousness, caring little what became of her, but as she recovered she felt once again a desire to live, and she used to wander over the countryside in search of dandelion leaves which made excellent salads, for the patients were inadequately fed. The doorkeeper kept rabbits, and to oblige him she gathered herbs to feed them. One evening he handed her a Red Cross letter from London. It was from me, my very first letter since our parting. Suddenly life held out new hope. There was something to look forward to. Her grandson had not been drowned, and the family had passed unhurt through the air raids. If only the war could end we might all be reunited.

On her return to Versailles, however, she suddenly discovered that my uncle was no longer able to give her hospitality, and she accordingly found herself with nowhere to sleep. Her fellow workers, shivering in tiny rented rooms, were unable to shelter her, but they all went about the town searching for some empty garret where she might at least spend the next few weeks. Finally they discovered an elderly spinster upon whom they prevailed to give her hospitality, but as soon as my mother arrived her hostess took possession of her ration book, and in order to regain it my mother was obliged to leave.

The sewing-class was under the direction of a Mme. Parisot, a widow of the First World War, whose son was living in Algiers. Before the occupation this excellent person had owned a small employment agency in the Avenue de St. Cloud, which provided her with a modest income, but as there was no longer any need for employment agencies, all surplus manpower being drafted to Germany, the one-roomed shop was empty and shuttered. Mme. Parisot now offered my mother her shop, and she gave her a camp-bed, a chair, and a stove. My mother's new home closed with a steel shutter which, by disuse, had become rusty, so that at night she was obliged to stuff the crevices with paper to hide the light of her candle, the German patrols being very strict about the black-out. Nevertheless she now had a room of her own, and she made her bed linen from the linings of soldiers' capes sewn together and hemmed. As the cold was unbearable she went every day into the park at Versailles to gather faggots, under the eyes of the German troops who stood in groups admiring the white statuary of the French kings.

She now thought it safe to write to Mme. Bayard, who expressed great joy at hearing from her, and who sent her from time to time some butter and a little meat from Normandy, which my mother cooked over the faggots on her stove.

And so she lived until the liberation.

My mother was confident that I would quickly arrive to rescue her from the cold shop with its steel shutters, but it was impossible for me to leave England, and I dared not advise her to go to Normandy, where, for all I knew, our farm might have been demolished during the landing.

Normandy was a battlefield, with the fires hardly damped and the roads still clogged with the dead. Christmas brought the Rundstedt advance into the Ardennes. All I could do was to send a few provisions to Versailles by courier, as people had done over a century ago.

The turn of the year presented a new problem. Mme. Parisot planned to leave for Algiers, to take up residence with her son and his family, and was therefore obliged to sell the shop in which my mother lived.

The shortage of accommodation was now even more acute than during the occupation, and I was not allowed as yet to send my mother any money.

Mme. Parisot's passport for Algiers was handed to her at the beginning of March, and her happiness was great at the thought of seeing her boy again. He was now in the air force and had a baby son. My mother helped her to pack on the morning of her departure; but as Mme. Parisot was preparing to leave, she received a telegram to say that her son had been killed in an airplane accident. She therefore set off in deep mourning, her eyes red with tears.

The shop was immediately sold, and my mother decided not to postpone her journey to Normandy any longer. The train service had just been resumed, though travelers made the journey in cattle-trucks and the trains went no farther than Lisieux. The day before her departure a young American officer, who had dined with me the previous night in London, arrived at my request in Versailles with a large box of provisions, with which my mother entertained her colleagues at the workroom. They had not eaten so well for five years, and the provisions were so generous there was sufficient left over for the party to have lunch the next day and to make sandwiches for my mother's long journey. Her colleagues rose at dawn to accompany her to the station in Paris, where passengers were obliged to queue for five hours before the departure of the train. Her friends busied themselves running round Paris to obtain the final permits. Then they stood on the platform to wave farewell.

My mother stood in the corridor gripping her poor belongings. The miserable parcels hardly held together because there was no string. They were made into bundles like dirty washing, knotted at the top. The train was so crowded that passengers clung to the sides, and my mother had seen nothing like it since the days of the collapse. As so many bridges and viaducts had been destroyed the train was obliged to make long detours to cross hastily constructed Bailey bridges. At many points the passengers alighted to allow the train to pass over alone, testing the viaducts.

At Lisieux the line came to an end.

Darkness had fallen and the passengers looked down on the ruined city too dangerous to explore. The war was not yet over, no bulldozers had cleared the tangled wreckage.

The unhappy passengers, cold, hungry, and exhausted, kept together for warmth in a corner of the waiting-room, one end of which had collapsed, allowing the bitter March wind to blow dust into their reddened eyes. After a sleepless night, cramped and dirty, they queued up at the buffet for barley coffee, in which they poured *calvados*, the fiery but invigorating brandy distilled from cider.

A good-natured inhabitant of Deauville, hearing that my mother was traveling in the same direction as himself, found her a seat in a rickety conveyance bound for that town. She hoped to find another bus to take her the same day to Villers, but there was nothing until the next morning, whereupon the kindly citizen took her home and implored his wife to give her hospitality. She slept deeply until the sun rose again. Then, through the open windows, she caught a glimpse of the sea. Surely now her troubles were nearly over!

Her coach drew up outside the Café Barbe, and my mother climbed down with her packages.

Her heart was beating strongly. She wondered if anybody would recognize her at the café. M. Barbe himself lived in the adjacent villa, one half of which was his residence and the other half his office. Before the war he had painted our farmhouse. Mme. Bayard's husband had always been his most trusted employee, but George Bayard was doubtless still a prisoner in Germany. My mother wondered if she should call on M. Barbe, but she was too shy.

She ordered a cup of hot milk, and asked the serving girl if she could leave her parcels while she walked up the hill. She would send to fetch them later. The girl did not appear to recognize her, but answered that she would be happy to keep the bundles.

Then my mother began the steep climb.

Glittering in the sunshine was the slate roof of the sixteenth-century farmhouse, but the two Italian poplars, which used to lift their arms skyward, were no longer there. My mother was about to pass under the cathedral arch of the narrow lane, when she suddenly changed her mind. Crossing the courtyard of the Poulins' farm she entered the buttery.

Mme. Castel looked up and exclaimed:

"Good gracious! Is it possible? Come in, my good lady."

Wiping her hands on her apron she hurried forward.

André, who was a few months younger than Bobby, was now peering at my mother from behind a yew tree. Mme. Castel appeared highly delighted to see her neighbor, and said that her husband had died a few days before the arrival of the Allies, so that she was now alone with her daughter Yvonne waiting for Ernest to be released from a prisoner-of-war camp in Germany. She went out into the courtyard and called her daughter. They invited my mother to lunch at the big table, and afterward Yvonne harnessed the pony trap to fetch the parcels from the Café Barbe.

My mother was extremely anxious to discover what had happened to the Goguets, but Mme. Castel did not appear willing to discuss the matter. Ugly rumors had reached us all about them, but neither my mother, nor I in England, could discover anything certain. A mysterious cloud hung over the orchard, in which stood our house and where the apple trees were beginning to blossom.

"I understand," said my mother, "that our farmer Goguet is no longer there?"

"That's true," answered Mme. Castel. "The Germans came to take him away during the autumn of 1943."

She paused, and then added: "It's a terrible story, a terrible story, a story of Judas, my good lady."

"Are Mme. Goguet's children with her on the farm?"

"The twins are there. They will be three years old next month."

"But the children we knew—Roger and Renée and little Robert?"

"The girl Renée is in service at Trouville and Robert is a farm-hand at Annebault."

"It's curious to think of Robert as a farm-hand!" exclaimed

my mother. "He was such a child! And Roger, Mme. Castel, what has happened to Roger, the eldest? He must be a grown man, twenty at least."

Mme. Castel averted her gaze.

"I don't quite know," she answered. "I think he is living at Trouville with his wife. You must ask Mme. Goguet."

"With his wife?" queried my mother.

But Mme. Castel only said:

"It's a terrible story—a terrible story!"

Then she added: "You'll be going along there now? Come here at milking time. If you need anything we shall be delighted to oblige you."

My mother looked over the hedge at our beautiful farmhouse nestling in the hollow, and exclaimed:

"Well, at any rate our house is intact! You know, Mme. Castel, I never expected to see it again!"

Mme. Castel laughed grimly.

"I am afraid," she answered, "you may find it rather changed inside."

The white gate was just the same, but my name had been removed. The high elm on the left was dead; it would have to be cut down. There were no cows in the field, and she bitterly regretted the disappearance of the Italian poplars.

Nevertheless, the scene was enchanting and the air smelt sweet. All the charm of this lovely country surged through my mother's veins. Every gnarled apple tree, every blade of grass, seemed to welcome her. In a fortnight's time the whole countryside would be pink and white with blossom.

As she advanced along the path she was very moved. The two houses, at right angles to each other, were as pretty as ever.

A wisp of smoke rose from the Goguets' chimney. An electric cable stretched to the hay loft. She looked back to where it came from. A cement pylon stood at the top of the field known as the Point. My mother remembered what a vast sum it would have cost before the war to equip the farm with electricity, and she was somewhat surprised to see these expensive improvements. Suddenly a flock of geese ran cackling toward her, their necks outstretched. She crossed the planks straddling the rivulet and surveyed the lovely garden. Roses still bloomed, but the rich earth was littered with dung and broken crockery. Something glittered at her feet. She bent down to pick it up and recognized the handle of a Lalique vase, a piece that I had treasured.

Before the flight to St. Malo I had handed my mother a key of the house. She now took it from her bag and opened the door of the big room. The door grated against the tile floor. From this room, once filled with the scent of freshly cut flowers and smouldering logs, came an appalling stench, which caused her to take a sudden step backward. Her eyes, not yet accustomed to the semi-darkness of the raftered room, surveyed the scene as through a veil. Then boldly she entered. A few pieces of furniture, a rusty pail, and a broken rake had been deposited in the center. There were cobwebs everywhere, and some of the panes of the windows had been smashed. She picked her way carefully into the kitchen. The Aga stove had been taken away, and where it had stood there was a gaping hole staring at her like the eye of a Cyclops.

She flung open the kitchen door to let in the air. Then she went upstairs. All the bedrooms were empty. The cupboards where I had kept my dresses and my lavender-scented linen sheets had been stripped of their boarding. Thick nails had been hammered into the oak beams. There was nothing, nothing at all, for her to sleep on, and there were cobwebs everywhere.

She thought: "I must ask the Goguette for a broom and some water." Then she hurried downstairs and, crossing the *patio*, knocked at the door of the farmhouse. There was no answer. She lifted the latch. A log fire was burning brightly in the hearth. The living-room was clean and bright. An elderly woman she had never seen before eyed her from the corridor. She called out: "Is Mme. Goguet there?"

Silently, like a shadow, the Goguette emerged from the bedroom where she doubtless had stood to watch my mother walk across the field. Her appearance had changed and she looked as if she had suddenly tried to copy the fashion of the city. She said something in her deep voice, and as my mother went across the red-tiled floor to meet her, she caught sight of the twins in the bedroom, and ran to them. Then, before she could check herself, she exclaimed:

"Oh! You've got my grandson's little white chair!"

The Goguette turned on her angrily.

"It isn't his," she answered, her eyes flashing; "the chair comes from my sister at Caen."

"I'm sorry," said my mother.

Then she added:

"Would you be so kind, Mme. Goguet, as to pump some water into the tank in our house?"

"You've only to go down to the stream like we do," answered the Goguette.

"I have no pail," answered my mother. "But tell me, is there anything wrong with the well?"

"One needs gasoline for the motor," answered the Goguette sullenly.

"Why, yes, I forgot," said my mother. "Does that mean you haven't any?"

The Goguette turned her head and answered:

"Not for you!"

Then my mother knew that she had been unwise to say anything about the chair. The elderly woman was still standing in the corridor. My mother felt her penetrating gaze as she turned to go.

She could, of course, borrow a pail from Mme. Castel, but she would be obliged to make endless journeys from the stream to bring up enough water to clean out the house. She went through the rooms in search of a broom. It was just possible there might be one in the closet. She pushed open the door, and nearly fainted at its degraded state. On the floor lay a book from which the pages had been ripped for toilet paper. In spite of her abhorrence she stooped to examine it, and recognized the New Testament in French which my mother-in-law had given me. It had been wilfully defiled. The book was of a specially large format, with bold type, such as clergymen use in the pulpit, and my mother-in-law had chosen it because I was short-sighted. My mother picked it up reverently. I had turned to it a hundred times when waiting to deliver my son. Now the Gospel of St. Matthew was gone. What barbarians had passed this way?

18

As THE sun was going down my mother climbed wearily up the path through the orchard leading to Cathedral Lane. She had done everything possible to clean the house, but it was not yet habitable, and she had decided to ask Mme. Bayard to put her up for the night. My big-hearted charwoman lived on the main road to Dives, and my mother had no doubt that she at least would be genuinely pleased to see her.

Mme. Bayard knew everybody in the village. She and her mother, Mme. Blanchard, had delivered the mail during the First World War, which occupation had made them familiar with every farm and homestead for miles round. Mme. Bayard liked to recall her career as a postwoman, for it was thus that she had met her gentle, good-natured George. She had first seen him, a few months after the Peace Treaty at Versailles, loading up a horse-drawn van outside the railway station at Villers, where Titine (as everybody called her in the village) had gone with her mother to fetch the mail from the Paris train. George was driving for a carrier who had just set up business with a curious collection of chariots and covered wagons, which rumbled over the country roads delivering luggage or parcels too heavy to be sent by post. Titine fell in love with the good-looking young driver who had emigrated to Normandy from the beetroot fields of eastern France, and after their marriage they bought a plot of land which Duclos, the nurseryman, had used for rearing pear trees, for which reason Mme. Bayard had the best pear trees in the village.

My mother reflected that their son Jean-Louis must now be fifteen. I had much affection for the boy, and had begun to teach him English. How fortunate that he was still a child during the occupation! Mme. Bayard must have been sufficiently miserable thinking of her husband in the prison camp at Stuttgart.

As soon as my mother knocked at the door she felt better. She had no fears about Mme. Bayard's behavior during the occupation, for Titine's heart was stout and true, and she was incapable of any base action. Their friendship, based on mutual regard, was a splendid thing in these days of suspicion and revenge; and as soon as Mme. Bayard opened the door a great, enveloping, affectionate smile spread over her ample features. My mother's arrival was no surprise to her, for she herself had written to say that the time was ready for her return, and had she not been working all day she would certainly have called at the farm.

"Well," exclaimed Mme. Bayard as she helped my mother off with her coat, "a lot of things have happened since you were last here, my poor lady!"

"Yes, indeed," answered my mother. "I hear that Mme. Caffet's husband, accused of collaboration, was dragged through the village street with a halter round his neck! What will my son-in-law have to say about that? But you, Mme. Bayard? Did you go on working at the Caffets'? I remember you used to scrub their kitchen out every day."

"And so I did all during the occupation," answered Mme. Bayard. "You might say I was in the thick of it. And you know what a tongue I have! It simply won't stop wagging. I hardly know by what miracle I'm still alive. Sit down by the fire, Mme. Gal. We have still a little wood to put on it. What a misery, my poor lady, what a misery! Talking about my incorrigible tongue and the Caffets' kitchen, I was cleaning the pots and pans one day when Mme. Caffet came in with a fine young man, a real god, Mme. Gal, tall and handsome as you could wish. 'Let me introduced you to our new chauffeur!' exclaimed Mme. Caffet. He had the pleasantest manners, but after a few moments, started to be very rude about the Germans. You know I'm the last to echo such sentiments, specially with my Bayard in prison at Stuttgart, but I was just going to let myself go when I felt something cold round my stomach, and a voice from heaven whispered in my ear: 'Hold your tongue, Mme. Bayard, hold your tongue!'

"I bent my head over the pots and pans and rattled the handles to make a lot of noise, and I never said a word all the morning. When he had gone, Mme. Caffet said to me: 'Isn't he a nice fellow, our new chauffeur?' 'Perhaps,' I answered, 'but I never talk to strangers.'

"Well, you remember young Faneau, my good lady, the lad whose widowed mother has the carpentry shop? She made the chicken coop for your daughter just before you had to leave us. I wonder what happened to that chicken coop? Madame was very proud of it. Now who would have thought that young Faneau had so much courage? He drove round the country on his motor-bicycle delivering tracts for the resistance group, and the only thing wrong with him was that, being such an ardent patriot, he thought that nobody could be any less patriotic than himself. He talked rather too openly about what he was doing. Two days after the new chauffeur had walked into Mme. Caffet's kitchen, I was passing the *gendarmerie* when I saw a crowd standing round a motor-car drawn up by the gates. I guessed they were taking somebody away. You know what it is, Mme. Gal? These occasions made everybody nervous—even the collaborators, who never quite knew what was going to happen to them. I edged up a little and inside the car I saw our brave Faneau, his face as white as a sheet of paper, his wrists handcuffed, and behind him, lolling in the seat, was Mme. Caffet's new chauffeur, who had emerged as a member of the Gestapo! Yes, my dear lady, he had been brought into the kitchen to try to make me talk."

"What happened to poor Faneau?"

"We are never likely to know that," answered Mme. Bayard. "And there was Michaud, the dandy young coal merchant whose wife presented him with seven sons in as many years. Do you recall Michaud? Of course you do! He sold Mme. Madeleine the coke for her Aga stove.

"Michaud was in need of money and Caffet kept on saying to him: 'Why don't you drive trucks for the Germans! They pay well.' But Michaud answered: 'I don't like the idea,' whereupon Caffet used to answer: 'Don't be a fool, Michaud. I know you have a lot of mouths to feed.'

"At last Michaud accepted, and the Germans, who were not

sure of him, made him take his place in the middle of a convoy
to prevent him from deserting. They carried cement for the
Todt organization which was building the Atlantic wall. The
convoy was sighted by a Spitfire, which straddled it with machine-gun fire, wrecking Michaud's truck. I was in the garage
when it was brought back for repair, and believe me, Mme. Gal,
I nearly fainted, because the driving-seat was bespattered with
poor Michaud's brain. He was buried at Villers."

Mme. Bayard passed a hand over her forehead and continued:

"Yes, Caffet left great misery behind him. I expect M. Duclos,
the nurseryman, will be coming along to attend to your garden
soon. His handsome young grandson, Clément, who helped plant
the apple trees and the peaches in your private orchard, is still
covered with scars and bruises from the pounding and the beating he received from the Gestapo at Caen. That is a sorry tale,
Mme. Gal, and I must start at the beginning.

"The poor boy, who is nineteen or twenty, was ordered with
a dozen others to go to Caen to sign the register of young men
capable of being sent to Germany for forced labor. I must say
that these youths were extremely brave, and none of them revealed any fear when the coach, driven by one of Caffet's mechanics, left the garage.

"On their way back from Caen they picked up Quettel, the
beadle, who had for many years been a tenant of M. Allard.
Quettel was fond of a drop of apple-jack, and as the motor-
coach neared Villers he was feeling happy and started to make
the boys sing, whereupon Caffet's mechanic went out of his way
to drive past a villa occupied by German staff generals. The next
day all the occupants were arrested for sedition. The Germans
accused them of singing the *Internationale*.

"They were taken back to Caen, where all of them, including
Quettel, were stripped naked, pounded with rifle-butts, kicked
with hobnailed boots, and thrashed with whips, until they lay in
an immense pool of blood. Some of them were exiled to the
Channel Islands. The village was so horrified by this crime that
they were later released, but Quettel died from his wounds and
poor Clément is in a sad condition."

My mother was extremely moved.

"Tell me about yourself and about Jean-Louis."

Mme. Bayard answered:

"About Jean-Louis, yes. That is perhaps the strangest story of all.

"During the occupation the lad went to college at Caen. Bayard and I are not rich but, as you know, we are anxious to give the boy a good start in life, and there is no adequate instruction for children over twelve in the village. He is making splendid progress. If only your daughter could send him an English dictionary! That's what he needs. School books are quite impossible to buy.

"Last year, after the Whitsun holidays, I took him down to the main square to see him off on the coach to Caen, which stops outside Caffet's garage. While we were waiting on the pavement, Mme. Vincent, the notary's wife, came along with her two youngest children who, like Jean-Louis, were at college at Caen. They lived with their mother, who owned a house there, and they had been spending the Whitsun holidays with their father at Villers. The notary, because of his business, was obliged to remain here, but I believe he considered Caen safer in the event of an invasion.

"I cannot tell you how wonderfully the notary behaved. You should have seen him at the public auction sales defying the Germans—not openly, mind you, but with a word of sarcasm here and there which made them very uncomfortable. 'Here's a tin hat!' he would say. 'A fine tin hat! You'll need it soon, very soon, I assure you. What offers for this tin hat?'

"One of his elder sons was in the *maquis*. Yes, the notary was a great example.

"Mme. Vincent was a good woman, deeply religious and very strict about her children's education. She was good enough to speak to me at the bus stop, and after a few moments I said to her:

" 'What worries me, Mme. Vincent, are all these announcements on the B.B.C. about leaving the railway stations, the ports, and the coast towns, and all those personal messages which sometimes take ten minutes to deliver. I can't help thinking that the

English are ready to do something at last. It's a great worry, Mme. Vincent, to have my Jean-Louis so far off in his college at Caen. Supposing something *were* to happen?'

"She smiled at me so sweetly and answered: 'I shall look after your Jean-Louis, Mme. Bayard. I shall treat him just as if he were one of my own children, and if anything does happen he shall come to my house, and you will have nothing to worry about.'

"I was so grateful that tears began to wet my cheeks, and I thanked her. Then the coach arrived, and as if she wanted to prove to me that Jean-Louis was already a member of her family, she made him sit with her children.

"I came back home and kept on saying to myself: 'My Jean-Louis is in good hands'; but after two or three days that voice from heaven which had warned me about Mme. Caffet's new chauffeur whispered continually: 'Bring back your son, Titine. Bring back your son.'

"Of course, if Bayard had been here he would have laughed at me. But then, Bayard was in Stuttgart, and so all the responsibility fell on me, and it was more than I could stand.

"The next day I took the coach to Caen and brought my Jean-Louis home. Really I felt ashamed of myself. Even if the English were ready to do something, there was no reason to suppose that our part of the world would be involved. Besides, if the notary was content to allow his family to remain, who was I to think I knew better?"

Mme. Bayard hid her good, honest face in her hands.

Then she rose from her chair and said:

"Nobody has ever heard of Mme. Vincent and her two children since. Think of it! They have completely disappeared. No wonder that Maître Vincent never writes to your daughter! Sometimes he thinks that they were taken away as hostages by the Germans, that perhaps he will suddenly hear from them; but no, at heart he is certain he will never see them again. They lie under the devastation that was once his beautiful house at Caen. They were buried by those English bombs for which so often he prayed on his knees. But that such a thing should have happened to Maître Vincent, the one really patriotic man in the village! What irony, my dear lady! How *could* he write to your daughter? He still walks in a daze. He never opens a letter, still less answers one. Probably he says to himself:

" 'If a stupid, uneducated woman like Mme. Bayard thought of bringing back her Jean-Louis, am I not doubly responsible for what has happened to my beloved family?'

"Oh, my dear madame, what a cruel, cruel war!"

19

THE silent hostility my mother encountered on the farm began to affect her nerves. Her letters to London were filled with deep misgivings. She felt that her sudden arrival was unwelcome and had disturbed the plans of the Goguette, and she implored me to help her.

Bravely she set about cleaning the old farmhouse. In spite of her delicate health she made progress every day, and quickly reacted to the kindness of her neighbors, Mme. Castel and Yvonne Poulin, who supplied her with fresh milk and eggs. She used to arrive at the Poulin farm while the cows were being milked, and she would sit demurely on a stool in a corner of the low room listening to the conversation of all those who, like herself, were waiting for Yvonne to cross the courtyard with the creamy pails hanging from the yoke.

She did not dare again to ask Mme. Castel to enlighten her about the tragedy on her own estate. She knew that if she exercised patience the story would gradually be told her by the very people who just now were so circumspect. Already she knew the name of the woman who was living with the Goguette—a certain Marie who had arrived in the village after the last war to serve as cook to the man who started the carrier's business.

Marie had the reputation of being an extremely good cook, and during the occupation had been employed for a time by Victor Duprez at the Bruyères.

The Poulins were rather jealous that the Goguets had electricity on the farm, whereas their pump worked by hand, and their house was still lighted with oil lamps.

Mme. Castel explained that during the occupation the Duprez had built a transformer to equip the Bruyères with electricity, and had suggested that any neighboring farms so minded should take advantage of this opportunity to make use of the current. The Goguets had welcomed the idea, but Yvonne Poulin thought that in absence of Ernest, it was wiser to take no decision.

Victor Duprez furnished his house with nineteenth century pictures—he was a great admirer of Napoleon—and morocco bindings, and during the war entertained here members of his own family who were all gourmets. Marie had, therefore, what she needed to exercise her art, and at one time Roger Goguet had been employed on the Bruyères estate and served on occasion at table.

The remodeling of Berlequet into a lovely farmhouse, held up during the panic of the Exodus, was carried out during the Occupation, but when Victor attempted to eject Groscol, the furious farmer barricaded himself with his wife and five children in the pigsty where they remained till hunger drove them out.

At one time the beautiful new farm was offered to Roger Goguet but there was such a coming and going of German soldiers that Roger was sent back to his father on my farm. Marie, the cook, also went to live at Berlequet for a short period.

Now the scene was almost ready for the tragedy that was to make my farm spoken of in hushed tones all over the Pays d'Auge, as far as Pont L'Évêque, Lisieux, and Caen. The crime will be told over hearth fires for many generations. So far, however, my mother merely sensed it. The pink and white orchard had a heavy atmosphere.

Mme. Castel went to a cupboard, and taking down a pretty pewter milk-pail that I had once brought over from London said:

"You will be able to take your milk away in it every evening."

To my mother it was something more than a useful receptacle to carry away the milk, for of all the things I had brought from London to furnish my beautiful farm it seemed the only one left. Everything else had disappeared, everything but the New Testament in French which, outrageously sullied, now reposed on a chair beside my mother's couch in the big downstairs room. She turned to it with love and respect, reading a few verses by candlelight before retiring. The couch had been lent to her by Roginsky, the furniture dealer, who, alas, had very little left in his shop, but what little he had he offered unhesitatingly and without thought of gain.

My mother had brought from Versailles the sheets she had so roughly made from the linings of military capes, and as it was impossible to obtain new ones she was obliged to go on using them. She had no blankets, but was patiently making a patch quilt of many colors from all the small pieces of wool she had collected during the last two years. She had hardly any crockery, and her knife and spoons of cheap metal would not have found grace with the poorest person before the war. She owned one frayed dish-cloth. When the Goguette hung out her washing to dry in the March wind my mother saw many splendid pieces of pure Irish linen which had once lain in my lavender-scented cupboard, but she dared not say anything.

The house was becoming cleaner every day. Though my mother's hands were crippled with rheumatism, she felt that at last she was working constructively, and she told everybody she met that I would soon be arriving to put the estate in order. Thus even from a distance my influence was beginning to be apparent, and Mme. Castel kept on making veiled references to the future of the farm. People appeared to take it for granted that the Goguette would be leaving at Christmas, and Mme. Castel, ambitious for her daughter and son-in-law, would have liked to obtain the use of some of my orchards.

Goguet was commonly believed to be in Germany, and we knew that on his return he would be in a position to claim the privilege of all returned prisoners who, even if their contracts had expired, could return to their farms for a term equal to that which they had passed in captivity. The Goguette's decision to leave at Christmas was dependent on this factor. Meanwhile her antagonism was making my mother's situation intolerable.

Some days after her arrival my mother went for a long walk to inspect the property. What she called the grand tour required the best part of two hours, but the sun was so warm and the grass so tender and fresh that she set out full of excitement to renew contact with the orchards and woods.

Every now and again from the direction of the coast there

came a great explosion which made the birds rise into the crisp air. These explosions reminded her of the aerial bombardment of Le Havre during the last weeks before the collapse.

Now German prisoners under a French armed guard were exploding the mine-fields they themselves had laid. The straw-haired youths in *feldgrau* who, during four years of occupation, had walked proudly through the village, were marched through the country lane in ragged processions, and often they were to be seen carrying bunches of wild flowers to place on the graves of their comrades killed when a mine had exploded under them.

When the Germans entered Villers, the *Kommandatur* installed itself in two villas facing each other at the top of the Rue Pasteur, the steep road leading from the village to a spot known as the Meeting of the Four Ways, high up on the plateau, a few minutes' walk from the Poulins' farm.

The *Kommandatur* proper occupied a pretty house with a balcony and a flight of stone steps overgrown with moss roses, which led down into an untidy but picturesque garden where the *Kommandant* liked to smoke his cigar after dinner in the cool of the evening. This villa was known as The Rosary. On the opposite side of the road was a strange habitation built at the close of the last century to resemble a medieval castle. The name of this villa was The Dungeon, and it became the headquarters of an artillery regiment.

The Meeting of the Four Ways was an excellent observation post. My husband and I had stood there just before midnight on the eve of our departure.

Our own lane was heavily mined, doubtless to prevent any surprise attack against The Rosary and The Dungeon from the direction of the plateau, and my mother, who knew nothing of this, nearly went along it on the day of her arrival. Mercifully she had desisted because of the brambles and barbed wire. In the grounds of an estate belonging to M. Salmond, a Paris doctor, she came upon two graves surmounted by steel hats, both beflowered with hydrangeas. A Canadian and a German had fought to the death, and lay, nameless, side by side.

As my mother walked through my orchards she noticed how many fine trees had already been cut down. If Goguet had not been arrested by the Germans he would doubtless have done us even greater damage, for wood was fetching high prices, but the Goguette was not strong enough to fell many trees herself, and it had become difficult to obtain laborers. Nevertheless, my mother looked bitterly at the tall stacks of fine logs which my farmer's wife stood in the courtyard. The logs in her possession had been stolen from the estate, and my mother reflected that it was a little hard that she herself had nothing to burn while the Goguette enjoyed the results of her theft.

But on the whole these were minor vexations, trivial indeed when compared to what might have happened to the farm. Even the pillage of the house would not have appeared so sinister if my mother had received a friendly welcome. This antagonism hid something much deeper than she could guess for the moment.

Gradually the beauty of the scene charmed her. The new farm which had risen magically on the site of Groscol's former house was really quite fascinating, and as she passed it a Polish laborer, who was the new farmer, touched his cap and greeted her amicably. She opened the white gate leading to the Big Valley, and it was splendid to see how the young trees had grown strong and straight, no longer requiring the protection of the steel corsets. Now the cows could safely rub their backs against them. Sturdy roots attached them to the soil. The hay-field stretched as far as the eye could reach and the sun brought out the perfume of wild flowers. This country was a paradise.

When first she had walked through these orchards seven years ago, the Goguette's children had romped round her, pointing out everything of interest with shrill voices made harshly musical with the Norman intonation. Little Robert, the youngest Goguet, held her hand when they passed the field where Robin, the bull, glared at them fiercely through the hedge where the bees made honey. Renée was a lithe, olive-complexioned girl who had not yet made her first communion. Roger was awkward, but so astutely close to the earth that it was easy to forget his baser instincts, to see only what was picturesquely peasant in his character. They had taught her where the wild strawberries grew and which trees yielded the most luscious nuts in autumn. They had filled her mind with country lore and curious superstition. They had dragged her to the big wood which I had bought from Victor Duprez for only a few dollars because in those days woodland had no value. Now she trod the same path, and over the hedge could see the field in which Victor had put sheep to graze: unheard of fantasy in peace-time, but now the sheep gave forth their wool to soften the rigor of cruel winters. The big kitchen garden of the Duprez home was superbly tended and cunningly laid out. Peaches grew against the red-brick walls and the vine prospered in the low glass-houses.

The big wood had no real opening. One entered it as best one could, being careful not to tear one's stockings against the brambles. Almost virgin, a clear bubbling stream ran over a pebble bed at the bottom, and I had always dreamed of building a log hut for my son in this fairyland where the trees grew so tall that it was difficult to see the topmost branches.

My mother could hardly believe that she was home. The sunshine and the clear air, the new freedom and the sweetness of the day, gradually chased away the misery of her life at Versailles.

By the time she arrived at the Poulin farmhouse, the cows had already been milked, and Yvonne and her mother were standing in the center of the excited crowd. The high-pitched voices stopped at her approach and the little crowd turned to her with greedy, expectant eyes.

"Well, my good, poor lady," exclaimed Mme. Castel after a moment's silence. "Tell us all about it."

"Yes," echoed the others, "tell us all about it."

My mother felt her cheeks turn warm. Her incorrigible shyness was unable to overcome this unexpected interest in her person, and she could only answer:

"But about what, Mme. Castel? I've been down in the wood these two hours."

They looked at her uncomprehendingly, but the naïveté of her expression soon told them that she was ignoront of the stupendous events which had just taken place.

Then little Mme. Castel said importantly:

"Mme. Goguet, your farmer's wife, has been arrested by two *gendarmes* who marched her off between them down the lane."

"Past our front gate," said Yvonne Poulin. "She was wheeling her bicycle, and as she went by she turned her face away from us."

"A pretty first of April," put in Mme. Castel. "Things should happen now, for, believe me, she'll not be the only one to spend the night in jail. There are others whose conscience will not be at ease today. That's what comes of being so sure the Germans would win the war. Others also will be sorry that the Germans are no longer here to protect their infamy. It's a terrible story, a terrible story, a story of Judas, my good lady."

My mother's hand trembled as she held out the little English milk-can, for it could not escape her that there was something oppressive in living alone in the old farmhouse, whose walls had obviously echoed to the sounds of this intangible wickedness to which the Goguette might or might not have been a party.

She returned thoughtfully home, but her relief at being rid of the Goguette was somewhat blunted towards nightfall upon seeing Renée arrive to take her mother's place, for Marie, being unversed in the art of milking, had sent for the girl, now turned almost into a grown woman, to supervise the farm. And was this not the same Renée who had tried to stone her daughter?

Before retiring for the night my mother wrote me a long letter recounting the emotions of the day.

Within forty-eight hours all the Pays d'Auge appeared to be occupied with the drama that had started in my orchard, and about which as yet my mother had been able to gather so little. The occupation might have taught our neighbors to be discreet. Then again, the sacking of my lovely house had undoubtedly been on a large scale. Perhaps others beside the Goguets had been involved, and that even those whom my mother thought her friends were trembling lest she should discover too much. To know whom she could trust was her worst predicament. Her intuition told her that Mme. Castel and her daughter were true friends. They might not have dared prevent the systematic sacking of my house, but they would not have participated in it. But what connection had there been between the looting and that crime which seemed to have put a curse over my orchard, that Judas crime? And when did the looting take place—before or after the crime? These were the problems that kept my mother awake at night. Obviously her sudden arrival on the scene had disturbed whatever the Goguette was doing. That would explain the woman's antagonism, her desire, until her arrest, to make so difficult my mother's life.

The next morning it became known that the Goguette, who

had spent the night in the village police station, had been taken to prison at Pont-L'Évêque. This town, about ten miles away, was almost completely destroyed, but the law courts still functioned. Then news reached my mother from Trouville that the Goguets' eldest son Roger had been arrested there. He lived with a woman many years older than he in the high part of the town where he was in semi-hiding. Roger also was taken to Pont L'Évêque and put into jail.

Clearly Roger had been the central figure in the crime, whatever that crime might have been. Mme. Castel hinted that although he had enjoyed a good deal of the loot from my house, his crime tormented him, and that at night devils appeared to him in such terrible garb that he filled the lodging-house with his screams.

He had, of course, always been strange and readers will remember how, when my husband and I discovered the farm, Robert, the Goguets' second son, then a very little boy, was almost drowned in a cattle pool while his big brother had in the most inexplicable and cowardly way looked on, sucking his thumb, his cap pulled down over his eyes. There had been other incidents. In an attempt to bring out what might be good in the lad I had once taken him along the lane by Dr. Salmond's house, but there he had suddenly begun to tear the paling down out of a sort of sadism.

Mother and eldest son were now in prison at Pont L'Évêque, and slowly the law was being set in motion. Then suddenly in the evening, when my mother went, as was her custom, to fetch her milk at the Poulins' farm, news reached them of an even more frightening event.

On the Saturday afternoon when the Goguette had been marched down Cathedral Lane and Roger had been arrested at Trouville, other *gendarmes*, this time from Dozulé, had been sent to the picturesque village of Annebault to arrest the Goguette's father, Old Man Hommet, in the cottage where, by popular belief, he was supposed to concoct his spells. Peasant superstition held him in respect, and children ran and women made the sign of the cross at his approach. For months past stories of the drama at my farm had been whispered over log fires in every cottage. The sorcerer, who had beaten his first wife to death, had apparently incited Roger to do his evil deed, and so when the *gendarmes* marched down the little street with its rose-covered thatched houses the people of Annebault were very excited.

Hommet, hearing the tread of feet, looked through the parlor window, and then hastily dispatched his wife to meet the men at the door. He listened to their conversation through a crack in the timbering, and when he heard them ask for him, he climbed quickly to his bedroom, seized a knife, and cut his throat. He was not even heard to groan, but was found dead in a pool of blood.

In the low buttery of the Poulin farm this news came at the end of two days of great excitement. My mother recalled the many, many times Hommet had walked with Goguet from the farmhouse to the cider press. His wizened second wife, the Goguette's mother, was apparently left alone in her cottage at Annebault, where she was hourly expecting her own arrest. She was too frightened to wash the blood off the oak timbering of the bedroom, but spent long hours crouching by the fire, her mind occupied with dismal thoughts.

20

WHEN in June I made an application to go to France I was told that women were not yet being given permission to travel. I therefore insisted that my husband should go for a few days to see my mother and look after my interests.

The first person he met in the village was Mlle. Lefranc, the young midwife who had helped to bring our son into the world. We had last seen her very late in the evening in the darkened main street on the eve of our flight. Her car had stood by the curb at the back of Roginsky's house, and she was piling up her suit-cases ready to leave as soon as her last patient had been delivered safely of her child.

She had changed not at all since this last meeting, and immediately took up the story.

Madeleine Montague, Ernest Poulin's sister, who lived with her husband on a small farm on the road to St. Vaast, had been expecting her baby at any moment, but the new member of the family appeared to be in no hurry to make its appearance, and finally Madeleine Montague, with several other women in her condition, were evacuated to a village beyond the great bridge across the river Orme.

Mlle. Lefranc was thus left free to look after herself.

Instead of going to Lion-sur-Mer, just above Caen, where she owned a cottage, she decided to drive to St. Nazaire, where her sister was married to a naval engineer.

She proved to be one of the last people to leave. The farmers, having killed their cats and dogs, had allowed their farm animals to roam at liberty, with the result that the main square was filled with rabbits, hens and cows, which made a strange picture in the dim light of dawn. The Roginskys had preceded Mlle. Le-

franc to Bayeaux where they intended to spend a few days, but
when Mlle. Lefranc arrived in this town she discovered that her
friends had gone and that the road to St. Nazaire was closed. She
therefore followed in the wake of a British convoy bound for
Cherbourg, but the Germans caught up with her and made her
turn back.

She re-entered Villers on July first, having crossed the Dives
over a wooden bridge which the Germans had just built. Most
of those who had merely tried to hide themselves in the surrounding country were already back, and the open-air café of
the Hôtel de France, which faces the sands, was filled with German soldiers drinking champagne.

Mme. Bayard had just returned from a ludicrous adventure.
Herself, Jean-Louis, her two married sisters with their children,
and old Mme. Blanchard, stricken with the evacuation fever, had
all clambered into an uncle's truck which was to take them to
safety. When they were comfortably seated on kitchen chairs,
they discovered that not one of them knew how to drive. Mme.
Bayard's eldest sister, Mme. Mazure, had a boy of seventeen who
was to be a schoolmaster. He was the only male in the truck, or
at least the only one to wear long trousers, and accordingly the
shy youth, goaded by these laughing females, turned the knobs
and buttons and managed to start the vehicle on its zigzag journey. After covering half a dozen miles, he brought the truck to
a standstill by the ditch.

Night was beginning to fall, and old Mme. Blanchard announced that she had no intention to sleep in an orchard under
the stars. "After all," she added, "I'm not a cow! We came here
to escape the Germans. So far we haven't seen one. I prefer to
face a problematical death than to catch a cold!"

Her daughters all said:

"Mother Blanchard is right. Let us go home."

They climbed back into the truck and young Mazure managed to turn it round, but after a while, seeing a bridge in front
of him, he refused to negotiate it a second time, and again
brought the truck to a standstill. Then everybody jumped out
and walked home.

Meanwhile the Goguets had borrowed a horse and cart from
Mme. Woolf, a neighbor.

M. and Mme. Castel, and Yvonne Poulin and her son, drove to

Fromentin in the pony trap. Both families soon tired of their wanderings and returned to their respective farms almost at the same moment. The giant Groscol, drunker than ever, was barring the entrance to the Poulin farm with a scythe.

"Welcome home!" he exclaimed. "If anybody had tried to come in, I would have chopped his head off."

Then, raising his voice loud enough for the Goguets to hear, he screamed:

"There is the Goguette! I have chased all her cows into the road!"

On July second, Mlle. Lefranc met Mme. Goguet in the main square of the village and said to her:

"I've been thinking, Mme. Goguet, that it would be a good idea for me to come up to the old house and take away some of the more valuable things for safe custody. Of course I could not take everything, but we might save the beds and the linen and madame's valuable coats."

"Oh, you know, they didn't leave me a key!"

"We might get over that difficulty. Suppose you signed a paper to say that you witnessed my act and that it was for the best. That would certainly satisfy madame when she returns."

"No, thank you, mademoiselle, I prefer not," answered the Goguette.

A week later Mme. Goguet saw Mlle. Lefranc in the main street and said to her:

"You can come up to the farm now. We found a German sleeping in madame's bed. They have taken a whole lot of things."

"No," answered Mlle. Lefranc. "If the house has been broken into, I refuse to have anything to do with it."

Exactly two years later the midwife was called to the farm, where the Goguette was in childbirth. The accouchement was so simple that when the farmer's wife was delivered of the first baby, she was not even aware that there was another.

"As the twins lay in the bed," said Mlle. Lefranc, "I looked up and exclaimed: 'Why, there is little Bobby's cot!' 'No,' answered the Goguette, 'it belongs to my children.'" But Mlle. Lefranc, having nursed my child for more than two months, well remembered the white cot with its Pompadour roses, and it reminded her of the cosy room in the farmhouse where she and I had spent so many hours.

When Mlle. Lefranc was ready to dress the twins, she was handed a pile of Tetras napkins. "Oh!" she exclaimed again. "These are madame's napkins." "No," answered the Goguette, "they belong to my children." Mlle. Lefranc went to the cupboard and opened the drawers. Everything was just as she had seen it on her last visit to the old farmhouse. Even the ointments were English. She was offered the scales on which every day she had placed Bobby at a time when he refused to put on any weight because I was breast-feeding him. They were of a type normally only found in hospital. She recognized all the linen and the eiderdown with the flowered design which I had bought from Roginsky.

Young Mathieu, the fair-haired son of the village plumber, who in June 1940 had so courageously driven us all on the first lap of our journey to St. Malo, was now back from Germany. He found on his return that his father had parted company with his former associate Dauvilaire, who had set up a business of his own elsewhere, that there was hardly anything to sell in the shop, and that until the prisoners returned from Germany there would be no labor. Orders were pouring in, however, from all the people whose villas had been damaged or looted. What young Mathieu wanted most was a suit of clothes and a pair of shoes which, just then, no money could buy.

He told my husband that the Aga and the refrigerator from my house had been removed by the Germans to a requisitioned farm above Blonville. The estate was owned by M. Foyer, a very honest person, who would certainly be delighted to return them. The transportation of the Aga was, of course, a major difficulty, but Mathieu thought he could manage it if my husband went first to inspect the cooker at M. Foyer's farm.

It was almost as much of a problem for my husband to transport himself to M. Foyer's place as it was for young Mathieu to bring back the Aga, but by a happy coincidence he met in the market-place the *gendarme* Aimable Rihouey whose soft blue eyes considered the question a moment. He said: "If we turn the engine off every time we go downhill, then I think there is just sufficient gas in the car."

This was Rihouey's afternoon off, and the fine weather

tempted him into the country lanes. He liked the idea of having somebody new to talk to, and he was conscious of the fact that he cut quite a dashing figure in his light brown linen uniform. The events of the last five years had passed lightly over Rihouey's fair locks, for he resolved all matters of conscience by the comforting reflection that the authorities were always right. He felt capable, therefore, of passing judgment on each matter with complete impartiality, and this detachment gave spice to his conversation.

Blonville is a hamlet halfway between Villers and Deauville, but it also gives its name to the rich pasture land on the plateau above sea-level. An avenue of fine trees led to M. Foyer's comfortable residence, but the house was obviously in some disorder, and the master and his family were busy cleaning out the rooms. They came into the courtyard to greet the *gendarme*, their faces covered with dust, and when they were acquainted with the purpose of the visit, M. Foyer himself led the way into the cellar where the Aga, as bright as ever, reposed under a white sheet. From all appearances it had suffered not at all, though the refrigerator which stood next to it was chipped and yellowed.

M. Foyer took leave of his guests at the limit of his land, and Aimable Rihouey drove my husband over the rough ground, past a barbed-wire barrier where once a German sentinal had stood proudly at the entrance to an encampment of wooden huts. What a decadence of German might! Soon they emerged by the railway station at Villers, which in pre-war days stood like a colored toy halfway between the farmhouse and the Louis XIII château. This station, far removed from the village, always had the most beautifully tended gardens. During the "phoney" war a large number of luxurious Blue Train sleepers and Golden Arrow cars were parked on the sidings which run alongside the cemetery.

There was nothing much left of the station now except the shattered platform. Aimable Rihouey claimed that on three occasions the Allies sent twenty-five bombers to blow it to pieces, but not a single bomb hit the target. Most of them fell in the cemetery where a gravedigger was once hurled into the depths of a tomb opened up by the explosion, and buried alive. Nénette Riquet, who during the bombardment of Le Havre had hanged herself by a bull halter in the cart-shed, was buried here.

Her grave was ripped open and her remains scattered over the railway siding. Thus she did not even find peace in death. Her tombstone remained intact, and as it was a pity to waste it the family placed it over the grave of M. Castel when he died a few days after the liberation, for by then gravestones were not easy things to acquire.

"You will agree," said Aimable Rihouey, "that it was strange to send seventy-five heavy bombers to plough up a cemetery. A few days later the R.A.F. sent over two small machines which blew up the station with a single bomb."

Aimable Rihouey drove my husband back along the avenue leading to the village. He began talking about Peter Gravé, the rotund rubicund builder who had put up Goguet's house and the stables before the war. Apparently the Germans treated him as a harmless eccentric. He took to growing a Hitler moustache, and during the "V for Victory" campaign stopped a German lance-corporal and said to him:

"Take care, my good man, that you are not arrested by the Gestapo," and he pointed with an accusing finger at the soldier's stripe. "I do believe you're wearing the V sign."

Aimable Rihouey claimed that even the German officers laughed at his practical jokes, but he met his death in this same station avenue where he had made so many people merry. Cycling home one day after a long spell of inebriety, he skidded into a poplar tree, and died the same night from a fractured skull.

My mother was doing wonders with the old house, and though only the big living room was furnished, the entire place had been thoroughly cleaned. A few pieces of furniture had been rather mysteriously returned, such as the grandfather's clock, though the key was missing, and a large cupboard of Norman design in which my mother stored the dainties I was able to send her every time a willing acquaintance crossed the Channel. She had now a modest store of tea, coffee, and chocolate—very little, of course, compared to English standards, but she was so extraordinarily economical where her own needs were concerned, that they seemed to last for ever. My husband further enlarged this shelf of good things, but as he watched her poor hands putting each packet carefully away, he felt ashamed that he had not brought twice as much. My mother was obliged to wash her scanty linen with the ashes of the burned logs to save the price-less bars of English soap treasured for important occasions. How resourceful my mother had become, cooking all manner of appetizing dishes in two or three smoky saucepans over the faggots! She had even learned to make charcoal, which she was putting away against the time when the Aga would return. She lived in her almost bare house like Robinson Crusoe on his desert island, making use of everything that nature provided, for it was impossible to buy anything in the shops, not even a plate or a fork. But she was so gay, so confident, so brave; and now that the Goguette was no longer there to mock her, she was beginning to feel the effects of this open-air life. The bitterness she had for a moment felt against these farmers who had enriched themselves throughout the occupation had disappeared. Instead of coveting her neighbor's wood, she marked the dead trees on the estate and employed a woodman to cut them down and saw them into logs. She gathered her faggots, and made a little jam for the winter with the plums and greengages in the garden. She was avid for news from London, and spoke continually of her grandson whom she had not seen since he cried for her on the ship at eleven months. Her efforts would make the old house worthy of him as soon as I could bring him there.

For the first night my husband slept on an osier chair in the empty bedroom where our son was born, but in the morning he was so bruised that Mme. Castel offered to place at his disposal her well-furnished spare room. The high peasant bed with its four mattresses of pure wool refreshed him after the long journey, and during the morning, when he was back in the old farm shelling peas, a long procession of vistors arrived. Déliquaire brought a slab of freshly made butter and a dozen eggs. His eldest son was of an age to marry, and the Goguets' house would have suited the lad admirably, for he was serious and hard-working like his father. The Pole who lived at Berlequet came to say that he would like to set up for himself, but my husband pointed out that the farm was mine and that he had no authority in the matter. M. Barbe sat down at the big table, and holding the stub of a pencil in his mutilated hand, estimated the cost of repainting the house from top to bottom. Prisoners were returning from Germany. Huge feasts were taking place in all the farms. Bayard, the faithful Bayard, was back and it was a pleas-

ure to see the joy of his wife. My mother was delighted to think
that this brave fellow would do most of the painting in the house,
and M. Barbe promised to begin in the early autumn when the
apples were being picked. The electrician arrived to see about
wiring the house, for though the Goguets had put the current
everywhere, even in the pigsties and the cattle-sheds, they had
not wired my house.

Aimable Rihouey saluted at the door.

He was paying an official call to take an inventory of the
things which had disappeared from the farm, for it was necessary to take action against some unknown person or persons. He
brought out a shining note-book from his breast pocket and,
licking his pencil, wrote a long and careful report in labored
and official language. From time to time he broke off to tell a
story of his own.

In the thatched farmhouse Renée Goguet, grown almost to
womanhood, moved about quietly. My husband had never seen
her so subdued.

At the Bruyères Victor Duprez and Simone, his pretty, intelligent wife, lived in comparative magnificence.

Since the death of his father, Victor Duprez had become a
very important person in the village. There was not a farm for
fifty miles around with whose history he was not minutely acquainted. He was for ever hurrying from Caen to Lisieux or
from Deauville to Pont L'Évêque. He knew exactly the value of
a field and the price that a house would fetch. He was acquainted
with all the foibles of the Norman peasant, and had learned from
childhood to treat them with exactly the right degree of firm-
ness and familiarity.

My husband, who went over to pay his respects to the Duprez,
remained to dinner, in the course of which he was invited by
Victor to accompany him to Caen, where he had business the
following day.

The battle of Caen, so mighty in consequence, was the hinge
against which the Anglo-Americans coming down from the
Cotentin threw all their weight, and when the door was pushed
open they fanned out southeast, leaving Deauville, Villers, and
Cabourg untouched to their left. The little car which Victor

Duprez's handyman drove soon reached the outskirts of Caen. Locomotives lay-on their backs along the side of the road, and lines of·charred trucks looked like Chinese dragons. The heart of the city was an arid mass of bricks over which blinding white dust swirled in eddies. While Victor Duprez went about some business my husband looked round. He told me later that he had the sensation of being sent out alone into a blizzard, but suddenly his nostrils were filled with the perfume of lime trees in flower, and he saw a green avenue leading to a church. It was like a strip of fertile land on the fringe of arid, burning sand.

For the first time he became aware of people. They were walking along the avenue to the top part of the city, which was practically untouched. A man was whistling. A mechanic was mending a punctured tire outside a garage. Church bells rang, and half a dozen children stood on tiptoe round an ice-cream barrow.

His heart warmed. He felt as if he had walked from death into life.

The Rue Guillaume le Conquérant, narrow and crowded, led to the spires of the church of St. Étienne and he hastened there as for a solemn pilgrimage, for in this church, perhaps the most beautiful in the whole of France, thousands of people lived during the long nightmare of the bombardment, not daring to leave its sanctuary by day or by night. The church stood in front of a quiet square, in a backwater, to the left of the busy street.

A farmer dozed in his chaise by the sculptured door, and as my husband entered the church he was overcome by the magnificence of the nave and the solemnity of the scene. Hushed and empty now, the population of a city in anguish had prayed here with tears in their eyes. They had slept and many had died on the stone floor. Women had writhed in labor; children had searched for parents they would never see again. As he looked upward, where the beautiful pillars rose into the half light, he saw that the whole of the triforium was decked with French flags, making a panoply of blue, white, and red. There was a saying, known to every Norman, that the day the church of St. Étienne suffered harm, the crown of England would come to an end. It had been repeated a thousand times since the invasion to show the link which existed between this ancient church and

the British monarchy, for had not William the Conqueror reposed here for a time after his death? This magnificent edifice,
built five centuries before my farmhouse, looked down with
pity upon the stricken town under whose ruins lay poor Mme.
Vincent and her son and her daughter.

Commander Gille, a young lawyer, and Mlle. Louise Boitard,
alias Janine, were standing in front of a long trestled table laid
for lunch. On the wall behind them was a large French flag, on
which these words were embroidered in gold:
"I was the first to wave with pride over liberated Caen—9th
July 1944."
Under the flag, in bold lettering, were quotations from the
historic speeches of Winston Churchill.
Commander Gille placed my husband on his left, and about
twenty people sat down to the simple meal. Victor Duprez and
his handyman sat opposite him; a young cousin of the Michelin
family sat at the far end of the table.
The conversation turned immediately on the returning
prisoners.
Mlle. Boitard had gone to the station that morning to meet a
man released from one of the German horror camps.
The Michelin lad was back from Manthausen, where the
German commander used to bring his children as a treat to see
the prisoners thrown into a pond, where the wardens hit them
over the head with iron rods each time they rose to the surface.
The Michelin boy turned to Victor Duprez and asked:
"Did I hear you say you come from Villers?"
"Yes," answered Victor. "Did you ever meet anybody from
there?"
"I did," said Michelin, "a farmer by the name of Goguet, but
I had no chance to speak to him because he was in quarantine."
Goguet at Monthausen!
This was so sudden that my husband no longer felt able to
take any part in the conversation. He could think of nothing
but my cunning, lovable peasant torn from his Norman orchards
in that November 1943, when the apples were lying stacked in
the cider press, to start the dreadful journey to the German
prison camp!
Whose venomous tongue had sent him there?

Two days after the visit to Caen, my husband called on Maître Vincent, the notary.

The villa by the sea was now abandoned, because the Germans had requisitioned most of the promenade to make pill-boxes and fortifications, and the notary lived with his two remaining sons in a small white house at the bottom of the Rue Pasteur. His clients sat on a row of chairs outside his study, waiting their turn to see him. Jean, the eldest, was twenty-four. He welcomed my husband and talked to him about the *maquis*. The clerk was scratching away on a parchment.

They had thus been conversing about an hour when the heavy door opened, and Maître Vincent appeared on the threshold, looking very small and wan. My husband hurried forward. The door closed, and the notary, without a word, buried his head in the bend of my husband's outstretched arm. He remained thus a moment, sobbing. Then he drew himself up and turned his features to the wall to hide his tears.

My husband could do nothing to lessen the grief of this broken heart. He could merely clutch his friend affectionately by the shoulders, and as he closed his eyes he saw again the arid desolation of Caen stretching away to infinity, beyond the ruined church of St. Sauveur. There, perhaps, under the rubble, lay the notary's beloved wife and two children.

Maître Vincent sat down. There was no massive oak desk, only a table piled high with unopened papers. He spoke in short phrases and his voice was so low that at times it was only a whisper.

"I know, I know," he said, "I never wrote to madame . . ."

And then he waved his arms in the direction of the table as if to show that the great mass of papers upon it weighed him down.

My husband was rising to take his leave when there was a knock at the door, and the *gendarme* Aimable Rihouey, cap in hand, walked into the room. He seemed surprised to see my husband because of the lateness of the hour, but after excusing himself for breaking in, he added, in a voice that tried to conceal his emotion:

"Goguet is dead!"

"Oh!" said the notary with sudden interest. "That will change everything."

Aimable Rihouey beamed with satisfaction at being thus the bearer of such sensational tidings, and added:

"The examining magistrate telephoned the news from Pont L'Évêque less than an hour ago."

He took from his pocket the note-book he always carried about with him and, turning the pages with a moistened thumb, came upon the notes he had made at the police station, and said:

"G. Warin, 15 Rue de Grisy, at St. Pierre-sur-Dives, returned prisoner from the German horror camp of Ebensee in Austria, yesterday furnished the examining magistrate with a statement made to him by Goguet on his death-bed."

These words, read out in a police court drawl, were followed by a painful silence. The notary had turned his head and was staring out of the window. My husband suddenly felt a great sadness steal over him. Goguet had been part of the farm. My husband could not imagine the place without those gay, malicious eyes, that deep, picturesque Norman intonation. He had loved him for his very failings. Would not my husband have shed a tear to see some splendid oak on his estate torn down by a gale? He was still lamenting the two Italian poplars, with which he had fallen in love the first day he set eyes on the farm. But what was the loss of a tree compared to the soul of these enchanting meadows? One would have needed to be hard indeed not to be moved. Goguet in the horror camp of Manthausen! Goguet, ill (he must have been ill to have been in quarantine), pitchforked into some abominable cattle-truck and shipped to Ebensee. Goguet, kicked, beaten, starved, and dying, robbed of air and sunlight, he who had spent his life between the green grass of his orchards and the blue sky above. Oh, misery!

Maître Vincent turned his eyes on my husband. Once, long ago, we had known them to be mocking.

Quickly, with the back of his hand, the notary stopped a tear from falling down his cheek. Was the tear for Goguet? Or was it merely that the cup of suffering was too full? Now that the war was over, the wreckage was beginning to be apparent.

Maître Vincent said:

"Yes, it changes everything. The position will become much more serious for the accused."

He turned to my husband.

"We shall have to see. Perhaps you had better go to Pont L'Évêque."

But how could my husband go to Pont L'Évêque? The only train left Trouville at six in the morning.

As he walked out into the sunshine, he met Victor Duprez who, with his usual generosity, said:

"We will fetch my car."

Pont L'Évêque had been a sleepy little market town. Apart from the fact that it gave its name to one of the most famous cheeses in France, my husband knew hardly anything about it. True there had been occasions before the war when, because Caffet was otherwise engaged, my husband had returned to Dieppe by omnibus and train. The journey was appallingly long and dusty, but he never minded that because these rural buses, filled with peasants, butter, eggs, and fowl, allowed him to contemplate at leisure the beautiful countryside with its thatched houses, irises, apple orchards, and busy farmyards. These journeys had generally taken place on Sunday night. One omnibus would take him to Trouville, another from Trouville to Pont L'Évêque, and another to Rouen where he could catch the train to Dieppe.

His knowledge of Pont L'Évêque was therefore confined to the bus stop, which was outside a dreamy, old-fashioned inn whose exterior was covered with climbing roses. Obviously it had not changed at all since the days of the stage-coach or diligence, and from the kitchen at this hour of the evening there came the most appetizing smell of chickens roasting on the spit. Plump commercial travelers dined at the table-d'hôte and tasted knowingly the cider and apple brandy.

In Victor's car the journey was extremely rapid, but by mutual consent they did not talk about the tragedy. Victor Duprez had known the Goguets long before my husband, for it was he who had given them their first chance to make good.

As they drove into Pont L'Évêque, my husband recognized the inn outside which he used to wait for the omnibus on Sunday evenings. It stood in a long, narrow street by a crossroads beyond which stretched the town. The inn was there, the street was there, and so were the crossroads, but beyond nearly everything was in ruins.

Somewhere on the edge of this devastation there stood an absurd Louis-Philippe replica of a Greek temple with fluted pillars. Much too shallow to suggest usefulness, it resembled one of those arbors that wealthy financiers built in their spacious parks a century ago. One wondered curiously why it had not collapsed gently in the course of that tornado which laid low so much of the town. There was a courtyard in front, and here Victor Duprez brought his car to a halt.

"This," he said, "is the Palais de Justice."

They climbed, unchallenged, a narrow, circular staircase to a balcony on the first floor. They walked along a dark paneled passage, and knocked where there was a chink of light. A tall, broad-shouldered man crossed the room to meet them. He wore American-style tortoise-shell spectacles.

"Yes," he said, "I am the examining magistrate."

He looked much too young for such a grave office, but when he heard the reason of their visit, he went to his desk and, taking up a thick dossier, shook it violently in both hands and exclaimed:

"It's an astounding story, one of the most appalling of all the appalling stories that it has been my unhappy task to disentangle since the departure of the Germans. Mme. Goguet has been here today for one of the longest interrogations so far, and she sat quite unmoved during the entire proceedings, as if it was nothing to her that her husband had died in torment, her father had cut his throat, or that the son might hang."

His words came out in a torrent, and as he spoke he walked rapidly up and down the tiny room as if he were trying to work something out of his system. From time to time he broke off his continual pacing to open the dossier, which he would straightforth close again with a bang.

"This G. Warin, of St. Pierre-sur-Dives, is in no state to be questioned at length, for he is much enfeebled by his long suffering," he continued; "but we know that Goguet died from dysentery at the Austrian camp of Ebensee on the twenty-ninth of December 1944, and that on his death bed he dictated an impassioned appeal to his fellow prisoner Warin, saying:

"If you get back alive, see that justice is done. Such is the request of a dying man!"

"Ebensee was liberated by the Americans on the seventh of

May last. They found a number of people alive, or rather half alive, and a great quantity of corpses heaped in a tunnel, into which the Germans had prepared to drive a locomotive and a wagon filled with dynamite to hide all traces of their crime. I would say that the octogenarian Eugène Hommet who cut his throat at the moment of arrest, and the youth Roger Goguet, bear the chief responsibility of the denunciation. These matters will be brought to light when the case is tried at Caen in September."

He threw the heavy dossier on the desk, where it slid across a dozen others, and added:

"Yes, it is by far the most horrible story I've come across up to now!"

Night had fallen by the time my husband was back in the old farmhouse, where in front of the log fire he told my mother the details of Goguet's death.

"Do you remember," asked my mother suddenly, "how on Christmas Eve during the phoney war, Goguet brought us the traditional piece of elm, so large that he could hardly carry it? He said to Madeleine: "There's a piece of wood that will last you all day and all night.""

She added:

"What do you suppose Goguet revealed to Warin on his deathbed?"

"We shall be the last to know," answered my husband. "What struck me most was to hear the magistrate saying: "It's an astounding story, one of the most appalling of all the appalling stories it has been my unhappy task to disentangle since the departure of the Germans." Does that remind you of anything?"

"Why, yes," said my mother. "Mme. Castel has almost the same refrain: 'It's a terrible story, a terrible story, a story of Judas.' "

My husband shuddered.

"It will be wiser not to ask too many questions," he reflected. "We must wait until the case is tried at Caen."

Then he remembered how curiously he had looked at the Palais de Justice, in that nightmare city where little was left but the law courts and the church of St. Étienne.

"The Germans marched poor Goguet off to Caen," he put in without translating into words his train of thought. "The Goguette and Roger will be taken there by the French. To think Madeleine made such splendid plans for her farmers!"

21

Two months after my husband's return to London I suddenly received all the necessary papers to cross the channel.

My joy was immense. I was about to see my mother for the first time since our poignant parting at St. Malo, and I would take possession again of the farm which was mine, bought with my own earnings.

With womanly foresight I decided to take over as much food and clothing as I could carry. It must not be too heavy, for I had been warned that there were no porters at the Gare St. Lazare and that transportation in Paris itself was not obtainable for a person like myself. Only the military and the various government officials had cars. I therefore filled two leather cases, a wicker basket, and innumerable string bags.

The train was scheduled to leave Victoria at ten in the evening and I was due to reach Paris the following evening at six.

I was rather frightened and much more excited than I cared to admit, for these journeys to Paris had once again taken on all the romance and uncertainty of bygone days when people traveled by stage-coach and sailing barque. Almost anything could happen on the way. I had spent some time wondering what to wear, and finally chose a black tailor-made and a cotton blouse. This was the first time I had ever left my child, and I was torn between the anguish of leaving him and the joy of seeing my mother again. I filled a linen bag with all the small things I had forgotten at the last moment, and then realized that this was the one I had brought away with me during our flight in 1940. It had contained the baby's feeding-bottle and some cans of Nestlé's milk. Now it was scorched on one side where I had laid it over the lamp on my writing-table during one of the worst raids of the war. I had not believed my child and I would live to see morning.

As soon as I arrived at the station, I became aware of the bustle occasioned by this strange continental boat train. The registered baggage was being weighed and ticketed in front of the florist's shop, whose windows were ablaze with light. Senior American officers stood beside carts filled with important-looking cases sealed with the embassy stamp. Foreign languages struck the ear, for there were Frenchmen and Poles, Belgians, and even a Chinese couple with their children in native dress. All these people talked at the tops of their voices and ran this way and that, gripping their passports and their tickets as if they were already frightened of being late. The porters answered the same questions a dozen times, sorted out the baggage, and stacked it on electric carts which they drove with a clattering of bells to the departure platform. My little boy who had come to see me off, charmed with the glamour of the nocturnal scene, chattered and danced with the excitement that was a prelude to his tears. The colorful picture, the clashing of strange tongues, and the whistle of the distant locomotive made his blue eyes sparkle.

The platform was even more picturesque, for in this confined space, patrolled by the military police of all the allied nations, the passengers were engaged in last-minute conferences or fond farewells. Bright-eyed A.T.S. girls leaned out of carriage windows and apostrophized the crowd. American army trucks raced down the ramp, to stop with a grinding of brakes in front of the open luggage vans where an R.T.O. officer with a melodious Virginian accent sang out his words of command. Although the train stretched the entire length of the platform, there was hardly a seat to spare, and a small group of new arrivals ran with their baggage behind an inspector who, key in hand, had promised to open a number of reserved compartments.

The locomotive gave a prolonged whistle and as I hurried to my seat in the packed compartment, I felt horribly alone. The radio had that evening given renewed gale warnings, and I was haunted by the fear of finding nobody in Paris to help me with my luggage.

Gradually I began to inspect my companions.

In the far corner was a distinguished Frenchman accompanied

by a young woman who was presumably his wife, extremely dark, very pretty, with a complexion that by its color and texture resembled the camellia flower, and hair dressed high above the forehead. He was broad-shouldered, with blue eyes and wavy hair, of the type one finds in the Jura mountains. They had settled down to a game of cards. The woman looked up at me and gave me a youthful, friendly smile.

On the seat exactly opposite was a middle-aged business man deep in a novel. Two Frenchmen in civilian clothes were discussing the modern school of painting, and now and again they would exchange information about the fate of well-known artists during the occupation. I closed my eyes and saw again the features of my son with the tears rolling down his cheeks. If the train had stopped I would have got out and taken the next one back to London. I wondered whether my husband had taken the boy back in a taxi, or whether they would cross the park together by moonlight. I wondered if he would miss me or whether he was already happily laughing with his father. I thought of him in his little bed with his teddy bear grasped firmly in his arms. The train thundered through the night.

It was nearly midnight when we reached Newhaven harbor, and the wind was howling across the marine station where the dim lamps creaked in their sockets. A porter took me to the baggage hall where the registered luggage was being assembled under the different letters of the alphabet, so that its owners could pass it quickly through the Customs. There was a group of French youths being repatriated by their Government. Half a dozen middle-aged men, wearing the U.N.R.R.A. badge, discussed tropical diseases, and a diplomat from Uruguay explained that he was being transferred to Paris from Sweden where he had been stationed during the war. The Chinese couple moved silently like shadows, surrounded by their children, whose dark straight hair was cut short like the wooden dolls we played with in our childhood. The woman told me that the baby in her arms was born in India, for they had taken six months to reach Europe from China.

Immediately in front of me a dejected-looking Pole was being subjected to a searching examination of his luggage. The customs officer was just then diving into his hold-all, from which he brought out a collection of miserable treasures. Some of these

—they were very harmless in effect, and consisted chiefly of small packages of tea, coffee, and soap—were stuffed into the soldier's socks, boots and shoes, or neatly wrapped inside his underwear. Seemingly without pity, the customs man withdrew each article of clothing and proceeded to shake out its contents on the long wooden table, after which he methodically undid each paper parcel.

The unfortunate Pole covered his ears with his short plump hands, and turning to me exclaimed plaintively:

"Oh, madam, I am indeed miserable! How shall I manage to do up all my little parcels again?"

Touched by this cry of distress, I helped him to repair the damage, and when he had gone I asked, turning to the customs official:

"I hope you are not going to do the same thing to me?"

He answered, laughing:

"Not if you tell me what those two leather suitcases contain."

"More or less what our friend the Pole had," I answered; "tea and coffee and sugar and clothes—but they are not for me. I'm taking them to my mother."

He made a cursory examination of the luggage, and said good-naturedly:

"You would never guess what some of the Polish soldiers manage to take out of the country. They think nothing of hiding a couple of dozen spark plugs. Everything has its price in Paris."

He chalked up my luggage and added:

"There, because you're a woman I'm letting you off lightly."

One o'clock struck, and in spite of the high wind the night was clear.

The channel steamer, dimly lighted, creaked against the side of the quay. It was my old friend the *Worthing*.

"Why, I've traveled on this ship a score of times!" I said to the porter.

"I expect you have," he answered. "But she's the only one of the fleet left. The others are at the bottom of the sea."

He added:

"I'm not supposed to tell you, madam, but during the war she was a commando."

He winked and repeated: "Yes, madam, a commando."

"When do we sail?"

"At seven," he answered. "You'll have time to sleep."

All the private cabins had been booked in advance, and there where so many women and children that, in addition to the usual women's quarters, one of the men's lounges had been taken over. Even so there were not enough bunks. A Swiss woman, married to a Czech, was returning to the country of her birth with three infants huddled together on a mattress while she reclined on a deck-chair beside them. Her children were recovering from whooping-cough. A young woman from Manchester, married to a French engineer, was returning with her two little girls from a visit to her parents. She had been in France during the occupation, and said that the only time her mind was more or less at rest was when the girls were at school, because the Germans respected the schools, but during the holidays every time they left the house she was never sure they would return. She had frequently seen workmen hanged in the street where she lived, and was continually giving refuge to those who dared not go home. "I shall never understand what you people went through during the air raids," she said, "but those of you who spent the war in England will never understand the mental torture that we endured." Her two girls had been fitted out with new clothes by the grandparents in Manchester, who had sacrificed all their coupons to send them back to France reasonably dressed. She added that her engineer husband had been in the resistance movement.

The two little girls were on the bunk above mine, and had fallen asleep almost as soon as their heads touched the pillow. Now and again the young mother, as she was talking, looked up at the children, and each time the rough blanket slid to one side she would tenderly cover them up. A portly W.V.S., passing along the crowded lounge, had attempted to engage the Swiss woman in conversation, being filled with compassion for the three mites sleeping beside her, but when it was clear that they could not make themselves understood, the W.V.S. called the stewardess over and said gently: "Poor woman. She has her hands full. Look after the tots, won't you?"

What a long night this was going to be! I said to my companion:

"I suppose you were living in Paris most of the time?"

"Just outside it," she answered, "in the factory district of Boulogne-sur-Seine, but my husband was from Ussel in the Corrèze. We often went there."

The name of this rocky, picturesque little town reminded me of that hot day in the 'twenties when Mme. Sardou and I, having dispatched Pierrot to his father, broke our car journey there to visit a young woman called Jeannette, who was dying of consumption, a story I tell in *Madeleine Grown Up.* I was wakened from my reverie by my companion, who continued:

"Ussel passed through martyrdom during the occupation, because the wild country round it was ideal for the *maquis.* The Germans perpetrated the most dreadful acts of revenge. They took a youth and hanged him from a window in the street with his arms and legs nailed to a cross, like Jesus, and so he remained until the carrions ate his flesh."

We stopped talking and I must have dozed.

I was wakened by a sudden lurching of the ship. We had left harbor and were running into the full force of the growing gale. The Swiss woman and her three little children all had their heads bowed over the same basin. The Chinese baby and its small brothers and sisters were sprawling over a bunk on which, during the war, some begrimed commando, armed to the teeth, must have snatched a few hours' rest before hurling himself against the enemy-occupied shore. Now a stewardess with stiff white collar and cuffs was handing out lifejackets to her senseless, agonizing passengers. She said:

"There's really no danger, ladies, but just in case we hit a mine."

Toward eleven next morning I struggled into the passage. The wind had dropped slightly, and the Polish officers had formed groups to talk politics. Two of them were giving, in English, a lecture on foreign policy to a meek and spectacled member of U.N.R.R.A. On deck a few passengers were sheltering behind a tarpaulin, to examine the outline of the French coast through the haze. Nobody spoke. The vessel cut through the swell toward the land where men fell that it should be liberated. Narrow white houses ran down to the sand, and on top of a hill was a gutted church. This was the scene of the historic commando raid during the summer of 1942 when so many Canadians were massacred. The cross-channel steamer, her bows covered with spray, made a glorious picture. There was something triumphant in the way she bore down on the distant harbor, at the bottom of which lay one of her sister ships, dive-bombed and sunk by the Luftwaffe when all the world trembled before the German onrush.

There was a strident whistle. The *Worthing* was entering harbor.

When I came on deck again, holding one of the Swiss woman's children by the hand, the sun was shining. The mother was carrying the youngest. The third was being looked after by the pretty brunette whom I had noticed in the train on the way to Newhaven. Suddenly the mother remembered that she had left her hat, for which she had paid $6, on the bunk in the lounge, and leaving her two eldest children in the care of their respective guardians, she hurried away to fetch it.

"My goodness!" exclaimed the elegant Frenchwoman, "how this child is coughing!"

"Yes," I answered, "it appears that they are all recovering from whooping-cough."

"Misery!" said the lady. "To think I am on my way to see my grandchild of seven months. Must I be a criminal and abandon this child? Or must I be a worse one and carry the whooping-cough to my grandson?"

She laughed and continued to look after the child. The ship was already tying up. The Paris train with its heavy locomotive was waiting on the quay. In a few moments I would once again step on French soil. I was singularly moved. During the war a secret agent, returned from a mission, had brought me back a handful of earth and a few wild flowers from this forbidden land.

The repatriated Frenchmen went down the gangway first. I watched them curiously. I half expected they would kneel and kiss the ground. But no, they hurried off with their fiber cases, their hats pulled over their eyes. I said to myself: "I'm absurdly romantic. People don't do things like that any longer."

The Swiss woman hurried back and as soon as we were on the

quay a *gendarme* took charge of the mother and her children, hurrying them through the customs.

Then started those interminable formalities, the customs man peering into my things and inquiring: "Have you anything to declare?" I answered: "I have three hundred cigarettes."

I smiled at him naïvely and took out a packet of twenty. He placed it on the edge of the counter with several others, and immediately chalked up my luggage. Then he pointed to an adjoining room and said: "Go and show your passport, madame."

The porter, who had gone off in search of a seat, came back and said:

"There's not a place left on the train. We shall have to wait until they open up a second-class coach." He added: "You won't be leaving for an hour."

Dejectedly I returned to the customs hall, not caring very much what happened. It was midday. I had been violently sick and was without food and drink since leaving home. In a corner of the hall the pretty brunette was seated on her luggage pecking at a bunch of grapes like a graceful bird. She smiled at me, handed me the paper bag and said:

"Do, please, help yourself. I've lost my husband and my porter but I found these in the town."

"There is your husband," I said, seeing the tall young man hurrying toward us. He seemed quite unperturbed and announced:

"As I couldn't be the first, I decided to be the last."

"That is all very fine," answered his wife good-naturedly, "but it appears there is no more room on the train."

On the quay the heavy locomotive was letting off a cloud of black smoke. Had it been chased by Spitfires during the occupation? At the Bar Dieppois, in front of which the R.A.C. man used to park travelers' cars during the days of peace, at fat lady was serving coffee and glasses of white wine. From a side street came a pathetic funeral procession on foot, the bier carried by four men, with only half a dozen mourners behind. The porters came back and said: "They have opened the second-class coach. We've put your things together. You'll have a compartment to yourselves."

When finally the train began to crawl along the quay, past

the various basins, I had my first glimpse of the mighty destruction caused by our bombers on port installations on the Continent. Cement blockhouses had been shattered, and here and there the funnel and masts of a sunken vessel emerged from the water. The fishmarket, where in pre-war days I had seen the fisherwomen in their lace caps, was wrecked and idle, and as the train cautiously entered the town station I saw geraniums growing where once there had been busy halls.

We now saw a crowd of townspeople on the platform, and as soon as the train stopped a number of portly women dressed entirely in black, carrying an immense quantity of bags and parcels, and accompanied by a little girl of seven or eight, edged sideways into the compartment, where they puffed and chattered and spread out their belongings without taking the slightest notice of us. Their clothes, dyed a cheap black, smelt acrid under the burning sun, and with harsh Norman accents they began an excited conversation through the open window with their numerous relatives on the platform who had come to bid them a safe journey. Then all the females together, pointing to a fiercely mustached gentleman outside, shouted to the little girl:

"Say good-by to Mimile. Throw a kiss to Mimile."

"But I can't see Mimile!" cried the little girl.

The pretty brunette's husband who, from his corner seat, had been watching all this with an amused smile, lifted the little girl in his strong arms and, holding her up to the window, said:

"There is your Mimile. Take a good look at him. Throw a nice kiss to Mimile."

The child turned big, wondering eyes at her knight-errant and then waved to to Mimile.

"There!" exclaimed the pretty brunette's husband. "Now that you have had a good look at Mimile, hop! Down you go!"

The train was beginning to move and the family on the quay ran along with it. As the *gendarmerie* came into sight with the republican flags flying from the colored roof, the *gendarmes* hurried out to say good-by to Mimile's daughter, for Mimile was obviously in the police force.

The locomotive gave a shrill cry and the ladies in black, by common accord, opened voluminous bags of American oilcloth, from which they produced their knitting. They held their needles, peasant fashion, at arm's length, the large balls of string-like *ersatz* wool reposing against their ample breasts.

The little girl was fidgeting. She was adorably pretty and already quite grown up in her ways, but she said in that piercing Norman intonation:

"I forgot to bring my doll!"

Her mother answered:

"You can have the towel I wrapped my knitting in."

The child took the towel and, as in Victor Hugo's *Les Misérables*, knotted it within a few moments into quite a life-like doll which she began to nurse against her shoulder. She looked a real little mother. Now she tidied her hair and straightened her skirt.

I looked out of the window at the cows grazing peacefully in the green Norman orchards. In the distance was the hamlet of Totte in which Guy de Maupassant laid the scene of *Boule de Suif*. You remember how the occupants of the crowded stage-coach arrived, during the war of 1870, at the gray stone inn where they were held up by the Prussians until Boule de Suif abandoned her virtue to the Prussian officer. Presumably Totte was only just recovering from a second occupation, for on the wall of a farmhouse was a notice printed in German.

The pretty brunette's husband asked the little girl's mother:

"Were you in Dieppe, madame, during the commando raid in 1942?"

She looked up from her knitting and answered:

"Not only were we there, but in our house on the high ground, and we saw it all. Hundreds of those poor Canadians were buried in the sand. The Germans waited until their bodies turned black in the scorching sun. Then the male population was rounded up to wheel the corpses in wheelbarrows through the streets to the cemetery. They wanted us to have a horror of the British. A week later, not satisfied with this gruesome procession, they made our menfolk dig up the corpses a second time and bury them elsewhere. Were we there, my good gentleman? I assure you we shall never forget it."

Now the train began to travel faster.

"I'm hungry," said the little girl.

Her mother produced another large bag from which she took out, wrapped in a snow-white napkin, an enormous *brioche* which filled the compartment with a delicious smell of Normandy butter. The other ladies also busied themselves searching their belongings for food, and soon they spread out a great quantity of farm produce and American chocolate.

But it was the succulent, golden, buttery *brioche* that fascinated the three weary passengers who had been without food since leaving London.

I turned to the husband of the pretty brunette and asked in English:

"What would you say if they offered you a piece?"

"My goodness," he answered, "they wouldn't need to ask me twice."

To keep my mind from the pangs of hunger I turned to a copy of the *Figaro* which I had picked up at the station. This newspaper was now, like every other French newspaper, limited to a single sheet, but as I glanced down its columns I noticed that a good deal of space was still devoted to what was called society news. This column had always vaguely amused me. I used to discover who was at Deauville during the season and what dresses had been seen at the Grand Prix.

These aristocratic names again figured in the Carnet Mondain —but in what a poignant manner! Entire families—father, mother, young sons, and daughters—had been burned in the furnaces of the German death camps of Buchenwald, Dachau, Osnabrück, and Belsen, and distant relations were now praying for their souls that they might repose in peace. Here was a marquis in his teens, "fair hair, blue eyes, tall," of whom there was no news since he had left the camp of Sachsenhausen (Oranienburg) in February 1945. His mother was asking for news of him.

A young mother bearing the ill-fated name of Antoinette had died in captivity on March third at Ravensbruck. An old lady of eighty with three grandchildren, not one of whom had reached ten summers, a brother and a sister . . . tortured, maimed, starved to death. A young lieutenant in the resistance massacred, a little girl, doubtless like the one eating her *brioche* opposite, torn from her doll and stifled to death in a railway wagon.

The newspaper dropped from my hands. The Grand Prix, Deauville, Belsen. What an appalling mockery. Not even Robespierre had brought such a flood of tears.

The train was jolting over switches and I looked out of the window.

We were passing a goods yard, and a shunting engine was pushing a whole collection of trucks. I had never seen anything like it before. These trucks had been strung together from every corner of Europe—German trucks, Dutch trucks, Belgian trucks; trucks from Turkey and Spain, Austria and Italy. Long trucks, short trucks, tall trucks, low trucks, and many with their superstructure blown to bit. Now they were pressed into service by the French Government, whose own rolling stock had either been wrecked or stolen.

The boat train slowed up as it ran though a station. There was no roof, no waiting-rooms. A giant locomotive lay on its side in a ditch. The steel carcass was rusty and holed by bullets. Grass was growing over the tender.

The country became flatter and there were some cornfields.

From time to time the train would pull up, and then start again very cautiously. Then the passengers would move toward the windows and somebody would exclaim: "Another Bailey bridge." These American and British bridges had everywhere replaced those which had been destroyed by bombers before the invasion of the Continent. The wreckage was still visible. Twisted steel girders hung across blasted cement piles, and often the old track stretched down into swiftly running water. Buildings on both sides of the river had been gashed open by the near misses.

The heavy train crawled forward as if testing the strength of the new bridge.

Asnières. Double-decked suburban trains filled with people showed that Paris was ending its day's work. They looked curiously at the train whose passengers had started their journey over twenty hours ago.

Suddenly the Eiffel Tower came into sight, shimmering in the setting sun, and all the ladies in black led Mimile's daughter to the window to show her this first glimpse of the capital. Then, slowly, houses hid it from view, and the train entered the Gare St. Lazare.

In the turmoil of the arrival, I bade farewell to my friends, who were to be met at the barrier. For a few moments I re-

mained by the door of the compartment, hoping to catch sight
of a porter, but there was none. The young woman from Manchester ran into the arms of her husband, who kissed her on
both cheeks and then embraced his daughters. He had arrived
with a home-made push cart, on to which he proceeded to pile
their luggage. The military were being taken care of by their
respective R.T.O.s, but nobody took any notice of the woman
standing forlornly alone with her string bags. My two heavy
suit-cases were among the registered baggage, but I realized how
useless it would be to claim them until I had found somebody
willing to help me.

Gradually the crowd began to lessen and, almost panic-
stricken, I remembered that M. Marin, the manager of Brown's
in Dover Street, had told me that if I were hard put to it, he
had a friend who was in charge of the Terminus Hotel. I therefore dragged myself to a newspaper kiosk to ask the way. The
woman, who was friendly and eager to help, said that it was
necessary to cross the whole of the Cour la Reine to reach the
main entrance, but she thought there must be a short cut
through the station buffet. In the noisy brasserie the white-
aproned waiters were serving beer and *ersatz* coffee, but beyond
the cash-desk a number of women under the eyes of a captain
were washing up the glasses, and having acquainted one of
these with my predicament, the worthy woman rolled down her
sleeves and led me through the underground labyrinths of the
hotel, to the main entrance.

The uniformed porter considered her from behind his desk
and said:

"You can't stay here. The hotel is commandeered by the
Americans."

"I'm not asking to stay here," I answered. "I should like to
see M. Caron."

He grumbled, but led me up some stairs where we came upon
M. Caron in person.

"Why, of course!" he answered after I had explained my
visit. "M. Marin is my best friend."

Then turning to the hotel porter he said:

"Have a commissionaire take this lady's luggage into town
on his bicycle."

Then he bowed and said that he would be always at my service.

Half an hour later the commissionaire and I sallied forth into the streets of Paris. The commissionaire was wheeling his bicycle to which, by some miracle, he had attached with a stout piece of rope that I bought the previous day in London, the two leather suit-cases, the osier basket, and my numerous bags. This pyramid of heavy luggage was balanced on the handle-bars, and the commissionaire turned and twisted beside it like the strong man in a circus. Such a picture would have drawn a crowd in any London street, but in Paris nobody looked up.

The Galeries Lafayette was closing and the Rue de Rome was full of laughing shopgirls. This was my first sight of Paris for six years—since before the birth of my son—and I was trying to take in everything, with an eager thirst for discovery such as I had not known since I was a girl. What struck me most was the difference in appearance which the changed fashion gave to the women. They looked tighter in the waist, fuller in the skirt, more top-heavy on the head. The contrast with London was so unexpected that I felt like an explorer coming upon a strange land. At home the silhouette was still straight and tidy as it had been before the French collapse. Here wooden soles made a din and clatter on the cobbles. A young woman swept past with her golden hair built up nearly a foot high. No hat could have sat on this cliff which rose so abruptly from the forehead. The birds of the air might have perched on the summit. I suppressed a smile, and could not decide whether it was absurd or becoming. The strangeness of it took my breath away.

A kindly government had arranged for my accommodation at the Castiglione which, during the occupation, had been requisitioned for pilot officers of the Luftwaffe, and which now had become an annex to the British Embassy situated on the opposite side of the street. All manner of people, from high officials to blonde little typists, stayed there—some for days, others for months.

The agile commissionaire leaned his bicycle against the wall and untied the baggage. I offered him a hundred francs, but what he mostly coveted was the rope, which I had not the heart to refuse him.

The Castiglione was a moderately up-to-date hotel built between the two wars—narrow, high, and compact, with the almost unheard-of luxury of constant hot water. The foyer was dimly lit and the porter, having consulted a piece of paper nailed to the wall, took charge of my bags and led me to the elevator.

Because of the shortage of accommodation in these government requisitioned hotels it was the custom for short-term travelers to occupy the apartments of our Treasury or Foreign Office officials who, for some reason or other, were obliged to leave Paris for a few days. I was thus quartered in a very dignified suite, in which the owner had left all his belongings with a most touching assurance in the honesty of his compatriots. His literary tastes proved him to be a man of discernment. He liked the poems of Aragon, the works of Boileau and the Lives of the Saints, in addition to which he studied a variety of voluminous reports issued by His Majesty's Treasury. His suits were neatly arranged in the wardrobe, at the bottom of which reposed his brightly polished shoes. On the dressing-table he had left one of those massive gold watches favored by Victorian gentlemen, together with a gold chain and several hundred cigarettes.

I was somewhat intimidated to find myself in the home of this stranger who had left so much of himself behind. At every step I found myself unwittingly prying into his character. His silk dressing-gown hung on the only peg in the diminutive hall, his particular brand of soap and hair-oil greeted me in the bathroom, a novel lay by the bedside lamp, his slippers stood on the rug. I almost hesitated to put out my own lingerie and dresses in case he might return unexpectedly and believe himself compromised.

Freshened by a hot bath, revived by a simple meal, I went out on the balcony. Paris lay at my feet, and as I looked across the roof-tops at the close of this splendid autumn day, the famous monuments and avenues lit up one after the other as if to cry their welcome. I saw them glittering like a diamond necklace—the Eiffel Tower, the Arc de Triomphe, the Invalides, the Champs Elysées, the Place de la Concorde, and the Palais Royal.

The church bells were chiming nine, and I could not resist the temptation of going out for a walk. I thought it would be fun to call on M. Schwenter of the Meurice, who never retired before midnight. How surprised he would be to see me!

Often during the nocturnal raids on London I had thought

of him. Like the brave agents who made secret trips to Paris, I would have liked to be wafted to the Meurice, to peep at the Nazi overlord who presumably slept in King Alfonso's bed. I used to wonder what M. Schwenter would say if he suddenly saw me walk into his office.

I closed the door behind me and slipped the key into my handbag.

In the hall the night porter was dozing.

The august mansions of the Faubourg St. Honoré were gray and somnolent, but some of them were pockmarked as if there had been a street battle. There was a line of official cars outside the British Embassy, and the tricolor floated over the Palace of the Elysée where President Lebrun had lived with his numerous family until the collapse. The little luxury shops which have always been a feature of this quiet street were sufficiently well lit to make an inspection worth while. There was a roll of material apparently not for sale, a few metal trinkets, and a cotton blouse which would have cost a dollar in New York. I looked at the price in francs, and after making a rapid calculation, discovered that it would cost $75.

I crossed the Rue Royale and in less than five minutes faced the entrance to the Meurice. This was the scene I had pictured when the bombs were falling over London. Why should I feel excited? The reception clerk said to me:

"M. Schwenter? Certainly M. Schwenter is still here, but he goes to bed early. I will tell him in the morning that you called, madam."

Schwenter in bed early! That was something I had not envisaged.

The streets were so deserted that I regretted the impulse which had driven me out of the hotel. A man can walk slowly and enjoyably through the half darkened streets of a great city at night, taking in the mysterious scenes that unfold before him, dreaming strange dreams, peering into multitudinous secrets. These experiences are beyond the reach of a woman. We are not able to walk alone at night. I was already imprudent. If only I could have found a man to take me with him! I should have known better. There was a warm glow on the opposite side of the street which appeared to come from a restaurant. I crossed over and amused myself by looking at the oil paintings which the owner had grouped round a bowl of fruit in the window. This combination of restaurant and art gallery was not without charm, but though the interior looked inviting, I only saw one customer whose back was turned to me. I was about to continue my way when something about his shoulders made me look at him a second time. Then he looked round and our eyes met. He threw down his napkin and ran to the door:

"Madeleine! Of all the people in the world!" he exclaimed. "How long have you been in Paris?"

"Charles d'Ydewalle!" I cried.

He took me by the arm and led me to his table, where he offered me a glass of wine, saying: "The pears aren't ripe, but the greengages are splendid. My goodness, what a surprise!"

This tall, adventurous Belgian, who had been our constant visitor in London following his escape through Gibraltar in 1942, was always well posted with the latest news, and it was he who had given me the most vivid pictures of Paris under German occupation. I had often wondered how a man of such striking stature could have escaped capture, but some people seemed to benefit by an invisible cloak during their clandestine activities. Charles had left London a few days before the invasion of Normandy, and for several months we had been without news from him. Then he returned to London for a short visit, having followed the armies to the Rhine, visited his family near Bruges, and spent a short time in Paris.

Charles wore one of those vague uniforms which apparently allowed him to go anywhere. He explained that he had left Brussels that same morning by road, had gone to a theater but had left after the first act because it was dull. He seemed to think that Providence had made him choose the dullest play in all Paris with the sole view of making this reunion possible, and he was so anxious to recount his adventures that he started a dozen subjects without exhausting one.

We had not been together a quarter of an hour before the waiter arrived with the bill, for it was past the official closing hour. The days of leisurely meals were over in Paris, or at least they had not yet returned. In all other respects this place was not unlike those friendly restaurants I had known before the war, but it had apparently sprung up overnight, for Charles had come upon it by chance, which made our meeting even more remarkable.

Because I had as yet seen nothing of the capital, Charles offered to take me for a stroll before escorting me back to the hotel.

As we walked toward the boulevards, he told me how he had been reunited with his family on the outskirts of Bruges.

The Allies were just moving in; the Germans were covering their own retreat with a sporadic bombardment.

Charles, in battle dress, reached the garden of his little home. His eyes turned quickly to the house for a glimpse of his wife. He had looked forward to this moment for months, dreaming how it would be. Suddenly from a slit trench in the garden bobbed up a blonde little head.

"It's a Canadian!" cried the child.

From another trench cautiously emerged the head of the elder brother:

"No!" cried the second voice. "It's daddy!"

The returned soldier clasped his children and asked anxiously for news of their mother. They told him she had gone on her bicycle to a neighboring village to call on some cousins. Charles borrowed a bicycle and rode to meet her. They met halfway along the dusty road.

"Oh, that first evening spent together round the table!" Charles exclaimed. "We no longer took any notice of the bombardment. Often when you used to give me hospitality in London, I wondered if I would see them again."

He described the house, gave me all the details of the first meal, and said:

"My wife and I had just gone to bed when the telephone rang. The instrument was downstairs and she asked me to go and answer it.

"I must have taken a few moments to put on a dressing-gown because before reaching the bottom of the stairs, I heard my youngest boy reply to the caller in a shrill but certain voice: 'Don't worry. I'll ring up the fire brigade. Everything will be all right.'

"I leaned over the banisters and called: 'What's the matter, son? Is there a house on fire?'

"He ran up to where I was standing and said in a low, confidential tone: 'It's nothing, daddy darling. Mme. J. is expecting a baby—almost any moment. You see, the fire brigade are the only people to have a car, so I am just going to ring them up to tell them to take the doctor round to Mme. J.' He added: 'Now go to bed, daddy. I never worry mother for little things like that.' "

We had cut across the Place Vendôme, and every now and again I stopped to look at the window displays of the Rue de la Paix.

"The prices are staggering!" I exclaimed.

"The aftermath of war produces a very congenial atmosphere for people with their wits about them," answered Charles. He added with a wink: "That applies specially to some of my compatriots. If you traveled as often as I do between Brussels and Paris, you would learn that this simple journey, which takes but a few hours, can earn any person so inclined at least $1000."

I was not surprised to find Charles well versed in these matters which always puzzled me. The black market, like the resistance movement, was clandestine and romantic, though its motives were, alas, less disinterested. I knew Charles well enough to suspect that his inquisitive nature kept him eternally on the alert.

What was happening on the black market was of interest to everybody just then. Life on the Continent centered on it.

Charles could assume the accent of a Bruges peasant or an Ostend fishwife to a nicety. As we walked toward the Opera, he began to describe how the Belgians who lived along the frontier near Lille crossed on bicycles every morning to work in the mines or help in the fields. Belgians liked to work in France because they earned more money and because they could augment their wages by smuggling tobacco, a profession which had always been dear to their hearts.

On Saturday nights they collected their pay in French francs, brought the notes home to Belgium and sold them at a discount to agents from Brussels who gave them Belgian money in exchange. Every week, therefore, wealthy operators in Brusesls collected vast sums of French paper money which they had bought cheap.

These French notes were then smuggled to Paris where they were used to purchase gold sovereigns.

"It's a queer thing," said Charles, "but the good English sovereign can generally be bought a trifle cheaper in Paris than in Brussels. My countrymen like the touch of gold. Besides, they have lived through so many devaluations of their currency.

"These gold sovereigns, therefore, bought in Paris are smuggled to Brussels and sold at a profit. This trade, which is illicit at every turn, produces fortunes which would stagger you. There are, of course, many variations. Gold pieces bought in Switzerland are sold in Brussels for three times what they cost at Berne or Zürich. And how long does the journey take? A few hours by car.

"The Brussels night-club owner does a deal with a British major. Send three army trucks to Rheims to collect champagne from a man he knows and there will be one load for the mess and two for the night club. The night-club owner did precisely the same thing with a Nazi major under the occupation, and he is the man who buys the gold sovereigns which were bought at a discount in Paris with French paper money bought from the peasants under par. Now, my little Madeleine, do you still wonder that prices are high?"

His big, hearty laugh echoed across the Place de l'Opéra, where the lights were full on and where a line of American trucks was parked along the avenue. An American G.I. leaned from the back of a truck, and whistling to Charles called out:

"Cigarettes? Eighty francs."

"A month ago," said Charles, "they sold at one hundred and ten. The market is soft."

"But why do they sell their cigarettes?" I asked.

"Because," answered Charles, "the dollar-franc exchange is so adverse that they cannot buy anything with their pay. The Frenchman, on the other hand, wants cigarettes, for he has none of his own."

When I was younger I loved to walk along the boulevards in autumn, because of the booths that displayed their wares and side-shows along the curb, under the trees whose leaves were turning color.

With a cry of joy I noticed that there were booths all along the curb and that their lights glared as far as the eye could see, but the cafés were closed, their upturned chairs ranged against the plate-glass fronts, and there were soldiers, soldiers, soldiers.

The entire American Army might have been ambling along the boulevards. The sight of them filled my heart with joy. How smart and virile these Americans looked! What real men! Most of the civilians had disappeared with the last subway train, for after that there was no method of going home.

So the G.I.'s passed from booth to booth, where they occasionally tarried to shoot at clay pipes with rifles, at five francs a time, as if they regretted that their sniping days were over. Sometimes I saw a strange figure from the *maquis*, still armed heavily, showing his girl how he handled a gun. Now and again a convoy of American trucks would thunder along the road, a jeep with a couple of white-helmeted M.P.'s would cruise along the curb, or a German Mercédès would glide past carrying erect, beautifully groomed Russian officers.

Here was the teeming activity which I had missed in the quiet *faubourg* and the deserted Place Vendôme. I felt grateful to my male escort.

At the corner of the Rue de Richelieu, steeped in the history of the French kings, five taxi-cyclists were resting over the handle-bars of their machines. They wore Alpine berets and open-necked brick-red shirts, and their muscles were strongly developed. Their vehicles, which consisted of an open tub on wheels harnessed to the back of their bicycles, replaced the non-existent taxicab. They had been a feature of the occupation, and were the modern equivalent of the sedan chair which most of the houses in the Rue de Richelieu had looked down upon long before the boulevards were built, when the link-man still walked the streets.

"Now," said Charles, "choose your driver and let us go to Montmartre to see the fair."

The fair was back again for the first time since the war.

It stretched all the way from the Place Blanche nearly as far as the Gare du Nord—one immense highway of blinding light, merry-go-rounds, booths, switchbacks, giant wheels, and fortune-tellers. But it was like a film in the silent days, for there was no music at all, and canned music is half the fun of a fair.

The inhabitants of Montmartre had come down to join the crowd of Americans who had tramped up from the boulevards. The Moulin Rouge, converted into a picture house, retained something of its ancient glamour, and here and there some landmark recalled the glory of the jazz-mad twenties, but mostly it was a vast playground for the boys on leave from those battered cities of Germany whose *herrenvolk* had so lately marched with their conquering boots along this selfsame street.

The taxi-cyclists parked their machines in the Place Blanche at the top of the Rue Fontaine, and they had the place to themselves, for a few nights earlier the police had swooped on the private cars drawn up outside the newly opened night clubs, and by a strange coincidence all of them had been using army gasoline! The sinewy pedalists, resting from their long climb from the heart of the city, were therefore enjoying the prospect of better business, and they passed on the good news while puffing contentedly at army-ration cigarettes.

The seasoned night-hawk prefers to seek his enjoyment in the night clubs and cabarets dotted about the dark and winding streets below the Place Blanche and the Place Pigalle, rather than join in the more vulgar crowd seething round the fair. The artist delights in these contrasts of aged houses and neon signs, mysteriously curtained windows, and blind alleys.

Save for the Moulin Rouge, Liberty's Bar, and the Théâtre de Dix Heures, the great white way might be another Coney Island, but the Rue Fontaine and so many others, encrusted with the grime and dignity of centuries, make that charm which brings visitors to Paris from all over the globe. They were doubly mysterious now because there was no traffic. Only a few lovers walking arm-in-arm, a girl standing under a domed archway, an hotel of ill repute whose soft light shone on the pavement.

Charles led me through these labyrinths. This was the Montmartre of my girlhood. I rediscovered shadows and smells. Then came later memories—memories of young womanhood. In the boom years friends had driven me in their rapid and shining limousines up these precipitous streets, to finish the evening in one or other of the gay cabarets where Parisians sipped crème de menthe and danced the tango. They were coming back, these little cabarets, not always in the same place, but much as they used to be, with their façades built up to resemble a barge, a farmhouse, or a caravan. Their lights shone brightly against a house on the opposite side of the street. The sound of jazz issued from a half-open door, in front of which stood, not very smartly, a commissionaire dressed in red and gold. This was the Montmartre that so many people dreamed about when, during the occupation, Paris was a forbidden city. Partly because of the police swoop, these places appeared to be half empty, but who could tell that in a year or two Montmartre would not experience once again the mad popularity of another pleasure-seeking world? At any rate, this was a sign that France was shaking off the shackles of servitude. One cannot weep for ever.

We turned a corner and suddenly I gripped my companion's arm.

I could hardly believe the sight that greeted me.

Charles had led me into the narrow street in which stands the Bal Tabarin. The famous music hall was lit as in another age, and all along the curb in front of it were horse-drawn cabs and barouches whose veteran drivers nodded sleepily over their reins, their shining toppers reflecting the glimmer of gas light.

"Oh!" I cried, "this might be the aftermath of the war of 1870! It's a period piece!"

"Consider," answered Charles, "that you might never again see such a picture. This state of affairs started in the spring of 1942, when I was being hunted by the Gestapo, but even so I took pleasure in looking at this page out of a history book. Those horses come from the Barbary coast. They belonged to a brigade of Spahis quartered near Belfort during the phoney war. When France collapsed the two regiments crossed the border into Switzerland, but in 1941 they were expelled and took refuge in Vichy, where the men were disarmed and the horses seized by the Germans who, finding them too old for service in Russia, put them up for auction in Paris. If I remember rightly they fetched over $1000 each and were bought by the cabbies, who searched all the French châteaux as far as the Aisne for forgotten landaus, barouches, victorias, broughams, and coupés—anything, in fact, capable of being pressed into service.

"The cobwebs were brushed off and the copper lamps burnished. The cabbies rescued the toppers worn by their fathers and their grandfathers, spat on them, polished them, and put them on their aging heads. Look what a lovely picture they make! Notice what a soft light those candles give!

"Could there be anything more romantic for a background than this famous music hall with the poster of the can-can, that seductive dance, so evocative of the Second Empire?

"Yes, Madeleine, you're looking at something you never expected to see. It's as if you had said to a magician: 'Let me spend five minutes—just five minutes—in the past.' We are the only people in this narrow, dark street who spoil the effect. I should have a beard, and you, Madeleine, should have a little red jacket with leg-of-mutton sleeves, and a long skirt touching the ground. But then, if you were an honest woman, Madeleine, I'm afraid you wouldn't be hanging round the entrance to the Tabarin at midnight. What do you say to that?"

"Look at the name of the show!" I cried suddenly.

"*Happiness is Here Again.* Well, let's hope it's true."

The two athletes who had brought us up the steep climb to Montmartre now pedaled us back to the heart of the town through the silence of the night.

It was a strange and exhilarating experience.

The curious vehicles turned briskly past the Opera House into the Boulevard de la Madeleine, where once again I thought I must be dreaming.

On both sides of the boulevard the wide pavements were covered by recumbent figures in khaki—so many that they appeared to make a living carpet, on which one saw from time to time the red glow of cigarettes.

Then, from the direction of the Madeleine, would thunder a heavy army truck. It would draw up by the curb, sway a moment, and then drive off again, having sucked up a part of this human mosaic like a carpet-sweeper.

I watched this operation repeated a score of times as our driver pedaled slowly along.

The great army of tired but happy G.I.'s was being taken back to camp at the end of twenty-four hours' leave in Paris. The six-wheeled trucks thundered along the boulevard like express trains. Gradually entire stretches of the distant pavements were cleared of weary limbs and sore feet. The cigarettes had been sold, the cognac drunk, the clay pipes shattered by toy rifles, and eyes were heavy with sleep. Tomorrow these men would recount their experiences in the gay city—that same city which their fathers had told them about when they were children, for this was the second generation to have liberated French soil. Could we ever thank these Americans enough. How I wished I could tell their womenfolk. Might their sons be spared the task of again liberating Europe!

The limousines outside the British Embassy had driven off.

Charles bade me good night at the entrance to my hotel.

"Tomorrow," he said, "I'm going back to Bruges. I forgot to thank you for all the things you gave me in London for my family. My wife has been cutting up the material and sewing shirts for the boys. She wears your cardigan, and the shoes fit her perfectly. My goodness, but isn't the world small? I haven't yet got over meeting you in that restaurant!"

I watched him folding his tall limbs into the miniature trailer which glided off along the deserted street.

The next day a shaft of sunshine streamed through the open windows, and during those first moments of semi-consciousness, I enjoyed the sensation of waking up in Paris.

For once I would not have to cook the breakfast. Somebody else would make the bed.

There was no sound in the hotel except a distant radio giving the news in French. I missed the noisy motor-car horns whose high-pitched symphony had always wakened me in Paris in the old days. What a strange thing was a modern city almost bereft of traffic.

I rose lazily and made a tour of the apartment by daylight. What a luxury to have a sitting-room—even if it was not quite one's own. The gentleman from the Treasury had been buying some curious oil paintings, which were stacked in their walnut frames against a leg of the writing-table. Did he intend to take them back to London? Why, he had even left his fountain-pen beside the blotter!

This experience of sleeping in a man's bed, surrounded by his things, and not even knowing his name, will count as one of my strangest experiences. How little does this Treasury official guess that I was his ghostly mistress for a night!

I went to the window.

In a room in the building opposite half a dozen young girls were stitching dresses.

At the corner of the Faubourg St. Honoré quite a well-dressed man was examining the contents of a garbage tin.

I washed and ironed my blouse, put on a tailor-made, and went down to breakfast, taking a seat at a table where already three young women were eating their porridge and cream. There was an orange beside each plate, and the menu included eggs and bacon, and toast and marmalade. These copious rations were supplied by the United States Government under Lend-Lease. Many a Londoner would have envied them, but here in Paris they seemed an unbelievable contrast to milkless, sugarless acorn and barley coffee with which most citizens contented themselves.

My companions worked at the British Embassy. All three were Londoners, and one had come from Rome, where she had spent the early part of the year. They were a little tired of the food, and said how dull it was, because of the exchange, never to be able to buy anything in the shops. That alone took away most of the fun of living in Paris. The lack of transport prevented them from going out much in the evening, and they were always wearing out their shoes which, by special favor, they might send back to London to be mended.

In this room had breakfasted the senior officers of the Luftwaffe, back from their raids on London, Liverpool, Coventry. . . . Here straw-haired pilots must have boasted of looking down on Piccadilly while the bombs fell.

Now that the British Government had taken over the hotel, the guests were all civilians—secretaries, typists, diplomats, members of the Supply Departments on short visits, officials of the B.B.C., and an occasional cleric. The waiters were French. Most of them had come back from labor camps in Germany. Their Government had given them a few francs and a suit of clothes made from wood pulp.

As I crossed the hall, the porter came up to me and said: "There's a telephone call for you, madame."

He led me to a booth next to the operator's switchboard.

With some emotion, on taking up the receiver, I heard M. Schwenter's voice. "I'm sorry about last night," he said. "But I'm expecting you for lunch. What do you say to midday?"

"Oh, yes," I answered. "You can't think how I'm looking forward to seeing you."

As I left the booth the telephone operator looked round.

"Everything all right?" she queried.

She was an angular woman who spoke excellent English though with a slightly guttural accent, which surprised me.

"Where do you come from?"

"From the Lorraine," she answered, picking up her knitting which she worked at intermittently between calls. "Almost on the border."

"Then you speak German also?"

"Yes, of course. I've always been in this business. Languages are essential."

She dropped her knitting, put in a plug as quick as the flash that had appeared on her board, and while dialing a number continued:

"I worked at General Electric with the Germans. All the rest of the girls on the switchboard had been sent over specially from Berlin. I thought I was quick, but you should have seen *them!* And what they didn't know about our exchanges! Full of tricks too. They had worked out a system whereby they replaced the first three letters of the exchange by the numerals. They claimed it saved one second on every call, and we found they were right. (Yes, sir, you want the British Embassy? Certainly, sir.) I've never known anything like that switchboard. Every night we dealt with calls from every city in Europe. The first intimation I had that the Germans were nervous about the outcome of the war was when two generals discussed a new Russian tank appearing on the eastern front. One of them said: 'We keep on bringing up new weapons but these tanks are larger and more powerful than anything we have at our disposal.' (Speak up, sir, you're through to the British Embassy.)"

She took up her knitting again and added:

"Their organization was wonderful, but they never prevented British intelligence officers, dressed as Germans, dining in the mess. Every time they sent a new fleet of trucks out, the convoy was bombed by the R.A.F. fifty miles out of Paris."

She talked as fast as she worked. "Some of the truck drivers were Russian prisoners," she continued. "They had volunteered because of the food, and many shot themselves when the Germans left Paris."

I looked with interest at this woman. She seemed to have turned so naturally from working for the Germans to working for the British.

Warm sunshine filled the Faubourg St. Honoré as I left the Castiglione. The street was crowded and now and then I looked back to examine the fashionable hats, to which I was now accustomed. Some of these headgears resembled dishes of fruit or plates of whipped cream. I wondered how these women wore their hair, for obviously one had to choose between the high hats and the high coiffure. I liked the high coiffure, though it still puzzled me, and as I walked through the sunshine I began to feel that it would be a good idea to go to a hairdresser myself, to repair the damage of the long journey.

I crossed the Rue Royale by the pedestrian crossing that faces the tea-shop where in pre-war days one found such excellent cherry cake. Obviously there was no more cherry cake, and doubtless no tea, but I did notice a hairdressing establishment in an adjoining building, and having a couple of hours to waste before lunch I went in.

A lady in a black satin dress sat behind a table on which were exhibited some of those immense tortoise-shell combs that were the fashion in Edwardian days. She said: "The hairdressing saloon is on the first floor."

I sat down in a cubicle and asked for a shampoo and a set.

They called a little girl (she turned out to be sixteen summers) in a white linen overall. Perched on immensely high wooden shoes, her hair was dressed upward like an open fan above her forehead. She was thus all in height! Her least movements were rapid and graceful and she had all the exuberance of budding youth.

As soon as my hair was washed and combed, Yvette (for so she was called) came back, to take over from her colleague who had been responsible for the shampoo. She came back in no normal way: I had been smoking a cigarette, decided halfway through that I did not like to smoke, and threw it aside. Like a bevy of young starlings, half a dozen girls flew into the cubicle to try to seize the cigarette for their fathers or brothers, and Yvette, being faster than her colleagues, won the prize. This comedy started up the conversation, and as I had brought some sweets from London, I opened my bag and gave one to each.

Yvette ate hers at once. The others kept theirs for their sweethearts.

"They are English sweets," I explained.

"My goodness!" exclaimed Yvette. "You are lucky!"

"Don't you get many?"

"It depends," answered Yvette. "Sometimes we are given a special ration. You see, we are all J.3's."

"You will think me very stupid," I said, "but I've been away so long I don't understand. What is a J.3?"

"A J.3," they all said at once, "is an under nineteen. We were given that appellation during the occupation because we have special ration cards. We are what the Americans call junior misses."

I soon found all my young friends seated on manicure stools around me. There was no work that morning because of the elections.

The fact that I had arrived from London invested me with a halo. Everybody wanted to examine my coat and skirt. Was it possible that one could obtain such magnificent material in England? The great fashion in Paris was a tartan skirt. Yes, Scotch tartans were very popular, though of course they were not of real wool. We discussed the difference in prices, and my friends affected great surprise at the cheapness of clothes in England. Then Yvette asked:

"How shall we dress your hair?"

"In some new way," I said. "I should like to have it dressed straight up in the air like yours."

"It will suit you wonderfully," said Yvette. "And your hair is just the right thickness for it."

She took the comb and started to work at tremendous speed, and as she built up the edifice, so she talked about herself.

Yvette lived at Asnières, the Paris suburb through which the boat express had run on its way to the Gare St. Lazare. She traveled up and down each day in one of those double-decked suburban trains which I had noticed from my compartment window. She left her warm bed at five o'clock every morning to work on her coiffure, and it took her exactly two hours to erect the scaffolding, curl by curl. She confided in me that her hair, not being thick enough or sufficiently luxuriant for any to be left over by the time she had made the open-fan effect in front, was attached by a postiche at the back which, in turn, had to be curled every evening before she retired for the night. Moreover these postiches had to be renewed fairly often, and as they were expensive they accounted for most of her pocket-money.

Her dream was to be a film star, and every now and then she went to the Printemps to be photographed in every imaginable pose. Asnières was full of Americans, and when Yvette was not engaged in uncurling or curling her tall Hawaiian coiffure, she danced the jitterbug and the swing. Whatever the rich Parisians felt about the American invasion, there was no doubt that the J.3's were delighted to have them in the town.

I had never seen such dexterity in a hairdresser. This girl of sixteen was a Chopin of the comb, and it amused me to reflect that, whereas after the last war we had all rushed to have our tresses shorn, to shorten our skirts and become unfeminine, the great idea of Parisian girls after this war was to copy the head-gear of Marie Antoinette and proclaim the triumph of femininity.

When the masterpiece was finished the J.3's all came to inspect it, and I was escorted like a heroine to the door.

As I walked down the Rue Royale in the sunshine, I felt terribly self-conscious, but it became obvious I had merged into the atmosphere of the capital. I went directly to the Meurice, and having announced my arrival stood for a moment in the hall.

I looked round to see if anything had changed, but nothing appeared to have disturbed the air of quiet dignity that I had always noticed. The show-cases still displayed their wares, the mirrors were polished, the marble pillars, strong and unblemished by time, upheld the tradition of this royal hotel.

Then I saw M. Schwenter approaching from his office. I thought he walked more slowly and that his broad shoulders were slightly bent, but as he came up to me his voice was the same, quiet but affectionate.

He led me into his office and offered me a chair beside the massive desk with its silver ink-pots. I looked round almost nervously, as if expecting to see the ghosts of the successive

Kommandants of Paris whose grim, sardonic rule had been exercised from here. The thought of these cold, calculating butchers with their haughty manners and fine uniforms gave me a sudden chill.

In front of the desk was still the colored picture of those lovely Edwardian ladies with their wide hats and parasols, taking tea in the foyer. As my eyes followed the wall round I suddenly exclaimed:

"Why, there they are! The Prince of Wales, Prince George, and the King of Spain! I believe you never took them down?"

"No," he answered. "They are just as you saw them last, but alas, two have passed away. King Alfonso . . . the Duke of Kent."

I rose and looked at the signature *Edward* with the graceful under-sweep of the first letter.

"What did your successive *Herr Kommandants* have to say about that?" I asked.

"Nothing," he answered. "They pretended not to see them.

"Yes," Schwenter continued, "I closed the hotel on the ninth of June, and the Germans arrived on the fourteenth.

"Three weeks earlier—on May twenty-sixth, to be exact—my wife and I had a motor-car accident in the Bois de Boulogne. Several of Mme. Schwenter's ribs were fractured and were still in plaster, while I had a broken wrist, but as soon as I knew that the Germans were on their way, I asked Mme. Schwenter to receive them at the hotel while I went round to the Grand and the Prince of Wales which, as you probably remember, come under my jurisdiction. The director of the Grand had taken fright and run away, so that I was obliged to appoint the assistant manager to the post. As there was nobody available at the Prince of Wales, I took along a young man from the reception desk here and gave him the post.

"I had spent most of the morning running from one place to the other, and it was eleven by the time I returned. The Germans had already arrived.

"They were strutting about the foyer under the nervous gaze of my wife, and after they had looked round for a few minutes, they came up to me and exclaimed:

" 'It would be a shame to billet troops here. The hotel is far too beautiful. We will make our report and let you know later.'

"We heard nothing more until the evening, when we were warned that Von Briesen had just arrived to take up the post of *Kommandant* of Paris, and that he would make his headquarters at the Meurice."

Thus it was that this hotel, where by a strange coincidence during the war I had left a box full of spring and summer hats that I had worn during the state visit of the king and queen to Paris, became the home of the Prussian commander who had power of life and death over every citizen in the capital.

Beneath the blue hat-box hidden in a corner of the attic had tramped the heavy boots of the tight-lipped invader.

How that delicate tulle, those pretty flowers, those soft ribbons, must have shaken!

"My wife and I shut ourselves up in our apartment and waited," M. Schwenter went on. "There was nothing we could do. The Germans ran the hotel.

"I had a notice painted on the door of my flat (I will show it to you presently) with the word PRIVAT, but I gave orders that the word should not be centered but placed a little on one side, to allow me to turn it into English as soon as the Germans had gone. You may think that rather childish, but we were reduced to these absurdities to keep up our spirits.

"Von Briesen did not stay with us long. He was sent to the eastern front and was killed.

"His place was taken here by Von Schaumburg, a *junker* with features of stone. He took over Alfonso's suite, the one I so often gave you before the war, but he seldom slept there, for he commandeered the Villa Coty in the Bois de Boulogne, turning it into a wonderful private residence. His was a reign of terror and it lasted three years.

"By the time he was replaced by Von Boineburg there were signs that the Hitler regime was meeting with opposition. Before long Von Boineburg himself was accused of having sympathies with the generals who tried to assassinate Hitler in Berlin, and only a few months after arriving in Paris he was removed to Dijon. Von Choltitz then became *Kommandant;* but in due course Von Choltitz discovered that his best friend had been executed in Berlin for his share in the *putsch,* and to this fact the city of Paris today owes its existence, for Von Choltitz

decided that in order to revenge his friend he would not defend
the capital.

"On the eve of the liberation of Paris, Von Choltitz summoned his staff to the drawing room—the one between the foyer
and the dining room. I knew that our fate depended on the result of that meeting, and I stood in the corridor where I could
hear what was being said.

"Von Choltitz gathered his staff round him and announced:

" 'We must defend ourselves until the last man. Nevertheless,
as long as I remain with you, I shall expect you to obey me implicitly.'

"He spoke in this way because he had decided not to destroy
Paris. Though an enemy, he loved the city. His temporary con-
cern was to keep a tight grip on his men. That is why he said:
'I shall expect you to obey me implicitly.'

"The date was August twenty-fourth, and already the tricolor
was flying from the *hôtel de ville* and Notre Dame.

"That evening nothing happened. Though Von Choltitz had
exhorted his staff to defend themselves to the last man, he refused to give a single order, with the result that there was a
great silence in the hotel.

"The streets and bridges of Paris were mined. A word would
have blown them up, but Von Choltitz dined frigidly in the
corner of the restaurant.

"The following day a senior French resistance officer telephoned to him from the *hôtel de ville* with a request for his
surrender. The *Kommandant* answered:

" 'I cannot surrender because the *Fuehrer* would kill my family. We must have an honorable battle.'

"During the morning there were frequent and earnest con-
versations in the foyer between the Swedish consulate and the
German staff, but again Von Choltitz went to his accustomed
table in the restaurant, where he lunched alone.

"Then the French brought up machine-guns in the Rue de
Rivoli and a few shots were exchanged in the gardens of the
Tuileries.

"The French now stormed the hotel's Rue de Rivoli entrance.
The first Frenchman to break in was an Alsatian, Lieutenant
Karcher, who, seeing nobody, fired his pistol at the portraits of

Hitler and Goering which hung in the hall. Then he looked round, wondering what to do.

"You remember the Rue de Rivoli entrance, I expect. We shall pass it in a moment on our way to lunch. In front of the restaurant is the elevator built like a sedan chair.

"Lieutenant Karcher stood facing this elevator with his smoking pistol in his hand. There was nobody in the elevator, but on the balcony, behind some sandbags, a German soldier was crouching with his rifle. The German could have shot the Frenchman long ago, but he held his fire because he had received no orders from the *Kommandant*, Von Choltitz.

"Suddenly Lieutenant Karcher looked up and saw the German. He raised his pistol and shot him dead.

"Then all the German officers came down the wide staircase with their hands above their heads, and they gave themselves up in the foyer on this side of the hotel, the one that faces the Rue du Mont Thabor.

"Von Choltitz remained alone in his room.

"A French officer went up to fetch him, and drove him away in his jeep.

"Half an hour later a detachment from Leclerc's Division arrived to search the hotel. The soldiers went everywhere, even in the attic. (By the way, that reminds me! I believe I have a hatbox belonging to you.) All the German kit was brought down in the foyer, not only the leather boots, beautifully shined, and the uniforms, but great quantities of silk and woolen underclothes.

"As soon as the French troops left, the hotel was entered by a vast crowd of youths claiming to be members of the resistance movement. They swarmed everywhere, looting all they found. Within a few minutes the leather boots and the underclothes had disappeared, but there remained the *feldgrau* uniforms, reaching to the ceiling. One of the looters shouted: 'What's wrong with these? They only need to be dyed!'

"There was a rush and soon not one was left."

M. Schwenter rose.

"That's about all," he said. "General Billotte, who was in London for so long with General de Gaulle, slept here with some of his officers. But the next day, which was my birthday, he left to camp in the Bois de Boulogne. After that we were requisitioned by the Americans."

He put a hand on my shoulder.

"I often thought of you," he said.

"And my hat-box?" I asked, laughing.

"I'll send for it," said M. Schwenter. "Unless some soldier has thrust a bayonet through it, I shall expect to find it intact."

He added:

"Now let us have some lunch. The chef won't like it if we keep him waiting. Things are not easy for him these days."

We walked through the corridor, past the drawing room where Von Choltitz held his final conference. Just now the room was filled with American officers watching a film. I peeped through the lace curtains and saw the shaft of light from the cinema quivering above the heads of the young officers.

"This is where I stood," said Schwenter, "when Von Choltitz spoke to his staff."

The elevator built like a sedan chair was just as I remembered it.

The attendant recognized me and smiled. The sandbags had been removed from the balcony and were replaced with flowers and ferns.

"Nobody would ever think," I said, "that this was the scene of so poignant a drama."

"There is a bullet hole through one of the mirrors of the dining room," he answered. "A waiter clearing up after lunch was injured."

We had reached the door of his apartment.

I read the notice: PRIVATE.

"You see," said my host, "the E is painted in a slightly different color. I had it added as soon as the Americans took over."

"I am afraid you are going to have a poor lunch," Mme. Schwenter said to me.

"On the other hand," said M. Schwenter, "you shall have a bottle of champagne. Like your hat-box, I was able to hide a few treasures from the Germans."

As he lifted the bottle from the ice, he added:

"I expect you will want to know who occupies King Alfonso's apartment now. Well, we are the headquarters of the

SHAEF mission, and so General Lewis (U.S.A.) and General
Redman (Great Britain) sleep on either side of the late king's
drawing room."

He smiled: "You see, one has to be a diplomat. They share
the honor."

"Tell me about yourself?" I asked, turning to Mme. Schwenter.

Pride lit up the gentle features of my hostess.

"I am entirely engrossed in my infant grandson," she said.
"Perhaps you noticed the perambulator in the passage? My
daughter is married to Colonel Granval who, with Pierre Brossolette, was one of the most romantic figures in the *maquis*."

"Granval!" I exclaimed. "But of course! Pierre Brossolette
mentioned his name a score of times in my presence. I believe he
met him each time he crossed the channel."

This indeed was a strange coincidence. Brossolette, alias La-
voisier, had been among the few who made the *maquis* far too
glorious for its name to be sullied by those who afterward
brought it into ill repute.

I knew now that if, as I had dreamed so often, I had been
wafted to the Meurice during the occupation, I would have been
in safe hands.

An hour later I returned to the Castiglione with the hat-box
under my arm.

These frivolous memories amused me, for they had proved
stronger than the successive *Kommandants* of Paris whose reign
of terror was finished. Von Briesen's dried bones must have been
scattered over the blood-seeped fields of the Ukraine. Von
Schaumburg, Von Boineburg, Von Choltitz, had come to a pitiful end. Mme. Agnès's satins and ribbons had fared better than
they. I laid the hats out on my bed and their gay colors contrasted with the serious surroundings of these rooms lent to me
by the gentleman from the Treasury. The doll's hat with its
blue and pink feathers shimmered in the breeze from the open
window.

"Perhaps," I thought, "they are not so frivolous after all."

A radio announcer and an engineer who were arranging a
broadcast from Caen to tell the peoples of the world what the
stricken city now looked like offered to drive me in their car

as far as Lisieux. The announcer had a soft caressing voice and the gentlest manner. He had been sent over from London to arrange broadcasts of this kind, whereas the engineer, though English by birth, had spent most of his life in France. They shared a passion for French poetry of the Resistance school, in which they gave proof of their intelligence, for it had reached great heights of emotion and beauty.

The car left Paris by the Bois de Boulogne, where the Villa Coty, deserted since the eclipse of Von Schaumburg, faces the Longchamp racecourse, accidentally bombed during a race-meeting.

Leaving the park we followed the wide and leafy avenue beside the river Seine, and ahead of us the sun sparkled on the new white bridge of St. Cloud. The driver brought the car to a standstill in front of a row of splendid houses whose gardens reflected the russet autumnal tints behind wrought-iron gates.

"It's only a tire," he said, turning round. "We shall not be delayed more than a few moments."

I left the men and walked across to the towing-path to admire the wide river which flowed majestically at my feet. A few men were lazily fishing between pontoons that led to gaily painted houseboats, in the nearest of which a woman was hanging out her washing, and a man was watering the geraniums in the stern.

Could any sight be more peaceful than this?

"Lucky people," I thought, "they do not appear to have a worry in the world."

For a few moments, in my cotton blouse and black skirt, and shoes with tall cork platforms, which all the women in Paris were then wearing, I stood behind a fisherman, day-dreaming.

To my left the sun was reverberating on the blinding white bridge; to my right, a third of a mile down stream, lithe figures were diving into the water from the springboards of an aquatic school. In the distance, beyond the farther bank, rose a miniature mountain fastness whose granite face dominated the capital.

"What is that place?" I asked the fisherman.

He followed my gaze, shading his eyes with a withered hand. Then he looked at me and said grimly:

"That's the Mont Valérien. Maybe you were not here during the occupation. Yes, my little lady—a knock at the door, a

summons, a few tears, and then, an hour later, a shot behind
the damp walls of that old fortress. It looks pretty in the sunshine, doesn't it?"

He gripped his rod again and turned his eyes steadfastly to the
red and white float bobbing up and down among the reeds.

The houseboat was the prettiest thing I had ever seen.

It had a front door just like a doll's house, with a brass
knocker and a letter-box. I wondered if I would like to live in
a houseboat. I was always dreaming of the simple life, but in fact
I was much too feminine, too much a townswoman, to appreciate it.

The man in the stern had finished watering his geraniums
and, having picked up a bucket, now started to walk across the
pontoon. He looked at me as he passed, and I, without attempt-
ing to turn away my eyes, said simply:

"You keep your boat bright and neat."

He put down his bucket and answered:

"My son bought it before the war for $42. An old landing-
stage for the Seine pleasure-boats, that's what it was. Only the
other day a gentleman from Paris offered us $750 for it, but you
see it's the only home we've got. My wife and I are refugees
from Dunkirk. Do you remember Dunkirk? The British pulled
out from there in 1940. Well, we thought of the son's houseboat. We put our things on board and took her up the Seine to
escape from the Germans when they entered Paris, but they
caught up with us and harried us all the way to Mantes. In the
end we were given permission to return to Paris and tie up here.
It's not ideal, especially in winter, but it only costs us a dollar
a year in dues, and the electricity is laid on."

He took up his bucket.

"Fresh water, that's the only problem; but the houses opposite
are always willing to oblige."

The chauffeur was klaxoning in the avenue.

The car passed over the bridge and entered the yet unfinished
St. Germain *autostrade*, one of the most modern arterial roads in
Europe, cut through dense woods, and having something of
French elegance about its construction which made it a thing of
beauty as well as usefulness. From time to time it was crossed
by very pretty bridges carrying other roads, but some of them

had been dynamited, and occasionally a powerful German anti-aircraft gun stood in the long grass by the side of the road.

Then· came the dusty, poplar-shaded *route nationale* which since Napoeonic times has led into Normandy by way of Mantes and Lisieux.

Now the fair fields of France stretched away on either side. Along this road thundered opposing tanks after the allied breakthrough in Normandy, and now and then a maimed Tiger tank reared its ugly wreckage in the ditch. Beneath these leafy poplars the allied convoys had thundered to the west, fed by gasoline pumped from England through the giant pipeline over which the bramble grew and the poppy waved its head. "Beware of the pipeline," said the notices posted at frequent intervals. "No naked lights."

Here, half hidden by the ripening corn, was the wing of an airplane, whose fuselage, a hundred yards distant, still hung from the smashed roof of a farmhouse. "Pot-holes ahead! Go slow!" was the warning nailed to a telegraph post whose wires sagged to the level of the cornflowers edging the fields with blue. Doubtless that German airplane, before the final burst of fire which winged it to destruction, had machine-gunned the road, which now made me clutch the side of my seat to steady myself as the car bumped its way over the uneven surface.

American convoys still used this highway. We passed them grouped for a mile or more along the side of the road; or we crawled near the ditch to let them thunder by at sixty miles an hour, swaying like express trains, throwing up the white dust which blotted out the country—concentrated tons of flashing metal borne along on brand-new tires which did not puncture at every turn like those the French used.

At the entrance to a village a cordon of police stopped all but military vehicles bound for the capital. They were searching for contraband butter from the rich pasture lands of Normandy. Nobody understood why they did this because, if it was solely due to the lack of transport that Parisians were without dairy produce, one might have thought that whatever was brought in by private means would ease the situation. Perhaps the big dealers looked upon the private motorist as a competitor. Certainly, whereas the police minutely searched private cars and hay-wagons, they stepped politely aside to allow a hundred-weight of butter to go through in a truck. These matters were too abstruse for a woman like myself to understand, and I would have needed the expert knowledge of Charles d'Ydewalle.

The sun was reaching its zenith and the little stones on the road glittered like diamonds. Two burned-out trucks, their chassis locked together, stood rampant like rusted phantoms against the trunk of a withered tree. A cross of wood, a tin hat, and a bunch of faded wild flowers marked the spot where a man was buried.

The announcer recited quietly:

> "Je meurs et France demeure
> Mon amour et mon refus
> O mes amis si je meurs
> Vous saurez pour qui ce fut."

The engineer added:

> "Et si c'etait à refaire
> Je referais ce chemin."

The chauffeur said:

"I've heard men in the *maquis* recite Aragon when they were armed and drunk with fatigue and liquor. I've heard his verses taken up from mouth to mouth while a candle flickered in an empty bottle. Ten minutes later a train blew up."

So far I had not counted more than a few private cars on the road, but now I was beginning to see a few open trucks of antiquated design, remarkable for the large number of bicycles grouped behind with their driving-wheels in mid air. These vehicles were the counterpart of the creaking wagon of Tristram Shandy's days. The driver, having delivered his load in some distant town, was now returning in leisurely fashion to his base. For him the roads were paved with banknotes, for every few miles he would be stopped by weary pilgrims with sore feet or aching limbs who would be glad to give him a hundred francs to continue their journey in greater comfort. They stood or reclined on the straw-covered truck and one saw the wizened peasant woman in whose osier basket cackled goose or hen, exchanging gossip with the bicyclist whose plus-fours reached to his ankles.

And past them, all the time, roared those supermen from

Illinois or Arizona at the driving-wheel of their four-tonners equipped with double rubber tires.

Gradually the aspect of the country changed.

The wheatfields gave place to orchards surrounded by hedges, and occasionally one came upon an airport, all the buildings of which had been utterly destroyed by allied air attack. A hundred yards farther along new buildings had been put up. The airport carried on under new management.

Almost every miles one came across a French car broken down at the side of the road. The driver had spread his gear on the grass and one wheel of the vehicle would be jacked up.

Never had the country looked more beautiful.

Sleek cows lay under the apple trees and children played in front of the farms. Here was the rich produce that Paris never saw except in the black market. In the distance the tracks of the railroad shone in the sunshine. Road and rail were beginning to converge.

Without any warning the car suddenly came to a crossroads.

White dust lay upon them and they looked unreal. A couple of American military policemen stood in the middle and the road signs were in English and French. All the beautiful fields, the apple trees, and the cows seemed suddenly to belong to another world. I gasped at the desolation, the horror, and the nakedness of the sight. The white dust was a shroud.

"Where are we?" I asked.

The driver turned round and answered:

"Lisieux, madame."

Then he looked at the announcer and asked:

"Would you like me to show the lady what is left of the town?"

"If you can," answered the announcer.

The car skidded down a track between mountains of white rubble. Nothing had been cleared. It looked as if trucks and trucks filled with broken brick had been emptied on an immense stretch of waste land. But here and there, like wooden crosses over dead men, were notices that read: "So-and-So. Chemist," or "Such-a-One. Notary," and I wondered whether the wording referred to the chemist or to his shop, the notary or his office. There was not a person in sight. No other car thought it worth while to break itself to pieces on these shapeless boulders. I felt the white dust clog my nostrils and blind my vision.

"For heaven's sake, let's go up again!" I shouted. "I can't stand this feeling of loneliness."

The car turned round a corner, and as I peered through the window I saw towering above this graveyard, high up on the hill, the undamaged basilica of Sainte Thérèse de Lisieux.

22

Before leaving Paris I had telephoned to Victor Duprez, who promised to meet me at the station at Lisieux. My friends accordingly drove me to the entrance of what had once been a modern and well-appointed ticket office.

Thunder clouds had suddenly obscured the autumn sun, and big drops of rain were falling on the white dusty surface of the station yard. The express from Paris to Caen had passed through about a quarter of an hour earlier. I looked at the clock. It was a few minutes past midday.

I stood sheltering with my luggage under the cement portico whose blasted walls gave but scant protection from the wind and the rain. This was real Normandy weather—weather that blew the ripe apples from the gnarled trees and kept the grass green and luxurant.

A slow train, the only one of the day, was about to leave for Trouville, whence there was a connection for Villers. There was no sign of Victor Duprez, and I reflected that if for any reason he did not arrive I would be left stranded in the stricken town.

I began to feel rather miserable in this almost deserted station, and feared to have misunderstood Victor Duprez on the telephone. Perhaps he had already called for me, and finding nobody had driven home.

A taxi driver, whose vehicle was drawn up by the station entrance, came over and asked me if I was waiting for somebody.

"Yes," I answered, "I am waiting for M. Victor Duprez."

"Toto Duprez from Villers?"

"That's right. Have you seen him?"

"Not this morning, but I know him well, madame. If you wish, you may take shelter in my car. You are only wearing a light cotton blouse, and I'm afraid you'll get wet here."

"Thank you," I answered, "but my wicker basket is almost more important than I am. There is a blanket inside which I have brought all the way from London."

The driver took the basket under his arm and said:

"Don't worry, lady. There is room for you both."

I ran across the wet asphalt in the smart wooden clogs I had bought the previous evening in Paris, and as soon as I was seated in the car I heard the Trouville train puffing out of the station.

"If Victor Duprez does not come," I said to the driver, "I shall have to sleep in the ruins."

He turned round and answered:

"You've no need to do that. I can drive you to Villers."

It had not struck me that he would be willing to go so far and I asked how much he would charge.

"Eighteen hundred francs," he answered.

I translated this sum mentally into dollars and decided that even if I was obliged to part with my last $30, the expense was justified.

"Very well," I said to the driver. "There appears to be no alternative."

He was about to start his engine when one of his colleagues appeared from the ticket office and ran to him through the rain. The two men entered into a whispered conversation about cigarettes, and my driver opened a small flap in one of the doors of the car from which he produced a varied collection of cigarettes, some American, others French. I watched this black market bargaining with an amused smile for a few moments. Then a Citroen with mud-bespattered yellow wheels drove into the courtyard from the main road and came to a sudden stop beside them.

"Oh!" I exclaimed. "There he is! There's Toto Duprez."

The taxi driver answered:

"That's too bad. If I had left when you asked me to, I would have been eighteen hundred francs the richer!"

"Never mind," I answered, opening my hand-bag and handing him a packet of English cigarettes. "You may add this to your collection."

Toto Duprez soon made me forget my tiresome wait. He was
a candidate for some regional election and had apparently been
detained at the polling station.

The rain had stopped now, and the hedges were garlanded
with silver drops shining in the warm sun which had once again
emerged from the clouds. We drove rapidly across the plateau
by way of Blonville, and as we approached Cathedral Lane I
felt my heart thumping against my ribs. I was longing to catch
sight of my own land.

Toto Duprez drove me to his own house, the Bruyères, where
he lent me a servant to carry my luggage to my farm. Thus I
walked toward my own gate, preceded by a farm-hand wheeling my belongings in a barrow.

My mother stood framed in the entrance of the half-timbered
house.

She appeared very small, very slight, in her carpet-slippers,
her hair waving in the wind. A log fire was burning brightly in
the immense stone hearth. The cats, frightened at our approach,
slid into the garden and jumped over the white gate.

I ran into my mother's arms. She was too moved to say very
much.

Then she looked at me and exclaimed:

"Why, you are wearing the same little cotton blouse that you
wore when we said good-by to the house five years ago! Did
you return in it on purpose?"

"Why, no!" I answered. "I never gave it a thought."

It was a simple blouse with white numerals on a blue background that she had made for me out of a remnant. The blouse
had cost a shilling.

My mother recalled all this in a flash and added:

"You remember how hot it was! That's why you chose the
blouse, to keep cool on the journey to St. Malo. Yes, it is curious
to come back in it!"

The farm-hand was on the gravel path, twisting his cap in his
bony hands. He had deposited all the luggage on the tiled floor
of the big raftered room and was waiting to be thanked. He was
a typical, angular Norman. I gave him a packet of cigarettes,
and he went off very pleased with himself.

My mother had gone over to the hearth, where she was balancing a blackened saucepan over the curling flames. As I came back into the room she said:

"I'll make you a cup of tea. I have so much to tell you that I am afraid I can only think of the stupidest things to say."

I opened the heaviest of the suit-cases and began to put some of the provisions I had brought from London into the large Norman cupboard in which my mother kept her stores. Then I inspected the odds and ends on my mother's work-table. There was a pretty pincushion, with some snapshots of Bobby taken in the Green Park, but they were all quite recent pictures, and I asked suddenly: "What have you done with the ones we took of him in the garden when he was a baby?"

My mother looked up from the fire.

"I burned them at St. Malo, every one of them," she said.

Her voice was rather unsteady.

"I was so frightened the Germans would find them in my bag and that in some way he would be made to suffer. I was foolish, but I threw them all into the fire at the hotel in the Place Chateaubriand."

"You poor thing!" I cried. "How you must have suffered!"

I walked slowly round the room.

"Oh!" I cried. "You have electricity, and to think I never noticed!"

Then I ran into the kitchen:

"And the Aga is back and looks just as lovely as when we left!"

"Yes," my mother answered, "young Mathieu brought it up last week from M. Foyer's farm. Barbe was to have started painting the house today, but I put him off a week so as not to inconvenience you."

"You have done wonders!" I cried. "Everything is so peaceful that I can hardly bring myself to believe that so many horrors happened here during the occupation. What news is there of the Goguette?"

"The Goguette is back. You will see her at milking time."

I turned quickly on my high wooden heels. I felt my throat suddenly parched. I repeated:

"The Goguette is back?"

My mother pointed to a newspaper on the big table and said:

"You will find an account of the trial in there. Roger, your little Roger, to whom you once wanted to give the farm, has been sentenced to penal servitude for life."

I gripped the side of the table.

How often had he come to the door with his cap pulled over his eyes to beckon me. I had been so sure that with patience I could make something of him. At one time I forbade him to wear a cap. I washed his head in a bucket of rain water in the garden to drown the fleas. I had burned his horrible greasy jacket and knitted him a pullover.

Now Roger was to spend all the rest of his life in prison!

"When was the trial?" I asked.

"Three days ago. You just missed it. I myself have hardly seen the Goguette since her release. She keeps very quiet, though they killed the fattest goose to feast her return. The girl Renée has been sent away again."

"And Mme. Hommet?"

"Mme. Hommet was arrested. It had something to do with Goguet's last statement—the one on his death-bed. But she also was released, and she is here with her daughter on your farm."

Now that everything had been discussed in court, the drama on my farm was no longer confined to hushed allusions. Nevertheless the story, which had blown like a hot, evil wind over the countryside, had left a feeling of horror that nothing could dispel.

To what extent the rich contents of the beautiful sixteenth-century house had prepared the terrain was not possible to assess. The farmhouse was broken into a few days after Mlle. Lefranc had first met the Goguette in the village square. Cart-loads of linen and furniture were removed by night, and the police heard vague reports of my fur coats changing hands in the neighborhood. The Germans themselves took the Aga and the refrigerator, but the house must, by then, have been practically empty. The fact that German troops put their horses to graze in some of the fields for a few days, and were known to be moving freely about the property, confused the issue.

Whereas the Goguette liked money for the pleasures it procures, Goguet had the peasant's ingrained desire to amass wealth under the mattress and in secret places. If he had always hated his eldest son Roger, it was merely on account of the trifling expense the lad's ill health in childhood had occasioned. There was also, of course, the unpleasant knowledge that the day was soon coming when, by Norman law, he would be obliged to render the boy his due.

The peasant's avariciousness had, in normal times, undoubted advantages. He worked not only untiringly but also unceasingly, both on his own land and on occasion on other people's, hiring out his services by the hour. To his credit it must be said that he kept the fields in splendid condition. His personal wants only cost him the labor of his brow. He drank gallons of cider and a great deal too much *calvados*, which is potent and deadly, but both the cider and the brandy were made from his own apples in his own cider press and did not therefore appear to him as costing any money at all. Goguet did not know what it was to take a holiday, and the only occasions on which he had been to a moving picture was when the holiday camp at the Pelouses, to which he supplied milk every day, invited him and his family to the open-air cinema they gave on the eve of their departure.

In giving him an extra cow and many unusual advantages, I had hastened Goguet's advancement. The fortune was not yet made, but the foundations were laid for acquiring it. The pity was that the hardworking Norman must also be crafty, and even while his house was being built for him by Gravé, Goguet could not keep his hands from stealing the bricks to sell to his neighbors by night.

At heart he was not a bad man. He was prone, however, to listen to the counsel of others, and the sorcerer Hommet, with whom he spent long hours tapping the sides of the aged casks in the oak-beamed cider press down by the trout stream, proved too often his evil genius. The apple brandy, responsible for stunted children and hangings in desolate farms, made Goguet a prey to those whispered invitations to make a little more by some act of cunning. The nine hundred and ninety-nine francs, with one more added to it, would produce a new one thousand-franc note, blue and crisp from the bank, to lie snugly with the others in the hidden woollen sock underneath the bottom mattress.

The war had left him king of his rich domain. The woman who owned it had fled and, as with the Spanish galleons of old, rich booty lay within. When the contents of the house had disappeared, Goguet himself marched down to the *Kommandatur* to announce to the occupants that the land upon which he worked belonged to an Englishwoman. He supposed that such frankness would put him in well with the new masters. The Germans thanked him politely, but though they traded with him they never ceased to respect the owner's property, and once a month a high officer motored to the farm to look at the tiles on the roof to ascertain whether Goguet was keeping the exterior, at least, in good repair. The farm was enemy property.

Never could the former cowherd have believed, however, that money was so easy to earn. The war had passed him over, almost by a mistake. The fact that he had been sent back from Dozulé, unwanted, at the beginning of the phoney war, was a piece of good fortune that does not happen twice in a man's life. Most of the farms were now without men. Ernest Poulin had been captured in the Maginot Line and was in a prisoner-of-war camp in Germany. Goguet could drink his soup at night with all his family around him, and when he was in need of a little help, he could send for Old Hommet and his wife from Annebault. Roger was working as butler and farm-hand at the Bruyères, and Renée was also bringing in money. London was being burned to the ground by the Luftwaffe, and the Englishwoman owner would never return to seek her belongings or call for her rent.

The opportunities for amassing those blue banknotes were now almost without limit. True enough the Goguette had cut her dark hair, and in spite of having two infants to look after, was growing very particular about her looks. In his drunken moments he beat her, which he had never done before. He could not bear the idea that, in some way in which he was unable to ascertain, money was escaping from his hands.

The German regime had brought to the village a mixture of cupidity and fear. A few people who all their lives had prided themselves on being good patriots, people of normally amiable character with fine records in the last war, went out of their way to voice their desire for a German victory. A sense of bitterness for the defeat of their own country may not have been altogether foreign to this attitude. Others made the presence of the enemy an excuse to loot and pillage deserted farms and villas, on the excuse that what they did not acquire for themselves would be commandeered by the Germans; but the most common failing was for the shopkeeper or the farmer to sell his goods or his produce to the Germans for no other reason than that the men in *feldgrau* paid the highest prices.

To rob the German became an honorable act, though it left such honest souls as Mme. Bayard without food or clothing. Many a farmer in the Pays d'Auge took the cream off his milk to sell to the Germans before supplying the women and children of the neighborhood.

The drama took place on November twenty-sixth, 1943.

It was a misty, damp evening; and Goguet, having returned from the fields, took it into his head to wind up the grandfather's clock in the living room. This clock had found its way there from the old farmhouse, where Roginsky, the furniture dealer, had placed it at the foot of the stairs leading to the bedroom where my son was born. The clock was made of polished oak in the Norman style, and the massive key usually hung on a nail inside.

Goguet therefore opened the tall narrow door to take out the key, whereupon, in the spacious cupboard of the grandfather's clock, he discovered, hidden under an old newspaper, a liter of *calvados*.

Goguet's apple brandy was the most valuable commodity that his imagination could conceive. Its distillation from cider was a long and difficult business.

Old applejack was a rarity that not even money could easily buy, and the apples on my farm were among the best in the neighborhood. These matters must be appreciated to realize Goguet's wrath when he discovered that somebody had been tapping his keg and drawing off *calvados* for sale to the Germans behind his back.

Wrenching a bar from the nearest chair, Goguet went to his wife, who was cowering against the wall, and beat her savagely about the head and shoulders. Her piercing cries brought help from a nearby orchard; a farm-hand dressed her wounds and took her down to the village, where she lodged a charge of assault against her enraged husband. The *gendarmerie*, accus-

tomed to these family scenes, advised the Goguette to return
to the farm and try to make matters up with her spouse.

Unfortunately no reconciliation was reached that night. This
was not the first time that Goguet had beaten his wife, and indeed on several previous occasions he had thrown her almost
senseless into the cowshed. The next morning, therefore, the
Goguette wrote a letter to her father, Old Hommet, asking him
to come to her rescue and take her back with him to Annebault.

The sorcerer took his bicycle and hurried to Villers. Goguet
was not at home when he arrived, having gone down to the
village, where he confided to an acquaintance that he had the
impression of being driven into a trap. Accordingly, in his
absence, a family council was held in the living room, during
which the Goguette appealed for a separation.

After the matter had been fully discussed, Old Hommet, taking his grandson Roger by the arm, led him down the orchard
toward the cider press. On the way he said to him in a low
voice:

"Has your father got a gun?"

"Yes," answered Roger, "he still has the shot-gun he used to
hang against the oak beam in the sixteenth-century house. He
refused to hand it over to the Germans in spite of the death
penalty for owning a firearm. It is hidden behind a rafter in the
cider press."

Old Hommet asked again:

"How far away is the *Kommandatur?*"

"Less than ten minutes' walk—the big villa on the left by the
Meeting of the Four Ways."

Old Hommet said:

"That's good. He won't make us spew tonight."

Then Roger guided his grandfather to the *Kommandatur*,
where the boy denounced his father to the Germans.

"You realize the importance of the charge?" asked the German officer. "Are you quite sure that your father's gun is where
you say it is? If you mislead us the responsibility will be upon
your head."

"I am quite certain," said Roger.

The Germans led him to the door and said:

"You may go. We don't need you any longer. You are no
more use to us."

But they kept Old Hommet.

Roger walked back toward Cathedral Lane. Suddenly, as the cool air blowing from the sea smote his cheeks, he became aware of the enormity of his crime, and thought that if he ran fast enough he would have time to warn his father.

So he ran over the path moistened with damp leaves.

But when he came level with the white gate leading to Dr. Salmond's estate, he was overtaken by two German patrols riding bicycles. They stopped him and said:

"You don't need to go home. Come with us and we will give you a dish of meat. If your information is correct, we shall pay you for it."

And they led him back between them.

While Roger was being given supper at the *Feldgendarmerie*, officers of the Gestapo drove up to the farm with Old Hommet, who was to act as their guide. They walked down the field past the old house to the cider press, where Goguet was cutting stakes by the edge of the stream. Goguet looked up, axe in hand. He probably thought they had come to buy some apple-jack. He did not suspect anything, because of the presence of his father-in-law.

But Old Hommet turned away his gaze, and one of the Germans asked Goguet:

"Have you got a gun?"

"No," answered Goguet.

They climbed the rickety staircase leading to the hay loft, and found the gun exactly where Roger had told them.

Then they manacled Goguet and took him away.

When Roger had finished his meal, the German police set him free and told him he could return home. He knew that it was too late to warn his father, and he was looking forward to the reward which the Germans had promised him if they found the gun in the place he had indicated. He wondered how he would spend the money.

When he reached the farm he found his grandfather talking to a neighbor. The old man was in high spirits and patted his grandson on the back. Then, rubbing his hands together, he exclaimed:

"We've done a good day's work. He won't worry us any more."

Meanwhile the girl Renée, having heard what had happened, slipped into the hay loft, where she knew her father had hidden a box of cartridges. She thought that if she could dispose of them before the Gestapo made another search, her father's situation would become less serious. She found the box under a heap of straw and, taking it to the trout stream, threw the cartridges into the water.

After Goguet had been taken by the Gestapo to Caen, Roger was given his blood money. He bought a motorbicycle which it had been his ambition to own for several years, and he drove along the country lanes, smiling at the Germans whom he met on the way.

But Old Hommet thought of the blue banknotes which Goguet had hidden for so long in some secret place, and this treasure which he was unable to discover obsessed him to such an extent that he went back to the *Kommandatur* and pleaded with them, saying that the family was unable to run the farm properly because his son-in-law had hidden the money, which was not his alone.

"Make him tell us where he has put it," said Old Hommet.

The Germans telephoned to Caen and Goguet was beaten until he divulged the hiding-place.

Then the blue banknotes were unearthed and Old Hommet also touched his thirty pieces of silver.

Roger now lived without fear of his father in the farmhouse, where he defiled the New Testament which my mother-in-law had given me and in which, when my mother found it, her eyes fell on the story of Judas Iscariot.

"After the liberation," wrote the paper I held in my hand, "the odious old man, the chief culprit, at the moment of his arrest, took advantage of a moment's inattention on the part of the *gendarmes* to cut his throat. The son Roger now bears the heavy responsibility of his father's death. In spite of his age when the crime was committed, and a brilliant address by his counsel, Maître Richard, he was condemned by the court to penal servitude for life. The widow Goguet and the grandmother Alphonsine Lebreton Hommet were both acquitted."

I looked up, and unconsciously my eyes turned to the place where the grandfather's clock used to stand.

"But it's there! It's there!" I cried. "Am I dreaming?"

"No," answered my mother. "Renée Goguet gave it back to me. The key was missing, but Jean-Louis Bayard made me another."

I walked toward it and touched the polished oak with the tips of my fingers. Then I said:

"I feel the need of some fresh air. I think I shall take a turn in the garden."

I picked a King William pear from the tree against the house and started to eat it. Then I heard a voice crying out:

"Bonjour, madame!"

Looking round I saw the Goguette on the other side of the white fence.

"Good afternoon," I answered. "You've grown thinner."

The Goguette laughed in rather a forced way.

"Well, you know," she answered, "I've not had a very amusing time."

"How are the twins?"

"Well," answered the Goguette.

"Can I see them?"

"Of course you can."

I opened the gate and passed between the two houses where, behind the cattle trough, Mme. Hommet, with one eye hidden by a black pad, was watching like a cat.

The twins were playing on the sunlit porch of the thatched house, and I knelt down and took them in my arms, one after the other. I kissed them on their foreheads. The twins caught sight of my long red fingernails and of my rings and played with them like kittens. Then I open my hand-bag and gave to each of them a sweet. I turned to the Goguette and said:

"I don't suppose you ever thought the twins would have English sweets?"

The Goguette looked uncomfortable but said nothing.

Mme. Hommet gave a slight cough as if she were anxious to attract my attention, and said: "I've a cataract in my eye."

Then the Goguette announced in a humble voice:

"I'm leaving at Christmas. I should like to settle the arrears of rent."

"That's very kind of you," I answered. "You must see Maître Vincent."

Night was beginning to fall, and I was crouching in front of the log fire in the big room. My mother had gone to the Poulins'.

There was a knock on the door, and then a gruff, hearty female voice:

"Whatever you do, don't put yourself in fright, ma'am. It's only Titine and her man!"

I rose quickly and welcomed my faithful friends. Titine took off her heavy coat and revealed a beautiful sky-blue pinafore. Her gray eyes were laughing with mischief, but soon they became damp with tears of affection, and I clasped the big frame in my slender arms.

George Bayard stood a few paces behind her, screwing up his cap.

"You haven't changed at all!" I said to Titine.

"You have become thinner, ma'am, and I must say that it suits you," answered Mme. Bayard, wiping a tear from her cheeks. "And now, tell me what you think of my Bayard?"

"I am terribly glad to see him safely back."

Then turning to Bayard:

"You were made prisoner in the Maginot Line with Ernest Poulin, so I am told, and then you were taken to Stuttgart where the traitor used to broadcast his treacherous talk? Is that so?"

"That's right, madame. The first year was hard, very hard, but afterward I had the good fortune to be placed on a German farm where they looked after me well. Louise, that was the name of the farmer's wife. She was an honest woman. . . ." He nodded his good, kind head in the direction of Mme. Bayard, and added: "A woman just like you, Titine."

Titine's features took on a puzzled expression, as if she were trying to assess the value of this compliment, but she knew that her husband was only joking, and immediately she was all smiles again.

I asked gaily:

"Tell me everything, Titine, everything! What did you do when you saw the Allies marching into the village?"

Mme. Bayard gave a deep laugh which shook her comfortable person.

"They were all in battledress," she said, "and so I said to myself: 'Titine, here come the English. You must embrace one of them!' You see, ma'am, I thought of you and your husband and the little boy in London. I broke through the ranks and kissed one of the soldiers on both cheeks. Then what do you think happened? He answered me in French, ma'am. He was a Belgian! Yes, the Belgians were the first to march in."

I smiled.

"But there were some Canadians, I fancy?"

"Yes," answered Titine. "They were quartered at the Pelouses, where the little refugees from the Spanish civil war were put up in your time. I sent my Jean-Louis round to practice his English on them. The first time he came back and said: 'Mother, all the little boys of the village are queueing outside the gates asking for food. I came away because I am not a beggar.' I said to him: 'But you do not need to beg, Jean-Louis. Go and talk nicely to one of them. Say you are pleased to see him.' But when he went back, the Canadians were already moving off and the villagers were scrambling for the stores they were leaving behind. My Jean-Louis as usual was too honest to take anything, but as he was going away he saw a neat little box on the ground, and thinking it might contain something good to eat, he brought it back to me."

Bayard, who knew the story, laughed behind his cap.

"Well, Titine, what did it contain?"

Mme. Bayard bent over and whispered confidentially: "Contraceptives, my good lady. And beautifully packed!"

"My poor Titine!" I exclaimed. "You really do have the worst possible luck!"

After Titine and Bayard had taken their leave, I remained talking with my mother by the fire until the small hours. Then, because there was only one mattress, we lay down together by the dying embers.

In the morning we went across the trout stream, past the cider press, to call on Déliquaire.

Déliquaire himself was named René like poor Goguet, with whom he had never had anything in common but his Norman talk and ingrained love of the black earth.

I felt increasingly inclined to rent the farm to Déliquaire, but the new decrees which governed owner and tenant were such that it was practically impossible to give a farmer any lease under nine years. The problem was therefore more than usually difficult, and I decided to take no definite action for the time being. Also I could never feel quite sure that the Goguette would not find some excuse for not leaving at the appointed date, though she had again confirmed her intention of doing so.

We had been talking for some time in the courtyard of Déliquaire's farm, when I said, laughing:

"To think that the war is over and I have not yet seen a German soldier! I suppose I ought to consider myself lucky!"

My mother, who was looking in the direction of the orchard, exclaimed:

"There is one coming along now!"

Déliquaire followed her gaze and answered with a chuckle:

"No, ma'am, that's my eldest son. He is wearing a *feldgrau* uniform those gentlemen left behind. There's not a stitch of clothing to be bought in the village, and so our lads must make do with what they found when the Germans hurried off."

He said that as soon as the Germans left the *Kommandatur* and The Dungeon, the population flocked there to empty the two villas. Some of the farmers drove up with hay carts, which they filled with clothes and bedding. The German army sheets were made of blue and white check gingham, and within a few days these had been cut up into window curtains and aprons for the little girls. Indeed the entire village, the surrounding farms, and the feminine population were decorated with this material.

My mother and I walked slowly back to our own house across the orchards. From the high ground we looked across to Le Havre, which I had last seen when it was being attacked during the summer of 1940 by relays of German airplanes.

From here I had watched the giant liner *Normandie* proudly moving across the blue water on what was to prove its last journey to New York. Now it was being broken up for scrap iron. By the wooden gate we had met the woman from Rouen trudging up the hill with a child in her arms. She had given us the first news that German tanks had entered the town. What bitter, poignant memories were revived by the sight of this orchard, where Déliquaire's cows moved gracefully in the long grass, and where the hedges were filled with ripening hazel nuts. The red autumn sun was breaking through the haze, and all was peace and content.

So much had passed, so little had changed. Already I felt the charm of this beautiful country flowing warmly through my veins. We clambered over the trout stream and went a hundred yards out of our way to inspect the marshy ground where Goguet grew mustard and cress. Then we climbed toward my private orchard, where the young apple trees were exactly Bobby's age—straight and sturdy, full of promise.

The Goguette was walking down to the cider press.

She said:

"There's a pear tree yonder, madame, full of splendid fruit."

"Is that so?"

"If you would care to pick some . . ."

"No, Mme. Goguet. They belong to you. But if you would like to pick some for me, I should be grateful."

We continued our way back to the house, and while my mother was preparing lunch, I started to dig in the garden.

The grandfather's clock struck twelve. I counted the strikes. I had counted them one stormy night when I was writhing in childbirth. I had counted them all through the night, and not until twelve o'clock struck again did my son come into the world. What a time I had! The grandfather's clock! I had heard it strike eleven when Britain declared war on Germany. I had heard it carillon farewell when I left my farm like a refugee. Its oak cupboard had proved the death of Goguet, the imprisonment of Roger, the suicide of Old Hommet, the breaking-up of two families.

I bent over my spade. Then I heard childish voices crying out in unison:

"Bonjour, ma'am."

The twins were standing at the white gate, each carrying a basket of ripe pears. They trotted in and presented them to me with a little bow.

23

Toward the end of September, Barbe sent two men to paint the house, and soon the walls shone dazzling white which gave the raftered hall that clean, healthy appearance which had made it so neat and pretty when the child was born. George Bayard, delighted to work for his friends, felt that his honor was committed to repair, as far as he could, the damage done during my absence, and every evening he stayed a little longer to beautify the lovely bedroom whose wide window opened out on the bay of Le Havre and the Louis XIII château, where the trees were beginning to take on a copper tint. The wardrobes, stripped of their three-ply linings, were mended by his agile hands and repainted to tone with the room. Young Mathieu overhauled the furnace, the water pipes, and the central heating, reglazed the broken windows and tested the Aga stove, which had required no fewer than six men to bring it from the farm where the Germans had taken it after the house had been broken into.

Now we began to make the old farmhouse habitable.

My mother, who continued every evening to fetch the milk from Mme. Castel, learned that this worthy person was disposed to sell a mattress, which was indispensable if I were to take possession once more of my own quarters. Mme. Castel was rich in bedding because, during the last two years, she had come into quite a lot of furniture by the timely deaths of many distant relatives, not the least wealthy of whom was that old gentleman from Le Havre whom I had seen at the Poulin farm at the beginning of the war.

As soon as my mother came into possession of the mattress, she hurried over to Titine's house to tell her the good news, and the next day Titine came down the path accompanied by her mother, the widow Blanchard, pushing her carding-machine over the tufted grass.

Mother and daughter, amongst their many other accomplishments, were the most expert mattress-makers for twenty miles round. They worked as a team—in the open air when there was not too much wind, or otherwise just inside a hay shed—at whatever farm mattresses required to be remade. The widow Blanchard's machine looked like a wheelbarrow with props to stand it up, and she sat between the handles, swinging to and fro the teethed roller which disentangled the wool and threw it out in fresh and airy strands on the grass or on the floor. This ancient handiwork, old as the world, is extremely picturesque, and as it throws up a considerable amount of dust, the carder wears, as Mme. Blanchard did, a scarf twisted like a turban round her head, and an apron round her waist.

As the widow threw out the white strands, her daughter picked them up and laid them on a trestled table on which was the material she would sew up with her curved needle and twine. I would thus have a mattress of the finest wool to fit the undermattress which my mother had discovered at an auction sale and which Jean-Louis brought to the farm on his wheelbarrow. The bed had been made specially by the widow Faneau, whose young son, you will remember, was driven off manacled by the Gestapo under the eyes of Titine for his part in the resistance movement. Now, at last, the poor widow Faneau knew she would never see her boy again. Too many months had passed without news of him. Her carpentry shop was being carried on by her son-in-law who, having made the bed, gave it to George Bayard, who painted it.

The cider-apple crop was one of the worst within living memory. Normans expect two years in three to give poor yields, which fact is compensated by higher prices, and it was some satisfaction to know that the following year would doubtless prove excellent. By that time the widow Goguet would have left.

My private orchard, however, gave forth pears in plenty, and my mother was very proud to think that she was free to negotiate for their sale—the first piece of farm business she had ever transacted. What a change had taken place in her life since she had decided to hurl herself against the rocks at St. Malo! She talked the matter over with Mme. Castel, who purchased the crop, with the promise that Ernest Poulin would come to glean the fruit and carry it off in a farm cart.

My mother's needs were few, and I admired her stringent economy, the more remarkable because of the big change that had taken place since the beginning of the war. Butter now cost a hundred francs a pound instead of eleven, milk seven and a half francs a liter instead of one, and an egg twenty francs instead of fifty centimes. Occasionally one of the Goguette's hens flopped over the garden gate and laid seven or eight eggs amongst the logs at the back of the old farmhouse, and the sight of them made my mother more than ever determined to have chickens of her own as soon as my farmers had left.

There was no longer any doubt about the Goguette's plans to leave at Christmas, for almost every day she could be seen making her way up the path behind a wheelbarrow filled with her belongings, and now and again a cow would be taken away for sale. The Goguette had quite changed her tactics and was almost friendly. Her physical endurance was as remarkable as ever, and she trimmed the hedges and dug round the apple trees to give air to the roots, as she was required to do by contract, in an obvious effort to leave the farm in good condition. Every morning also she spent an hour or more taking down the mistletoe from the boughs of the fruit trees.

Great quantities of apple props began to leave the farm, and a number of these pieces of stout wood, which hold up the branches when the trees are heavy with fruit, were undoubtedly mine; but I preferred not to make any objection, knowing how impossible it would be for me to prove their identity. The Goguette would cut them up for firewood, which would sell for big prices in the village, where there was still no coal. Dudouy, the laborer, informed me that he was about to clean the cattle pond at the top of the field, where, because of the drought that summer, there lay a film of stagnant green water.

By the end of November Chouquet, the cider merchant, arrived at the farm with his cart and team of two horses, to take away the cider from the old thatched press. The women had made enormous quantities of cider since the farmer had been led away by the Gestapo, and as they never drank by themselves, the barrels had lain untouched for several years. Cider now sold at about twelve francs a liter instead of half a franc as at the beginning of the war, and the Goguette's reserves therefore represented a good deal of money.

There was something medieval about Chouquet's heavy cart, whose axles creaked and groaned as it lumbered down the field, and Chouquet left one of his horses by the gate to browse on the frosted grass, so that the animal would be fresh to help its fellow draw up the cart when the barrels had been stacked upon it. I watched this performance with something like sadness in my heart. The path that Goguet and Old Hommet had made by their repeated journeys between the farm and the cider press had now quite disappeared.

So the days passed, and every day something new left the farm.

Toward dusk one afternoon, on my way back from the Castels, I came upon the Goguette, accompanied by Marie and the twins, setting off for the village behind a wheelbarrow.

Renée had been called back by her mother to the farm to help with the cows, and I had not yet seen her. Since the incident of the stone-throwing, when my baby son had so nearly been killed, I had refused to speak to her. Often in London, during the war, I had wondered what my reaction would be if I came face to face with Renée again. My bitterness was such that my shaking limbs almost gave way beneath me as I walked slowly toward the farmhouse.

But instead of going to the old house, I went to the thatched cottage and knocked at the door.

As I expected, a voice bade me enter, and I found Renée sitting behind a beautiful sewing-machine, cutting a tartan skirt from a paper pattern.

"Good evening, Renée."

Five and a half years had passed since we had seen each other. Renée was now a young woman.

Her scissors poised in her lifted hand, she looked up and answered:

"Oh, madame, I would hardly have recognized you."

"Have I changed so much?"

"You are slimmer, madame, and you do your hair differently."

She was obviously fencing to gain time.

"Well, Renée, are you going to pelt me with stones again?"

My question had escaped from my lips with a hiss. It contained all the bitterness, the resentment, and the loathing, yes, the loathing, which I had nursed in my breast for so long, but as soon as the words had been uttered, I suddenly became aware that my hatred was dead. My features relaxed and I found myself actually laughing as I added:

"Because, Renée, if you throw any more stones at me, I'll return them with bricks."

There was a moment's silence. Then I asked softly:

"Do you remember?"

"Yes, madame, I particularly remember how you twigged my ears."

"But what had I done to you? Why did you want to kill my son?"

Renée shrugged her shoulders and muttered:

"I don't know."

I sat down.

"You have become a very beautiful woman," I said, "but, heavens, how you resemble your father! You have his eyes, his mouth, that same perfect oval, and your hair grows low on your forehead as his used to!"

Involuntarily tears started to moisten my cheeks, and I asked:

"Do you often think of him?"

Now it was Renée's turn to cry.

She bent over the tartan on her lap and sobbed.

"Do you remember your first communion?"

"Oh, yes, madame, I still have the white woollen shawl that you gave me to wear at church."

She lifted her head and pointed to the top of the cupboard.

"I keep it there. I never allowed anybody to touch it."

I remembered how I myself had dressed Renée for the service, placing the shawl under her veil so that it fell in a point about her corsage.

"I still have everything you gave me," said Renée. "Do you recall the dolls' tea-service you brought us from London and

in which we all used to drink tea at the farmhouse? Do you
recall the day when little Robert drank twelve cups?"

She rose from her seat and opened the cupboard:

"Look, madame, there it is!"

She was half crying and half laughing.

"And the pullover you knitted me with the Seven Dwarfs on
the buttons? I have that also. It was because you knitted one for
Roger. We were so jealous."

"Yes. We all used to go to the woods together—you, Roger,
Robert, my mother, and I. I was expecting my baby. My mother
used to pick long garlands of ivy and convolvulus and deck
them round you. You were the queen. Robert was the king.
Your dress had a train and Robert had a crown made of ivy.
You held each other by the hand and we all sang the march
from the Seven Dwarfs."

"I remember," said Renée. "Roger used to march behind, with
you and your mother, and you all carried axes and saws; and
then the dog would start barking, and the geese would come to
meet us at the top of the field; and we could come into the old
farmhouse for tea with sugar and cream, and home made cakes."

She looked up, almost ashamed of recalling so much happiness.

"We used to paint the colored books you brought from London, madame. They were in the big wooden box you gave to
Roger. How proud he was of it!"

"I wanted Roger to have the farm when he was of age. Where
is he, Renée?"

"At Poissy jail, madame."

Her features had suddenly become serious.

"His punishment is dreadful!" I cried suddenly. "He is paying for——" I suddenly checked myself and asked: "Don't you
think they may reduce his sentence?"

"What?" answered Renée harshly. "After all he has done?"

"But perhaps your grandfather, Hommet, was mostly to
blame?"

Renée closed her eyes and said: "One evening, after they
had betrayed my father, Hommet was sitting at the foot of the
pear tree yonder. He called me over and asked: 'Are you not
going to say good evening, Renée?' 'No, never,' I answered."

She remained silent a moment and then added:

"I don't even know where he is buried, madame, and I don't care!"

Now we were both looking out of the window at the flicker of light which the lamp threw on the old pear tree.

"You must have wished me dead many times during the bombing of London, Renée?"

"Not *I*, madame!"

The accent was too spontaneously placed on the first person not to give me a cold shock.

Then I rose and, taking Renée in my arms, kissed her.

And without a word I left the cottage.

The following evening I was sitting with my mother in the big room of the old house, when I heard somebody lift the latch of the garden gate. I half expected to see a farmer coming to inquire about the land which would be free at Christmas, but when the door opened I saw Renée on the threshold, her slim figure lit by the flames from the log fire, and a few steps behind her, in the darkness, a youth I did not at first recognize.

"I've brought you the boy Robert," said Renée.

I rose from my chair. My heart was beating with emotion. Little Robert had been my favorite child. He was scarcely more than seven when I had last seen him, and I remembered him in his red and white check gingham overall, stealing up to peep at my baby in the perambulator.

Now he was dressed in black, with trousers that were both too long and too short for him. He was no longer a child, but not quite a man. He looked somehow like a chimney-sweep; but his face and ungloved hands were white and bloodless, and his skin had the transparency of wax.

He hesitated for a moment, and then pulled off his black cap and, as he had done when he was a child, lifted up his cheek to be kissed.

He looked more like a skeleton than a little boy.

Then he sat down on the edge of a chair by the wall, his knees close together, his little hands folded upon them, his head to one side with an expression of tremendous fatigue, as if saying: "Life isn't all roses. I've a pretty load to carry."

"Draw your chair up to the fire, Robert. You must tell me all about yourself."

"I'm working on a farm the other side of Annebault," he said. "I milk the cows and help cut the hedges."

His voice was still the voice of a child.

"Have you come on your bicycle?"

"No, lady, I walked the eight miles. I haven't a bicycle."

"Are you happy, Robert?"

I felt my voice falter as I put the question. I wanted to cry.

"They pay me four hundred francs a month, lady."

Four hundred francs a month! Such a pittance was unbelievable when one thought of the immense sums of money which had passed hands at the cottage. What a misery!

I would have given anything to see the child smile. Could he smile? I asked him:

"Do you like your little twins, Robert?"

His features seemed to light up a moment as he answered:

"Oh, yes, lady."

Renée, who had been standing in the background, was vibrant with life. She had the immense advantage of being a girl. She put in:

"They are bonny enough now, the twins, but you should have seen them, madame, when they were born. They weighed but a pound and a half each, and were more like dolls than children, so that when we put them in the cot, instead of placing one at each end, we arranged them side by side, and there would have been room for another. All the baby-clothes were too large for them. Why——"

She checked herself suddenly and turned her face to the wall. Yes, the baby-clothes I had left must certainly have been large for them.

"They say you have become an enthusiastic dancer? Is that so, Renée? I can hardly blame you. I was the same at your age."

"Oh, yes, madame, I adore dancing. The swing, that's what I like best. I could dance it all night, whereas the waltz make me giddy."

Her face flushed with excitement and she explained how, when her mother was in prison, she used to go to the *bal musette* on the road to Dives on Sunday afternoon, and have to rush back to milk the cows and divide the cream, after which she would run up the field again to rejoin her partner.

"What will you do now, Renée?"

"I shall have to work as a maid at Trouville, but soon, madame, I shall learn hairdressing. I'm sick and tired of the sight of cows. I shall never work on a farm again, never. It's too hard, too hard."

Her laughter had turned to tears.

"It's too hard!" she repeated.

Then her youth regained its inherent hope and she added:

"I think I've a gift for hairdressing, madame."

"That is possible. Your hair is prettily done."

There was a moment's silence, and then Renée said:

"We must be going, madame. Robert must be up before dawn to walk back to be in time to milk the cows. You see, it's hard, isn't it?"

"Yes, I know. What are you going to have for supper?"

"Pumpkin soup and cream, madame."

"You are lucky. I haven't tasted the cream from our farm for many a day."

Renée took her brother's hand.

"Good-by, the lady," said Robert.

He turned toward the door, and in the half light his face looked like candle-wax.

24

A CRISP red sun rising over the château of Villers was beginning to warm the icicles which during the night had formed on the boughs of the naked apple trees. The grass in the orchards, though hard underfoot, was still a deep green, and the sky was a Mediterranean blue. The morning air smelt good and was invigorating, but the farm was strangely silent.

I came in from the garden and shook off my heavy wooden clogs on the flagstones. Two gnarled logs, each four feet long, were crackling merrily in the huge fire-place, and my mother was bending over the coffee-pot, balanced at a dangerous angle on the tripod amongst the white embers, close to which her cats were curled up for warmth.

The drama had come almost to its close. This miracle had happened, that the war was over and I had lived to see my farm handed back to me. Dreamily I thought about the future. I still felt a young enough woman to brave new ventures: it was now that I first seriously determined to work unceasingly to take my place among contemporary women writers. Life had so many beautiful experiences to offer. I should taste again the exhilaration of refurnishing my house, perhaps of increasing the property, of being not only a townswoman but also a countrywoman. I was thankful for my femininity, thankful that in London my six-year-old son would be waiting for me. How would the next so important phase of my womanhood work out?

I liked these lazy Sunday mornings, which gave me an opportunity to inspect the orchard and idle away an hour in the loft where the dessert apples, growing wizened, lay on trestles under the oak beams. The house was beginning once more to have that clean lived-in appearance. The half-timbering made the rooms a dazzle of black and white, and there was a smell of lavender and burning logs, of toasted bread and freshly made coffee.

The holly trees were full of red berries, and I had cut half a dozen branches to decorate the house. I laid them on the stone floor and said to my mother:

"The farm has suddenly become deserted. Marie and the twins have left the cottage, and nearly all the animals have gone."

"The Goguette wanted it that way," answered my mother. "She disposed of almost everything in advance of the sale this afternoon. She will be gone by the end of the week."

There was something terribly sad in these final preparations for departure.

I could hardly think of the farm without the Goguette. I always imagined that Goguet himself might appear one day along the path leading to the thatched cider press. The idea that his poor emaciated body had been burned in a German horror camp was too repellent for belief. Now that my bitterness was swept away, I reflected that every memory of my dream farm was in some form or another connected with the Goguets, and that it would never be quite the same without them.

Normally the sale would have taken place on the farm, but the Goguette wanted it otherwise. She had emptied the place cart by cart, wheelbarrow by wheelbarrow, beast by beast. Life had gradually ebbed away from the once busy farm until only two cows remained—Rescapée and the one-eyed animal wounded by shrapnel during the battle of Caen.

The Goguette had announced her intention of spending Christmas at a small house in the village, where she would remain until she put her affairs in order. She would never work on a farm again.

Renée was to be a maid at Trouville. Little Robert, almost forgotten, was already with strangers. Roger's poor wife had gone to live miserably near Poissy jail and was expecting a baby. The family, like the beasts on the farm, was breaking up.

Now Maître Vincent had arranged for what was left to be sold in a public auction-room after lunch—but the remainder merely consisted of Rescapée, poor dear Rescapée, the one-eyed cow, and the bright red machine for dividing the cream, which had once been the pride of the buttery. The furniture in the cot-

tage had nearly all been taken away to provide for some future
home for the Goguette and the twins.

The sun had become a large red ball, and we were silently
drinking our coffee, when there was a tap on the window, and
the Goguette arrived with a bowl of fresh cream which she
put down on the table, crying out:

"It's the last one!"

As usual she showed no signs of emotion, but merely added:

"The Renée told me you would like some, and so, as I won't
be making any more . . ."

"Why, thank you, Mme. Goguet, thank you."

It was I who felt like crying.

The Goguette went back into the garden, and I listened to her
footsteps on the gravel path. The cream in the bowl was so thick
that the spoon stood upright in it.

I rose and went up into the bedroom to do my hair. The view
from the window soothed me, and I began to think with great
tenderness of the day when I would bring my son to see the
house where he was born. I hoped he would arrive at the farm
when the apple trees were in bloom, and that would open a new
chapter in its four centuries of existence.

I allowed the morning to slip idly through my hands. Then
from the courtyard I heard the voice of Dudouy, the laborer,
calling out:

"Will it be long enough?"

"Perhaps it will, but perhaps it won't," cried the Goguette.
"Give me a little more in case."

I heard the laborer's heavy hobnailed boots, and the cows
trampling the hard earth as the rope was fastened round their
horns.

My thoughts traveled to the village auction-rooms, where the
ceiling was hidden by festoons of chairs hanging with their legs
downward. I pictured Maître Vincent, small and impeccably
dressed, moving among the bedsteads, the pots and pans, the
crockery, and the oil lamps which would presently come under
his hammer. All the farmers would be there—Yvonne Poulin, the
Déliquaires, the Montagues. I preferred not to mix with them on
this occasion, but I should like to have kissed good-by to Rescapée, on the forehead, between the horns, as she stood with all

the other cows in the yard. What new owner would milk her to-night and tomorrow?

My mother was calling from the big room. It was time to fetch the milk from the Castels. I threw a coat over my shoulders and hurried down the narrow stairs where the grandfather's clock pointed to ten minutes before midday.

We spoke little on the way, but as we stood in front of the Poulin farmhouse waiting for Mme. Castel to make her appearance, we saw a strange procession coming along Cathedral Lane.

First there was the laborer Dudouy, with a truss of hay tied on his back, and in his left hand he held a rope. Behind him was the one-eyed cow, greedily nibbling the hay. The rope had been passed round her horns and behind her, in turn, similarly attached, was Rescapée, who, having no feed, kept on wandering to one side or the other of the lane, to see what she could pick up from the hedges; and last of all came the Goguette, with a stick in her hand and across her shoulders the yoke from which dangled the shining milk-pails.

The Goguette was dressed all in black with the exception of a shawl of the same color as the sky, a deep sustained blue. From time to time she talked to Rescapée.

"Hey, the greedy one, first it's ivy, then it's fir, and what next? Teu! Teu! Teu!"

Slowly the procession passed by.

I watched it turn this way and that until it disappeared under the arched boughs of the naked trees. But through the crystal air came the Goguette's cries:

"Teu! Teu! Teu!"

Until they were drowned by the bells of the village church, down by the sea, ringing the angelus.

PART IV

THE DAYS OF PEACE

25

ERNEST POULIN was repatriated from Germany where he had been fortunate enough to work on a German farm. He found himself at the head of a magnificent farm with an only son, André, five years old, ready to love and admire him.

My mother and I, on the other hand, increasingly gave the impression of complete poverty. I could not yet bring any money from England. We ransacked the cider press for wood to make a table, and searched the hay lofts in the hope of finding some new piece of furniture that our plunderers might inadvertently have left behind. The Goguette walked brazenly through the village unmindful of the fact that her eldest son was serving a life term. My furs, dresses, linen and skirts would occasionally be seen in a mutilated state in other people's homes but the police refused to act. Too many people had been plundered. The police were bored with them. Then again, could Maître Vincent be expected to sympathize with a woman whose house had been plundered when, speaking of his own tragedy, he would cry out: "I have not even a grave over which to shed my tears."

The fact that my rich orchards were now idle turned rapacious eyes in my direction. With the price of butter fixed low by the government and the rent of farmlands pegged to it, farmers who sold all their butter at fantastic prices in the Black Market did not hesitate to rent every acre of land they could acquire.

Insolent farmers came to insult me, woman that I was. In an effort to force my hand, they would exclaim: "Do you realize that the country needs food?"—whereas they themselves were doing everything to starve it. Two women are easily intimated, especially when the law works for the dishonest against the weak. A rich farmer from Dives, alleging that a bomb had destroyed his pigsties, threatened to have me dispossessed. He used the same bullying tactics as the communists who set up tribunals to grab what they could. I picked up a stick and raised it against the farmer from Dives who fled in a panic. As soon as he had gone my legs gave way under me and doubtless due to the emotion I came out in a nettle rash.

Ernest Poulin, of course, aware that my land everywhere touched his own, and not having nearly enough grass for his magnificent herd of cows, coveted my twenty-four acres which would practically have doubled his property and made him the most consequent farmer on the plateau. I admired the Poulins, especially the women, but Ernest had come back from Germany so imbued with modern methods that I was suspicious of him. Our orchards remain fabulously rich so long as they are farmed in the old way. Increased yields with us would impoverish the soil. It is perhaps my womanly nature that makes me cling to the sweet goodness of the past.

I had merely to walk through my orchards to realize how fortunate I was. They were by far the richest in this rich land. If only I could pull out like weeds from my mind all the bitterness I felt for the theft of my furniture, my linen, my hats, my dresses and my furs!

Secretly I had by now quite decided to make Déliquaire my tenant farmer. I had a great affection for Madeleine, his wife, and their two boys, Roger and Jacques.

I now returned to London to fetch my son, Bobby, who was anxious to see the place of his birth. As I planned to spend several months in Normandy I also decided to bring my pekinese, Pouffy, who had been our companion during the whole war and whom I had dragged, together with my son, from shelter to shelter throughout the bombardments. Bobby would be six in June. The Pekinese was a few months younger. On the long night journey between Dieppe and Paris, the permanent way being only partially repaired, the child slept on the seat beside me, the dog snored underneath. Dawn broke while we were on a siding. I dared not close my eyes for there were two youth in the compartment of whom I was not very sure, and also the cold of the night had fallen on the steel compartments so that from time to time I would delve into my bag for some woollen garment to throw over the child.

When the train began to move again, the ticket collector arrived. The child did not wake but the dog, whom I was trying to hide, emerged furiously and woke up the whole compartment. In Paris there was still no transportation. It was 7 A.M. when we emerged into the wide courtyard outside the Gare St. Lazare— a Paris with the shutters still closed, no milk, no coffee, nothing warm to drink. The hotels were filled with G.I.'s and one could not buy bread without tickets. The child never complained. His blue eyes seemed to watch with joy and wonderment all these French people who spoke a language that hitherto he had merely heard from my lips in exile. As soon as we took our places in the Lisieux express, he babbled with excitement, lisping in that delightful way that was soon to charm film audiences all over the world. As the sun rose and the train rolled slowly on, we passed alternately through rich orchards and devastated towns.

We changed twice before reaching Villers. Then at last we stepped out on the platform, a woman with as many bags as she could carry, and a child who in turn dragged a panting dog. Waiting for the train to pull out before we crossed the line, I did not immediately see my mother. I thought she might not have been able to hire a car. There was so little gasoline. When the last coach slipped away, I saw her hurrying toward us with a man to fetch the luggage. She kissed her grandson whom she had not seen for five years and took his hand, while the pekinese, released from his lead for the first time since he was in France, jumped for joy.

I called at the town hall for our ration cards. When I came out my mother looked very sad.

"He calls me Madame," she gulped. "Each time I ask him something, he answers very politely: 'Thank you, Madame.' I, his grandmother who looked after him for the first eleven months of his life am a stranger to him! Did you never talk about me in London?"

She spoke petulantly like a little girl trying to be brave. One had the impression that the discovery was beyond her comprehension. She could not appreciate that the baby of eleven months who was Bobby when they parted on the gangway of the transport at St. Malo, could not remember what his grandmother looked like. She stroked the pekinese, saying:

"The dog is affectionate. He licks my hand. Do you suppose my grandson will ever love me?"

I had no doubts about this, but I did not wish to hustle my son. During the last twenty-four hours he had looked avidly at such a multitude of new things that his mind was dazed.

We drove to where the narrow road forks opposite the low wall of the Poulin farm. The dogs barked, and Émile, the farmhand, who was rubbing down the white mare, slowly touched his cap while gravely looking at the boy born in the adjoining house and only a few months older than André, the son of his master.

One behind the other, we walked down Cathedral Lane, carrying our bags. The oldest elms had gone so that the arch high above our heads was pierced with blue sky. Here, on our left, was the white gate leading into my orchard, the home orchard that sloped down to our yet hidden house and thatched cottage. Oh, what a lovely day! This was June in all its splendor. A few apple trees still had garlands of blossom but in most cases the fruit had just begun to form. This was summer as one dreams of it—the sweet smell of grass and honeysuckle, the singing of birds, the high-pitched drone of a myriad insects, a shimmering haze over the earth. Cows lowed, geese, ducks and turkeys wandered unconcernedly between the hooves of the lazy cows.

My son looked up and asked me timidly:

"Mother, are we here?"

"Yes, my darling. You are on our own farm."

"Do you mean that it's ours like the Green Park in London is ours?"

"More so," I said. "This orchard and many others belong to me. You do not need to come and go. You are here. Our house is in the hollow."

"Ah," he murmured, trying to understand.

There was a pause, and then my mother said to him, as my grandmother said to me at Blois when I was a little girl:

"Do you think you will like it here, my child?"

For the first time, he answered with unrestrained joy:

"Oh, yes!"

She smiled down at him and he smiled back. They were no longer complete strangers. Then suddenly the half-timbered house, its white plaster and black beams dazzling, its slate roof shimmering, broke out from behind the foliage of the tall pear tree. The child, not expecting this magic apparition, gave a cry of delight. A tall rose tree under which he had slept in his perambulator as a baby, had a deep red rose as large as a baby's face, and as it swayed in the breeze on its tall thick stem, it seemed to be welcoming the little master, pleased to see him back.

I opened the garden door. Marigolds ran a blazing golden trail across the unkempt paths. Miquette, Mme. Goguet's cat, who had taken refuge with my mother, ran indoors to hide. Bobby followed me into the tiled kitchen, and asked with his usual sweet timidity:

"So this is the house, the house that is ours?"

"This is our house, the house where you were born. Do you not find it pretty?"

He looked up eagerly:

"Not pretty? Oh, but yes, it is pretty. I just wanted to know."

"Would you like to take your coat off?" asked his grandmother. "You could play in the garden while your mother and I make lunch."

She undressed him and he went to the door, but he could not decide whether he wanted to be in or out. Then, because he was by adoption a little Londoner, accustomed to the London parks, he asked if he could touch the flowers. He advanced timidly a few paces, and then came running back to say that he had seen a tree with the beginnings of cherries. We laughed. He looked puzzled, but then enquired if next time he could go a little further.

"But of course," said my mother. "Go right round the house to the gooseberry bushes. There is nothing to fear. You won't lose yourself. Look! Your little dog is already much braver than you are."

"Then come, Pouffy," he cried. "Come with me!"

But the pekinese smelt steaks on the fire and returned hastily into the kitchen.

I had brought some Irish linen from London, and I laid the meal at the end of the table. There were potatoes in their jackets and cider. The child tasted the cider and winced but when we asked him if he would prefer milk, he answered: "No. I shall soon learn to like the cider." His eyes kept roving to the open door through which he could see the garden, and after a while my mother sent him there to play while she made pancakes. She was determined to win his affection. On his return, she admired a tiny watch with a narrow red strap on his wrist.

"Oh, what a pretty watch, Bobby!"

He looked at it gravely, and explained:

"My father gave it me in London for my sixth birthday before we left. Would you like to hear it tick?"

He placed the watch against my mother's ear, but she said:

"I think it has stopped."

"Oh!" he commented, without surprise.

She wound it up for him, and he suddenly fled back into the garden. He was proud of his first watch but as he could not yet read the time, it was immaterial to him whether the watch went or not.

The next morning we took him all round the orchards. We showed him the successor of Robin, the bull I had fed with sugar from my handbag when my husband and I first discovered the farm. The Little Valley and the Big Valley in which I had planted hundreds of young apple trees before the war were now fine orchards with excellent grass and plenty of shade. My Burgundy hayfield was sweet with clover and tall daisies. The woods were full of sturdy trees. The stream, clear and cool, banked by buttercups, orchis, moss and forget-me-nots, delighted him.

The most striking change was the consolidation of Victor Duprez's estate. The Picane which, when horses grazed on it, was said by Goguet to be poor grass, was now vastly enriched, and the Cour du Cerf, on the opposite bank of the stream, had been drained at tremendous expense and planted with hundreds of young trees, while at Berlequet, where Groscol once lived, was the modernly equipped farm so pretty and feminine (Victor's wife, Simone, had designed it) that it put one in mind of Marie Antoinette's Petit Trianon. The low house, stables, garages and barns, all fitted with electric light, were colorful and doll-like. Except that Victor's estate was better looked after than mine, it was not much larger. However, he entertained, kept servants and a bailiff, and was always planting the best apple trees. Just now he was on the point of becoming mayor.

From the Burgundy hayfield, my son (with the pekinese racing ahead) ran to the Molière, and from the Molière to the wood. I took him to see where the fox had his lair in the bracken. I had wanted to be buried here if I died in childbirth.

I would have liked my farm to be larger, even more beautiful, for whenever we came upon a new orchard, and my son asked: "Is it ours?" and I answered: "Yes," he opened his eyes in wonderment, like the king in the gold coach when Puss in Boots kept on telling him that the fields through which they passed belonged to his master, the Marquis of Carabas.

I took him also to the big wood across one of Mme. Anger's fields in which Dudouy, the laborer, lived in a small and curious house. Dudouy was said to prowl about the orchards at night, though this did not prevent him from being extremely active by day.

We did not like him much because of the help he had given to Mme. Goguet in removing the plunder from my farm, and when Goguet's death became known, he had tried to marry her. He was therefore, as far as I was concerned, in the enemy camp. Moreover I suspected him of cutting my hedges for faggots.

He would hire himself out all day, working with old-fashioned skill, but drinking far too much apple-jack so that he was difficult and quarrelsome. His little house was empty until nightfall, except for a dog tied to a chain that barked terribly whenever anybody came near. There were also some white rabbits in a cage, leaping from corner to corner, as penned-up rabbits always do.

As soon as Dudouy came home at night, he would lift the

latch of his wooden gate, and if the wind was in the right direction, we would hear his little dog barking for joy. Half an hour later we would see a thin wisp of smoke rising from the chimney. We supposed he was cooking his lonely supper.

26

DÉLIQUAIRE was now my tenant farmer, and every evening I went to his place to fetch the milk. We went down by our cider press, across the stream and up the next orchard. The entrance gate was on the road to St. Vaast.

His farmhouse, like ours, was in the middle of an orchard. The walls were half timbered, the roof had lovely slates, and there was a garden all round fenced off from the orchard to prevent the cows from eating the flowers.

As in all true Norman farmhouses, the door led straight into the main room where, both summer and winter, a fire of elm logs burned between stone pillars. Madeleine Déliquaire boiled her water in a black cauldron over this fire, on which she threw twigs when she wanted to cook under the wide chimney. The dogs slept on the red flagstones with which the room was paved, and the men ate at a long table under the window at meal-times, served by Madeleine who never had time to sit down herself. There was no electric light, no running water. One stepped back a century or two in time. The family was entirely happy, finding all its satisfactions in the age-old cunning of their hands and in the amazing richness of the land. The butter and cream were magnificent, the eggs large and strong of shell. There was no radio and, of course, no telephone. If ever there was foot-and-mouth disease in the neighborhood, the Déliquaires would call in a sorcerer to cast magic spells. They believed also in the art of bonesetters and healers, and when the master went to bed at night, his favorite dog jumped in also and slept between the bed-clothes.

The cows liked to amble as near as they could to the front door. Madeleine Déliquaire treated them like daughters and could tell the state of their health by the feel of their udders. When they caught a chill or a cough she tied blankets round their waists which made them look very curious. There was a donkey who carried the milk churns on a special saddle when the family went milking in a distant orchard. On their return home in the evening, walking slowly in single file, the Déliquaires, the donkey, and lastly a servant girl carrying a three-legged stool, created an effect that was almost Spanish. When the donkey was not working he liked to remain near the farmhouse, rubbing his back against the garden fence while the chickens, the ducks, the geese and even the sow with the piglets came and went as they pleased.

A little white dog was tied to a kennel half way between the top of the orchard and the house. His business was to bark at strangers. He would emerge from his kennel, which was really a hollowed-out tree, and pretend to look very fierce. Dogs can become very fierce when they are never allowed off the chain, but no animal at the Déliquaire farm was ever unhappy, and it was a great wonder that they did not all sleep with the master and mistress between the bedsheets.

"Ah, Ma'am Henrey, so there is your big lad!"

She seized him in her arms and he, by sudden impulse, kissed her on both cheeks.

"It's in his blood," she said proudly. "After all he was born here."

She led us into the house. What was nice about the big room was that one set of windows looked out on the stables, the rabbit hutches, the cider press, built in 1555 like our own, while the other set gave one a magnificent view of the sea. One could watch great liners steaming into and out of Le Havre. It seemed to bring New York quite near.

Although I was hampered by currency restrictions, I quickly refurnished my house. The Bank of England showed immediate understanding as if they knew about the farm and wanted to help. My hope of making a pretty, feminine interior to this jewel of a place did not, however, materialize. I constantly had before me memories of charming farmhouses in England and America. I would have liked a kitchen with wide windows and American planning and a living room with gay chintzes and English easy chairs. In my mind everything appeared reasonably simple. I still think that many women would have triumphed. I was granted certain gifts when I was a little girl. Perhaps this one was missing.

The low room should have been a museum piece. The huge fireplace and the round pillars of Caen stone were worthy of a Renaissance castle but as one walked straight into it from the garden and as it was practically the only room in the house one could sit in, except the kitchen, the men came in with their mud-soaked clogs, dirtied the flagstones and threw their damp clothes over tables and chairs.

Milk, thick creamy milk, has for all time been the thing that mattered in this fabulous corner of Normandy. Not an inch of soil is ploughed. The grass is far too valuable. The grass grows damp and luscious as if by magic. It is a crime even to grow a small square of potatoes. Thus the farmer's wife for centuries has milked her cows in the orchard and brought the pails on a yoke straight into her low room. Our farms in this respect are unique. We need no outhouses, no granaries. The farmer need only cut a little wood, make a little hay and occasionally dig round the base of the apple trees to let in air. The woman is the person who matters. She must originally have inspired these fairy tale houses so that she could be in the very center of her herd. In and out she goes, calling her cows by name. She will slip on her clogs as she goes into the grass, kick them off as she steps back on the tiles of her low room. When she cooks, she goes out to fetch faggots to make the fire blaze in the huge hearth. Her baby sleeps in a Norman cot, snug and warm. The hens come in and peck the crumbs.

Thus the fault was entirely mine. I was punished for wanting to live in a peasant woman's house, in a fairy tale house, in Cinderella's house, and I was angry with it because my miserable townswoman's pride wanted the beauty and comfort of a sophisticated American woman's home.

My Aga stove was reconditioned by experts from Caen and its gentle heat now warmed us night and day. Anxious to have no more strangers, no more Renée Goguets, to throw stones at me, I repainted the cottage and used it as an annex to my own house. We used its main room to store apples, grain and potatoes. I set up a subsidiary kitchen with an electric range in case something should happen to prevent my using the Aga. The two bedrooms could be turned into guest rooms when I could afford to do so, but I had so many urgent matters to attend to that it was not yet possible even to think about hospitality.

The village artisans, who before the war had been so anxious to group themselves round me, were no longer eager for work. Giles Mathieu continued as a favor to send me a plumber when I needed one urgently and with the help of M. Massard he electrified my water system and made a modest addition to my central heating, but inflation and an orgy of social relief, from several thousand francs for the first baby to the equivalent of an ambassador's pay if one had eight or nine children, had entirely destroyed the value of money. I was asked more, even measured against gold, to repair my cider press than I had paid for the entire farm. I was therefore obliged to allow this sixteenth century splendor to fall slowly to pieces. On the excuse that gasoline was expensive, no tradesman or artisan would willingly come to me. The mile that separated me from the village was too much of an effort. Also, there was no road between the top of my orchard and the house. Trucks would get bogged in the soft earth. A horse and cart or a wheelbarrow were the only safe ways to bring sand, bricks or coal.

People told me to build a cement drive across the orchard to my house. They said I was a stupid woman to prefer the beauties of nature to the conveniences of a modern world. There were moments when I agreed with them, but for centuries my orchard had been considered the richest, the most milk-yielding of any, and it seemed a crime to destroy its medieval charm. It would also have been bad economics, for in Normandy people do not count the value of a house, but only that of the pasture land, and if ever I had needed to sell my farm, a road down to my house would have quite destroyed the value of my orchard.

Thus my problems sprang entirely from the fact that I was half a woman of the town, half a peasant woman. I would suddenly be obliged to exchange a rough dress for a tailor-made, and fly to London on business. I could not live without the inspiration of a great city, whether London, Paris or New York. The noise of the city kindles within me a desire to create.

Two years after our return to the farm, I was asked to bring my son to London to make the film which, in due course, was to make him famous. I was not anxious at first for him to make this film. We flew direct one autumn morning from Deauville to Croydon and an hour later he was facing the movie camera in Belgrave Square. Then began for both of us a fairy tale which led the following year to cheering crowds in London and Paris and our presentation to Queen Elizabeth, now the Queen Mother.

The throb of the city kept me young but with increasing frequency I hurried back to Normandy to seek on my farm the satisfaction that Marie Antoinette must have looked for at the Petit Trianon. But it never proved a rest as it must have done in the days when a woman could have servants. I did not even keep up with Mme. Bayard. I could not afford her. I wanted the money more urgently for steaks for my mother and my growing son. As a result I did the housework myself and soon began to yearn for the town.

My kitchen garden was also a preoccupation. For the first two years I had a gardener but he cost me more than I spent to run the entire house. I had watched him carefully to learn as many of his ways as I could, and then dug the ground myself, pulled out the weeds, planted the vegetables and the strawberries, built great tanks to have water always at hand and obtained some amazing results. My mother, crippled with rheumatism, not content only to do the cooking and look after the considerable farmyard, was so anxious for us to produce all our own vegetables that she ended by doing more work in the kitchen garden than I did. For I was always being called to Paris or London, and on my return the weeds would have undone my labors.

I planted hundreds of fruit trees every winter—even elms and chestnuts for shade along the lanes. The cider-apple harvests consisting of many tons each year did not fetch the prices they used to. There was a tendency for young people to drink wine. Also, the English cider firms who used to buy heavily from us, presumably because our apples were better than those in Devonshire, had ceased to do so because of the difficulties of foreign exchange. I therefore replaced many cider apple trees as they died with the best eating apples or even, and this was a very new and daring thing to do in a Normandy orchard, with black plums, greengages, quinces and cherries. I had a fixed idea that the land must support us, not only in money, but with all the food we needed.

But a woman has a different outlook from that of a man. She does not find it easy to plan great things for future generations. Tree planting on a big scale is expensive and one has to wait so long! I got a lot more fun out of our strawberry beds. We ate them with cream from the cows in our own orchards, made open tarts and many pots of delicious jam for the winter.

There were days when my mother and I would set about cleaning the house until it shone like a new dime. We might even keep it thus for half the week. Then suddenly we would start something enormous in the kitchen garden, something that would require all the rest of the week, so that the house would gradually assume a ragged appearance, dust would settle on the furniture, and at this very moment important visitors would arrive in our orchard, and the weather until now so fine would turn to rain so that we could not even entertain our visitors in the garden but must needs bring them into the house. I would say all kinds of things against my poor house to anybody who had the patience to listen. I would look at the roses withered in their bowls, the water all dried up, and I would say to myself: "There is a thing you should not have neglected. What will your visitors think?" I would remember that I had passed an entire morning trying to save the life of a baby chick which I had rescued from a water trough into which it had fallen, placing it for warmth between my breasts inside my dress. If I had not done that, if I had not saved a chickling's life, my house might have been in order.

Every day something extraordinary took place in this house in which nobody expected anything to happen, in which they all thought I must be very bored. My mother and I spent a whole day looking for a flock of turkeys. We walked miles. We not only searched in orchards and along roads but we looked up into the trees where they sometimes spend the night, and all this time the wicked birds were looking quietly at my house from the garden hedge. So that day neither my house nor my garden had anything done to them. But how happy we were, my mother and I, to find our turkeys again!

We would worry if one of the cats did not turn up for the evening meal. My mother would say: "The poor thing has been caught in a trap or in a gin, and perhaps it is in pain and calling for us." Then my mother would slink out and patiently go all round the hedges till night caught up with her and she could no longer see anything. And I would feel nervous and go in search of her. Hours later we would come sadly home and the silly animal would be asleep on the Aga stove, but we had wasted the whole evening.

We imagined at first that we were just two silly sentimental women, mother and daughter, but we soon discovered that Madeleine Déliquaire, who was the best farmer's wife I have ever known, the cleverest, the hardest working, was just the same as we were. A sow would have gone through the gate and disappeared along the road to St. Vaast, and it was not merely that the sow represented a small fortune, a real sack of gold lurching along the country road, but she treated all animals like members of her family.

Roger, her elder son, was now married, but his young wife was a dressmaker, the daughter of a man who was both grocer and market gardener. Jeanine thought our village was the hub of the world and she refused to leave it for life on a farm. She looked at me with pity because I lived in the middle of an orchard. She felt superior because from her parents' grocer's shop she could see the funerals and the weddings and, best of all, the christenings entering and leaving the church.

So Roger left the farm, and the Déliquaires were a man short. Up till then Déliquaire had managed with his wife and his two sons. They liked it that way because with no strangers in the house, the doors and cupboards could all be left open. Besides, they could have their meals as they pleased, and even skip a meal if there was a lot of work. Then Jacques was called up to do his national service, and because he had in his veins the blood of the old Norman adventurers who set sail to discover Quebec and New Orleans, he volunteered for service in Indo-China, telling his mother that he would see something of the world, learn a litte engineering and even put a few thousand francs aside.

The Poulins' farmhouse was not Norman, and there were moments when, as a housewife, I envied Yvonne Poulin's large, sensible rooms and parquet floors. The house was of brick in the nineteenth century French style and was put up by the village chemist whose son, a wealthy and clever notary at Breuil-en-Auge, now owned the Poulin farm. The Poulin farm was everything one expected a flourishing French farm to look like, and when the house was first built Villers-sur-Mer was a place of wealthy summer estates, many of them owned by members of the French aristocracy, or writers and musicians famous in Paris, and the church, since pulled down, was true Norman dating from the time we were a fishing village.

Of course, Yvonne Poulin had her difficulties. The house was of the kind that needed servants. Thus she and I both suffered from having to adapt our different houses to present needs, she having to keep a large house clean without servants, I trying to turn a peasant's fairy tale house into one in which a townswoman could find the minimum of comfort and hygiene.

Ernest Poulin, glad to be home from captivity, took over from his wife and mother-in-law and quickly assumed his authority as the man. He and André made nearly two men, his small son learning to copy his father, going about everywhere with him, even shouting at Emile, the servant. Yvonne now started to have a baby regularly every year, and each time it was a girl. Soon there were five little girls, and it was prettiest thing in the world to see this bevy of little girls led by Yvette, the oldest. When anybody commiserated with Ernest for having so many girls and only one boy, he would say: "Well, at any rate, they will be able to dust the furniture and polish the floors. The big farmhouse needs women. When my father was the master, my mother and three sisters worked in it from morning till night, and the floors shone like mirrors. Girls grow up quicker than animals but one can keep them longer on the farm, and they are even more useful. You will see how my house will shine in a few years time. Yvette, at six, is already a little woman, tidying up, putting things away, helping her grandmother, Mme. Castel, with the wash. Too much outside labor takes the profit away from any farm, and besides—I do not want strangers prying into my affairs."

The Poulins tried very hard to do without a maid. Yvette worked till each baby was almost born, and Mme. Castel, frail and tiny, busied herself even at night because she could not sleep, but I soon saw a procession of servants coming and going, each being tempted away by the hotels in Deauville which wanted chambermaids or by shops which needed girl assistants. The five Poulin daughters were still too young.

Our nearness to Deauville, which prevented us from having help for the farms, was nice all the same because we could sell our produce more easily and at higher prices than inland. The French government tried at first to impose all sorts of restrictions which our farmers immediately disobeyed. They claimed that good men do not obey bad laws, and the housewives agreed. In England women were too patient in the face of ridiculous man-made laws that were an insult to us as women. Thus while rationing continued to poison the lives of women in England, it was immediately swept away in France.

The only thing our farmers did was to sell a portion of their milk to a syndicate. Déliquaire bought a smart truck and went round collecting this milk, and he enjoyed this enormously because it supplied him with gasoline for his threshing machine and for his automobile on Sundays. He also had priority to buy a new truck each year, tires, and accessories. Most of all he thus assumed the role of troubadour, penetrating into each farm, listening to their stories, placing farm-hands with farmers and obliging farmers with farm-hands, discovering which farmer had a vat for sale, a horse or a donkey. Now that, in addition to his own land, he rented so much of mine, he was an important farmer, as important as Ernest Poulin, and because of his knowledge of what went on in other farms, he could sometimes tell in advance when prices were going to fall or to rise.

After the London and Paris premières of my son's film, I brought him back to Normandy in time to spend Christmas on the farm. My house was now acquiring a personality of its own, and though I may not have been a very good housewife, I had stamped every room and corner with my own form of feminine untidiness. The following April, forgetting all about the excitement of the city, though perhaps unknowingly inspired by it, I began to write *The Little Madeleine*, the story of my girlhood, sitting in bed with a writing pad on my knees every morning from breakfast till my mother called out that lunch was ready. I would then hurriedly do my hair, slip on a jumper and a skirt and come down to the kitchen, looking quite worn out and very different from the elegant woman whom strangers expected to find when they inopportunely came to the farm. Except for a fortnight when I was obliged to take my son to London for an operation, I worked on my girlhood story till the middle of August, and had the pleasure of seeing my apple trees turn from their spring blossom to the full ripeness of their fruit.

This period was more than a long spell in the house that was beginning to love me. This was the first time that I had written a book deliriously as if inspired by some force other than my own, and it brought me the calm, certain realization that I had it within my power to become a woman of letters. My mother, with a tact all her own, never once questioned me on my writing. She would occasionally say: "If that is what you wish to do and if it brings you in a little money, I entirely approve. Only please don't ask me to read anything about the hard days. I want to forget all about them."

My career as a woman writer was thus affirmed strongly in the room with the big stone pillars in which I had given birth to my son before the war. My house was not merely a fairy tale abode but a place full of accomplishment where twice, first for my son and then for this narrative of girlhood, both destined to make ripples on two continents, I had tasted the exhilaration of giving out a living part of myself. Is it not a woman's joy to create something which she hopes will be lasting? The important thing was to keep the house friendly so that I should not too quickly know sorrow within its walls.

We spent the winter in Vienna where my son made his second film, and it was June again when we returned to Normandy, this time with a governess whom I lodged in the cottage which, though repainted, was still not as pretty and gay as other women would have made it. Potatoes cluttered the floor of one room, and another served for our bicycles.

We made strawberry jam, bicycled at low tide along the sands as far as Deauville, bathed whenever we had time and I filled the house with roses from the garden. I see from my diary that I bought a leg of lamb for my son's birthday and that the galley proofs of *The Little Madeleine* were beginning to reach me from London.

The cows were in our home orchard. They were to stay a week with us and I looked forward to a week of pure joy, for I loved to have them. They wore heavy chains connected to steel bracelets round their legs; all this armor was to prevent them from raising their heads high enough to tear down the apples from the trees, for quite apart from any concern we might have for the apple trees, cows are greedy for apples and when they eat too many can choke to death.

The cows moved slowly, dragging their chains, enjoying the tender grass. At night they came brushing up against the stakes protecting our garden, and I could hear their breathing, and sometimes their coughing, and their presence so near to my bedroom was very comforting to me. In the morning, the Déliquaires arrived with the donkey, the churns and the three-legged stool. Then I would run down in my nightdress, throw a coat over my shoulders, slip my feet into clogs, and hand a jug over the fence to Déliquaire for my breakfast milk hot from the cow.

This was July sixth and Déliquaire was talking softly to the cow he was milking for in spite of the early hour flies covered its mouth and eyes.

"Yes, ma'am," he said, offering me his fist to shake as is the custom in our country. "It will be a hot day, and small wonder, for we shall soon be celebrating the Sainte Madeleine, your name day and my wife's. After that the days will grow shorter and then look out for autumn! Our little grandson has been very sickly these last few days, ma'am. The doctor sent last night for a specialist from Caen."

Jeanine had taken Roger to live above her parent's grocer's shop in the village. Thus as she sewed and fed her baby, she could continue to watch the funerals, weddings and christenings gathering in the church parvis, but the rooms were small and hot, and quite unsuitable for a baby in summer.

From down by the stream on this hot, misty morning, came Madeleine Déliquaire's voice:

"Hurry! Hurry! Roger and Jeanine have sent for us."

Mme. Déliquaire had become terribly fond of her baby grandson. She said it was the first time she had watched a baby growing up, for when she and her husband had their children, they were so poor that they had to leave them with others while they both went out to work. Roger had not lost any money by leaving the farm. By hiring himself out to build a road or drive a truck, he could earn big money, and Jeanine could remain happily with little Alain. The poor child was difficult from the start. At three months, he had asthma, and now pneumonia—a child who was not yet a year old. But Déliquaire, kicking the milking stool aside, and preparing to follow his wife, said hopefully:

"Nowadays there are so many new inventions and drugs, and the doctors are so clever that one has little to worry about."

We had just finished breakfast when the church bell started to toll, and the sound on this lovely July morning increased our feeling of fear. We tried to tell ourselves that it was not for Alain, and Thursday being market day, and the morning promising to be so hot, we had more than one excuse to go to the village earlier than usual. The Poulin's governess cart, with the mare between the shafts, was tied up outside the church, and beside it stood Déliquaire's light green truck, the one he used for milk. We hurried into the grocer's shop to inquire about Alain but as soon as we saw Jeanine's mother, her eyes swollen, we knew that tragedy was in the house. She said between sobs:

"Oh, Mme. Henrey, it's all finished. Even as M. Déliquaire was milking the cows in your orchard, the little angel flew away to heaven."

He lay in his narrow bed, in a long baptism robe, his tiny arms still pink. His mouth for the first time was closed. The fierce struggle to breathe was over.

Jeanine and Roger were crying like big children in a corner, but poor Mme. Déliquaire's grief was tremendous. All my heart went out to her and my tears flowed with hers. When at last, leaving the stricken house, I emerged into the hot sunshine, jostled on the pavement by indecorously dressed holidaymakers in shorts, I felt a fierce desire to slap the girls' faces for their indifference in the presence of this tragedy they could not possibly suspect.

A few days later my mother complained of a painful rash. Thinking she must have been stung in the long grass, I painted her lightly with iodine. She hardly slept at night, but continued to cook in the morning. This summer, which began with ripe cherries and sea bathing, suddenly stifled me with unknown fear. Alain's funeral was on Monday, and André Poulin was one of the choir boys. After mass, the little coffin was put on a sort of stretcher and four choirboys, in red cassocks and white lace surplices, began to carry it to the cemetery a mile and a half away.

From time to time the cortege halted by the side of the long white road, and four other choirboys would relieve those who were carrying the stretcher.

On our way back from the cemetery, we were joined by the Giles, our neighbors on the south, and then came the schoolmaster with a group of scholars. A young priest passed us with the eight choirboys carrying the stretcher from which the white linen sheet bordered with lace had been removed, and they were walking fast for the church clock could be heard striking midday. Women and children passed us carrying long loaves of bread and bottles of wine. The scene, painted brightly by the sun, was quite gay, and having cried so much during the last three days, I was now ready to laugh again and feel pleasantly hungry. A white flower lay in the middle of the dusty road. I picked it up and though it had been trodden upon, I decided to place it between the pages of my Bible.

27

I SENT for Morin, the carpenter, wishing him to construct an elegant barrier on the two open sides of my courtyard at the back of the house, made of dazzling white rails like those that one sees at smart race tracks.

The back of my house stood at right angles to the thatched cottage, the stables and the cartshed. The rabbits had their hutches here, and the ducks, hens and turkeys congregated round the open stable doors. I dreamed of double gates, wide enough for a hay wagon, to lead into the orchard, and of another gate, of more modest dimensions, to lead into the kitchen garden.

Morin arrived and drew up a plan. We agreed on the price. Robert had come from London and so, for once, my small family was complete.

The doctor had diagnosed my mother's rash as shingles. She was in agony, not merely from this unfortunate illness but also from the arthritis in her hands, which was chronic. I could not bear to see her poor fingers so stiff, fingers once so pretty and supple, so clever at sewing lace blouses and dresses for me when I was a little girl. She would now walk with her arms stretched down against her sides, fighting growing stiffness. The doctor gave her injections for the shingles. The rash followed the line of the nerve in a design of fantastic form. She reacted quickly to the treatment, continuing to look after the ducks and hens in spite of the fact that Morin turned the courtyard upside down, and dug trenches many feet deep into which to cement the base of his oak posts. He was a conscientious worker and wanted my barrier to last a lifetime.

My mother would remark with a touch of annoyance that I

could not have chosen a worse time to complicate her existence. In her presence I was always a rather timid little girl, and on this occasion I felt she was right. I was appalled also by the growing importance that the work assumed and by the fact that the estimate, large in the first place, was being continually surpassed.

My authority on the farm was virtually absolute. I was able for the first time to learn by a process of making mistakes but there were occasions when I realized the inconsequence and futility of my feminine mind. I would save ferociously in my daily purchases for weeks on end, and then embark on a farm improvement program that would quickly run out of hand. This was not altogether my fault. Anything fashioned out of wood was absurdly expensive. The making of a five-barred gate cost so much money that as soon as I had ordered one, I would not sleep at night. I wanted to take a man's decisions but I was terribly sensitive about what people would say or think, and at heart I was too thrifty a woman to spend money easily on my own whims.

My husband never interfered with the running of the farm. His love for it was such that in his opinion nothing was ever too good for it, and he approved all my decisions. The trees were his particular interest. He would occasionally persuade Besnard to plant forest trees in the hedges for the fun of seeing them grow, and his other passion was to fill the front garden with rose trees.

One day after lunch I was talking to the workmen in the courtyard when a window opened and my husband asked me to come up and see him. He had a rash on his chest and a slight temperature and I called the doctor and put him to bed.

Our old friend, Dr. Lehérissey, who, with the help of Mlle. Lefranc, brought my son into the world, appeared surprised at the virulence of the rash that by now covered my husband's back but diagnosed chicken pox brought about by contact with my mother who had shingles, pointed out that this childish illness was occasionally a little stronger with an adult than with a child, but said that by the next day the temperature would undoubtedly begin to fall.

I had put my husband in a very beautiful spare bedroom at the end of the passage where he would be quiet and as far as possible isolated from the child. It was Friday. I went with the doctor to the garden gate, had a short talk with my mother and returned to the courtyard to finish my business with Morin. I felt no anxiety about my husband. The rash would follow the usual pattern and in a few days all would be well.

But the next day the temperature, instead of going down, began to rise, though still not enough to alarm me. I telephoned the doctor several times asking what I could give my patient to eat, and in the afternoon I took my bicycle and went down to the village for some Evian mineral water.

On Sunday the temperature was still rising and following my report, the doctor arrived at the garden gate, puzzled, I fancy, that I should disturb him for so simple a case, but when we went up into the bedroom, the sun shining strongly on the bed, we suddenly noticed that the spots which a little while ago were transparent, had now turned yellowy white—and what is more my husband was covered with them thickly from the top of his head to his toes. His face presented a lamentable sight, the eyes scarcely visible, the cheeks swollen.

The doctor spoke about giving penicillin urgently and made a first injection.

In my own room, where he came afterward to speak to me, he looked white and grave.

"I can't make it out," he said. "I am suddenly overcome by the terrible fear that in England from where your husband has just come, inoculation against smallpox is not insisted upon by law, and that there is at this precise moment a serious outbreak in Britain. There have been several deaths. I must vaccinate everybody in the house, yourself, your mother, your son and the young English governess. I shall be back in an hour. Please have everything ready."

So we were all vaccinated, even the doctor who announced his intention of vaccinating his own family as soon as he returned home.

"You know," he said, "there's not much one can do about smallpox, except to wait."

I was now plunged into despair. What could I do? Merely wait? That is the hardest thing of all. My mother was admirable, overcoming both the after-effects of shingles and the pain of arthritis to take charge of the house, and even to search the orchard for herbs to make soup for the patient. My mother possessed a witch-like gift, doubtless inherited from my grand-mother of Blois, for discovering health-giving herbs for her soups. She would bend over the simmering saucepan for hours concocting these marvels of past centuries. They were in tune with her nature that loved everything done slowly and carefully by hand, whether a piece of lace, a blouse or a lovely dress.

My husband would drink the soup. He admired what my mother did and liked sorrel, but when I looked at him, his poor tormented body made me want desperately to weep. Could I read to him? Yes, he would like me to read the Acts of the Apos-tles but in English, not in French. Though he was perfectly bilin-gual, and had been since earliest childhood, he wanted me to read from the Bible his mother had given me. The hours dragged. We finished the Acts. Had I ever read the Book of Job? Why must he choose the Book of Job? When I came to the part where Job is smitten with sore boils from the sole of his foot unto his crown, and when I realized that this description so horribly fitted the living picture in front of me, my courage abandoned me, and like Job's three friends who, having come to comfort him and not recognizing him because of his sores, wailed and tore their clothes, I wanted to do the same.

My husband said suddenly:

"My father's birthday was on August second. The next day was my parents' wedding anniversary."

He spoke of his parents as if they were still both alive, and I began to wonder if he was delirious but I think that, on the contrary, he was extremely lucid, envisaging with the utmost calm, and almost with an aloof indifference, the possibility of his death. He did not know that the doctor feared smallpox, or perhaps he knew it and was never particularly concerned with this aspect of the case for I never hid from him the fact that we had all been vaccinated. He seemed already to be floating in a more elevated plane. He was mildly vexed that I had not shown more concern about his illness at the beginning, but now sud-denly dismissed me, saying that he wanted to be left alone.

A little rain was falling but the countryside had taken on that tired look that comes over it during the last days of July and the approach of the August Bank Holiday. The hot sunshine of strawberry time and cherry time had burned the tenderer colors, and already the grass was less green, while a few yellowed leaves spiraled down damply from the trees in the hedges, making gold blotches on the orchard. The black plum and the greengage underneath the window were full of wasps, even a few hornets, and the roses were in full and riotous bloom at the foot of my bedroom wall which was covered with huge ripening peaches.

Our birthdays, Robert's and mine, fell on consecutive days in the middle of August, and I was certain that he would not live to see them. The doctor came again during the afternoon to administer a second injection of penicillin. He had been trying to contact a specialist at Caen, some thirty miles distant, but most of them were on holiday. The patient's temperature was alarmingly high but he was still perfectly lucid, almost frighteningly so. He asked me how my barrier looked and if the work was nearly finished, but as it was Sunday, Morin had not come.

"It will be very pretty when it's finished," he said. "I'm so glad you had it done."

But I thought:

"What was the good of having had it done. He'll never see it."

Nearly a month had passed since that hot morning when I had handed my milk can to Déliquaire and he had told me that Roger and Jeanine were waiting for a specialist from Caen for poor little Alain. The cows were back in my home orchard and I could hear the little procession coming up from the stream— M. and Mme. Déliquaire carrying their stools and the donkey with the heavy churns on either side of the leather saddle.

"Teu, Teu," called out Mme. Déliquaire.

The cows ambled toward her, dragging their chains. She would begin to milk them under the cherry tree against my garden rail. I went out to meet her with my can. She was in black, and asked me for news of my husband, saying with infinite sadness:

"Oh, Ma'am Henrey, you and I will not quickly forget this lovely summer."

"Dr. Lehérissey is trying to get a specialist from Caen," I said.

"Then let us go on hoping," she said, "but as far as I'm concerned, I'm finished with drugs and specialists."

On my way back to the house, I met my young English governess. I was in a great state of alarm lest she might at any moment fall ill, and then I would have felt the heavy responsibility of having brought this on her so far from her mother in Exeter, but I found her admirable in this crisis and though fully aware of the gravity of the illness, extremely calm.

I went up to my husband again and tried to tell myself that he was a little better, but was it merely that I was by now accustomed to his terrible appearance? In no circumstances would I have allowed my son to see him thus. Whatever happened, the child's memory of him must not be spoilt.

The Paris suburb of Arcueil had already sent a first batch of children to their holiday camp at the Pelouses (Green Lawns), and because the wind must have been in the right direction, there came across the evening air a great singing of rumbas and sambas. My son had told his grandmother there would be fireworks at ten o'clock on the beach. Night fell slowly over the orchard. The rain had stopped and the birds were flying low. The first bats swooped under the eaves. Insects and moths wheeled round the lamp beside my husband's bed. I began to worry about the specialist who showed no sign of coming. Had Dr. Lehérissey not been able to contact one after all? He would surely have found one in the end but perhaps his car had broken down on the way? The traffic must be appalling this evening, the last Sunday in July. Between the intermittent rumbas and sambas of the noisy Arcueil children, I could hear distantly the roar of traffic on the Caen-Trouville road, cars bumper to bumper climbing the hill, others going down.

I read aloud a little to my husband but absent-mindedly.

Then at last I heard the slamming of a car door at the top of the orchard, and my heart beat so violently that in an attempt to get up, I almost collapsed. I leaned out of the window, and I soon saw in the gray dusk the figures of two men coming toward the house across the grass, talking, laughing, hidden from view now and again behind the trunks of apple trees, then reappearing a few yards nearer.

I hurried down to open our little garden gate. Dr. Lehérissey introduced me to his young colleague, and as my mother had come out of the kitchen door, Dr. Lehérissey explained that she was only just recovering from shingles.

"Yes," said the specialist thoughtfully. "With shingles in the house . . ."

He entered the low half-timbered room where my husband was lying, and cried out with surprise at the sight which met him, the entire body covered with abominable pustules. But he was categorical. This was not smallpox.

To begin with, he said, the patient was reacting to penicillin.

"Then again, my dear doctor," he explained, turning to Dr. Lehérissey. "Pray look at the palms of the hands. They alone are free of pustules. That is a sign. Continue with penicillin. I have never before seen such a virulent form of infected chicken pox. We must give thanks to penicillin. Dear madam," he continued, turning to me, "penicillin has saved your husband's life. Go on taking good care of him. The kidneys are the things to watch. But have no fear. The crisis is over."

They went off gaily through the garden gate into the impenetrable night, laughing as they picked their way between the trunks of the apple trees by the light of a torch, and I, returning to the house, felt the dawn of another day.

28

A WEEK later Robert began a very slow convalescence, punctuated by long sleepless nights during which he ceaselessly walked up and down his room, and Bobby developed a very normal chicken pox with no untoward infection. I now needed all my energy but unfortunately my vaccinated arm became swollen and extremely painful so that I ended by suffering nearly as much as my patients.

August came to an end and my husband returned to London. The cider apples ripened on the trees, and the sands, emptied of holiday makers and at their loveliest, beckoned us for bicycle rides and bathing.

Now that Jacques Déliquaire was in Indo-China and Roger drove a truck for a firm of cider makers in the village, the farm was short of hands. New faces would appear at milking time and then suddenly go. Bernard, for some reason, lasted a little longer than the others, a simple soul, sixth child of an alcoholic father and of a mother who was no better.

He called Mme. Déliquaire: "Ma patronne," which could reasonably be translated as: "My boss," and as soon as he came in to her low room with a bundle of faggots or a pail of milk, he would exclaim:

"Well, boss, is it that you have no desire to talk at this hour? Don't worry. I'll talk for two."

He had arrived from his native village on the other side of the Seine estuary with nothing more than the trousers he stood in and a kerchief round his neck.

"You will have to buy me a trousseau like a bride," he said. "For instance, boss, you can use my first month's pay to buy me a pair of shoes. I shall not be tempted in that way to spend the money. All I need is a packet of cigarettes."

His cigarettes filled poor Mme. Déliquaire with terror. She would get up in the middle of the night and climb into the attic with a torch to see if he had not gone to sleep with a lighted cigarette between the sheets. The good-natured half-wit was always nearly setting the house on fire. Thus Mme. Déliquaire, who normally had such an excellent temper, slept hardly at all, and began to lose her serenity. Sundays also became sad days for her. She was in the habit of cooking a chicken and making fritters for her assembled family. Jeanine had brought the baby. But now when Jeanine and Roger came, it was to cry their poor eyes out.

At about this time I first heard that Victor Duprez was going to sell his farm.

The bailiff came to say good-by to us and the next we knew was that a chicory manufacturer from Dunkirk had bought the Bruyères and all the land. Victor Duprez, now mayor, had entertained there quite a lot. He loved the place, loved it so much that at one time he naïvely confessed that he hated me for not selling back to him my little farm which had once been his. He had dreamed of combining the two estates.

Just after the war he could certainly have done so. His orchards were beautifully kept up, his hothouses and kitchen garden were those of a country squire, and people who had seen my mother return so miserably to our pillaged house felt sure that our land would soon belong to the Bruyères. Simone Duprez was still the chatelaine in those days. She was exactly as I had first seen her when, seated on a high-backed tapestried chair, she told me about the little house that was to become mine. The war years had not changed her at all. She entertained charmingly at the Bruyères, and it vexed me not to be able to return her hospitality, but how could I compete against her modern house, her excellent servants, her Vosges linen and her lovely silver? I then saw less of her. She was nearly always in Paris. Soon we learned that Simone and Victor had separated, each planning to marry again. The breakup of the Bruyères was complete.

M. Courcot, the new owner, was married and had a little boy. He had sold his chicory factory in Dunkirk to buy Victor's farm, but the person who bought the factory was not able to pay for it with the result that M. Courcot spent an uneasy eighteen months between Dunkirk and Villers.

Not quite knowing where to turn, he hired as a sort of bailiff a man called Duchemin, a giant of a man, with a square head, blond hair and blue eyes who, like Dudouy whose friend he was, could do the hardest tasks to perfection, as men did them in the old days, binding hay, trimming hedges and making beautifully porportioned faggots, but refreshing himself so liberally with apple-jack and often, which was worse, with pear-jack that he would become quarrelsome and violent. We were careful not to contradict or thwart him on these occasions for he was tenacious in vengeance.

During the war he had married Mme. Pinson, that strange woman I had met at the Poulin farm in 1940 when I helped Dr. Lehérissey to bring André into the world.

The Duchemin administration could not have been very fortunate for the Bruyères. In May 1951 news reached me in London that M. Courcot had decided to sell at least part of the property, and it struck me that I might never again have such a good opportunity to acquire magnificent orchards bordering my own. I had, of course, no use at all for the Bruyères itself but fate was offering me for the second time the orchards of the Paul estate that I had not been rich enough to buy when Victor's father had pressed me to take them before the war. These included the Cour du Cerf (the Field of the Stag) and the little Marie Antoinette farm, called Berlequet, which Simone had so tastefully done up on the site of Groscol's old house and which, being contiguous to the Point, would give me a large island site of unrivaled beauty between my home orchard and the Bruyères. There was also the famous Picane which had always belonged to Victor and on which he kept his ponies in Goguet's days. As the Picane and the Cour du Cerf faced each other across the stream, their acquisition would be of immense value to my farm.

The Bank of England, where I applied personally for the necessary foreign exchange, showed again the most human un-

derstanding, and within four days I was able to confirm my
offer to Maître Vincent. The matter then went to the Bank of
France for their permission to purchase. On June eighth, M.
Courcot and I met in the notary's office and after the usual formalities, the contract was signed.

I had thus added the most important of Victor Duprez's orchards to mine. While M. Courcot offéred me a glass of champagne at the Bruyères, the news, kept very secret till then,
hurtled down the main street of the village. The hands of the
clock had turned again. My mother, who had returned so hum-
bly to my farm, being forced to suffer the insults of the Goguette, even being refused fire and water, could now lift her
head. My farm was one of the richest on the plateau.

Déliquaire hurried round to know what I was going to do
with my new land, for I had it in my power to enhance very
considerably the prestige and importance of whatever tenant
farmer I chose to favor. I could, for instance, have made Ernest
Poulin immensely powerful. Yvonne and Mme. Castel had been
charming to my mother when she had no friend to help her.
But I was too pleased with the Déliquaires not to help them.
They had become part of my own family.

Déliquaire's face assumed an expression of infinite pride and
satisfaction. I told him I would keep the Marie Antoinette farm
for his son Jacques so that he could set up an establishment of
his own on his return from Indo-China, and that in the mean-
time Déliquaire himself could farm the land. He rolled his eyes
and gurgled. Clearly what he wanted most was to run off and
spread the news of his important advancement among his friends.
He had never guessed that such a thing could happen. This was
indeed the most exciting event for a long time. He really must
go and tell everybody.

The Bruyères, shorn of the Marie Antoinette farm and its
sweetest orchards, had reverted to what it was in M. Allard's
day, a very pretty country house with a kitchen garden and
enough pasture land for two cows. This was just the sort of
thing that playwrights and musicians, as well as titled women,
had loved to own along the coast in the 'nineties and the early
part of this century. When Paris became uncomfortably hot,
they came to Normandy with their servants and carriages, and
drove into the woods or took tea on the lawn. The novels of

Gyp, so beautifully illustrated, describe these charming house parties. Their flavor permeates the triangle love plays and the enchanting operettas of the period.

M. Courcot was not sure whether he would keep the Bruyères. M. Duchemin would look after the place during his long absences at Dunkirk. He had not sufficiently realized, he said, that country houses like the Bruyères were luxuries of another age. The countess of Béarn's place near the sea must have been very lovely. Now it was a vacation center for poor Paris children. So was the Pelouses. So were all the other former country houses. Perhaps that is how Bruyères would end. The only economic way to live in the country was to have acres of rich pasture land and practically no house, to live as I did in the house of a peasant, and have no servants. That was like owning bars of gold in a bank and sleeping on them. It might not be very comfortable, but one's money was safe. Maître Vincent had warned him. Never buy houses that need servants. Buy land.

"But, of course, one doesn't cut much of a figure," I objected. "I am always in a jumper and an old skirt, and there's mud on the floor."

"Well," he answered, "the important thing is not to have to sell."

I was almost more frightened than pleased by my acquisition. My mother, after a moment of pride, found occasion to remind me that she had not yet realized her life's ambition of owning a wardrobe with all tall mirrors, and it seemed a little strange to her that I should go about buying up orchards and then skimp on the butcher's bill.

M. Courcot went back to Dunkirk. I spent a good deal of time looking over my new Berlequet farm. This low house with honeysuckle creeping up the walls, with its stables, warm lofts, modern garage and beautiful kitchen garden, was reached directly from the lane. The vivid blue of its shutters contrasted with the pure white of its walls, the red tiles in front and the russet roof. Carnations and peaches mingled with the vegetables in the kitchen garden. Miniature apple trees were trained along the beds. Then, beyond, was the prettiest orchard, on such high ground that one could see the bay of Le Havre. The low farmhouse, colored like a set from a musical comedy, seemed to stand guard outside the garden of Hesperides.

I was not certain what kind of arrangement M. Courcot had made with his sinister bailiff. Sometimes as I came up from the village, Duchemin already slightly drunk but trying to hide his small misdeeds under much politeness and gallantry, would start a conversation that terrified me, for ever since my girlhood I have had a horror of violent men.

"And how are you today, ma'am?"

"Very well, thank you, M. Duchemin."

"Do you know, ma'am, that by the merest coincidence I have some red tiles just like the ones on the roof of your new farm-house. If we have storms this winter, the tiles will blow down and you will need to replace them. Would you like to buy some of my tiles?"

"I will think about it, M. Duchemin."

"I was talking to M. Courcot the other day, ma'am, and he said: 'M. Duchemin, ask Mme. Henrey to lend you the key of her new cider press. I rather fancy we left some of our barrels inside.' So ma'am, if it would not inconvenience you, may I come and borrow your key?"

"I regret, M. Duchemin, but I gave the keys of the farm buildings to M. Déliquaire. I think it would be wise for you to discuss the matter with him. You manage these things so much better between men."

He smiled. I had touched off in this giant a natural pride in his virility. He knew that he could always win some small advantage over me. I was, after all, only a woman.

I understood perfectly the working of his mind. He had made himself so much at home on the estate as when M. Courcot had originally taken it over. At dawn he would walk across the orchards with a gun, shooting rabbits, gathering himself a dish of mushrooms, and picking up anything which he found on the way. He would probably go on doing this, for how could I, a woman with a house to run, prevent him from poaching at dawn?

He had a son-in-law who owned a small café in Deauville, and on Sunday afternoon, dressed in a black suit, a clean shirt and a blue linen cap that made a violent contrast with his round crimson face, he would take the bus and when, as sometimes happened, I took the same bus on my way to the airport, he would look at me, obviously dressed for a journey to Paris or London in a tailor-made, high heels and a hat, and whisper in his sly way:

"So you are going to leave us for a while, ma'am? You are going to exchange our calm orchards for the life of a woman about town?"

"Oh, only for a day or two," I would answer blushing. "I shall be back very soon."

I would have liked to invent some story about only going as far as Deauville but his eyes would rest on my dressing case, and he would go on:

"Very smart, the air travel labels, ma'am! I suppose that in an hour's time you will be right above us?"

He referred to the Bruyères, now as *his* Bruyères, *his* farm, and he bullied poor Mme. Courcot who was often left alone for weeks while her husband was at the factory in Dunkirk. She was probably as frightened of him as I was. He knew just what to say to make us feel that we were women temporarily without the protection of our husbands.

He must have done rather well out of M. Courcot's two cows for he bought a motor bicycle and we heard him racing, back-firing, hurtling through our narrow lanes. He came up and down down the hill at all hours, and those of us who were mothers, Mme. Poulin, Mme. Courcot and myself, decided that he had become more menacing than ever.

Then one Sunday, on his way to Deauville (for he no longer took the bus), he was overtaken by his son-in-law driving a friend's truck, who, recognizing him, slowed up the truck by the side of the road, signaling his father-in-law to stop. Perhaps Duchemin did not understand the signal. He drove straight into the rear of the truck and hit his forehead against a small nut which killed him. "If it had not been for the nut," said some-body at the inquest, "he would not have died. It was such a small thing." Like the stone hurled from David's sling, it hit the giant where he was weak.

This man who had terrified us, who had beaten his wife, made scenes of violence in our country lanes, and poached our rabbits, had ceased to breathe. Those of us who were women had the impression that our orchards would at last be our own.

At about this time I had the well that Tavernier made for me electrified.

All these years it had worked with a small gasoline engine which lifted the water up into two tanks, one in the attic of the cottage and the other one, a good deal larger, under the beams of my house. When the tanks were empty, a great cry would go up from my mother and from me, and somebody would be sent to the thatch-covered well to put on the motor by turning a handle as in old fashioned trucks and automobiles.

If my husband happened to be at the farm, all was well, but in fact he was not often there. The farm was entirely my domain. I used it as a retreat where I could be with my mother, write my books, allow my son to run wild, and seek the rest I urgently needed between exhausting spells in town. I considered it also in the light of an insurance policy, as some women buy diamonds in case anything should happen to them. Having been poor in my girlhood I was haunted by the fear of being poor again, poor in old age when I had no longer the vivacious ways and pretty face that so successfully lifted me out of poverty when I was a girl of twenty.

I always saw myself spending my last years in a humble cottage with a cow to give me milk. This idea came from the opening scenes of a book I had loved when I was a girl. Thus at the beginning of my life I was already looking ahead, beyond success, to what might happen toward the end. People may call this French realism. Perhaps it was, but so many women who were great actresses, singers, dancers, writers have ended in poverty. Can one do anything to avert it?

I tried from the beginning to make the farm a place in which even if I suddenly lost every cent I possessed, I could still live in reasonable comfort. Déliquaire provided me with milk, butter and cider in return for the grass of my home orchard. For the other orchards he paid me in cash, sufficient to cover my taxes, my electric light, my telephone and a few groceries. I retained for my own use the apple crops of my home orchard. They totaled about five tons and I either sold them or asked Déliquaire to turn them into extra cider. My mother's farmyard provided us with eggs, many of which we sold, chickens, ducks and turkeys. Grain was expensive and we probably ran the farm-yard at a small loss but I was sometimes able to compensate for this by the sale of our cherries, plums, strawberries and peaches.

Most years therefore we could exactly balance our budget. The acquisition of the new orchards put me, of course, in a much stronger position. My rent roll was almost doubled. But there were the improvements which every year seemed abso-lutely necessary. The electrification of the water system was the most important. The old gasoline engine had countless times driven me to tears.

My mother's hands were so full of arthritis that she could only cook a little, feed grain to the farmyard and run up a dress for me to finish. She used to follow me pathetically to the well while I bent down and tried to start the motor. Alas, I have never been anything but an entirely feminine, physically weak woman. I would turn the handle frantically for a moment, pray-ing God that I would have the strength to accomplish that last half turn that would set the motor roaring. If I was successful I would weep with joy and pride, but on most days nothing, neither my prayer nor my biggest efforts, could start the en-gine. I would draw back panting, disheveled, furious, and my mother would look at me in silent commiseration, her poor hands hanging limply at her side. These were our black days for we knew that we were women without strength, at the mercy of any passer-by.

When the pump was electrified, it was a wonderful thing for us to listen to the sudden click which told us that the tanks were being automatically refilled. We felt strong. Our water, how-ever, ran as yellow as pale beer. Our tanks had not been scoured since Gravé had put them up before the war, and as the water was now being pumped in much faster, rust was coming down. We could no longer rinse our sheets for they would have been dyed yellow. If we took a bath, which only happened on rare occasions, we went in white and came out brown, and then the belt above the well, for some reason, kept on slipping so that the motor turned for a whole night once without pumping up any water.

My house was improving but things were always happening to me that did not seem to happen to other women.

Jacques Déliquaire came back the following winter from the war in Indo-China. He had sent a cable to his mother saying that he was sailing home on the *Campana,* and we followed his progress every evening on the French radio which give the shipping news, starting with the training ship *Jeanne d'Arc,* followed by the cruisers and submarines on active service and ending up with passenger liners and cargo ships sailing on the seven seas. Our proximity to Le Havre and Cherbourg gave us all the mentality of sailors' wives, mothers of sailors or just potential travelers, women hoping one day to cross the ocean to New York. We became, if not proficient in geography, at least familiar with place names full of romance and poetry like Mozambique, Madagascar, Saigon or Santiago de Chili, distant names which in our orchards, amidst the clucking of the hens, the quacking of the ducks and the singing of birds, made us often dream. Jacques on his *Campana* reached Colombo, and finally Marseilles, whereupon the Déliquaires, no longer able to contain their excitement, decided to meet their son in Paris, taking with them some nice warm clothes for the poor boy who would not be accustomed to the cold weather. Mme. Déliquaire, before leaving Villers, went to the hairdresser. Mme. Baudry, a Breton woman, who had a little house on the road to St. Vaast, would look after the Déliquaire farm, cook for the farm-hand and help milk the cows.

The departure was fixed for Tuesday. They lunched with the door closed because of a bitter east wind. There were big logs in the fire-place. The cows were in their warm stalls. The door opened, and Madeleine Déliquaire, serving the coffee, nearly fainted. Jacques was home.

He was burned a handsome brown, had grown taller and was beautifully slim. With his blue eyes and his light hair bleached by the fierce sun, he was terribly good-looking. He wore a sergeant's pale blue képi, was as carefully groomed as an American G.I. and had brought home some coffee from Indo-China, cigarettes for his father and a scarf made of native silk for his mother. They all began to question him at once, but he kept on repeating: "Oh, isn't it **lovely** here!"

"Could it be," asked his father slyly, "that you who were tired of the farm, who only dreamed of going thousands of miles away, still have a corner in your heart for farming?"

Jacques smiled.

Madeleine Déliquaire was happy again.

Jeanine was expecting another baby, and Jacques was much more affectionate, more patient, calmer. He took after his mother, had her beauty, and was as gentle as she, whereas Roger was strong and quick like his father, rough with the farm implements and even with the animals.

Jacques, the day after his home coming, filled a pail with water, stripped to the waist and gave himself an ice-cold shower in the little garden in front of the house. Mme. Déliquaire let out a cry of alarm for this was a thing that she had not seen done before. Jacques smiled back at her, filled the pail with water again, and proceeded to give himself a second shower. The army had revised his ideas about physical fitness. He had learned to swim and to dive.

"How the boy has changed, Mme. Henrey!" said his mother. "But it's all for the better, and I feel that it will not be long before he chooses a nice little wife and settles down. Would it not be charming to have another wedding in the family!"

Funerals, weddings, babies. . . . How occupied are our minds with these events! For the career woman, the city can bring success and fame, but it is in the country that, as women, we live with intensity. What happens to the neighbors assumes gigantic proportions. We tremble, we weep, we quiver with rage. We become conscious of the amazing vocation of womanhood! We gossip, not out of wickedness but because of our vital interest in one another. A death brings the entire village together for a moment at church. We weep sincerely with the bereaved family. We pray. We are a hundred women all in black, kneeling between stone pillars, widows, mothers, wives, shaken by thoughts common to us all because our functions are fundamentally the same. Then later we gossip because a death can occasionally mean the redistribution of rich orchard land. A wedding unites families. We crowd to see the bride in white with her orange blossom and white veil. Did we wear white ourselves or shall we eternally regret the magnificent moment that might have been? We unconsciously finger our wedding ring, we look at unmarried daughters wondering when their turn will come. Soon we shall be at the wedding lunch. The men will try to make us blush. And this joyful occasion will last until far into the night.

No wonder Mme. Déliquaire dreamed about the future of her son!

29

ONE September, before leaving for London where I liked to spend the Fall, I decided to build an outside wooden staircase leading from the orchard to the loft of my thatched cottage. The wall against which I planned to build it was rough-cast and windowless. The loft door merely stood gaping at the top. My mother and I were not strong enough to fetch a ladder when we wanted to go there, but we decided that it would be an ideal place to dry the sheets on washing day. My son, who was now thirteen, and about to go to the Benedictine School of Downside in England, knowing that we could not get up, used the loft as a hiding place, pretending not to hear us when we called. He had become intractable to feminine authority, engrossed in his own boyish problems, and would neither help in the garden nor allow me, because I was a woman, to give him lessons in French prose. Our cats had revealed his hiding place to me. He treated them abominably but they followed him. When I saw them peeping out through the open door, I knew he must be inside. He loved the farm passionately and, in these circumstances, I thought it best for him to do exactly as he pleased so that living in a world of his own, his adolescence might at least be colored by a strong imagination.

I told Morin that I wanted something reminiscent of a chalet in the Austrian Tyrol, with a balcony level with the loft door from which would hang, as in a suspended garden, geraniums, nasturtiums and roses. I thought it would be pleasant to sit on my balcony in the evening watching from this height everything that took place in my orchard.

Morin, as usual, was enthusiastic. He pictured me, he said, straining my eyes like Sister Anne in the story of Bluebeard, for the sight of a dusty horseman. The stairs would be painted white.

He asked 120,000 francs for this work, the exact figure I had paid for the entire orchard, including my own house and the cider press, two years before the war. Various devaluations had made the franc twenty times cheaper against gold, I believe, but even so my staircase was going to cost me a great deal of money.

Morin, as a gesture of goodwill, took away a five-barred gate, leading to my newly acquired Cour du Cerf, to mend. Three days later he brought it back in his truck and even changed the post, sinking it four feet into the ground and cementing it. He quite won my heart. My mother used to accuse me of giving work to all the glib young men in the village. Well, perhaps, I did, but does not a business man choose a pretty typist?

Morin was an artisan, working on his own account, capable of tremendous bursts of energy but as soon as he had a new truck, a new automobile, a new motor bicycle, he was like a child, driving up and down the roads for fun and when, on occasion, I would meet him, he would smile charmingly and exclaim:

"Good day, Ma'am Henrey. Your staircase is getting along fine. You will be delighted with it."

But on my return in December, it was still not put up.

"It's the weather, ma'am. The truck would never get down the orchard."

Déliquaire, seeing me worried and always anxious to help, offered to bring a team of horses to unload the staircase in the lane. So all went well. Morin arrived with his mate, a clever and much traveled man called Ernest. They had been working since dawn when suddenly the church bell started to toll, and an old woman came across the grass to ask Morin if he would make a coffin for her husband.

"What will you?" said Morin. "That is one thing that will not wait."

There was no further sign of Morin. Rain fell heavily. A mason was to build foundations for the two pillars holding up the balcony, and the bottom steps were to be made of cement. Rain falling soaked the cement bags and seeped down the sand pile.

This did not prevent me from making everything ready for

Christmas. My husband, who was to spend two days with us, promised to bring a tree from England. We would decorate it with ornaments I had first used during the nocturnal raids of 1940 when my son was eighteen months old and I expected that every night would be our last. Fir trees did not normally grow in the Pays d'Auge but my son, remembering his Christmases under fire, loved them so much that I told Besnard to plant a row of small ones hoping, if ever I had grandchildren, to provide them with trees from my own estate.

We cut armfuls of holly from the hedges. There was, to my shame, a great deal of mistletoe in the very old apple trees. Before the war we could be fined for having too much. Now, nobody seemed to care. It was even exported to Paris and London. My tiny house, beautifully decorated, became the evocation of a Grimm's fairy tale read in girlhood. Elm logs, four feet long, burned night and day in the old fireplace between the stone pillars. The cats slept on plaids in front of the fire.

Our evenings were quite delightful. Somebody would read aloud—the Nativity from the New Testament, *Little Women*, or a short story from an American magazine. I would knit a new jumper or sew a dress. The curtains were drawn and one would hear the wind howling round the old house. My mother would call to us from the kitchen where she was making a cake. Books and papers would sprawl untidily over the big table, on which, freshly gathered, were the last roses of the year:

"La rose d'automne est plus qu'une autre exquise," sang Agrippa d'Aubigné, Protestant friend of Henry the Fourth of France. Sometimes we would play the simple, old-fashioned card game of bezique, and my mother would become as red and angry as a little girl if she lost. The Aga cooker, burning Russian coal at sixty dollars a ton, gave forth its beautiful Swedish heat, preparing us for the hot chocolate and cream we would have before going to bed.

The cows were in Déliquaire's home orchard, and in the morning I forded the stream and crossed the road to St. Vaast, to fetch the milk. Madeleine Déliquaire was busily preparing pieces of black pudding and pork chops on grease paper. A pig had been killed on the farm the previous evening and these were choice morsels that Mme. Déliquaire proposed to give her neigh-

bors for Christmas, it being the custom in Normandy, after
midnight mass on Christmas Eve, to have a festive gathering at
which the family ate oysters and black pudding. The cats, seated
on the window sill, purring, watched the proceedings with green,
alert eyes.

"Ah, Mme. Henrey, so here you are collecting the milk yourself, this morning, and just in time for your share of the pig!"

I put down my can and sat on the wooden bench, looking at
the names written on the various pieces of grease paper. Here
were two chops for Mme. Baudry whose husband was employed
by the local council to lop the hedges and keep the roads in good
repair. He beat his wife who was twice his size, and dug his garden while she helped Mme. Déliquaire to keep the farmhouse
clean and milk the cows. Mme. Giles, deaf Gravé's daughter, had
a large roast for her family. When, in the spring, it was her turn
to kill a pig, she would do the same thing for her neighbors.

"Tell me all the news," I asked Madeleine Déliquaire, relax-
ing in the lovely warmth of her low room. She knew every piece
of gossip in the village, and as neither the Déliquaires, nor the
Giles, nor the Beaudrys yet had the radio, nor even electricity
in their homes, they had retained the ancient art of talking. Their
conversation, highly pictorial, full of wisdom, sometimes a little
ribald, had a delicious tang.

She looked up and queried archly:

"How goes the staircase, Mme. Henrey?"

"Not quickly," I answered.

"That is hardly to be wondered at," she said smiling, "for it was
your mason who came here yesterday to kill the pig. We heard
all the details of your staircase."

Ah, thought I, if I had pretended that everything was going
splendidly, what a silly woman I would have looked!

"That mason of yours," she continued, "is a wonderful
butcher, an absolute artist with the knife, but the pity of it is
that he drinks like a sponge. Is your carpenter not back yet?"

"He went off to make a coffin for an old man who died suddenly."

"And now the widow is in a bad way," said Mme. Déliquaire.
"I would not be surprised if she followed him before the New
Year. Those old couples can seldom get on without each other,
even though they squabble from morning till night when they

have the good fortune to be together. They pine away, that's what they do, Mme. Henrey."

Jeanine had safely given birth to her baby, a boy called Jean-Jacques, and Madeleine Déliquaire was now completely happy. Jean-Jacques was just beginning to walk. He was a darling but abominably spoiled, and who could blame the mother when her first was in the cold earth? Can one smack the one who has come to take his place? Jean-Jacques was unusually loving for a little boy. His kisses, in the words of Madeleine Déliquaire, were like warm bread, and they went to one's heart.

Madeleine Déliquaire had hurt her leg. It might not have been so bad if she had consulted a doctor, but she insisted instead on calling a sorcerer who burned herbs and recited magic words. I said: "Surely, Mme. Déliquaire, you don't believe in this sort of thing?" but she answered: "Of course, Mme. Henrey, how could anybody not believe? Don't you remember when there was foot-and-mouth disease and that sorcerer from Touques drew circles round the cows to keep them safe?" "But you inoculated them," I objected. "Yes," she agreed, "but that was merely as an extra precaution. We never lost an animal. You do remember, don't you?

"When I had to sit in an easy chair with my leg up," she was saying, "my knitting wool and my things to mend in a big basket beside me, Jeanine brought Jean-Jacques to keep me company, and the rascal emptied my basket, and the cats played with the balls of wool while I sat there unable to move, seeing my beautiful wool getting dirty. But the little fellow had such a good time, and there I was thinking of Alain. How pretty they would have been together!"

The dogs barked outside and Mme. Déliquaire, peeping through the red and white curtain, said:

"There comes old Troussel for his chops and black sausage."

Troussel lived in a half-timbered house, at least four hundred years old, in one of Déliquaire's orchards beyond the cider press. He was seventy-seven and had arthritis in the hip which gnawed at him continually. So he came limping in, dragging his poor body behind him. He sat down on the wooden bench behind the table and talked to us about the old man who had died and the widow who was so poorly, but instead of referring to them as old people, he was picturing them as they were when they were young.

Now suddenly he smelt the coffee that Mme. Déliquaire was making, and we could both see that he wanted desperately to stay. He knew that the men were out in my woods cutting brushwood. On their return they would have black coffee and pearjack, and perhaps Mme. Déliquaire would give him some light work. He was not paid much now but he had his pension. His eyes turned to the small stove in the form of a heart which Mme. Déliquaire used on Sundays for a roast and to make cakes. He could offer to saw some logs, and even if she already had plenty, she would not refuse. A compassionate farmer's wife does not like to disappoint a man anxious to do a little work. The coffee did indeed smell excellent and I wondered if it could still come from the sack that Jacques had brought back from Indo-China.

I got up regretfully. I love my farmer's wife and I am never tired of contemplating her calm, round features and her blue eyes. Yes, in spite of the fact that her nose is rather too long and the tuft of hair on her right cheek, no longer noticeable to those who know her, grows a little larger every year, I consider her a fine-looking woman. She is the spirit of the house. Her husband would not do anything without first asking her advice, and yet she always thinks as he does. She gathered up the little parcels of pork and black pudding, placed them carefully in a basket which she covered with a clean napkin, an elm log over the top to prevent the cats from getting in, and prepared the table for the men. She said to me:

"You know, Mme. Henrey, that accident to my leg was a real blessing. Jacques gets up early every morning, makes the coffee, goes off to milk the cows with his father and when they come back, while our young apprentice is passing the milk through the creaming machine, Jacques boils the milk and makes breakfast. He serves me in bed as if I were a lady. Then, when the men have gone, I get up slowly, as if I were going to the ball. I have never been spoiled like that!"

How radiant she looked!

Now the men came in. She looked up at her husband and said:

"I was just telling Mme. Henrey how you all spoil me. That is what comes of being a grandmother!"

Old Troussel was rubbing his hands, the color of wax, together. One could hear the bones cracking. It was as if the flesh had dried up but his eyes were fixed on the table and his nose twitched with greed.

How lovely to spend Christmas in the country!

30

THE SOUND of hammering woke me early. Morin, Ernest and the mason-butcher were putting the final touches to my ladder. My mother, who had already made the coffee, called me to kill and pluck a chicken for Christmas. Though I have become expert at it, I cannot stand killing our own birds, and Mme. Déliquaire and I always feel slightly aggrieved that this work is left to the women of a farm.

My mother was more than ever proud of her farmyard for in spite of the cold and the rain we seldom had fewer than twenty eggs a day, and Mme. Poulin, Mme. Déliquaire and Mme. Giles were very surprised. People came from quite a distance to buy our eggs and my mother felt important.

Having sent my son into the kitchen to make a cake for lunch with twelve eggs and some cream, I went to inspect the staircase. Alas, I made an alarming discovery. On reaching the balcony, which was to become my suspended garden with roses, nasturtiums and geraniums, I noticed that the high tension cable bringing power to my house, was only just above my head. I could easily stretch out my arm and touch it—and I am a small woman! I felt suddenly so angry with myself, so appalled by the thought of my incompetence, that tears clouded my eyes. Morin laughed at my fears. He said there was really no danger, and who would want to touch the high tension cables anyway? He made me a speech about insulated pliers and a wonderful pair he had stolen from an American soldier during the invasion. I hated him as much for his irrelevant story as for his mean theft. Since my girlhood the Americans had always appeared to me as heroes.

Then, descending my staircase, I noticed that a beam from the thatched roof was dangerous to anybody who might run down unthinkingly. I could see my mother gay but critical, wondering what would happen next, and I was so exasperated that I paid off the workmen and sent them home.

I had promised to meet my husband at the bus stop at the top of the road. He was coming from London to spend Christmas Day with us, crossing from Southampton to Le Havre by the night boat and taking the direct bus from there. My grandiose projects for embellishing the farm had all gone wrong, and I was humiliated. He would tell me that the French had not changed since the old wars with Italy, that they did things without due reflexion, and, of course, I would be furious.

The heavy bus stopped at the top of the hill, and my husband jumped down with an attaché case and an enormous Christmas tree. I had brought him Wellingtons so that he could walk comfortably across our muddy orchards. He was, as usual, perfectly charming, delighted to be in Normandy even for so short a time, and he started to enquire after all our neighbors rather like Bluebeard coming back from his journey, and I felt horribly like Bluebeard's wife, trembling that he should ask me about the staircase. I told him about my evenings with my mother and the child, reading or playing bezique, and about my morning visit to Mme. Déliquaire who was preparing her chops and black pudding, and thus we arrived within sight of home.

"Oh!" he cried joyously. "Your staircase is magnificent!"

"Yes," I agreed, ill at ease, "but look how near the balcony is to the high tension wires, and there are other things as well."

He threw down his case and the Christmas tree, and ran lightly up the stairs.

"The high tension cables present no difficulty," he said gaily. "The company will fix a longer arm. As for your beam, the thatcher will have to cut it, and roll back the thatch. One side of the cottage roof will be a little shorter than the other. That's all. I don't really see that it matters. The whole place is crazy. You would not want it to be otherwise."

"And then," I continued, loving him for so quickly dispelling my fears, "there is another dilemma. The cows will rub against the pillars, and nibble at the plants in my overhanging garden."

"They certainly will," he agreed. "Your carpenter will have to make you a small enclosure like the one at the back. You

could put a table and chairs on the grass, and we could lunch
out in hot weather. The cows would lean over the railings and
look at us."

Why, yes, of course.

"Things always seem so simple," I said contentedly, "when
one comes to country life fresh from the city."

I opened the garden gate and we went through. My son, with
flour all over his face and hair, cried out with joy at the sight
of the Christmas tree. My mother, delightfully self-conscious,
stood just inside the kitchen where the chicken and the three-
tiered cake were nearly ready for lunch.

The half timbering shimmered in the clear winter air.

Oh, these little farmhouses, hidden among the apple trees,
are they not too lovely for words?